I0602053

# Givers and Takers

Wings
Press, Inc.

# Givers and Takers

Jasmine's eyes well with tears. "My grandmother wept as she related what her own mother told her. Turkish soldiers broke into the family home, and even though her mother was only ten, she clearly remembered everything that happened on that horrible day."

Ani hands her a napkin to wipe her tears. "You don't have to go on with this, Jasmine."

Battia's eyebrows arch in anger. "No, I need to tell you." After composing herself, she presses on. "When the soldiers pushed open the door of the cottage, my great-grandmother got so frightened, she dashed into the nearby closet and hid. Through an opening, no larger than a slit, she watched them grab her mother and two aunts. The men ripped off their clothes and jumped all over them. She never forgot how fiercely the women kicked and fought to defend themselves. Through that slight opening, this ten year old child watched the soldiers beat and rape her mother and two aunts."

Jasmine takes the napkin, and again dabs her sad brown eyes. "Ani, I still see the pain in my grandmother's eyes as she struggled to tell her mother's story. It was as though she were reliving the trauma herself."

# What They Are Saying About *Givers and Takers*

Doctor Richard Berjian is an immensely talented writer who brings real issues to the page by drawing me in with characters I want to grab a coffee with and talk until dawn-- which is what happens when I'm reading one of his books. In *Givers and Takers*, Ani is an amazing mother willing to do anything so that Raffi can have a better life in America, and Dr. Raffi Sarkissian is a wonderfully torn hero. The Armenian Genocide is not an easy topic, but the author handles it with such care. Well done!

—Traci Hall
*USA Today* bestselling author

*Givers and Takers* is a fascinating read, written by Doctor Richard Berjian. The Armenian Genocide is a heartbreaking subject, but handled beautifully by this talented author. Wonderful characters and a great story!

—Patrice Wilton
*New York Times* bestselling author

# Givers and Takers

## Dr. Richard A. Berjian

**A Wings ePress, Inc.**
**Mainstream Fiction Novel**

# Wings ePress, Inc.

Edited by: Jeanne Smith
Copy Edited by: Christie Kraemer
Executive Editor: Jeanne Smith
Cover Artist: Trisha FitzGerald-Jung

Wings ePress Books
www.wingsepress.com

Copyright © 2019 by Dr. Richard A. Berjian
ISBN 978-1-61309-617-8

Published In the United States Of America

Wings ePress Inc.
3000 N. Rock Road
Newton, KS 67114

# Dedication

To my wife Sally, whose dedication and helpful advice sustained the momentum for this novel. To Traci Hall, *USA Today* bestselling author, who served as preliminary editor. To Mary Hakola, a friend, who offered insightful suggestions.

I am especially grateful to my friend Alex Selian, whose mother's real life story served as inspiration for this novel.

# Haig's Story
*Ankara, Turkey, 1980*

Captain Haig Sarian nervously drums his fingers on the worn oak desk, releasing a heavy sigh. A Russian Army officer versed in multiple languages, he has spent the last twelve months working as a translator at the Russian Embassy in Ankara. But after the telephone call from his undercover contact moments ago, he's convinced his work in the Turkish city must come to an end. The shocking news that his cousin Berj was arrested before dawn means it's only a matter of time before his own cover is exposed.

He leans over the desk and cups his forehead in his hands. His only unbearable regret is leaving Ani. Her image flashes before him and his eyes blur with tears. The striking Armenian translator has become his closest friend and lover.

From the first, he'd been attracted to her delicate features set on a satin olive face. Her hazel eyes pierce his soul, relieving his loneliness. Her laughter continually fills his heart, making life worth living. Generous with her love, she willingly gave her virginity to him. Now those intimate moments are over. Until Ani, all personal associations were superficial. He has acquaintances,

1

but nothing more. But even Ani's not aware of the role he plays in the world of international intrigue.

He checks his watch. It's nine o'clock Monday morning. With mixed emotions, he shuffles the papers before him, documents to be presented to the Turkish Department of Defense within the hour. His translation is almost complete, just needing a few corrections. He picks up his pen but hesitates, dropping it on the desk, consumed with the enormity of the decision facing him.

As a Christian Armenian born in the Soviet satellite of Georgia, he was courted by Moscow to undergo officer training in the Russian Army because of his excellence in languages. Now at the age of twenty-eight, he's attained the position of captain, a status most Armenians of his background would envy. More significantly, his assignment as interpreter for the delicate diplomatic interactions between Moscow and Ankara has placed him in a crucial position, vital to his covert espionage.

Despite his fluency in the Turkish language, his resentment is deep-seated against the government that mercilessly drove the Sarian family from their ancestral lands in Turkey sixty-five years earlier. More than a million and a half Christian Armenians living in the remnants of the failing Ottoman Empire were led to their deaths, either by starvation in the heat of the desert or by outright massacre. The year 1915 is embedded in his brain, as it is for most generations of Armenian families fortunate enough to have escaped the horror of the forced march into barren wastelands. That's why when his cousin Berj encouraged him to join him as a spy for the Brits, he accepted.

When he was two, he lost his mother and yet to be born sister in childbirth, leaving his rearing to Maritza, his widowed grandmother. Rather than telling fairy tales, Maritza imbued her grandson's young mind with her life's tragic events. She'd gaze into his eyes, holding his boyish shoulders firmly and say, "Haig, I tell you about my life so you never forget what the Turks did to our people." Maritza recounted her life story over and over again, until the ill-fated history of Christian Armenians living in Muslim Turkey during World War One became intrinsically woven into Haig's DNA.

He'd sit at the kitchen table watching his grandmother toil, stirring a pot of vegetables with chunks of lamb, a bandana holding back her grey wavy hair, recounting how she and her family survived. She was only thirteen, mature beyond her years, when the massacres began. In the dark of night, her father quietly loaded their few necessities into the horse-drawn wagon, padlocked the old wooden door of their village cottage and escaped Turkey with his family. They settled in nearby Georgia, only days before the onset of the coming storm of terror.

The jarring ring of the phone abruptly breaks into his thoughts and he cautiously lifts the receiver. The voice is familiar, hushed.

"Haig, get out now! Your passport won't be good much longer. They'll find you and throw you into the hell hole of a Turkish prison."

He sits motionless as the line goes dead and then seconds later, casts his translations aside. There's no reason to linger. A quick getaway out of Ankara to Geneva has to be made, with London his final destination. There his contacts would protect him.

Hastily he unlocks the lower desk drawer to retrieve his passport, pulls on his military jacket and heads toward the elevator. Down on the first floor he keeps a casual pace toward two armed guards standing in front of the Embassy and asks them to hail a cab. The taxi arrives; he enters, shuts the door and barks in Turkish. "Esenboga International!"

He peers through the cab window during the twenty mile journey to the airport, reliving the glorious days with Ani. Despite the present danger he faces, his thoughts dwell on his only love. How can Ani understand why he has to evaporate into thin air as though he never existed? He's convinced any communication with her will put her life in danger.

His throat tightens; he lets out a heavy sigh. Once things calm down, he vows to see her to explain.

## Ani's Story
*Ankara, Turkey, 1980*

Twenty-four-year old Ani Sarkissian shades her eyes from the morning sun as she peers through the window of the bus rumbling en route to the government building. She has taken this trip daily for three years, working as a translator for the Turkish Defense Department.

She exits the vehicle; her slim figure melds into the busy flow of employees entering the somber, gray stone building. Fingering the wrap on her head, she makes certain no hair peeks out as she moves through the massive doors, respectful of everyone around her. As a Christian Armenian, she is grateful to have this position and follows the traditional Muslim custom when in public. It's her talent as a translator in Russian, Arabic and Turkish that allows her to be a part of this government setting.

She enters the office cubicle located next to her superior and sits alone at her desk focusing on an article from a Russian political publication to be translated into Turkish by late morning. A knock on the door breaks into her concentration and she looks up to see the tall figure of the director, Colonel Orzan, standing before her. Catching the grimace cross his razor-sharp features, she feels a faint shudder of apprehension.

Orzan's tone is brusque. "Have you spoken to Captain Sarian this morning? We've had trouble reaching him."

"No, Colonel," she replies, aware he knows of their friendship. She reads the annoyance on the Turkish officer's face as he presses on.

"He promised to have the government's report ready for a meeting with the general."

Her mouth goes dry. "Have you called the Russian Embassy?"

Orzan raises his voice, his eyes flash. "Of course and he didn't answer. Did you not see him this weekend?"

Moisture collects on her upper lip. "I'm afraid not, sir."

Orzan's leather-soled boots echo on the wooden floor as he approaches and leans his hands on the desk, facing her. "This meeting is urgent and we can't continue without him. Are you sure you don't know his whereabouts?"

Her heart pounds, her voice faint. "I'll call you if I hear from him, sir."

The colonel brushes a finger across his mustache, his lips tight. "Captain Sarian's absence is most unusual. I must report this to security."

Ani feels a wave of panic, catching the sinister squint in Orzan's eyes. Is her Haig in trouble? Though neighbors, Russia and Turkey are not the best of friends. She catches her breath and blurts out. "Please, Colonel, I will do my best to reach him."

He taps his fingers on her desk for a moment as though considering her request. "Don't bother!" he finally says, storming out of the room.

Ani sits in silence, trying to contain her shock. Where is Haig—what could have happened? She senses trouble brewing. If he violates diplomatic protocol, he definitely will be ousted by the Turkish government and face severe penalties. Feeling a chill, she pulls her sweater over her shoulders. She plans to see him tonight and tell him the news. Her monthly period isn't just late—she's pregnant.

~ * ~

Weeks have passed since Haig's disappearance and Ani continues to face immense resentment from the colonel. Co-workers look upon her with suspicion as an assortment of stories circulate about the captain's sudden disappearance. She senses any trust she's shared with her supervisor and staff is destroyed. Alone in her office cubicle, she continues to work, speaks to no one, and after completing her tasks, takes the bus and goes directly home.

Each day, with pounding heart, she rushes to check the mail, but the inevitable disappointment of no word from Haig keeps her in a state of desperation. Possibly it's his secretive work that prevents him from contacting her. Still she doesn't give up hope. At night lying in bed, she sees his melancholy eyes, his firm jaw with a hint of a smile, his arms reaching out to her. Then she awakes, her nightgown clinging to her with sweat, only to discover it's only a vivid dream.

At first she attempts to shield her pregnancy, but attacks of nausea and frequent trips to the bathroom unmask her secret. At home, with her condition exposed, there is little support or sympathy from her father. The disgrace of having a daughter carry a child out of wedlock is a family embarrassment within the Christian Armenian community. No matter how Ani pleads to have the baby and raise the child at home, her father's stern manner, his cold treatment toward her each evening when she returns from work becomes unbearable.

Her mother provides concealed support for her out-of-wedlock pregnancy, but as an obedient wife, she refrains from quarreling with her husband, aware of his stubborn temperament. Thus Ani accepts her mother's silence and tolerates her father's blistering outbursts.

What is she to do? She lies in bed each night contemplating her alternatives: whether to stay in the only home she's ever known or leave to strike out on her own. Then everything comes to a head in her fifth week of pregnancy.

After a tiring day at work, a troubled Ani steps off the bus and reluctantly makes her way home, dreading to hear her father's scolding lectures. As she walks the winding streets, each step fills her heart with apprehension, a feeling of helplessness. She needs her Haig, her lover, but it's become clear he's out of the picture. She alone has to decide what will be best for herself and her unborn child.

Pausing at the front door, she plots to quietly flee to her room without being noticed. Anything to avoid facing her parents, who wait for her in the kitchen preparing dinner. The moment the door closes behind her, her father's commanding voice sounds, carrying a sense of urgency.

"Ani, come in here!"

Heat flushes her face as she removes her light wrap, aware of what lies ahead. Obediently, she enters the kitchen to see her father already seated at the table, his jaw firm with determination. She catches her mother's knitted brow, her eyes red from tears, turning to face her. For sure the usual argument about her condition was the topic before she entered.

Her father gestures to Ani with a sharp command. "Sit down; we now have a solution for your situation."

Ani flinches, reading the discomfort on her mother's face, and then takes her place at the table.

Her father presses on, his arms crossed against his chest. "Time is of the essence. You must get married before your stomach swells and gives away your secret and shame." He pauses and levels an intense gaze in her direction. His voice is firm. "You must get married *and soon.*"

Ani cries out in frustration. "The only man I want to marry is Haig and I don't know where he is!"

Her father's voice rises as he pounds the table. "I'm not talking about that scoundrel! There is someone who is interested in marrying you *right now.*"

Ani's mother leans over the table toward her daughter and lowers her voice. "It's Zaven, owner of the general store. He's

7

willing to marry you. It's the only way. Ani, you need a husband and the child needs a father."

Ani's eyes widen into an owl-like stare, and her breathing comes fast. "Mother, he's over fifty, more than twice my age!"

"Makes no difference," her father continues. "He has a well-established business and will provide a good home and security. He's an honest man, a good Christian, and most important, he's Armenian."

Ani bursts out. "I can't!"

Her father is quick to answer. "Yes you can and *you will*. There's no time to waste. I invited him to dinner tomorrow."

Ani's mother rises from her chair, and gently holds her daughter's shoulders from behind in an effort to comfort her. In a soft voice she whispers in Ani's ear. "Darling, it is for the best. He's been widowed for over five years and very lonely in that large house up on the hill. He's kind and will treat you and the child well."

Ani pulls away from her mother's tender touch and rises defiantly. "I know you want the best for me, but I must think about this." Without eating, she leaves the kitchen and runs to her bedroom, slamming the door behind her.

Lying on her bed, she cries convulsively into the pillow, but within a few minutes, she takes control of her frustration. She will leave Turkey before her child is born. No longer will she be her parents' problem. Her future and her child's well-being will depend on her own resourceful wit and confidence. Drying her tears, she rises from her bed, promising herself to begin the journey into the outside world. What that journey will be, only time will tell.

~ * ~

The betrothal dinner turns into a disaster. Ani refuses the merchant's proposal of marriage and flees from the table in tears. There is no peace in the Sarkissian family. Her father's wrathful challenge greets her each day as she returns from work. "Who will marry a woman bearing another man's child?"

The plan to leave her birth country occupies Ani's thoughts as she performs her daily translations. Working tenaciously, no project is too difficult—she has to be indispensable to keep her job and save money for the future.

By the third month, she becomes increasingly anxious. No word from Haig, and still no plan. But despondency changes to hope when a German document comes across her desk from the Swiss Embassy. The article questions if the Swiss government should agree with Turkey's militant position against the Kurds. Customarily, she'd complete the translation, submit it to her superiors and never deal with it again. This time, however, she decides this is the opportunity she's been waiting for and decides to take the bold step of contacting the Swiss diplomat who authored it. While she's aware communications of this nature are handled by higher authorities, it might very well be her link to Switzerland and freedom.

Hastily, she jots the diplomat's name on her pad along with his telephone number and rises from her desk to use the phone in the private office of her superior who has been called away for a meeting. Her heart pounds and she clears her throat to gain confidence as she dials the Swiss Embassy.

"Hello, this is the Turkish Defense Department. Is Mr. Rinehart Bruger available?"

"One moment please," a woman responds.

After a short wait she hears a mild, inviting voice.

"This is Rinehart Bruger."

She hopes she won't be rebuffed or even laughed at as the words spill from her tongue. "Mr. Bruger, I work for the Turkish Defense Department. I translated your statement regarding the Swiss government's position on Turkey's treatment of the Kurds. Is it possible we could meet? I would like to offer my translating skills to your government."

Silence follows, making her increasingly uneasy. Will he report her to the authorities? Has she risked too much?

He finally says, "Tell me why."

She has rehearsed her answer and replies with confidence. "Mr. Burger, I agree with your opinion in the article. As an Armenian, I share the sorrowful ways the Turkish government deals with the Kurds. I am fluent in Russian, Turkish, Arabic and some English and feel my expertise would be helpful."

She waits, his silence making her desperate. This is her only chance to escape her situation. "Please help me, Mr. Bruger."

A pause follows until he speaks. "Meet me at the Swiss Embassy after you leave work today."

She can't believe her good fortune and takes in a heavy breath. "I leave work at five—I can be in your office by five-thirty."

"Your name? I'll have you cleared at the front desk."

Ani's heart flutters, and she dabs the moisture on her brow with a tissue. She thanks him and then gently places the phone in the cradle, astounded by the straightforward success of the conversation.

That evening, Rinehart Bruger listens to her story with fatherly concern over her difficult family situation. He welcomes her transparency and agrees to arrange passport clearance and travel to Switzerland. By the end of the week, government employment in Geneva is secured.

~ * ~

A trickle of moisture rolls down Ani's forehead as she labors in the maternity suite of the Swiss Regional Hospital in Geneva. She braces herself for the next contraction, taking in deep breaths. They're coming more rapidly and stronger, but the joy of finally having her baby makes the pain bearable. She focuses on the future, distracting her from the agony of childbirth.

The obstetrical nurse draws the curtains and enters. "You've been laboring for several hours. I'll check to see if you're ready for the spinal anesthetic."

Eagerly welcoming the thought, Ani nods, anxious to deliver her child.

Satisfied, the nurse finishes her exam and peels off her gloves. "You're about ready."

Just then Ani feels a major contraction and lets out a sharp cry, causing the nurse's eyes to widen. "Don't press, dear. I'm calling anesthesia now."

With the anesthetic, Ani's pain dissipates and her body relaxes. She concentrates on the child she has bonded with during the last nine months. Who is this little one soon to be the center of her life? Her love is overwhelming, indescribable.

Within minutes, the wails of the newborn fill the delivery room. Ani can't believe after so many hours of labor, the baby came so quickly.

"You have a healthy baby boy," the obstetrician announces.

Ani struggles to break through the haze of sedation and asks, "Can I see him?"

"In a few moments," the nurse answers, carrying the infant to a table to suction its mouth.

The squeal of life is music to Ani's ears. Her prayer for a healthy baby has been answered. The swaddled infant is placed in her arms and she relishes the warmth, holding him close. At that moment, she makes a vow. Even though her son is fatherless, she will fill that void. Her journey is not yet over. Leaving Ankara so her baby would be born in Switzerland was only the first step. Despite rejection by her family and a vanished lover, she feels no remorse. It's her destiny to have this child and give him a bright future.

After being wheeled into her room, Ani prays that someday Haig will meet his son. But for the present, her child is the single purpose in her life. Her eyelids grow heavy and she drifts into a light sleep, overcome with complete joy.

~ * ~

Ani never gives up hope to be reunited with Haig. She names her son Raffi, his father's middle name. It's her way to keep a connection with the only man she's ever loved.

She feels blessed to have Mr. Bruger's fatherly support. On her arrival in Switzerland, he had arranged for an aide to help her settle into a tiny but clean second-story apartment in a boarding house close to work.

Her good fortune continued when the landlord living on the first floor befriended her. Frieda Knodler, a grandmotherly widow, consents to babysit Raffi during the day. Her chubby cheeks carry a cheerful smile. "Why not? My three boys are grown, and I miss the little ones. I'm only steps away."

Ani couldn't be happier. She returns home from the Swiss government offices each working day and dashes into Mrs. Knodler's apartment, excited to retrieve little Raffi. She hugs and thanks the widow, picks up her son and cradles him in her arms. His rosy coloring and the odor of talcum assures her that the widow knows how to keep her son clean and well fed. Each evening, she suctions breast milk, keeping it cool in the refrigerator. The following morning, she deposits it, along with her son and a tote bag filled with diapers, in the widow's apartment.

Raffi blossoms rapidly during his first year of life, gurgling and then muttering his first words. For the present, Mrs. Knodler is the perfect caregiver, but Ani promises herself that when her son reaches the age of three, she will pay for a quality nursery school where he can interact with other children. Education will be the key to Raffi's success and she saves diligently with that in mind.

Despite the positive moves in her life, she reminisces about her past in Ankara. She yearns to hear her mother's voice, to tell her she is a grandmother. After many failed attempts, she's excited when her mother finally answers the phone.

"Ani, it's you? Are you OK?"

"Hello, Mother! Thanks for speaking to me. How are you and how is Father?"

Hearing no answer, Ani presses on. "I wanted to tell you I have a son. His name is Raffi and he's two years old."

"Ani, your father will be furious if he finds I spoke to you."

She hears the tension in her mother's voice.

"He says you are dead to him. Please, you shouldn't keep calling."

Ani's throat tightens; she chokes a cry. Even the news of Raffi's birth doesn't soften her parents. "Mother, I sent you my address...at least please write to me." She hears nothing but silence followed by anguished sobs. "Mom, please don't cry. I'm happy here, have a good job and some friends...don't worry."

Her mother speaks through her weeping. "Remember, Ani, I love you. Stay well."

"I love you too, Mother." The call ends with a click. She senses this is the last time she'll hear her mother's voice. She slowly places the phone into its cradle, saddened that her life has turned out this way. No parents, no Haig. But she has her son, who fills her daily thoughts, giving her dreams for his future.

~ * ~

Both male and female workers are attracted to Ani as she walks the halls of the Swiss government building. Her olive complexion and large hazel eyes stand out in this city of fairer people. She's proud of her long ebony hair that falls past her shoulders. Some days she twists it in an upswept French knot which lends her an air of sophistication.

Despite the attention, she refrains from involving herself with any suitors. Her strict Middle Eastern culture keeps her from any casual association with the men she encounters at work. Why waste time with a provincial Germanic male, since her plans for Raffi don't lie in Switzerland? In her heart, America is her final destination and where she will raise her son to adulthood.

In two years, she's accomplished what she set out to do. She's well respected by her co-workers, makes a comfortable salary and has a few close female friends. She ignores the probing gazes from male workers and vows not to commit to a relationship that can deter her from her goal.

That is, until Gretchen, the typist in the secretarial pool, implores her to join her. "Ani, you miss all the fun at the

Christmas party each year. You must come with me this time. Cut loose and enjoy yourself. It's in the hall at the local tavern. There'll be music, dancing, and who knows?"

Ani enjoys going to the movies with Gretchen several times a month when her friend doesn't have a Saturday night date. She patiently listens to her chatter about the cute guy in some department, or her latest heart throb.

Admittedly Ani is lonely so she relents. "Yes, I'll go, Gretchen. It won't hurt to have a few drinks and some fun."

Gretchen's blue eyes sparkle, her full lips, accentuated by fire-red lipstick, break into a broad smile "Good girl!" she shouts, flipping her blonde hair over her shoulder. "I'll pick you up at seven, so wear that pretty pink chiffon dress. You are beautiful, Ani, if you would only use makeup. I'll bring some over."

A five piece band is playing Lionel Richie's "All Night Long," as Ani and Gretchen enter the hall. Ani is self-conscious; wearing the makeup Gretchen applied a bit too heavily. She straightens the satin sash around her waist as she gazes timidly into the room. The floor is crowded with dancing couples, swinging to the rapid rhythm.

Gretchen tugs Ani toward two men standing by the bar. "There's Helmut," she says. "He said he'd be looking for us."

Ani studies the men as they cross the room. The one of medium build and height has dark thick wavy hair and she knows he's Helmut, since Gretchen has a photo of him on her desk. The other, a tall, handsome, blue-eyed blond, towers over Helmut, holding a beer and laughing.

She pulls away, her gaze glued to the floor. "You go, Gretchen. I'll sit here at this table and have a drink."

"Come on, you party pooper. I talk to Helmut about you all the time and he's anxious to meet you." Gretchen takes her hand again and boldly walks up to the two men, Ani in tow.

Helmut looks to Ani and extends his hand. "Glad you came, Ani. I'm Helmut. Gretchen sings your praises and says you've been a good friend."

Ani smiles sheepishly and grasps Helmut's sweaty palm. "Pleased to meet you," she says, sensing a penetrating stare from the tall blond.

Helmut turns to his strikingly handsome friend. "Meet Hans. He works with me at the German Embassy." Before Ani can reply, Helmut swiftly grabs Gretchen's hand as the band begins playing "A Hard Day's Night." He calls out to Hans as he leads Gretchen onto the dance floor. "Don't let this great music go to waste. Get out here!"

Hans casts a warm smile at Ani. "It looks like we're left alone, so why don't we enjoy a drink together?" He gestures to a table nearby. "Sit here while I get you whatever you prefer."

Ani blushes under his scrutiny. "Thank you, Hans. Punch will be fine."

He smiles again, revealing perfect white teeth, and then leaves to retrieve the drinks.

Ani waits; her heart flutters with intense attraction to the polite gentleman. In the blare of the background music, she watches Hans fill two glasses at the buffet table and catches his smile as he returns. The sweet aroma of his aftershave tingles her nose as he leans over to place the punch before her.

Still smiling, he slips into the chair next to her. "Ani, I'm glad we're alone so we can get to know each other."

At first she's intimidated, wondering how her limited background could impress this obviously refined person. But after peering into his sky blue eyes she yields. "Yes, I would like that," she replies softly.

His full name is Hans Mueller and he comes from a family of privilege and connections. Ani, captivated by his charm, listens intently to his every word. When he asks about her, she decides to be honest and explains that she was born in Turkey and only came to Switzerland a short time ago. She hesitates a moment as her eyes meet his. "I'm alone here except for my toddler son."

When he doesn't inquire about the father, she smiles inwardly and lowers her guard, directing her gaze to the couples dancing.

After a few moments, he draws her hand into his. "They're playing the slow love ballads. Would you like to dance?"

She feels the warmth of his firm grasp; goose bumps rise up her arm. She nods her consent and stands to face him. He gracefully touches her waist, guiding her to the dance floor as the romantic music drifts across the ballroom. She follows his lead, feeling his strength as he draws her closer. She's unable to resist. For a moment, she's Cinderella whirling around in her chiffon dress with this handsome stranger.

In her own world, she clings to him, dancing until the music suddenly stops. Surprised, she laughs and says, "We're almost the last ones to leave. Where did the evening go?"

He guides her to the table, his touch still on her back. "Ani, I don't want the evening to end. Let's have one more drink."

She checks her watch; her face flushes with embarrassment wondering what he must think of her. Her voice is nervous, unsettled. "Thank you, Hans, but it's late and my sitter will be waiting. Where are Gretchen and Helmut?"

Hans peers into her eyes, casting a warm smile. "Everyone's drifted away, it seems, but us. It was wonderful dancing with you, Ani. May I drive you home?"

She feels too forward accepting his invitation, but relents, not wanting to walk alone in the dark. "Thank you, Hans, I've enjoyed the evening too. Yes, a drive home would be perfect."

He follows her directions to the apartment, parks and turns off the ignition. He lingers, gazing into her eyes.

She realizes he's waiting for a response, allowing her to set the pace. "Would you like to come in for a nightcap? I'll get Raffi in bed first."

"I was hoping you would ask," he replies. Quickly exiting, he darts around to open her door.

Raffi is fast asleep when Ani picks him up and thanks a bleary-eyed Mrs. Knodler as Hans discreetly waits in the hallway. Once in her apartment, Ani places Raffi in his bed and enters the living room to see Hans stretched out on her well-worn sofa.

"I have no schnapps, Hans. Will coffee do?"

"Most certainly." He smiles, his eyes surveying her.

Her eyes glow and she smiles back. "Make yourself comfortable. I won't be long."

She returns, places the cups on the table in front of the sofa, and sits next to him. "Do you take it with sugar and cream?"

"Black is fine," he says.

She senses a change of tone to his voice, less gentle, more assertive. His jaw tightens and the smile that entranced her all evening vanishes. She waits for him to say something, or even drink his coffee, but instead, he aggressively pulls her close, startling her. She feels the heat of his body on hers; his hand slides inside the neckline of her chiffon dress and onto her breasts. She panics, unable to push him away. "Hans, please don't do this!"

He has full control over her, holding her down, kissing savagely, squeezing her breast until it aches.

"No!" she shouts; his breath hot on her face.

"You know you want this as much as I do." His voice is hard, guttural.

She uses every last bit of strength to push him away, to escape, but his hold is strong. Her mind races, wondering how to get out of his vise-like grip. It's only after he pulls up her dress and tears at her panties that she instinctively twists sharply and jams her knee straight into his crotch.

He draws away, holding his privates, moaning in pain.

Ani makes a quick getaway toward the phone. "Leave or I'll call the police!"

He staggers toward her, eyes red with fire. "Bitch!" he curses, slapping her across the face.

She falls to the floor from the blow, but then instantly rises and dashes for the phone. Before she can dial for help, he yanks it away, throwing it against the wall.

"No need to call the police," he shouts. "I'm leaving!"

She trembles, touching the sting on her cheek. Shaken, she lets out an anguished cry, watching him storm out of the room. The door slams, confirming his exit.

Still quivering with fear, she quickly rushes to the door and turns the lock. As she stands, wiping away tears with the back of her hand, she realizes her vulnerability as a single woman—which means no further entanglements with men. Her goal is indelibly set in her mind and no romantic encounter will stop her from achieving it.

~ * ~

It's not until she witnesses Raffi at age three play with his friends in the park, laughing and shouting in German, that she becomes convinced it's time for her son to be well-versed in English.

Her ears have become attuned to the three languages spoken in Switzerland—German, French and Italian. It strikes her that English, the common standard of international languages, is not among them. She decides she has one more chore to accomplish before embarking on her final step to relocate to America.

Quickly she rises from the park bench, shading her eyes from the sun and calls out in German. "Raffi, time to go."

The beautiful boy, still carrying remnants of fine baby ringlets in his hair, halts at the top step of the slide, looks toward his mother and waves. His cherub cheeks are flushed from running and playing tag in the heat of the day.

Ani calls out again. "Raffi, you're allowed one more slide, and then we must go shopping."

Her lips lift in a smile watching his young body bravely slip down the long slide, imagining her Haig as a child. Father and son are both fairer than she and strikingly handsome.

On their walk home, she stops at the book store and purchases an English dictionary. She will teach Raffi everyday words in English. Her son will be fluent in the language by the time they arrive in America.

Ani wastes no time. The following week, she works overtime to complete a tedious translation project in order to remain at her office desk. After everyone leaves, she searches the massive directory listing international government agencies for possible translator positions. Her first choice is the United Nations in New York City. As she scans the directory, she spots a familiar name in the UN listings for Geneva. She quickly dials the site, asking for Helmut Schaeffer. A man answers on the third ring.

"Mr. Schaeffer," she responds in a polite tone. "This is Ani Sarkissian. We met at the Geneva government house when the Swiss ambassador to the UN was installed several months ago. I'm taking the liberty to call since you complimented me on my translations."

"Oh yes, Miss Sarkissian, I remember you well. How can I help?"

"I have a request; however, I would consider it a kindness if you would keep this conversation confidential."

There's a long pause until Schaeffer chuckles. "Certainly, as long as what you want is legal."

She clears her throat. "I intend to settle in the US and I'm looking for employment as a translator with the United Nations in New York. I speak Arabic, Russian and German fluently and some English. But I see no openings for translators in these languages. Do you have any connections at the UN to see if there is a position I can fill?"

Again there is a long pause before he speaks. "Yes, I can try, but openings are rare. I've heard how highly regarded you are by colleagues. . However, I will not ask why you wish to go to America."

A sense of relief floods Ani. "I assure you, Mr. Schaeffer, if I secure a position in New York, I will not do disservice to your recommendation."

Schaeffer lets out a gentle laugh. "I respect your sincerity and also your track record here, Miss Sarkissian. I don't promise, but give me some time and I'll get back to you."

Ani thanks him and hangs up, drying the moisture from her palms. Schaeffer's positive tone makes her heart race—even if it will take weeks and possibly months before he calls her. Living a frugal existence for four years, she has saved enough to purchase passage for herself and Raffi with a little left to cover the first few months of living expenses in America.

The wait is unbearable. She enters Raffi in a well-credited nursery school attended by children of many of her co-workers near the government complex. Each day she drops him off and then walks to her office, hoping to hear from Mr. Schaeffer. After six weeks, she becomes desperate, wondering if she should call him. Is her plan just an illusory dream? How many job openings could there be for a translator with her skills?

She finally hears from Schaeffer on the seventh week just as she's leaving the office to pick up Raffi.

"Ani, there might be an opening with the Saudi contingent at the UN."

Her heart races and she draws in a sharp breath. "When can I start?"

"Not so fast." Schaeffer chuckles. "First you must send your resume to Mr. Said al Salazar. I'll give you his full title and address."

Ani jots down the information while Schaeffer continues. "You mentioned you intend to establish permanent residency in the United States. Is that correct?"

"Yes, that's my wish. To raise my son there."

"I can recommend an immigration attorney who will smooth the way for you to get a green card."

Ani's voice rises along with her hopes. "Oh, many thanks, sir."

"Miss Sarkissian, I must caution you...as a Saudi employee, you might be required to cover your head."

"You mean like a hijab?" She remembers the long veil Muslim women are required to wear in public covering their hair, neck and shoulders.

"No, not that extreme. Just a small head scarf."

"That is no problem."

"Good. Write down the information for the attorney who will assist you with the green card."

At her desk, Ani records the telephone number and address of Mr. Warren Henderson with the law firm Henshaw, Goldberg and Henderson in Brooklyn.

"I can't thank you enough, Mr. Schaeffer. I promise not to disappoint you or the Saudis."

~ * ~

It takes close to a year before Ani's application is approved. After a successful interview by a Saudi Embassy official in Geneva, she signs her contract as an interpreter for the Saudi government located in the impressive UN building in New York City. Thanks to Schaeffer's influence, the Brooklyn immigration law office assures Ani that, although the process might take some time, they see no reason for her not to eventually be eligible for permanent status.

The day before she's to depart, Gretchen throws a surprise going away party at Mrs. Knodler's apartment. Tears, hugs and promises to write fill the living room of the boarding house that has become Ani's home and sanctuary for five years. The following morning, she embraces a tearful Mrs. Knodler, enters the taxi along with Raffi and two large pieces of luggage, and says goodbye to Geneva, the city that took her in and protected her.

Once at the airport terminal, she waits in line to check her baggage with her son at her side. Gently, she lays a hand on his head, caressing his soft curls. "Raffi, this is the beginning of our new life in America. Just as I promised."

~ * ~

After a long flight, Ani and Raffi arrive at La Guardia customs where their passports and visas are carefully scrutinized. Following the inspection, mother and son are cleared and directed to security. With formalities over, they leave the customs area, following exit signs to the main terminal lobby.

As they step off the escalator, Ani spots a tall man holding a sign with her name in bold print. As promised, Mr. Henderson has arranged a driver to meet and take them to their new apartment.

Once inside the taxi, Ani asks, "Where are you taking us?"

"Brooklyn, the Bay Ridge area," the driver replies.

Ani has no idea where that is, and persists. "Is Brooklyn in the city?"

The driver laughs as he turns to look at Ani. "Everything here is in the city, ma'am."

The multiple signs directing traffic out of the airport confuse her. Trucks, cars, busy highways, crossovers resembling webs of a spider. Signs for the Belt Parkway come into view and the driver speeds into traffic to keep in the correct lane. Ani sits white-knuckled holding onto Raffi while watching the driver dart around huge trucks. Making the sign of the cross, she prays silently that they will arrive safely at their destination after all they've been through.

After 45 minutes, the taxi slows as they drive onto a street lined with apartments and modest framed houses. It comes to an abrupt stop in front of a bright blue two-story wood-framed home squeezed between apartment buildings.

"You are now in Bay Ridge, Miss," he announces. "Mr. Henderson said this location will provide good subway access to the UN in Manhattan." He jumps out of the cab, retrieves luggage from the trunk and carries it to the front door. He tips his cap toward the young mother and her son before driving away.

Ani stands facing the house, still holding Raffi's hand, enchanted by what she sees. A brick walkway surrounded on both sides by patches of lawn leads to the front entrance. A cheerful artificial wreath of spring flowers is anchored to a bright yellow door. Ani's heart skips a beat as she and Raffi walk up the three steps. She embraces Raffi before ringing the buzzer. "Son, this will be our home now."

Suddenly the door opens, and a large-bosomed woman wearing an apron over a patterned house dress greets them. Her gray hair is pulled back in a bun, but despite her years, her skin is smooth and rosy. Childhood memories of her grandmother flash in Ani's mind. The woman has the same stocky build, the same welcoming smile.

The woman huffs, appearing to be out of breath from attending to some household chore. "You must be Mrs. Sarkissian, I've been expecting you. I'm Maggie Dooley. Please come in," she says, grabbing a suitcase. "Here, let me help you with the bags. After I show you the rooms, I'll get you something cool to drink." She speaks nonstop and Ani can't get a word in to thank her.

With the new tenants following, Mrs. Dooley leads them into a small foyer facing a narrow stairwell. They climb to the second floor landing with two doors at each end of the hallway. She pulls a key from the pocket of her apron and unlocks the door nearest the stairwell.

There's a warm glow on Dooley's face as she gestures Ani to enter. "This is your apartment. You have very nice neighbors occupying the one at the other end. You will meet them soon." She smiles at Raffi. "They have a boy just about your age."

Ani enters, Raffi at her side. Despite the encroaching darkness, a faint stream of remaining daylight filters through two large windows. The room, neat and simply furnished, carries the faint odor of a sweet air refresher. A wooden table with four chairs, and a kitchen with the basic needs for home cooking. A sofa and two cushioned chairs stationed in front of the windows.

Adequate, Ani thinks, walking across the room to peek into the two bedrooms, one smaller than the other.

The woman opens a door which Ani thinks is a closet. She announces proudly. "And here is your private bathroom. I had it installed last year."

Ani has never had a bath just for herself and turns to the landlady. "Thank you, this suits us well."

Mrs. Dooley's blue eyes squint into a smile and she places the key on the kitchen table. "Welcome to America, Ani."

Once she leaves, Ani opens cupboards while Raffi runs into the smaller bedroom and jumps on the bed.

He calls out. "Mommy, this will be my room! I like Mrs. Dooley and our new home."

Ani enters the room, sits on the bed, brushing a tear from her eye.

Raffi casts a worried frown at Ani. "Mommy, why are you crying?"

She wraps her arms around her son, holding him tight. "Son, these are tears of happiness." She then whispers a prayer of thanks in her native tongue, and makes the sign of the cross. The smooth transition to America is an unexpected miracle.

~ * ~

Johnny Pastorius, the boy next door, is a year older than Raffi, and like Raffi, an only child. The two boys quickly bond and are rarely apart. Together they walk to school, play, and have occasional sleepovers at each other's apartment. On school days, Raffi stays at the Pastorius home until Ani returns from work.

Ani quickly befriends the Greek Pastorius family. As Christians living for generations in the Middle Eastern Arab world, the Greeks had also been driven from their ancestral lands during World War One. Similar to the Armenians, they suffered under the despotism of the Ottomans and later, under the new Turkish government comprised of the Young Turks.

Ani returns home one afternoon earlier than usual and is surprised to see Raffi sprawled out on the floor watching TV. "Son, why aren't you at Johnny's house?"

Raffi's pleading look strikes a chord of fear in her. Was he in some kind of trouble?

His brown eyes widen as he stands up. "Johnny's busy with his violin lesson so I came home. Mom, I want to take violin lessons just like Johnny."

Ani smiles with relief. She has set money aside for occasions such as this. "We can manage that very well, but only if you practice every day."

"I promise I will, Mommy, every day."

Ani likes the idea, recalling Haig's love for music. Memories of him strumming Armenian love ballads on the oud cause her to take a hard swallow. Perhaps Raffi has his father's gift for music.

She hugs her son and says, "I'll check with Mrs. Pastorius tonight and make the arrangements."

As promised, after dinner, Ani calls Mrs. Pastorius. "Irene, Raffi wants to take violin lessons. May I have the name of Johnny's violin teacher?"

Pastorius, an earthy take-charge woman, lets out a hearty laugh. A Greek accent colors her speech. "Dear Ani, that's wonderful news! I'll arrange to have them take lessons at the same time since you work."

"Thank you, Irene. You are a good friend."

"Anything for you, dear Ani."

~ * ~

Throughout elementary school, Raffi's musical journey finally leads him to audition and acceptance to The High School of Music and Art in Manhattan. Ani learns that the public school is the first of its kind in the nation, established in the 1940s by Mayor Fiorello LaGuardia with a mission to enrich students with high academic grades with talent in music or art. Competition for entrance is stringent, and Ani is thrilled Raffi will be in an environment with other motivated students.

Her life is full, busy with work and fulfilling friendships from church. But when alone in the quiet hours of the night, memories of Haig surface. Where is he? Is he married or even alive? To find out, she checks the Internet at the library. Personal use of the computer at work would be too dangerous. She long suspects a secretive dark side to his life—a life in which she was never was allowed.

Her efforts bring no results and she closes the computer, discouraged. Possibly he carries an alias. After three attempts, she knows searching for him is a lost cause, and the demands of everyday living take priority.

Each weekday morning, she and Raffi travel the subway to Manhattan. They part ways, she walking the few blocks to the UN, and he, carrying books and violi

n to Music and Art. In the evenings, with a hint of a smile, she listens to him elaborate on his friendships with other students who share the love of music.

Ani discovers her son loves all types of music, both popular and classical. He plays violin, bass, guitar and occasionally drums, with student bands, earning pocket money. He even purchases a tuxedo from a consignment shop to wear when he plays violin with orchestras in well-known hotel ballrooms at an age when he isn't old enough to drink.

Besides music, Ani notices her son's aptitude in the sciences. Chemistry, biology, physics. It's in Raffi's junior year at Music and Art when in a matter of fact manner, he states, "Mom, I love music, but I've been thinking about becoming a doctor."

Ani's eyes glow with pride. "There could be no higher calling, son. It would be a good direction for you."

With her advice, he orders catalogues from the finest schools. She warns, "Now Raffi, it's important to attend a college of significance if you are to gain entrance to medical school."

As Raffi's high school years progress, she notices he spends less time with his musician friends. Instead, he studies into the night, earning high grades. Most evenings, their supper conversation centers on selecting colleges. Yale, Colgate, Cornell and Columbia top the list. How to pay? Ani's frugality allows her some savings, but not enough, so he applies for scholarships. Any amount, no matter how small, will help.

She'll never forget the day she retrieves the letter from the mailbox. Columbia University, Office of Admissions printed on the envelope. Her heart flutters; she's anxious to open it. In the kitchen, she places the correspondence on the table and waits for Raffi. He has orchestra rehearsal and will be home late. Too preoccupied to make a full meal, she scrambles eggs and sautés whatever vegetables she finds in the fridge and sets a portion aside for her son. She runs her finger over the envelope more than once, tempted to open it, but stops. Raffi's seventeen and she has to refrain from managing him.

As soon as he steps through the door, she thrusts the letter at him. They exchange apprehensive glances, and he slits the envelope open to remove a single sheet, allowing her to read over his shoulder.

Due to his excellent academic record, the Dean of Admissions congratulates Raffi Sarkissian on his acceptance to the undergraduate program at Columbia University. Raffi takes a hard swallow and reads the rest of the letter out loud. *"Because of your superior musical talent, we are awarding you a full scholarship to Columbia University on the condition you play viola with the university string quartet."*

Ani beams, wrapping her arms around him. Her mission is nearly complete. The rest of the journey will be his.

She continues working at the United Nations, and returns home to see Raffi's head bent over a textbook, studying at the kitchen table. At the end of four years, he graduates Columbia with honors, and in the late summer is accepted to the Cornell College of Medicine in New York City.

It's occasions like this when Haig's smiling face appears before her as she readies herself for bed. She has no photos, no traces that he existed, but she forces herself to remember his firm jaw, his sad eyes on a handsome face. In her heart, she still loves him.

It takes another four years for Ani to watch Raffi walk onto the Cornell University stage dressed in a black cap and gown, a colored sash signifying his doctorate degree. She sits in the auditorium, tears glazing her eyes. He has grown to look so much like his father. A lean tall frame, his hair darkened with maturity. Her thoughts return to Ankara and the wonderful days with Haig. How proud he'd be to see his son achieve such success. But she's learned to put that recurring heartache behind her. With tears of joy mixed with regret, she makes the sign of the cross, thanking God for making her dream for Raffi a reality.

# *One*

*Raffi's Story*

*Manhattan Medical Center, New York City, June 2011*

It takes nearly three tension-filled hours on Saturday night for chief surgical resident Raffi Sarkissian and his team to do the emergency repair of a ruptured abdominal aneurysm in operating room three. Raffi glances at the clock on the tiled wall. It's one o'clock Sunday morning as the junior resident places the last skin suture on the incision of the obese sixty-five-year old male. Nurses busily skirt around the operating room table disposing bloodied gauze into red hazard containers in preparation for Monday morning's elective eight o'clock case.

With surgery completed, Raffi's last duty before heading home to grab some shut-eye is to write postop orders. For a day starting before dawn, he and his crew are clearly exhausted.

He turns to Jeremy Jenkins, his junior resident, and to the first year intern. "Well done, guys. Let's roll the patient onto the

29

gurney and get him to ICU. Once he's stabilized and orders are written, we can go home."

They head to the Intensive Care Unit when Raffi's pager crackles. "STAT surgical consults request in ER."

The intern yawns, letting out a weary groan. "Christ, another emergency? We've got the busiest ER in all of Manhattan!"

Jeremy, Raffi's bright, dependable junior resident, grins as he keeps pace with the young intern, giving him a friendly nudge on the shoulder. "Don't sweat it, man. You'll soon get used to long nights with no sleep."

Raffi keeps a quick pace as he speaks to the anesthesiologist walking next to him. "Gail, get this chap squared away in ICU while I check the emergency in ER."

Her brow wrinkles, shooting him a concerned glance. "This guy's real shaky, so the sooner we get him in ICU, the better."

Before Raffi can answer, the overhead page blares. "Dr. Sarkissian, second call to ER, double emergencies! STAT!"

The intern speaks out, his eyes large as saucers. "I know the protocol...I'll write the orders."

Raffi looks to the young doctor who soaks up medical knowledge like a sponge. "Great, here's the chart. Write the postop entries and stay with the patient until he's stable. I'll check with you as soon as Jeremy and I take care of what's going on in ER."

"Sure thing," the intern says, and pushes the cart with Cheryl toward ICU.

Raffi and Jeremy waste no time taking the elevator to the first floor Emergency Room. Even at this late hour, the area is busy with patients.

The ER supervisor jumps on the two physicians as they enter, her brow knitted with concern. "It's a two car collision with serious casualties." She points to one of the ten curtained-off cubicles. "The fella in stall six is in pretty bad shape; better tend to him first."

Another nurse approaches, grabbing Raffi's arm. "Dr. Sarkissian, the woman in stall eight is Dr. Flint's patient. I just got off the phone with him and he demands the chief resident see her immediately."

*My luck.* The last thing Raffi wants is to lock horns with Flint. "No problem, Jennie. Jeremy and I will check her after we see the patient in six."

Jennie tightens her grip on Raffi's arm, lowering her voice. "Flint's on his way in, and if you don't see stall eight by the time he gets here, he'll blow his top."

Raffi flinches at the warning. Harold Flint, one of New York City's most prominent surgeons, carries major influence in the hospital. His social and political connections bring millions of charitable donations to Manhattan Medical, an attribute that simply can't be ignored.

Jeremy looks to Raffi with a shrug. "We all know Flint's temper. You better take care of his patient first. I'll tend to the fellow in six."

"Thanks, call if you need help." Satisfied that Jeremy is great under pressure, Raffi heads to Flint's patient and pushes aside the curtained drapes, hearing a painful whimper. A woman covered by a thin hospital sheet lies in a fetal position on the gurney. Her blonde hair is splayed across the pillow, her face turned to the wall.

The nurse hands Raffi the chart. "Name's Jane Smith."

"Thanks, Jennie," he replies, scanning the recorded entries. The woman's pressure is dropping, the red blood count dangerously low. He studies the x-ray hanging on the view box and detects free air in the abdomen, suggestive of a bowel perforation. *Gotta operate before she heads for a full septic infection.*

The light fragrance of perfume fills his senses as he approaches. "Miss Smith, I'm Dr. Sarkissian." He waits for her to face him, but instead, she moans without turning.

He motions for Jennie to remove the hospital sheet and leans close to the woman. "Miss Smith, I need to examine you."

She finally rolls over, and he catches a perfectly shaped nose on a beautiful face. Despite her grimace, she reminds him of classic Grace Kelly beauty, probably in her mid-twenties. Without speaking, he places his stethoscope on her abdomen and hears no bowel sounds. He frowns, pressing deeper, but she cries out, pushing his hand away.

He straightens and clears his throat, using his most professional manner. "Miss Smith, you have internal injuries. You need surgery."

Her blue eyes finally focus on him; her words are curt. "I want Dr. Flint!"

Raffi maintains a calm demeanor. "He's on his way in and will be the operating surgeon." He then turns to Jennie. "Call anesthesia, and have three units of packed red cells cross-matched for surgery. I'll check the patient in six before going to OR. Flint should be in by that time."

"The blood's ready, Doctor," Jennie replies.

Just then the nursing supervisor abruptly pushes open the curtain and pokes in her head. "Doc, the young man in six looks pretty bad. Dr. Jenkins put in a chest tube and it drained a steady stream of blood. Said to tell you he's taking him to X-ray for an emergency angiogram."

Raffi's brow wrinkles. *Blood in the chest signals vascular injury.* The angiogram will show if other major vessels are injured. "Thanks, Nellie. Have Jeremy call me with the angiogram results."

Jennie breaks in, locking eyes with Raffi. "Miss Smith's pressure is dropping again!"

Raffi studies the patient's pasty color, her lips a frightening blue. "She's bleeding out! Gotta move fast."

Jennie nods and with the supervisor's help, pushes Miss Smith's gurney into the elevator to the surgical floor as Raffi makes his way to the doctors' locker room. He changes out of his blood-stained greens into clean scrubs, but before he can enter the OR, the overhead speaker blares. "Code Blue, Code Blue, X-ray department!"

His heart sinks, aware Jeremy's patient is crashing. *Even if Jeremy needs help, I'm in no position to give it.*

He enters the OR, frustrated and conflicted. Whether he likes it or not, he has to tend to Flint's patient and scrubs at the sink. Charging into the OR with water dripping from both arms, he calls out to the circulating nurse. "Has anyone heard from Flint yet? He should've been here by now."

"Supervisor said he's on his way," the nurse answers, securing the ties on Raffi's sterile gown.

Gail, the anesthesiologist, stands at the head of the table; her eyes dart from the monitor to Raffi. "Hung two units of blood, but her pressure's too low to wait. Open her, Raffi!"

He winces at the thought. "Flint won't stand for that." It's a known fact the society surgeon restricts residents from operating on his private patients.

Gail flashes an impatient glare at Raffi. "You have no choice! She's under anesthesia, and with internal bleeding, it's too dangerous to wait."

Raffi admits Gail is correct. The patient's pallor shows evidence she's bleeding out. All traces of glamour are gone...blonde hair tucked under a paper cap, the plastic end of a trachea tube sticking out of her mouth. Whoever she is in Flint's star-studded patient world, any delay will place her at risk.

He paints the brown antiseptic on her torso in a deliberate manner, watching for Flint to appear. The sterile drapes are in place, and he checks the clock on the tiled wall. He can't wait any longer.

"Get started, Raffi," Gail urges.

His pulse quickens, aware Flint's name is on the consent form as primary surgeon. And Jane Smith sounds like an alias. *So who the hell am I actually operating on?*

Gail presses on. "She's sinking fast. Make the incision."

He peers over his mask and holds out his gloved hand to the scrub nurse. "Scalpel, please." Flint or no Flint, he can't stall any longer. He has to save this patient, and any thought of being sued for assault and battery quickly leaves him.

A loud thump shatters the tension-filled room as the swinging OR doors fly open. An unsteady red-eyed Flint staggers into the room, glaring at Raffi. "Take your hands off my patient and get to the other side of the table!"

Raffi moves quickly to the patient's left and holds out the knife. "Your patient is ready, Dr. Flint."

Flint wobbles unsteadily to the table, grasps the scalpel and hovers over the operative field while all eyes focus on him, waiting for the incision.

Raffi panics, realizing the man shouldn't operate in his inebriated condition. He watches Flint hold the scalpel with an indecisive wave over the patient. *Whether or not I have the authority, this is no time to argue.* Calmly, he says, "Dr. Flint, may I open for you?"

The surgeon shifts unsteadily on his feet, pauses, and squints at Raffi while everyone in the room holds his breath. Finally Flint hands Raffi the knife.

Raffi quickly makes the incision and the scrub nurse dries the field as he clamps and cauterizes the bleeders. He opens the peritoneum and an unexpected rush of blood spurts out, causing Flint to jerk back.

While the scrub nurse suctions, Raffi slips in a retractor to hold the wound open. Loops of intestines slide out, and he carefully packs them away to expose a crushed spleen, the bleeding source.

Flint abruptly brushes Raffi's hand away, thrusting his own his beefy hands into the wound.

The situation becomes a tug of war. Raffi forcibly grabs Flint's hands and positions them back onto the retractors. With the help of the nurse, he cuts the restricting ligaments and bands holding the fractured organ deep under the left diaphragm. He then raises the smashed spleen from the depths when Flint wildly grabs a clamp from the sterile tray.

"Watch out!" Raffi shouts, grabbing Flint's hand. "Don't clamp the tail of the pancreas."

Flint stops, confused, still focusing on the organ he nearly injured.

"I have it," Raffi says, gently releasing the clamp from Flint's hand. "I'll tie off the vessels."

With dazed eyes, Flint nods and steps back.

Raffi proceeds to clamp and tie bleeding vessels, and then searches the length of the bowel to find the perforation, the source of free air in the abdomen. Once identified, with the help of the nurse, he resects the injured portion and reconnects the small bowel. After washing the field, he takes in a deep breath, and faces Flint. "Everything's under control. Let's close."

From the corner of his eye, he sees Flint stand in a silent stupor, leaning on the table for support. Apparently, the senior surgeon is aware of how close he came to causing a dangerous pancreatic fistula, a complication all surgeons fear.

Once the patient is moved to the recovery room, Raffi peels off his gloves as he turns to the older surgeon. "Dr. Flint, would you like me to talk to the family?"

Flint mutters, stumbling over his words. "Uh-huh. I need to lie down."

Raffi leads him to the doctors' lounge, guiding him to the couch where he flops down and falls into a deep sleep. Raffi studies Flint's flaccid, wrinkled face, his low hanging jaw. *The man must be in his mid-sixties, close but not yet ready to retire.*

He leaves the room and shuts the door behind him, hearing the rattle of heavy snores. Ani's naïve respect for the medical profession comes to mind. Sometimes reality is quite different. *To think I gave up my musical career only to deal with the likes of a Flint.*

Prepared to speak to the family, he enters the surgical waiting room and instantly recognizes Candice Baker, the shapely blonde national anchorwoman for NBC. Dressed in a crisp, dark navy business suit accented by pearls layered on a satin blouse, she's slumped on the sofa, half asleep. She abruptly jumps up and approaches Raffi. "How is she?"

Raffi maintains a professional stance and replies, "She came through surgery fine. Are you related?"

Candice lets out a sigh of relief and extends her hand. "I was called as her closest friend since she has no family. Please tell me what happened."

"It was a two-car collision. That's about all I know. Maybe you can speak with Dr. Flint tomorrow—he's her physician."

"Where is he? I'd like to speak with him now."

Raffi puts on a professional smile to keep Flint's cover. "He's busy right now taking care of another emergency. But Miss Baker, rest assured, he took good care of your friend."

# Two

After a twenty-four hour stint into the wee hours of Sunday morning at Manhattan Medical, Raffi returns to his apartment and crashes, grateful he's not on call. He sleeps most of the day, microwaves a frozen dinner and spends the evening catching up on his surgical journals and watching Netflix.

Even before his alarm buzzes Monday morning, piercing wails of sirens awake him. He arises, shuffles to the window and opens the blinds, allowing early rays of dawn to filter into his second floor studio apartment. Located on Manhattan's lower west side, it's a convenient walk to the hospital, saving him the expense of owning and garaging a car in a busy city.

He stands for a moment, yawning, as he gazes out into the street below. All is still, no pedestrians, a few passing taxis and the sound of sirens long since gone. But within an hour, Monday morning bustle will resume and Manhattan's diverse population will fill the street in front of his doorstep. The wealthy, the workers, the homeless, all crammed into a patch of real estate no one can call his own.

He dresses in street clothes, then downs his usual orange juice and grabs a muffin before leaving the apartment to head to work. He walks to the hospital, breathing in the fresh air soon to be contaminated by the pollution of city traffic and honking horns. That's one reason he plans to leave the city once he completes his residency. He's all set to open a private practice in Sea Haven, a quiet seashore town on the Jersey coast.

But this morning is different. Nearing the hospital, he sees unusual activity in front of the building. TV satellite trucks are double-parked at the curb with people crowding the walkways. He hastens his pace, pushing through a small throng blocking his path. Two female reporters step aside but keep speaking into the video cameras aimed at them. Hospital security and New York's finest stand before the entrance practicing crowd control.

A policeman stops him as he approaches the front entrance. "Your identity badge, please."

"It's OK, he's a doctor," a hospital security guard speaks out, allowing him to pass through the barricade.

Raffi turns to the guard. "What's going on?"

Sticking his thumbs under a belt strapped below a round belly, the guard shakes his head, appearing irritated. "Man, ever since that socialite Traci Doss came into the hospital, the media's been all over the place."

Raffi recognizes the name. Traci Doss is the cigarette heiress the tabloids love to write about, gossiping over her every escapade. He's read articles about her in *People* magazine and newspapers. As the sole heir to multibillions she inherited from her father's estate, she's a well-known celebrity. With charitable foundations, university affiliations and global health initiatives linked to her name, her fame is legendary.

Instantly it hits him. Alias Jane Smith has to be Traci Doss. Someone in the hospital must have tipped off the media. He thanks the guard and enters, heading directly to her room before changing for the day's surgery.

As he approaches her door, a security guard stationed outside waves a newspaper at him. "Morning, Doc. I see you made the headlines. Somebody's really pissed at you."

Raffi grabs the paper and scans the front page headline. *HOSPITAL PLAYS FAVORITES TO SAVE HEIRESS.* A large photo of Traci Doss standing before Thunderbolt, her prize-winning race horse with its jockey at a society polo match, fills a good quarter of the page. He races through the article naming Raffi Sarkissian as Manhattan Medical's Chief Surgical Resident. *"He chose to save the life of wealthy Traci Doss, leaving a poor African-American laborer to die at the hands of a less experienced surgeon, junior resident Jeremy Jenkins."*

A smaller photo shows the black activist, Reverend Coleman Sanders, at a rally one year earlier, raising his fists. The article continues. *"Sanders is demanding an inquiry to investigate if the deceased man's civil rights were violated."*

Raffi's knees go weak and he steadies himself against the door jamb.

The guard retrieves his newspaper, shaking his head. "They really beat up on you, Doc, but Dr. Jenkins didn't get any high marks either, even though he's black. The reverend's using the race card again."

Raffi's shock turns to anger, recalling the events that occurred Saturday evening. Before leaving the hospital in the early hours Sunday morning, he and Jeremy had carefully reviewed the dead man's chart. Because he was wearing a seat belt, his diaphragm ruptured, his aorta lacerated and liver fractured. Every step taken was appropriate, and they both agreed no surgeon could have saved him. With no other information concerning the accident, Raffi is convinced the facts are on his side. He has to remain cool upon entering Miss Doss's room.

The heiress lies in bed, her head elevated, peering out the window. Pale without makeup, her matted long hair clings to her face. A naso-gastric tube hangs freely from her nose, connected to a long tube that suctions her stomach contents into a collecting device. She bears no resemblance to her celebrity photos.

He clears his throat to get her attention. "Good morning, Miss Doss."

She groans, her voice hoarse. "What's good about it? I feel awful. Where's Dr. Flint? I want to see him."

Raffi stands his ground not to be intimidated by her demanding tone. "He'll be here to check on you later. You're not expected to feel perfect just yet. Not only were you in a car accident, but you've had emergency surgery."

"The nurses told me my spleen had to be removed," she answers flatly.

He catches the sound of annoyance in her voice and decides to keep his distance. Wary of Flint's fanaticism, he plays it safe and keeps his reply brief. "Yes, Dr. Flint will fill you in on the details."

He turns toward the door when she calls out to him.

"Aren't you the doctor from the emergency room?"

He faces her scrutinizing gaze. "Yes, that's right."

She forces a smile and abruptly changes her demeanor, taking in his tailored jeans, Italian leather shoes and casual suit coat. "That's a cool jacket. You look different in street clothes."

Unaccustomed to such a direct examination, Raffi's face flushes. "Thanks for noticing."

She coyly pulls the covers to just below her chin. "Tell me, Doc. Can I live without a spleen?"

No way will he get into a tiff with Flint regarding his patient. "Miss Doss, Dr. Flint will discuss everything with you."

She brushes the hair away from her face. "How long do I have to stay here?"

Safe with generalities, he answers, "Maybe a few more days."

Her fingers tighten on the edge of the white sheet. "God! I'm supposed to fly to Hawaii tomorrow."

His timeline is short and he taps his foot impatiently. *I don't care whether she's going on vacation or doing fundraising.* "You might want to wait a few weeks for that."

She releases a deep sigh, her head cocking to one side. "You're probably right. I'd applaud Dr. Flint for saving my life, but I'm in too much pain to clap. Can I get more pain meds?"

As Raffi flips through the clipboard of medication, a knock sounds on the door. A lean, tall, well-dressed man carrying an attaché case and wearing a dark business suit marches in and a nurse follows. His demeanor is somber as he approaches the bed and places his briefcase on the floor. "Good morning, Traci."

Raffi throws a questioning look toward the patient.

Traci announces in a dry tone. "Meet Grant Perry, my personal lawyer," and then looks to the nurse. "I'm still hurting. I need a shot."

"Right away," the nurse answers, leaving quickly.

The lawyer stands beside the bed, his thin, lined face showing a flat expression. "Sorry to see you like this, Traci, but I've got some questions about the events of Saturday night."

Traci tightens her lips and scowls. "Not now, Grant. I'm hurting too much."

Perry appears unmoved, casting a sharp glance at Raffi. "Doctor, I have some personal business with Miss Doss. It'll take only a few minutes, so please wait outside."

Traci's eyes narrow. "Grant, whatever you have to say, spit it out. I'm really in pain here!"

Raffi takes Traci's side. "Mr. Perry, she's still shaky from surgery. Can't this wait?"

Traci looks to her lawyer. "Grant! The doctor stays! Just get this over with!"

The lawyer's lips tighten into a smirk; his voice rises with anger. "Traci, a woman's body was discovered in your guest bedroom by your maid the morning after the party. Police investigation is ongoing as I speak. You certainly will be questioned."

Traci moans and pulls herself upright, more alert. "Who died in my apartment?"

"Nancy Wood. What can you tell me about her?"

Traci presses a hand to her forehead. "Not much. She came to the party with Senator Olin Davis. I've seen her with him before, but I don't know her personally."

Perry presses on. "Is there anything else you need to tell me before you're questioned about your auto accident as well as the death?"

Traci crinkles her nose and flops her arms down on the bed. "Stop it, Grant! I can't handle all this bad news right now."

Raffi breaks into their conversation. "Sir, she's fresh out of surgery and needs her rest."

Perry throws Raffi an impatient glare. "Doctor, it's a full time job protecting Miss Doss from crackpot lawsuits and phony allegations. I must get the facts as soon as possible. The auto accident already hit the papers and lawyers will storm the court to file lawsuits. There's no telling what will happen when the media gets hold of Nancy Wood's death."

Traci waves her hand impatiently in the air. "Dammit Grant! Pay them off, get rid of them!"

The attorney's jaw hardens. "It's not that simple, Traci. Regarding the auto accident, any settlement offer will be viewed as an admission of guilt that you caused the collision. After all, you had a tire blowout, crashed into the other car and the driver died." Undaunted by Traci's annoyance, the lawyer continues. "As far as the woman's death in your apartment, that's under investigation. Is there anything you can tell me?"

Traci's face flushes as she grabs a tissue from her nightstand and wipes her brow. "There's nothing to tell. Just take care of it, Grant. You lawyers can do things we mortals can't."

The nurse returns with a loaded syringe and turns to the lawyer. "Please step out. You can return when I finish."

Perry steps outside the room and Raffi follows. "Are you the doctor who admitted her to the hospital?"

"Yes, I'm Chief Resident Sarkissian."

The lawyer clears his throat, getting to the point. "Questions will be raised and we'll need your deposition."

Reluctant to get involved with legal matters, Raffi's relieved when the nurse opens the door, and announces, "You can come in."

Perry looks to Traci on entering. "I've asked Dr. Sarkissian for his deposition."

Traci nods her approval. "Doctor, please answer whatever he wants." She rubs her red-rimmed eyes. "Grant, I feel lousy. Enough questions."

The lawyer picks up his case and faces Raffi. "I'll be in touch, Doctor."

With a full morning of scheduled surgery, Raffi says, "Miss Doss, time you get some rest."

As he heads for the door, she calls after him. "What's your hurry, Doc? I want to thank you for keeping me alive."

"All in a day's work," Raffi replies.

Her voice lowers; a flush creeps over her cheekbones. She lifts her hand, pointing to her naked finger. "I see you're not wearing a wedding ring."

He can play the game just as well and keeps a straight face. "Not married."

She brushes away a wisp of hair from her forehead. "You're very attractive. All the pretty nurses chasing you?"

Raffi hides a smile. The narcotic injection has taken effect, making her playful and flirty and kind of cute. Grateful for the ring of his cell phone, he answers and realizes it's his alarm. Thirty minutes to prep. "Miss Doss, got to head to surgery. Take care and get your rest."

As he moves to the door, Traci calls out, "I didn't get your name."

"Dr. Raffi Sarkissian," he answers over his shoulder.

Stepping into the elevator, he reflects how she's taking her good surgical outcome for granted. Despite coming close to death, she acts like the self-centered spoiled rich princess in children's storybooks. Never even showed remorse over the stranger's death in the car accident, or Nancy Wood.

The doors to the elevator open onto the OR floor, and the hustle and bustle playing out before him brings back reality. This is the universe he belongs to, far removed from the idle rich and society lawyers.

The desk secretary looks to him as he approaches the nursing station. "Dr. Sarkissian, before you start, Dr. Flint wants you to call him."

# *Three*

Raffi's pulse quickens as he enters the doctors' locker room. *Is Flint offended I took over in surgery?* Changing into his scrubs, he focuses on the double trauma Saturday night. His action was straight on target, even though he wasn't the operating surgeon on the consent. Everyone in the OR witnessed Flint's condition.

He closes the locker door and walks into the connecting room to dial up Flint before going into surgery. The lounge, where doctors relax, swallow a quick cup of stale coffee between cases, is empty. He drops onto the leather couch prepared to dial Flint and catches a female news reporter standing in front of Manhattan Medical on the TV screen.

She's talking into a video cam, gesturing toward the stone building behind her. "I'm in front of Manhattan Medical where Reverend Coleman Sanders continues to demonstrate, demanding an inquiry into the death of African-American Tommie Jackson, who died on Saturday night. The question raised by the black community is whether tobacco heiress, Traci Doss, received preferential treatment while Mr. Jackson was left to die at the hands of a junior surgical resident."

Raffi's gaze remains glued to the screen as he listens to the reporter mention several black activist civil rights groups. Again, his mind locks on Saturday night. *God damn! Jeremy and I reviewed Jackson's chart and agreed no patient could have survived what Tommie Jackson suffered.* They had written it all on the chart...hypovolemic shock, hemorrhage from a torn aorta, liver lacerations.

The page blares overhead, calling him to OR. He decides to delay the call to Flint. Bad news can wait until he finishes his surgery.

~ * ~

It's mid-morning by time Raffi walks out of the OR to an urgent message from the nursing desk.

"Dr. Sarkissian, Dr. Flint called twice. Sounds important."

"Thanks, Flo, next on my agenda." He returns to the lounge and dials Flint, still occupied with the TV news report. He could be drawn into a battle fighting a civil rights charge and has to tread lightly because Flint could also be implicated.

Flint's receptionist answers. "Oh, yes, he's right here, let me transfer you."

Within seconds Flint greets him in a heavy but sober voice. "I saw Miss Doss this morning and she's doing well. I want to thank you for taking good care of her."

Raffi's disarmed by Flint's compliment. The society surgeon's not the warm and cuddly type to toss out casual praise. "I appreciate that, Dr. Flint, but most of the credit goes to our crackerjack team at Manhattan Medical."

"I agree and thank them too, but there's something I'd like to discuss. Could you come to my office when you're free?"

Raffi's thoughts flare. *What does Flint want?* "Sure thing, Dr. Flint. I'm off Friday afternoon."

"Will three o'clock be satisfactory?"

"I can make that, sir."

"My office is in the Professional Arts Building, near Lexington Avenue at Six-thirty-four East Fifty-fourth Street. See you then." The phone goes dead.

Raffi dries the moisture on his palm onto his pant leg. *Has the meeting anything to do with the civil rights issue?* With only a matter of weeks left in his residency, he doesn't need that distraction just when he plans to start his private practice at the Jersey shore.

His cell phone rings and Ani's name comes up on the caller ID. She left a message earlier and he meant to call.

"Raffi, it's Mother, remember me?"

"Hi Mom, sorry I didn't get back to you."

"You're forgiven, but I'm expecting you for dinner on Saturday. Come at five, don't forget. There're friends I would like you to meet. An attorney and his wife and a newspaper photographer." She pauses, and lets out a repressed laugh. "I have news to tell, so I promise you won't be bored."

"What's the news?" He knows his mom keeps a secret better than anyone and no amount of cajoling can change her mind.

"When you get here."

Raffi gives a teasing chuckle. "Are you inviting an eligible young woman by chance?"

"No, but I should! You're over thirty and you know how I feel. It's time you meet someone, get married, start a family."

He taps the phone impatiently with his finger. "I've got to go, Mom. See you on Saturday." He slips the phone into his pocket and returns to the OR reception desk to check on his next surgery.

The desk secretary, wearing a questioning look, holds out a slip of paper as he approaches. "Doctor, Mr. Mays, the hospital administrator wants you to call his office for an appointment." She hesitates, then adds, "He sounded very insistent."

Raffi thanks her and tucks Mays' telephone number in his pocket. *Now what?* Any contact with administration is very unusual.

~ * ~

Tucked away on the fifth floor, the hushed atmosphere of the executive office contrasts sharply to the noisy activity of patient care areas. Raffi has never been invited to the administrator's office, and cautiously approaches the receptionist, still in his scrubs.

"I'm Dr. Sarkissian. Mr. Mays is expecting me."

"I'll tell him you're here," she says, rising to enter the inner office.

As he waits, his eyes wander over the soft beige Berber carpet set against ivory walls, giving the room a relaxed, clean appearance. The soft lighting creates a feeling so different from the harsh florescent glare of the unpredictable medical emergency room a few floors below. Plush leather sofas are separated by an expansive coffee table holding neatly arranged magazines. The orderly placement of furnishings reinforces Raffi's sense of the chasm existing between administrators and physicians.

The receptionist returns and gestures to the open door. "Mr. Mays will see you now."

Raffi enters, but Mays is not alone. Rather the meeting appears to be more like an investigative inquiry with the administrator at his desk facing three men seated across from him. He immediately recognizes the beefy African-American slumping back in his chair as Reverend Coleman Sanders. The thin balding middle-aged gentleman in heavy, dark-rimmed glasses waits at attention on the edge of his seat, a leather briefcase at his feet. The third is the only one Raffi recognizes: Harry Butler, Chief of Surgery.

Mays rises as Raffi enters. "Thank you for coming, Doctor Sarkissian. I'd like you to meet Reverend Coleman Sanders."

The stocky man remains seated, nodding grimly toward Raffi, and Raffi returns the nod.

"And this is Barry Gold, our hospital attorney."

The man with the dark rimmed glasses rises to shake Raffi's hand. "Glad to meet you, Doctor."

Having a minister and a lawyer in the room triggers an alarm bell in Raffi. He can't imagine the purpose of the meeting, certainly not for medical business.

Mays returns to his seat, bringing his fingertips gently together. "Dr. Sarkissian, we asked you here to help explain to Reverend Sanders your medical management of Tommie Jackson, the man who died after Saturday night's auto accident."

Reverend Sanders straightens in his chair, his steady gaze fixed on Raffi. "As you are aware, the two-car collision resulted in injuries to two people. They came into the emergency room at the same time. As chief resident, you took the society heiress to surgery and saved her while Tommie Jackson, a simple black laborer, died under the care of a lesser trained surgeon. We're rightfully questioning if Tommie's civil rights have been violated."

Raffi holds his breath, trying to keep his composure. *What can I say?* The truth already has been muddied by the media.

Butler catches Raffi's hesitancy and interjects. "The hospital takes no position that you did anything wrong, Dr. Sarkissian."

Raffi stands frozen in the deafening silence. He never saw Tommie at the time of admission. *No matter what I say, I'm already crucified by Sanders.*

The reverend unbuttons his jacket and eagerly leans forward, waiting for Raffi's response.

Raffi's jaw tightens in anger and he holds Reverend Sanders' gaze. It's apparent he's the fall guy, the reason for Tommie's death. "Sir, in my nearly five years at Manhattan Medical, I have never practiced nor ever advised anyone to triage patients based upon race, religion or economics. The man died because—"

The corners of Sanders' mouth turn up in a smirk. "Now Doctor Sarkissian, you are the chief resident, responsible for tending to the patient whose injuries are more severe."

Raffi knows the reverend's mind is closed to reason but he has to try a different approach. "Reverend, are you suggesting Dr. Jenkins isn't sufficiently trained to manage a case like Tommie's?" He pauses a moment and answers his own question. "That's absolutely not true. Jeremy's a gifted surgeon, the best I've seen during my years at Manhattan Medical."

The reverend's eyes narrow, his voice rises. "The man died, didn't he? Did you abandon Tommie because he's black?"

Butler stands up, cutting into the conversation. "Reverend, that's not a fair question."

Sanders is quick to answer. "It is to the dead man's family!"

Raffi continues to defend himself. "Tommie was not abandoned! His injuries were so massive that no surgeon could have saved him."

Sanders pulls his bulky frame from the chair and stands to his full six-foot height, staring down at the men. "We'll see about that." He gives Mays a brisk nod and heads to the door.

The administrator calls out, "Reverend, you're welcome to have your own expert review the chart."

Sanders throws Mays a piercing glare. "Tommie has two kids and a wife, and he's not here to fight for them. But I can." With that, he turns and leaves the room.

Mays gives the attorney a forlorn look. "Barry, what do you make of this?"

Gold removes his spectacles, wiping them with a handkerchief before responding. "I know Sanders to be one stubborn guy, so we definitely will have a fight on our hands." He turns to Raffi. "I understand your residency ends soon. This issue may not disappear by then, so be prepared to help defend the hospital. Unless you do so, Manhattan Medical will have no responsibility for any civil liabilities you might face." He rises, picks up his leather briefcase and faces Mays. "Arthur, I have another meeting pressing me, but I'll keep in touch."

Raffi watches attorney Gold walk out, closing the door behind him. Suddenly he feels like a ship without a rudder. It was Flint's order to take care of Traci, but he hesitated to state that fact. This wasn't the first time he had assisted Flint, but the man forced his hand when he arrived to the OR intoxicated. Whether Mays and Butler are aware of that fact doesn't matter. The society surgeon wields too much clout to be put in the crossfire. The discussion in the room tells him that he's alone in this battle.

# *Four*

The Reverend Coleman Sanders drops his massive frame onto the threadbare armchair across from Matilda and Odias Jackson, Tommie's separated parents. Their son's death will advance his political agenda, and he's come to get their support.

He faces Odias, who sits restlessly fidgeting on a saggy sofa beside Matilda. Dark and very thin, Odias jerks his head every few moments with a nervous tic, suggesting symptoms of drug addiction.

The reverend leans toward the couple with a solemn, sympathetic expression. "Odias, it's evident your son's civil rights were violated due to the color of his skin. The doctors at Manhattan Medical left him to die from his injuries while they took that rich white gal to surgery and saved her life." He shakes his head prophetically, and presses on. "We have here a clear case of racial discrimination, and you must take action."

A deafening silence ensues until Matilda speaks, glaring at Odias. "What's the judge gonna say when he hears Tommie never even saw his daddy for ten years after you ran out on us?"

Sanders patiently clasps his hands. "That's not the issue, Mrs. Jackson. You *both* lost a son because of an injustice and the hospital has to pay."

Odias speaks in a soft tone. "Did the doctors find any alcohol or crack in Tommie's blood?"

The reverend clasps his hands together. "Makes no difference, Odias. That rich girl plowed into his car, killed him, and she should pay."

Matilda bursts into tears, struggling to wipe the flow with the tissue she pulls from her apron's pocket. Angrily, she pounds her ex on the shoulder. "Odias, don't talk like that about your son! Tommie had cleaned up real good and was working hard to become a head cook."

Odias raises a hand to his face. "Matilda, I love Tommie just like you, but you know he had problems."

Abruptly, Matilda lets out an anguished moan, throwing her arms up in the air. "I miss my baby! Reverend, money won't bring Tommie back!"

The general shabbiness of the room indicates she could use the money. Sanders continues patiently, speaking gently to calm her. "Matilda, believe me, that's why you gotta sue to justify your son's death. That rich woman won't miss anything for what she pays."

Odias breaks in. "How much do you think we can get, Reverend?"

Instead of answering, Sanders rises and paces as if in deep thought, and then stops to lock eyes on the two. "I figure between Tommie's wife, two kids and both of you, about ten million with another five for pain and suffering."

Odias grins, revealing the few stained teeth left in his mouth. He slaps his leg with gusto. "Man! No way could Tommie make that kind of money as a cook."

A more composed Matilda clears her throat. "Reverend, have you talked to Tommie's wife?"

"Yes, I have, but she's too upset and confused. Told me to do whatever I think best." Sanders knows he has to take control. The lawsuit would bring him national attention politically and provide financial support for his agenda.

Odias leans forward, pressing both hands on his thighs. "So, if that's how much we can get from the hospital and the lady, what's wrong with that?"

Sanders can see the calculations flying in Odias's brain. "The civil rights charge will also be part of the death benefit settlement," he explains. "They serve to remind folks how unfair whites can be to blacks."

Matilda throws Odias a hardened glance. "You always thinkin' about money and dat ain't right. Tommie's boys will grow up not knowing their daddy. Dat's what you should be thinkin' about."

"But a court settlement is the *only way* to help the boys. Suing is the way to go," Sanders pleads.

Matilda's eyes narrow into a suspicious squint. "Reverend, how much you gonna make from this lawsuit?"

Startled, Sanders stops pacing, unaccustomed to being challenged. "Why, nothing," he answers.

"You sure?" Matilda questioned.

Sanders looks Matilda in the eye. "I'm only trying to help the Jackson family get what they deserve, nothing more."

Matilda looks suspiciously at him, offering a shrewd observation. "With that kind of money floatin' around, it wouldn't surprise me if some of it stuck to your fingers."

Odias bursts out. "Woman, what's wrong with you? Reverend Sanders deserves a share."

Matilda frowns, shaking her head back and forth. "Somehow I can't help feelin' we're being used, and you, Odias, don't give a shit."

Sanders interrupts, breaking the tension. "Look Matilda, Tommie's wife agrees, Odias agrees, and you should too. We can't bring Tommie back, but whatever you get will help the family."

"I'm with you, Reverend," Odias says, turning to Matilda. "I'm sick and tired seeing black folks jailed and kicked around like second class people. It's time we got our dignity back."

Matilda jumps up and puts her hands on her hips. "See! You always make it a black and white issue. Dat lady didn't know the color of Tommie's skin when she crashed into him."

Sanders comes to Odias's rescue. "That's true, but when Tommie got to the hospital, the doctors certainly knew. Why didn't they take him to surgery first? Why did he end up dead, waiting for the care to keep him alive?"

Odias whines, pulling her back down onto the sofa. "Come on, Matilda. The reverend's right, and we need the money."

Sanders remains quiet, studying Tommie's parents outstare each other. His experience observing human nature has taught him that self-interest is the primary motive when dealing with people. For sure, the money Odias wants is to feed his drug addiction. And Matilda clearly questions why this absentee father should profit from his son's death.

After a drawn-out silence, Matilda finally addresses Sanders. "Okay, Reverend, go ahead and make the arrangements. But before I sign, I want it clear Odias doesn't get an equal share. He never was a father to Tommie, so why now?"

# *Five*

Raffi carefully knots his tie and slips on a dark blue blazer in the doctors' locker room. Both of his surgical cases were performed with no delaying complications. He checks his watch. It's two o'clock Friday and Flint expects him by three.

As he hurries down the hall, a young trim-figured nurse with jade green eyes and crimson hair approaches. "Don't you look sharp, Doctor. Could I interest you in a quick cup of coffee?"

"I'd love to, Janet, but I'm rushing to an appointment."

"Oh, take a minute. We nurses are all buzzing about Traci Doss. What's she like?"

Her eyes sparkle, telling him she's interested in more than Traci. Outside of an occasional drink with her in the company of friends, he's never encouraged a personal relationship.

"Sorry Janet, I'm running late."

She smiles, gently touching his arm. "Then I'll take a rain check."

He moves toward the elevator. "Sounds good," he replies, hitting the down button.

Once outside, he waves to a passing cab that quickly pulls up to the curb, and within minutes, he's on his way to Flint's midtown office. When it comes to a stop in front of the turn-of-the century stone building, he knows he's in the high rent district.

A uniformed doorman directs him to the elevators and after the short ride he enters Flint's sleek contemporary waiting room. A vibrant abstract oil painting highlighted by halogen spots gives the space a feeling of drama. He takes a seat in a high-styled leather chair, assessing the powerful statement the room reflects on Flint's professional success.

The inner door opens and a uniformed nurse appears. "The doctor will see you now, Dr. Sarkissian."

Raffi rises promptly, following her down a brightly lit corridor between separate exam rooms.

The moment he steps into the private office, Flint questions, "What kind of a name is Sarkissian?"

Startled by his abruptness, Raffi replies, "Armenian."

Flint's brow wrinkles. "Is that like Romanian or Albanian?"

Raffi's head shakes. "No."

"Never heard of it."

He replies, knowing he's teaching Flint something new. "Armenia is known for its historical significance. It's where Noah's Ark landed on Mount Ararat and it is documented to be the first nation to establish Christianity as its state religion."

Flint throws a curious grimace, brushing fingers to his chin. "Very interesting, but I'm sure you want to know why I called you."

"Is it about the surgical consent for Miss Doss's surgery? I named you the surgeon when I dictated the case," Raffi replies defensively.

Flint chuckles and pounds the desk. "Hell, no! It's about your future, son. Your residency ends in less than a month. Have you decided what you're doing?"

"Yes," Raffi answers. "I have privileges at Monmouth Memorial down at the Jersey shore. I'll be sharing space with another surgeon in his office."

Flint rises from his chair and points to the large window offering a view of the Manhattan skyline. He smiles as he turns to Raffi. "You might want to consider staying in New York. How would you like to join my practice?"

Raffi's jaw drops in surprise. Is the offer because he saved Flint's ass?

Flint doesn't wait for a reply, and waves a hand. "Of course, you'll be on salary at first, but if we work well together, you'll be a partner in two years."

The unexpected invitation to treat New York's elite stuns Raffi. "Dr. Flint, I don't know what to say."

Flint approaches Raffi, placing a firm hand on his shoulders. "Say yes, you deserve it. You did the right thing the other night. How about a starting salary of two-fifty with a percentage of what you make tallied at the end of the year?"

Raffi remains silent, his thoughts racing. Accepting the offer would wipe out his medical school debts in no time and he wouldn't need that loan to purchase office equipment.

Flint returns to his desk, and presses on. "Of course, you'll be dealing with wealthier clients, patients you'll never see at the Jersey shore."

Raffi frowns, hesitating. "Sounds cool, Dr. Flint, but I need time to think it over." While living on a budget, he and his mother had never gone hungry or without. Money was never a driving factor in their lives.

"Certainly, but don't wait too long. Fixing your office, getting malpractice coverage, all that takes time." Flint gets up, signaling that the meeting is over.

Raffi takes the cue and rises, still bewildered by the possibility of changing his plans. He needs to consider all of his options and extends his hand. "Thank you, Dr. Flint. I'll get back to you early next week."

Flint gives Raffi a firm but friendly reassuring hand shake. "Call me Harold. I'll be waiting.

Raffi enters the elevator, taking his place next to an attractive middle-aged woman and gives her a friendly smile. Her styled silver hair complements the tailored powder blue suit she wears. Designer shoes and purse symbolize the prestige and wealth he could expect by associating with Flint.

When the elevator reaches the first floor, he waits for her to exit while doing a mental balancing act. Standing outside the building, he watches people scurry by. The seductive power of money excites him, but aside from Flint's alcoholism, he knows little else about the man.

As he turns the corner to find a cab, a bald-headed vagrant with a shaggy beard approaches, holding out his hand. "Spare five bucks for a hungry man?"

Raffi awakens from his trance, studying the frail figure. The beggar's tattered jacket and stained pants identify him as one of New York's homeless, probably addicted to drugs or alcohol. In a flash, he takes out his wallet and hands him the money, sensing the power of wealth. Maybe he'd be wise to accept Flint's offer.

~ * ~

The bus ride to Ani's apartment the following day takes longer than expected. What should take twenty minutes takes more than thirty-five due to heavy traffic. Realizing he'll be late, he dials his mother.

"Mom, I'm on my way but let me give you some good news. I got an offer from Dr. Flint to join his practice here at Manhattan Medical."

"Wonderful, Raffi! Did you accept?"

"Not yet, but I'm thinking about it. Now what about your news?"

"We'll talk about it later; just bring your appetite. There's someone I want you to meet."

Raffi steps off the bus and walks the short distance to Ani's apartment. It's a ground floor dwelling off Third Avenue in an old brownstone converted to two units. She has her own entrance in the basement, and the above ground floors are occupied by the owner. "This is just perfect for me," she had told Raffi when she rented it. "Although it's more than twice the price of Mrs. Dooley's Brooklyn flat, the convenience of the location is well worth it."

He skips down the five steps, and without hitting the buzzer, enters, heads for the tiny kitchen, taking in the aroma of his favorite Armenian dishes.

"Sorry I'm late, Mom. Traffic was heavy," he says, kissing her on the cheek.

Ani, still beautiful at fifty-six, has kept her figure, although a few fine strands of gray streak through her thick ebony hair. Her hazel eyes sparkle on seeing her son, and she hugs him tight.

"I made your favorites. Rice pilaf, shish kabob and borags."

He spots the triangle-shaped cheese-filled pastry sitting on the counter and pops one in his mouth. "Mom, as always, perfection!"

She laughs, shooing him away. "The guests are in the living room waiting to meet you. I'll be in shortly."

Ani's three friends are seated around the cocktail table covered with ethnic appetizers: tabulah, hummus and pita bread triangles.

"Glad to meet you all. I'm Raffi," he says on entering.

A gray-haired man of advanced age returns Raffi's handshake. "I'm Marty Dederian, and this is my wife, Lucy."

The third guest appears to be sixtyish, a bit older than Ani. He promptly rises and also greets Raffi with a handshake. "I'm David Frohman. I've heard so much about you from your mother."

The name is familiar. Ani had mentioned him on several occasions when he invited her to the opera and a Broadway play. He smiles at the good-looking man, wondering if his relationship with his mother is more than platonic. Is that her announcement? His mother's large expressive eyes still turn heads.

Ani returns from the kitchen, gazing pleasantly at her company. "Help yourselves to the appetizers. David, I hope you enjoy the kind of food I grew up with."

David offers her the chair next to him. "You're spoiling this bachelor, my dear. Everything's delicious."

Ani seats herself beside him, and then turns to Raffi. "David's a photographer for *People Magazine* and says he did a spread on Traci Doss, the heiress you operated on."

Raffi flinches, uncomfortable reliving the stressful news in the media and wants to distance himself from the controversy, "She's Dr. Flint's patient, not mine."

Dederian focuses on Raffi. "But you were mentioned in the news reports. As a lawyer, I believe what happened in your hospital will become a high profile civil rights case."

Ani butts in, shaking her head. "I don't like any of it! Doctors like my son are dedicated to helping people, not hurting them."

David pats Ani's hand sympathetically. "I'm convinced Raffi did whatever he had to do, but the sorry fact is the media's job is to sell papers. What better story than a rich cigarette heiress getting superior treatment over a poor black guy who died?"

Raffi breaks in, trying to stay calm. "Please, I've tried to make the truth clear, but the newspapers and TV reporters have a knack for sensationalizing. With the severity of his injuries, nobody could've saved Tommie Jackson."

The attorney shakes his head in agreement. "I understand, Raffi, but Reverend Sanders is looking for publicity and you and your lawyers might have a tough time defending your position. Race is a very big proponent of this issue."

Ani's face flushes, her voice rises. "I raised Raffi with Christian values. I trust in the integrity of his work as a physician, as well as in his personal life."

Raffi shifts in his seat, relieved when Ani changes the conversation.

She beams a smile toward her guests. "Enough of this talk. Raffi has some good news. Dr. Flint has invited him to join his practice."

David raises an eyebrow. "The surgeon catering to Park Avenue? I thought Raffi planned to practice at the Jersey shore."

Raffi catches the tone of familiarity in David's voice. *Is mom's relationship with him more than platonic?* Why else would she discuss their personal lives? He rises from his seat, pours himself a glass of wine and then scoops up hummus on a slice of pita. Before he sticks the morsel in his mouth, he faces David. "That's what I was going to do before Flint's offer came up."

Marty Dederian's tone takes on a lawyerly warning. "A word of caution, Raffi. If you go with Flint, get legal advice before signing a contract."

Raffi nods at the lawyer. "Thanks for the suggestion, Marty." An attorney would protect his interests from a powerful figure like Flint.

Ani's eyes dart around the room, ready to make her announcement. "I've brought you all here to celebrate the decision I've made about my future." She pauses momentarily. "After more than twenty-five years at the United Nations, I am pleased to say the FBI has offered me a position as a translator and I have accepted."

Stunned by the news, Raffi asks "Why, Mother? Are you unhappy at the UN?"

Ani speaks with conviction. "No, I love working there, but since the nine-eleven tragedy, the FBI needs translators in the Arabic language. With all the Islamic terrorist activities, I feel it's my patriotic duty to accept their offer."

Raffi rises and embraces her. "I'm so proud of you, Mom. The FBI picked a winner."

"I agree," David adds.

Ani stands up, straightening her skirt. "I'm glad you all approve, so let's eat."

A relieved Raffi joins the guests at the round dining room table positioned off the living room. His head spins with multiple thoughts. He thought his mom would work with the UN until she died, and for the first time since he can remember, she brings a man around. A decent guy, too, from the looks of it.

And now, after one infamous surgery, he's been offered an associate position in an upscale office in Manhattan by a well-known celebrity surgeon. As Marty hinted, the move also carries risks. He never would have faced Reverend Sanders if he hadn't been sucked into Flint's orbit. Before making a decision, he definitely needs good legal advice.

The vibration of his cell phone alerts him, and he rises to excuse himself. "I'll take this in the other room," he says, leaving the enticing aromas behind.

The tension in the nurse's voice is evident. "Dr. Sarkissian, this is Nurse Pritchard at the hospital. I'm taking care of Miss Doss and she's asking for you."

*Why is Traci asking for me?* "But I'm not on duty." he replies.

"I told her that, but she's quite insistent and upset. I think you should come see her."

The last thing he wants is to ruffle Miss Queen Bee's feathers, especially with litigation in the air. He gives an exasperated sigh. "Tell her I'm on my way."

Making his apologies, he leaves with one thought running though his brain. *If this is just a rich girl's tantrum, I'll straighten her out!*

~ * ~

It's close to eight o'clock when Raffi enters Traci's hospital room. Her naso-gastric tube is out, her golden hair pulled into a pony tail.

She looks up from the TV screen. "I'm so relieved to see you."

He maintains a professional stance as he scans her chart and smiles. "You're looking better for all you've been through, Miss Doss. Your tests appear normal."

Her mouth purses into a pout. "Except that I'm still in pain."

He studies her appealing appearance as she sits up in bed, wearing a flimsy nightgown. The few wisps of blonde curls fall on her forehead; her lips are a glossy red. To lighten the tension in the room, he says, "From what I see, you're confirming the lipstick theory."

Puzzled, she laughs. "What's that?"

He tilts his head, catching the coloring on her full lips. "It's not a scientific observation, but after surgery, women put on makeup when they feel better. That usually happens on the third or fourth day."

She frowns. "Looks can be deceiving, you know."

"Maybe, but let's examine you." He approaches, draws back the sheet and assesses her incision. The midline scar holds tight, skin clips appear healthy. He takes out a stethoscope from his white coat pocket and places it on her abdomen, listening. "Everything looks fine."

Her voice takes on a demanding tone. "Well, Doctor, I'm not fine. I need something for my pain."

Raffi's thoughts race suspiciously. Is she drug dependent, accustomed to the hard stuff? That could explain why she asks for more than the usual dose of pain meds.

He slips his stethoscope back into his pocket. *I'll not be manipulated with her demands.* "Miss Doss, I see no problems. Why don't we taper the narcotic dosage and combine it with an antihistamine? That should give you the same relief with less upload dependency."

Her tone softens. "Hope it helps, Doc." Within seconds, her face brightens as she gropes into the night stand and removes a small leather case. She holds it out to him and winks. "A nurse, whose name I'll never mention, told me you performed my surgery, not Dr. Flint. To show my appreciation, I'd like you to have this."

Surprised, Raffi hesitates. "I'm sorry, Miss Doss, you're very kind, but I can't accept this. Making you better is my job."

She insists, pushing the box toward him. "Please, open it. I'm thankful for what you did and hope you'll agree to be my personal physician."

Raffi carefully raises the lid with the Rolex logo engraved inside. A gold and diamond-studded watch glistens in the light.

"I can't take such an extravagant gift," he says, offering it back.

She crosses her arms, refusing the box. "Nonsense. Everyone who cared for me that night got one."

Raffi's thoughts teem with suspicion. She certainly is wealthy enough to afford it, but does the gift come with strings? If she's depending on him for future narcotic prescriptions, he has to tread carefully.

"Miss Doss, I appreciate the gesture, but remember, you're Dr. Flint's patient."

She lets out a hearty laugh. "Doctor, your secret's out! You're joining his practice and will be in the same office."

Raffi sighs, not knowing how to answer. It appears Flint has already made the decision for him.

# *Six*

Sunday morning comes too soon for Raffi. Flint expects an answer by Monday, but after a sleepless night, he still carries doubts about joining his practice.

What preys on his mind? Flint's aloofness, his subtle, elite arrogance, or Raffi's own apprehension dealing with an exclusive and possibly demanding patient population? Still, the tantalizing offer is too good to ignore.

He's confident he'll succeed in the practice. Whether due to Flint's advancing age or his inattention to newer techniques, Raffi has witnessed on more than one occasion the degree to which Flint's surgical skills have rusted. No doubt, that may be why the aging doctor wants a younger surgeon in the office.

Can he handle the heavier cases? Of course he can, but that might cause another problem. Surgeons are a competitive bunch and outperforming his senior colleague might lead to jealousy and conflict.

He smiles, thinking of Traci. She's already put her seal of approval on him, and it's flattering. He lies in bed, rationalizing.

Rich or poor, everyone deserves good medical care, so what the hell! Accept the offer.

He pulls himself out of bed, and by reflex reaches for the remote. Turning on the TV, the screen lights up, and a reporter stands in front of the 42nd Street Precinct, speaking into a mike.

"...*Police have not yet given any information, but one of the luminaries at the party was identified as United States Senator Olin Davis. The function, held in the private penthouse of cigarette heiress Traci Doss, raises questions. What led to the woman's death? The district attorney's office is withholding further information until the investigation is complete. Now let's turn to today's sports.*"

The mention of Traci triggers an electrifying bolt in his brain. The conversation between Traci and her attorney, Perry Grant, the other day in the hospital plays out in his mind. The woman must be the person Grant mentioned, the one Traci shrugged off as inconsequential. He sits numb, glued to the TV as a clip shows a shortstop in the outfield catching a baseball.

"Goddamn," he grumbles, turning off the TV. There's enough going on in his world with Reverend Sanders' civil rights accusations. For sure, the woman's death in Traci's home will add fuel to the newsmongers for a long time. He has to watch his step and not get sucked into Traci's life.

His preoccupation is interrupted by multiple rings of his phone, and he answers, hearing the excitement in Ani's voice.

"Son, your celebrity patient is in the news! A young woman was *found dead* in her penthouse the night of the accident. Do you think it's related?"

"Just heard it, Mom, but don't worry. It has nothing to do with me."

She rattles on nonstop. "I wonder if Traci Doss is involved. A lot of questions have to be answered. Who is this woman who died? And who else was at the party? One report suggests phone pictures were taken. If that's true, could they be used for blackmail? After all, Traci is one of the richest women in our country."

"Whoa, Mom, don't jump to conclusions."

Ani's voice trembles. "Be careful, Raffi. You don't want any additional contact with the Doss lady, so stay away from her."

He has never told her about Traci's Rolex gift. "Don't worry, Mom. I can take care of myself." From the time he was a kid, she was always there to protect him, whether staying up to the wee hours until he came home from a band job in high school, or insisting on meeting his friends for her approval.

Ani presses on. "And that Reverend Sanders. Is he really a man of the cloth? Your name is getting too close to him and his civil rights complaint."

Raffi casually slips, saying something he later regrets. "I met him the other day in the administrator's office."

"Raffi, you never told me! What was that all about?"

"Nothing important, Mom. The hospital just wanted me to describe what happened the night of the accident. Nothing more."

Ani's unrelenting in her questioning. "What about Jeremy, the resident you like so much? He's in the news as well—and he's black."

*Never heard her so stressed out.* "Look Mom, Jeremy and I will come out OK on this. So don't worry."

"I'll try not to." Hesitating a moment, she asks, "Are you going to accept Flint's offer? It'll open doors for you."

"I haven't decided yet."

"You can't stop living your life, son. These are very important decisions."

He blurts out defensively. "There's a lot on my mind, Mom." *That was not the right thing to say. Now she'll really worry.*

Instead, her familiar optimism returns. "Of course, it's your decision, son. I'm proud of you and what you've accomplished. You have no other family here to tell you that."

"I have you, Mom."

The yearning in her voice is clear. "Who knows, Raffi? Miracles do happen and someday you might meet your father."

He chokes slightly, recalling the childhood memory of his mother's sad face when he'd ask about his father and grandparents. He takes in a deep breath and replies, "I hope so, Mom, for your sake. Maybe someday it'll happen."

He ends the call and checks his watch. It's already ten o'clock and if he's to drive down to the Jersey shore, he'd better not waste any more time. He slips on his bathing trunks and pulls Levis over them along with his favorite t-shirt printed with bold letters: *Surfer of the Year.*

After downing a tall glass of orange juice and a bagel, he leaves his apartment, fortunate to have his neighbor's car available for his out of town trips. The symbiotic relationship works out well: emergency medical favors for their family in return for wheels that satisfy Raffi's transportation needs.

The early morning drive south is traffic free. The weekenders, already sunning on sandy beaches, are enjoying their one day holiday. The mass exodus of travelers returning north to their homes will begin by sundown.

Cruising south on the Garden State Parkway, Raffi ponders how to break the news to Ray that his plan to open a practice in Monmouth County might not happen. Ray Murphy had finished his nephrology residency at Manhattan Medical two years earlier, and when Raffi approached him about sharing office space, his good friend went all out. Even smoothed the way to gain hospital privileges for him at Monmouth General.

But now with Flint's offer, everything is on hold and he wants to tell his friend in person. After all, Ray went to bat getting him his staff appointment, and for that, he's grateful.

It's close to noon when he pulls up to the sun-bleached clapboard framed house and finds his friend sitting on the front porch waiting for him.

Ray approaches as Raffi exits the car, and gives him a bear hug. "Man, the surf is great today," he says. "Carol has lunch ready, so let's get a quick bite and hit the waves."

Raffi takes in a deep breath of salty air, and gives his surfing buddy a friendly grin as they enter the house. After delving into a huge turkey wrap, he finally tells Ray about Flint's offer, catching the dejection on his friend's face.

Ray pushes his empty plate away and looks at Raffi. "I'm disappointed as hell you're not coming."

"Ray, nothing's engraved in stone. I'm meeting Flint tomorrow. We'll see what he has to offer."

Ray's face brightens as he pushes back his chair. "Look pal, Carol and I wish you the best whatever you do. But until you decide, it would be a crime to let this perfect weather slip away."

Raffi looks to Carol. "Thanks for lunch. Want to join us?"

She winks, picking up the dishes. "Thanks, but no thanks. It's been so long since the two of you spent time together, and Ray's been looking forward to this."

"Me too. Thanks!" Raffi rises from the table and pecks a kiss on Carol's cheek.

The pounding surf gives rise to a salty mist as the two men race into the ocean, gripping their surfboards. Like two happy kids, they paddle through the swells to reach the crest where the waves form. After an hour of surfing, they make it back to shore and stand in the shallow water as the gentle currents lap against their legs. Close by, two children scoop wet sand into toy buckets while their mother lounges on a beach chair keeping watch.

Raffi gazes along the distant shoreline, catching his breath from the strenuous workout. Living at the shore excites him. He turns to Ray. "Man, this is hard to give up. I have a lot to think about."

The two friends stand silently, watching a beachcomber look for shells, or maybe a lost ring. A couple walks by arm in arm, making footprints in the sand, obviously in love. For a moment Raffi feels envious not having someone like that in his life.

In the hazy distance, three female figures stroll the shoreline toward them. As they advance, Ray remarks, "Babe alert."

Raffi focuses on the tall long-legged girl in the middle. Her tawny, sun-kissed hair blows in the ocean breeze as she walks.

Ray nudges him out of his trance. "Hey, man, you awake?"

"Just looking. The one in the white polka dotted suit looks real classy."

Ray chuckles. "Carol should see me now, gawking like a teenager—but I admit, that one is striking."

Raffi squints into the sun, watching the girls approach—close enough that he can see her tanned legs and long, honey brown hair.

Ray elbows him. "Go up, introduce yourself."

Raffi scoffs. "Are you out of your mind? She'll think I'm nuts."

Ray bumps Raffi's surf board. "You got no guts. You'll never get to first base this way."

Raffi gives his friend's shoulder a friendly punch. "Not interested, so don't rush me. Let's get in a few more rides before I have to head back."

# Seven

Instead of meeting Flint in his office, Raffi is invited for dinner at the senior surgeon's private club. A computer search reveals The Century Association is one of New York City's oldest and most exclusive watering holes. Mark Twain referred to it as "the most unspeakably respectable club in the United States."

It's located at 43rd Street between Fifth and Sixth Avenues, beyond walking distance from the hospital. Raffi decides to ride the subway rather than sitting in a taxi to watch a climbing meter, bogged down in midtown traffic.

He follows the flow of office workers rushing home, stepping around tourists who stare up at the numerous tall skyscrapers. Approaching the stately gray stone mansion, he's impressed with the building's ornate iron work and elegantly crafted trim. The three story building was constructed in 1891, although the club was founded earlier in 1847. Membership is by invitation only, and its prominent members include political figures from Franklin Roosevelt to Mayor Michael Bloomberg.

Raffi straightens his tie as he climbs the few steps and enters the reception area. A board on the wall behind a uniformed attendant shows the names of members. A wooden peg is inserted beside Flint's space, indicating he's present. *Probably a throwback to old school traditions.*

The male attendant greets him. "How may I help you, sir?"

Raffi takes in the formality of the club. *Good choice, wearing my dark blue suit and tie.* "I'm Dr. Sarkissian, a guest of Dr. Flint," he announces.

"Yes, he's expecting you," the attendant replies in a dignified voice. "Right this way."

He follows the attendant up to a landing that opens into an expansive gallery. Imposing leather chairs line the walls on two sides with an ornate billiard table in the center. The adjoining room opens up to a long oak panel bar with chairs and tables.

Having completed his mission, the attendant nods politely. "Have an enjoyable evening, Dr. Sarkissian," and then leaves.

Raffi scans the richly appointed room. Subdued lighting in a backdrop of heavy velvet drapes and opulent textured fabrics lends an atmosphere of old world refinement. The room is empty except for Flint, who sits alone at the bar, drinking and conversing with the bartender.

Raffi's stomach tightens as questions run through his mind. The awkward details of negotiation lie ahead and they have to be addressed. Will Flint agree to what he promised? This all has to be spelled out before he commits to him.

Flint spots Raffi and slips off the barstool to approach. He extends his hand and says, "I thought you'd enjoy the relaxed atmosphere of the club after a long day in surgery."

Raffi senses Flint's powerful handshake is sending a message. "Great choice, thank you, Dr. Flint." He follows Flint into the brightly lit dining room on the other side of the bar. Crystal chandeliers glow over tables with white linens and cobalt blue-rimmed monogrammed plates. Only five of the many tables are occupied.

"Monday is usually a slow night," Flint says. "What do you think?"

"Very elegant, although I always imagined a private club filled with cigar smoke."

"There's no smoking allowed," Flint replies, directing Raffi to a table. He sits across from him and continues. "That's been a sore point here. The city council banned cigars in an effort to protect employees from second-hand smoke."

Raffi lets out a friendly laugh. "No problem. I don't smoke."

Within minutes, a waiter enters leading a tall athletic man toward them. Raffi instantly recognizes him from pictures in the newspaper: New York Senator Olin Davis, appearing more handsome in person. His abundant wavy silver hair glistens under the indirect lighting.

Flint rises, extending his hand. "Glad you could make it, Olin."

"No problem," the senator replies. "Just a short flight from D.C." He turns to Raffi. "You must be Harold's new associate."

Raffi winces inwardly, and rises, politely returning his handshake. *Looks like Flint pre-empted my decision, making it public.*

The senator lowers himself into the barreled leather chair and unbuttons his navy blazer, revealing a crisp white shirt and red striped tie. The waiter returns with the order of scotch on the rocks and places a glass before each person.

Raffi studies the senator as he fingers the tumbler without drinking. *Surely he has to know about the dead woman in Traci's apartment?*

He sits quietly as an outsider, listening to the two men banter over their youthful escapades at Yale. Finally, the senator turns to Raffi.

"Dr. Sarkissian, Harold is like a brother to me. While I pursued politics, my good friend dedicated himself to mankind, healing the sick. You won't be sorry joining his practice. There's no better person with whom to be associated."

Flint takes a sip from his glass and nods. "Thanks for the compliment, Olin, but it's Raffi who stepped in the other night to assist on Traci."

The senator leans forward with a curious look. "You told me that, Harold, and now that I've met this young surgeon, I'm definitely impressed."

"Thank you for your confidence, Senator." Frustrated, Raffi bites his lip, waiting to get down to business. The unexpected visit by the senator is delaying the purpose of this meeting and he reflects on the advice from Mr. Dederian, Ani's attorney friend, he met the other day about firming up a contract. But Flint has already made the decision for him, and now the celebrity senator, as well as Traci, regard it as a *fait accompli*. He leans back, focusing on the two dominant men sitting before him. *Who am I to question them?*

Davis takes a mouthful of scotch, and then leans close to Raffi, lowering his voice. "Has the district attorney interviewed you yet about Traci Doss?"

The question startles Raffi. "No," he replies, "but one thing is certain, Reverend Sanders is demanding the Justice Department investigate the death of Tommie Jackson."

The senator waves a hand. "I heard, but don't take Sanders too seriously. He's known for making everything into a racist issue." His eyebrows abruptly arch and he asks, "Has Traci mentioned anything about the party the night of the accident?"

"It never came up," Raffi answers, keeping his response short. His instincts tell him that Olin Davis did not run into them casually at the club. He must have been invited by Flint. But for what reason?

The senator hesitates a moment, and then casts a cold narrow smile at Raffi. "I see." Abruptly, he rises and buttons his jacket. "Nice to have met you, Doctor Sarkissian." He turns to Flint, giving an affirmative nod. "You picked a fine man, Harold. Keep up the good work. Gotta catch the late train."

Raffi watches Olin Davis leave as quickly as he came. A single matter burns in his mind. *Did the senator travel all the way from Washington just to ask one question about Traci?*

~ * ~

Raffi joins Flint in practice. No contract is signed, only a handshake over dinner.

"Why go through the legal expense of a contract?" Flint tells Raffi, sipping his dinner cognac after the senator vanishes. "It's not public notice, but I plan to lighten my load and go part time as soon as you get comfortable in the practice. I respect your skill and work ethic and we should get along fine."

Raffi rationalizes that making a big deal about the contract would make Flint's offer disappear.

The elder surgeon's gaze focuses on him. "You and I have to be satisfied with our arrangement. I am, and if you are, a contract will only get in the way."

Flint's knack for making a convincing argument leaves Raffi with little choice but to accept.

The senior surgeon agrees Raffi will receive two hundred thousand a year along with payment of his malpractice insurance. Based upon performance, his salary will increase to two hundred twenty-five thousand the second year, and by the third, he could have a forty-nine percent partnership without making any capital investment in office equipment and furnishings. To a young hungry surgeon still burdened with a hundred ten thousand student loan debt, the enticing offer is impossible to refuse.

The following day, Raffi calls Ray between cases, promising to pay all the costs of the telephone hookup and Yellow Pages listings for the office he isn't going to open at the shore. He detects disappointment in the sound of his friend's voice and apologizes repeatedly. After ending the call, he decides to call his mother.

"I'm happy for you," Ani replies. "We'll celebrate Saturday night. Don't forget, you promised to join me and David for the Armenian Students' Association scholarship fundraiser at the Plaza Hotel. I have the tickets, so don't refuse."

"Don't worry, Mom. I'll be there."

"Are you bringing a date?"

"No, I'm coming alone." He loves to tease his mother about his love life, and adds, "Maybe I'll meet a nice Armenian girl at the dance."

Ani bursts out with a laugh. "So what's wrong with that?"

"Then you won't have to worry about me hooking up with some *Odar* nurse." He enjoys using the buzz word *Odar*, an Armenian expression referring to a non-Armenian.

"You're a grown man, Raffi; I want you to be happy."

"I am, but I'm between cases, gotta go." He ends the call, aware he's only going to appease his mother. As a single eligible male, he'll be the topic of conversation among her friends—which he hates. The only girls he casually dates are single nurses but so far no chemistry. Anyway, at the moment, he has too much going on in his life.

The overhead page blares out. "Dr. Sarkissian to OR six." He quickly transfers his thoughts to the emergency surgery waiting for him in the operating room. The bile duct of a fifty-year-old man was cut during a laparoscopic procedure performed at another hospital and needs repair. He has a lot of respect for re-operative surgery, since these cases deal with the unknown.

As he moves into the bright lights of the OR, his thoughts are far removed from his Spartan love life. He focuses on one thing: *Whatever you do, don't injure the portal vein and make this patient another statistic.*

# *Eight*

Bright lights illuminate the impressive façade of the Plaza Hotel Saturday evening as taxis drive to the front entrance, discharging and picking up passengers.

Raffi pays the cab driver and climbs the steps, moving around people clustered at the entry. He studies the smartly dressed men and women standing before him and buttons his jacket. He's dressed more casually, wearing his favorite blue blazer with light toned slacks. Approaching the gold-framed lobby bulletin board, he checks the listings to locate the fundraiser.

Young college students mingle at the entrance waiting to purchase tickets as the sound of rock music drifts from the ballroom. Raffi steps up to the woman seated at the reception table.

"Name?" she asks.

"Raffi Sarkissian," he replies, trying to avoid the revealing neckline of her emerald green cocktail dress. *Maybe coming isn't such a bad idea.* There's certainly some action here.

She scans the list before her and looks up at him with a smile. "Your ticket's paid for."

He enters the large ornate ballroom to the blare of Justin Timberlake's "Dead and Gone." Dozens of couples pound the dance floor amid the deafening sound. Cautiously, he weaves around the room searching for Ani's table when he hears her call out.

"Over here, Raffi!" His mother waves her arms until his eyes track her.

She stands out from the crowd, looking younger than her age. A tailored black sheath clings to her slim figure, and Raffi understands David's attraction to her. Is it her loyalty to him that's keeping her from fulfilling her life with a sound marriage, he wonders? Maybe David is the one to convince her that it's time for her to let go.

A broad grin crosses David's face and he rises from the table as Raffi approaches. "Glad you didn't chicken out. Lots of good looking singles here tonight."

Raffi gives him a sheepish look, kisses Ani on the cheek and then introduces himself to the other couple. He sits next to David with an unobstructed view of the dance floor. People of all ages gyrate to the driving beat. As he watches, he realizes devoting his energies to his professional life have left him isolated from New York City's dynamic Armenian social set. Since the time they'd stepped foot in to New York, Ani had encouraged him never to forget his roots. Wasn't that why he came this evening?

As he listens to the music increase in pitch and rhythm, Ani touches his arm. Her spirited eyes are radiant. "I see some real pretty girls in the crowd, Raffi."

Annoyed with his mother's attempts at matchmaking, he gets up from the table. "In time, Mom. What I need right now is a drink. What can I get all of you?"

David interrupts. "Stay put, it's my treat." He leaves the table and minutes later returns with a tray filled with glasses. "You look like you need this Scotch," he says, handing Raffi a tumbler.

Raffi eagerly grasps and holds it up. "*Salud*! To Ani and her good friends."

David clicks his glass with Raffi's. "After you finish that drink, I expect you to grab the loveliest girl in the room and hit the dance floor."

Raffi grins good-naturedly. "It's a promise, David," and then drains the tumbler.

When the band starts up with a slow ballad, David reaches for Ani's hand and leads her into the crowd of dancers, and the other couple follows. Left alone, Raffi wanders to the bar for another scotch, which he quickly empties. His head spins slightly as he stands studying his mother and David sway romantically to an old Cole Porter classic. A female soloist in a strapless long dress sings the haunting lyrics. Ani is laughing, enjoying David's company. Raffi sighs, suspecting if the man proposes marriage, she'll probably not accept. David isn't the first one to want a commitment.

He returns to the table, feeling a mellow remorse. Is it the liquor that makes him feel his mother has denied herself because of him? His eyes burn, thinking about the sacrifices she's made for him. But now with Flint's proposal, he'll be able to care for her just as she has for him.

The vocalist finishes, bows to the applause, and leaves the stage along with the band. Minutes later, another group of musicians walks on, carrying classical Armenian musical instruments. The clarinet is the only western one to be seen.

As the musicians prepare, Raffi recalls the church picnics Ani would drag him to as a youngster. He'd been a child running around with other kids playing tag while the adults intermingled eating from paper dishes and listening to Armenian folk songs reminiscent of his mother's life in Turkey.

Within minutes, the familiar sound of traditional folk music pierces the air, drawing Raffi's thoughts to the present. The clarinet wails its high pitched cries, the *doumbek*, a Middle Eastern version of the drum, covered with lambskin at one end, keeps a driving beat. The *oud*, a wooden pear-shaped guitar-like instrument, sets the pace as both young and old rush to the dance floor enticed by the rhythmic melody.

Raffi listens with nostalgia, reflecting on his high school days with his musician friends. He loves all kinds of music and drums his fingers on the table to the beat, wondering why he hasn't picked up his guitar since then. He misses playing but admits he's made the right choice becoming a physician.

He finishes his drink and leans back in his chair, gazing at dancers of various ages form lines, holding onto each other's hands like a tight community. In unison, they step to the long-established moves performed by many of their ancestors from past generations. In a snake-like pattern, the line of humanity weaves around the dance floor and in between tables. A college-age male with an athletic frame leads the line, vigorously twirling a white handkerchief in the air with the procession following.

Within minutes, a wide-eyed Ani rushes to the table and grabs Raffi's hand. "Join us, Raffi. The music is wonderful."

Raffi can't deny his mother's urging any longer. He breaks randomly into the line, taking a hand offered him and swings into rhythm. Dancing in step, he marvels he hasn't forgotten the communal moves after all these years. Looking to his right, he glances at the girl who had offered her hand. She definitely is attractive. Not missing a step, he keeps staring, wondering why she looks so familiar. He's seen her before, but where?

The music picks up a faster beat, and the clarinetist sways along with his instrument, producing melodic cries. The *doumbek* player's hands drum hard and fast on the sheepskin cover, keeping pace with the dynamic rhythm. The *oud* player's skill catches his attention. The music from the tear-drop shaped guitar blends beautifully with that of the clarinet and *doumbek*.

Raffi feels the driving pulse and lets loose, pounding his feet to the simple one, two, three kick step he learned as a boy. Moisture forms on his palm, but the girl dancing next to him continues to hold on.

The room shakes from the total multitude of feet stamping on the floor. Spectators stand by clapping in rhythm while the line leader directs the dancers, waving his handkerchief with ballet-like gestures. His moves encourage the followers to emphasize their steps with increasing intensity.

The sexy woman from the ticket table pulls a handsome young man with dark wavy hair from out of the line. Drawing him into the center, they move seductively as a couple while the long line of dancers circles around them.

Raffi's head whirls; he tightens his grip on the girl's hand who keeps in step, laughing in his direction. Her dazzling smile, her chestnut honeyed hair. Where has he seen her?

Suddenly the music stops and a massive uproar of joyous shouts and clapping erupts. As the line dissolves, Raffi keeps hold of her hand, breathless from the dancing and a bit intoxicated.

She wrinkles her brow, her face flushes. "Please let go, you're hurting me."

Raffi freezes as she pulls her hand away, unaware of his own strength. He drops his head, embarrassed. "I'm sorry, I didn't mean—let me explain."

Her gaze narrows. "What's to explain?"

"I've seen you before and I'm trying to figure out where." She rolls her eyes, but even that negative response is appealing.

She faces him with a questioning look. "You must be mistaken. I don't think we've ever met."

Raffi keeps staring, and suddenly the scene on the beach the day he surfed with Ray creeps in memory and he snaps his fingers. "Now I remember!"

She looks around, her face reddened with embarrassment. "People are staring at us. We're the only ones left on the dance floor."

Raffi turns toward Ani's table where everyone is watching. "You're right. May I get you a drink?"

She gives him a hesitant smile. "Why not?"

He holds her elbow, guiding her to a small circular table near the bar jammed with patrons waiting to place their orders. "White wine will be fine," she says.

Raffi apologizes. "Please, don't think I'm handing you a line. I'll explain after I get the drinks." Within minutes, he returns and places two wine glasses on the table. "I saw you last Sunday at the Jersey shore."

Her brow arches.

He leans toward her. "You were walking the shoreline with two girls. You wore a white bathing suit with black polka dots."

Her jaw drops and she breaks into a smile. "That's right. I was at the beach but I don't remember you."

"My friend and I were surfing. I wanted to talk to you, but didn't have the nerve. And now here you are. I hope you believe me."

"You are convincing," she says with a laugh, smoothing the strands of chestnut hair from her face.

Raffi hopes his story impresses her. "Let me introduce myself. I'm Raffi Sarkissian, a resident at Manhattan Medical soon to begin private practice."

She offers her hand for a shake. "My name is Lorig Balian. I'm a teacher and live in New Jersey."

He glances at her bracelet with its dangling charms. "I see a Phi Beta Kappa key on your wrist."

"Honors in history at Douglass College."

"Well, I'm impressed. You must have worked very hard to get that key."

She blushes and puts her wine down again. "I did."

"With honors in history, do you teach college?"

She frowns, staring down at the table. "After getting my degree, I decided to go for a master's in speech therapy."

"Why did you do that?"

"I have a brother with learning disabilities, that's why."

His face turns red. "I always tend to put my big foot in my mouth."

She's kind enough to let it go and gives him a hint of a smile. "Raffi, I decided to do something that makes a difference in the lives of innocent children with speech deficits, among other challenges."

Still embarrassed by his stupidity, he's relieved when the American band returns to the stage and begins playing the old Gershwin standard, "My Funny Valentine." He sighs, taking her hand. "That's one of my favorite old time ballads. Shall we dance?"

They dance right through to the last number. He doesn't know if it's the Scotch, or her graceful beauty, but he doesn't want the evening to end. He continues to hold her hand even after the music stops. "Lorig, are you with anyone?"

"Just a few friends," she says, pointing to several women waiting on the sideline near the door. "It looks like they're ready to leave."

Raffi takes her arm, realizing he doesn't have a car to offer a ride home. "At least I can walk you out," he says.

As they pass by Ani and David's table, his mother calls out. "Raffi, are you leaving?"

He knows he'll face a barrage of questions later, so thinks it wise to stop and introduce Lorig. He chuckles, "That's my mother who's been staring at us all night. Would you mind saying a quick hello?"

Lorig nods and casts a gentle smile. "I'd love to meet her, Raffi."

Ani and David rise simultaneously as they approach the table.

"Mother, this is Lorig Balian. Lorig, this is my mother Ani, and her friend David."

Lorig graciously extends her hand to Ani and then to David. "It's a real pleasure to meet you all. Raffi has entertained me most of the evening. I'm glad I decided to come tonight."

Raffi catches Ani's approving smile, convinced she's struck by Lorig's fresh natural beauty, her polite gentility.

David asks, "Won't you sit and have a drink with us?"

Raffi gazes at Lorig. "Would you like to stay awhile?"

Lorig gives an apologetic look. "Oh, I wish I could but friends I came with are waiting for me. Thank you."

Ani rises from the table and places a friendly pat on Lorig's arm. "It was so nice meeting you and I hope to see you soon."

Raffi feels heat under his collar, fearing his *yenta* mother's instinct for matchmaking. "I'll also be leaving," he chimes in. "Mother, David, thanks for inviting me. I'm glad I came too."

As they make their way out crossing the empty ballroom floor, Lorig says, "Your mother is beautiful. How nice to meet her."

Raffi bursts out laughing. "You have no idea what just happened."

"What?"

"Tonight is the first time my mother has seen me with an Armenian girl."

Lorig blinks. "The first time?"

Raffi nods awkwardly. "Yes, it is. And if you give me your telephone number, it won't be the last."

By the time she walks out of the door, he has her number and the promise of a dinner date. *Maybe she might be the one.*

# *Nine*

It's eight o'clock Monday night and after a full day of surgery, Raffi finally enters the doctors' lounge to pick up his mail. He stands in front of the cubbyhole shelves and sorts through the usual drug company announcements and advertisements when a heavily textured envelope with gracefully scripted handwriting catches his attention. Quickly, he slits it open and reads the engraved invitation from Traci—to spend the weekend with friends at her New Jersey farm.

Of course, he's tempted to go, but Traci's name most surely will come up at the police interview the following day. Socializing with her would definitely compromise his testimony. He has to refuse and pockets the invitation just as Jeremy enters.

Still in his scrub greens, the junior surgeon lets out a tired sigh. "People say I shouldn't give up my day job, but this is my day job."

Raffi chuckles at his friend's humor. "A day in a surgeon's life. My case ran late, too."

Jeremy speaks as he removes his mail from the box. "Figured you were held up too. Saw them cleaning your room when I finished." He pauses, and throws Raffi a sly grin. "Hey, I checked my schedule and I can take your Saturday night, if you're still planning to go out on that dinner date."

"I'd like to but haven't called her yet."

"You say she's a knockout, so don't blow it."

Raffi winks, recalling Lorig's warm smile. "Good advice, Jeremy. Thanks for covering my call."

Jeremy sorts through his mail, pulls out an envelope and lets out a grunt. "Son of a bitch!" He reads out loud the multiple names listed followed by 'Attorneys at Law.' "I bet it's the civil rights lawsuit."

Raffi exchanges glances with the junior resident, wondering if he'll receive the same letter. He remains silent watching Jeremy's brow wrinkle into a frown as he rips open the envelope with his forefinger.

"Shit! I'd like to tear this up and say it never came."

Raffi grabs the letter and reads the painful message. The family of Tommie Jackson has filed a lawsuit against Jeremy along with Manhattan Medical. They claim discrimination and medical dereliction of responsibility caused the death of their son.

Jeremy slams his fist on the counter. "Dammit, Sanders pulled me in with all his civil rights bullshit."

"Easy Jeremy, you did nothing wrong. You can fight this."

"Sure, but even if I win, I lose. Sanders is setting off fireworks. It's no longer a medical issue. It's become a political pow-wow, and how do you fight that?"

Raffi doesn't want to labor the point at the late hour. What Jeremy needs is good legal advice and he pats his shoulder. "Look friend, every time we walk past the reverend's picketers in front of the hospital we get dissed. But the facts are on your side. You're a good surgeon, and chief resident in a few weeks. They'll have a hard time making a case against you."

Jeremy leans against the counter, breathing a heavy sigh. "Just blowing off steam, Raffi. It's not every day a lawsuit greets me in the mail." He pockets the rest of his mail with a soulful look. "Thanks for listening."

Raffi gives him a sympathetic nod. "That's what friends are for."

The fire in Jeremy's eyes softens. "Man, do I have to ask again? You better call that girl about Saturday night."

Raffi removes the invitation from his pocket and flashes it at Jeremy. "I also got something in the mail. Traci wants me to spend the weekend at her Jersey farm."

Jeremy breaks out laughing. "It's no farm with little ducks and chickens. I used to drive past her place on my way home to the Bronx from med school in Philly. It's pure country, Raffi, miles of farmland, and I hear her estate is humongous."

Raffi scratches his head. "The invitation is pretty fancy. Sounds like fun."

Jeremy's lips curl into a smile, remembering his visits to Traci's hospital room. "I got real friendly with her. Tried to keep her positive with all my jokes."

Raffi put the invitation back in his pocket, giving it a pat. "With all the publicity, I'm not going. Don't want to taint my testimony with the detectives tomorrow."

Jeremy sighs and throws up his hands. "Detectives, lawsuits! When do we do what we're trained for? All this bullshit about civil rights."

Raffi's brow arches in disapproval. "What's with Sanders? Instead of pulling *you* into the battle, he should regard you as a role model for young black men."

Jeremy shakes his head, his jaw tight. "Raffi, you have more faith than I do. Amazing how my people fall for his line. Growing up in the Bronx, I've seen drug pushers, pimps, even the Muslim Brotherhood and the New Black Panthers. They all try to get into your brain."

Raffi studies the pain on his friend's face, aware of his share of unspoken frustrations. "How'd you manage?"

"I had a tyrant of a mom who set me straight at an early age and saved me."

"That's good, Jeremy. Sounds just like my mom."

Jeremy wiped his brow. "Yeah, when two of my friends died in gang wars, I knew I had to get out. Cracked the books and studied, lucky to get accepted to med school away from home."

"So you did it, and look at you. That's why I don't understand how Reverend Sanders can attack you."

Jeremy pulls out the attorney's letter and waves it. "The reverend and his civil rights lemmings keep reminding my people that we're always victims. Now in my professional world, these attorneys are trying to make me a victim as well. No matter what, I'm screwed."

What kind of advice can Raffi give this colleague who has become his loyal friend? Jeremy is striving to make his mark in a world outside the ghetto. But now even his own people are out to get him.

~ * ~

The following morning, Raffi finishes rounds by noon and enters Radiology to review CAT scans. A sense of unease keeps him from concentrating. Detective Daley's interview regarding Traci's emergency room admission is in an hour and Flint's earlier call carried a warning.

"Raffi, watch what you say when you meet the detective. Don't quote Traci, don't speculate if she was intoxicated and don't even hint you met Senator Davis."

Flint's threatening tone plagues him as he heads to the cafeteria for lunch. The fact Lorig agreed to the Saturday night date is the solitary positive thing in his personal life.

Munching on a turkey sandwich, he thinks about where to take her. Dining at a noisy Manhattan restaurant doesn't appeal to him. A quiet intimate place where they'll talk and get to know each other, that's what he wants. Better off in some small neighborhood eatery.

Halfway through lunch, the overhead page calls him to the administrative offices. He rises quickly, empties the tray into a refuse barrel and moves to the elevators, preparing for the interview.

Hospital attorney, Barry Gold, ushers Raffi into the conference room and introduces him to Detective Daley. The officer is a portly middle-aged man carrying a twinkle in his eyes consistent with his Irish heritage. His suit jacket bulges at the elbows, showing effects of long wear.

Gold addresses Raffi. "Officer Daley is here to gather information regarding the Jackson family lawsuit. Remember, Doctor, you're not under oath. I'm here to protect the hospital."

Raffi sits in a chair facing Daley, detecting a heavy odor of tobacco on his breath. The detective's eyes squint into a smile. "Just have a few simple questions, Doctor. When you first saw Miss Doss in the emergency room, did she show any signs of alcohol intoxication or did she appear to be under the influence of drugs?"

Raffi's answer is swift, to the point. "I noted none of those signs. I found her in the ER, curled on her side, moaning in pain, afraid to move because of her belly pain."

"Were any blood alcohol levels drawn?"

"No."

"Why not?"

"Detective, she was bleeding out and surgery was urgent. There was no time to do tests. I smelled no alcohol on her breath and she had no signs of drug intoxication."

Daley scribbles on his pad, the smile never leaving his face. "I see. Did she give you any details of the accident?"

"No, she could hardly speak. The medics said she had a blowout, crashed and rolled the car."

"Did they comment about anything she might have said to them?"

"No."

Daley stops writing, raises his head to gaze at Raffi. "Do you know Senator Olin Davis, or have you ever met him?"

Startled, Raffi remembers Flint's warning. "I'm here to answer questions of a medical nature, Detective. I can't speculate about non-medical issues."

Hospital attorney Gold adjusts his glasses on the bridge of his nose, prepared to come to Raffi's defense. "That's your privilege, Doctor. You're not under oath."

"It's a simple question," Daley persists. "Do you know or have you ever met Senator Olin Davis?"

Raffi's pulse races, and he searches for safe words. "I have no professional relationship with any senators."

Daley frowns, indicating his dissatisfaction, but to Raffi's relief he doesn't press. "OK, Doc, enough for now." He gets up and turns to Gold. "I had to fight my way through the picketers outside the hospital. Looks as though the good reverend is doing one hell of a publicity promotion for his civil rights organization."

"Demonstrating is within their rights, Detective," Gold replies. "But neither doctor did anything wrong and we're prepared to defend the hospital against Sanders' claims."

As Raffi leaves the room, his shirt clings to his back with moisture. *Were my answers convincing? Especially the one about Senator Olin Davis?*

# *Ten*

Raffi drives the Saturday night bumper-to-bumper traffic on the upper deck of the George Washington Bridge heading to New Jersey. Lorig lives across the river from Manhattan, several miles south of the bridge. He begs off on Traci's invitation with an apology, explaining he has a previous commitment. Although tempted to discover how the other half lives, he hesitates joining the horsy social set.

Once off the bridge, he follows signs south on 9W, just as Lorig directed, and turns onto her street, a short block on the bluffs of the Hudson River facing New York City. Vintage traditional two story homes built before World War II sit on wide expanses of lawn surrounded by lush rhododendron shrubs.

He parks in front of her home. It's just as she described—a large two-story Colonial with stately columns and a wide wraparound front porch. Perched close to the cliffs, the house overlooks the Manhattan skyline. According to Lorig, the film industry originated in Fort Lee and her home is an original built in the 1920s for a movie mogul. Raffi approaches the massive oak door and rings the bell.

A well-groomed woman, possibly a bit older than his mother, greets him. "You must be Raffi. Please come in. I'm Alice, Lorig's mother."

Mr. Balian and Lorig's two teenage brothers wander out of the kitchen and introductions are made. Slightly uncomfortable under their scrutiny, Raffi smiles, shakes hands and exchanges pleasantries.

Then his heart takes a leap. *She's even more beautiful than I remember.* Lorig skips excitedly down the long curved stairway, her hands sliding on its rich mahogany railing. Her full-skirted dress floats along with her.

Hurriedly, they say goodbye to her family, and once settled in the car, Raffi asks, "How about a quiet restaurant for dinner?"

Lorig smiles, apparently pleased with his suggestion. "There's a quaint little roadside place I think is a hidden gem. I teach school with the owner's daughter. He and his wife do all the cooking, authentic northern Italian style. You'll love it."

"Good choice, just direct me."

She points to the right. "Go back on 9W and head north."

He drives as she chats about chaperoning a group of fifth graders on a class trip to the Metropolitan Museum the day before. "One of the ten-year-old boys wandered off and got caught up in the prehistoric dinosaur exhibits." She laughs for a moment, hesitating. "Sounds funny now, but at the time I was darned scared. Who knows what might have happened to the kid?"

He studies the way she wiggles her nose, and tries to keep up the conversation. "Can't say my day was as exciting as yours. I worked surgical call, and lucky for me, my junior resident is covering the rest of my shift tonight."

He continues to drive, following directions as he mulls over their different backgrounds. He, growing up in a small Brooklyn flat with no father, and she accustomed to a more affluent life surrounded by family and relatives.

His thoughts begin to fly like wild fire. For the first time in his life, he's actually thinking about a long term commitment.

*Could she survive in my crazy unpredictable world of emergencies, sleepless nights and on call weekends?*

"A penny for your thoughts," she says, catching his attention. "Never mind, you'll have to tell me later," she continues, and points to a small roadside framed building. "There it is, Casa Luna."

She leads him into the modest Italian family restaurant, gesturing to the booth in the back which suggests she wants privacy as much as he. The jovial bald owner approaches wearing a wraparound apron across his rotund abdomen. "Lorig, good to see you. Tonight's special is your favorite, *osso bucco.*"

Lorig beams at Raffi. "Mr. Tony makes the best. You gotta try it!"

Her spontaneous enthusiasm appeals to him. "If you say so."

As they dip freshly baked Italian bread in pungent garlic olive oil, he gazes at her, the flicker of candle light highlighting her cheekbones. *God, she's perfect!*

She dabs the corner of her mouth with a napkin, her eyes tracking his. "So, Raffi, tell me about yourself."

He leans forward, resting his arms on the table. "I was born in Geneva, Switzerland, and came here with my mom when I was six. The rest is pretty boring—undergraduate school and then med school. I'm finishing my surgical residency at Manhattan Medical in a matter of weeks."

Her eyebrows arch, her eyes widen. "I saw your name in the newspaper. Did you really operate on the cigarette heiress, Traci Doss?"

"I only assisted. Dr. Flint was her primary."

Her head tilts, her long chestnut hair slides over her shoulders. "You and a Jeremy Jenkins are mentioned in the news along with that reverend...what's his name?"

"Coleman Sanders." It seems he can't get away from the man.

"So, what's the fuss all about?"

Raffi taps his fingers on the table, reluctant to open the topic. "It's just political crap. Has nothing to do with medicine."

Wanting to change the subject, he says, "I see you're close to your family, still living at home."

She dips another piece of bread in the garlic oil before answering. "There's a financial reason for that. With what I'm paid, I don't want to keep an apartment and go into debt."

He peers into her eyes, searching to understand. "With your credentials, there must be opportunities that could earn a higher income."

She shakes her head in disagreement. "That's not how I look at it, Raffi. Working with these kids satisfies me. For now, that's enough."

Before he can reply, the waiter arrives with their meal, pours the Chianti, and beams with satisfaction. "*Mangiare*," he says and leaves.

Raffi raises his glass, aware once more he's stuck his foot in his mouth. "Thanks for putting up with my stupid questions. I see you're sincere in purpose and not motivated by money."

"I'm a pretty simple woman."

To Raffi, she's anything but. The meal progresses and between mouthfuls of the rich Italian dinner, he speaks about his early life in Brooklyn. He catches her saddened expression when he mentions the only family he's known is his mother. She listens patiently, absorbed with Ani's story. He's certain Lorig will like his mother and Ani will adore Lorig.

They eat and talk without stopping, connected by stories of their common ancestry living through the horrendous Armenian Genocide.

Lorig frowns and put down her fork. "My mother talks about what her grandparents went through to survive in Turkey, but I was shielded from all that."

Raffi nods in agreement. "We have to appreciate the opportunities this country has given us. We couldn't have done it without the generous spirit of America." He waits until the dinner plates are cleared before approaching a subject he's dying to ask her. "So, is there anyone special in your life?"

She grins sheepishly. "No one serious. What about you?"

*My luck she's unattached.* "Don't date much. My schedule keeps me busy."

"Come on now, that's hard to believe," she chuckles.

"No, it's true. You're the first Armenian girl I ever dated."

She smiles coyly, running the tip of her finger up the stem of the wine glass. "Then you've had a relationship with a non-Armenian?"

He laughs, memorized by her slender hand wrapped around the glass. "I dated a girl in med school, but it was short and sweet. Too much on both our plates at the time."

"You're one serious guy, Raffi—extremely focused."

He sits back in the booth, feeling uncomfortable talking about himself. "What about you?"

She sighs and puts down her glass. "The summer before my first year at college, I met a senior from Georgetown." She pauses to take a sip. "He overwhelmed me with flowers, fancy restaurants, came to visit whenever he was on break. He was generous with his wealth, but it didn't work out."

"What happened?"

"I got cold feet. I was only eighteen, and he talked as if our future was all planned. I just got scared."

"What did you do?"

"I talked to my parents about it. My father's warning saved me from making a huge mistake."

Curious, Raffi asks, "And what was that?"

"He said the most important decision I will make in my life is who I choose to marry. Right then and there, I knew I wasn't ready to make such a commitment, so I broke it off."

A pang of jealousy hits him. "Were you in love with him?"

Her gaze becomes distant, and she hesitates before answering. "That's a good question—I don't think so. I felt controlled by him and realized he probably wouldn't change. Why should I expect him to?"

"That's a lot of wisdom for an eighteen-year-old."

Lorig leans forward and rests her chin in her hand. "I've come to the conclusion the world is made up of two kinds of people." She holds his gaze. "They're either givers or takers."

"And you thought this dude was a taker? But wasn't he giving you things?"

"That's what's so seductive about receiving stuff. It's only a diversion. People like that are really taking. They steal your self-confidence, your independence, anything to control you."

Raffi takes a last swallow of wine, intrigued by her comment. "You're a smart lady, Lorig. So tell me, am I a giver or a taker?"

"Do you really want to know?" She leans over the table, her eyes sparkling. "Raffi, I don't know you well enough to answer."

He reaches for her hand, her fingers warm. "Then by all means you must get to know me better. Can I see you again?"

The corners of her mouth turn up with a flirtatious smile. "Why not?"

# *Eleven*

Raffi awakens to the buzzing alarm Sunday morning with new-found energy. No question, he enjoyed the date with Lorig the night before and lies in bed pondering their discussion. *Am I a giver or a taker?*

Jeremy had taken his shift on Saturday, but today is his call, so he climbs out of bed, shaves, dresses, and leaves for Manhattan Medical. Hospital rounds have to be made, emergencies have to be covered. Like all surgeons accustomed to working on Sundays, he long ago learned illness and accidents don't take vacations, even on weekends.

He walks his usual short distance to the hospital, breathing in the clean air of early morning. The hum of heavy street traffic and human activity hasn't begun yet, and his thoughts turn to Lorig. Before the day ends, he wants to talk to her again.

As he approaches the hospital, he notices a lonely figure sitting on a step at the front entrance. A thin teenage black boy in baggy pants and a t–shirt three sizes too big leans on a wooden crate. At his side rests a large sign declaring in bold print, "MEDICAL RACISM."

The kid's dark brown eyes widen as Raffi approaches.

Surprised to see a protester this early, Raffi greets him with a smile. "Good morning. Where are your friends today?"

The young demonstrator jumps up and holds the sign. "They're comin'," he replies. "I'm saving our spot."

Raffi catches distrust in the boy's expression. No more than thirteen and already jaded. "Have you had breakfast yet?"

The kid tightens his lips and his hold onto the sign but doesn't answer.

"I guess not," Raffi says. "How about I send out something for you to eat?"

The teenager gives a cautious shrug.

"I'll take that for a yes." Raffi wonders what the boy knows about race wars. No matter the color of his skin, his is about poverty.

Raffi enters the building without looking back and heads to the cafeteria. He grabs a can of Coke, a bagel with cream cheese and two donuts along with a couple bottles of water, and places them in a cardboard container.

He returns to the lobby and approaches the security guard at the entrance. "Do me a favor—would you take this to that boy outside?"

The guard frowns. "You mean that troublemaker with the sign?"

Raffi nods. "He's just a kid, looks hungry."

The guard shakes his head and takes the tray. "OK, Doc, but the reverend's organized a big demonstration today. Let's not feed the whole mob—they'll never leave."

"I get your point," Raffi chuckles, "but maybe we can make one friend."

The guard leaves on his mission and Raffi heads to the doctors' locker room to change into scrubs and a white coat. The headline of a newspaper lying on the bench catches his attention.

"POSSIBLE DRUG OVERDOSE CAUSE OF DEATH AT DOSS PARTY."

A sudden rush of negative thoughts crush his positive mood as he reads. *The deceased female is identified as Nancy Wood with a Washington, D.C. address. It's reported she was a guest of Senator Olin Davis.*

Angrily, he tosses the paper onto the table. For a moment he even feels sorry for Traci. The media loves to pick on the poor little rich girl. Is that why Senator Davis came to see him at Flint's club? Unfortunately, Flint's warning came too late. Senator Davis's link to Nancy Wood is now public knowledge.

He has no control over these explosive developments and tells himself to stay focused. Picking up the phone, he pages the surgical intern. "Meet me on two west. We have a full load today."

~ * ~

It's late in the afternoon when he finishes rounds, reviews a CAT scan report with the radiologist and finally leaves the hospital to take a call from his mother.

He steps outside the building, puts his phone in his pocket when he sees a small army of demonstrators walking in a circle, carrying signs. In unison, they repeatedly chant, *"No justice, no peace."*

Raffi reads posters scrawled in large letters. *"What happened to Tommie's civil rights?" "Who does Manhattan Medical Serve?"* Reverend Sanders stands on a portable podium with a group of Amen supporters, vigorously responding to his taunts.

A large cadre of New York police guides visitors through the barricades as Raffi moves past the line of sign-carrying demonstrators when a hospital security guard approaches. "Dr. Sarkissian, let's get you back inside."

Raffi nods a thank you to the guard just as a man flashes a press card toward him.

"Dr. Sarkissian, I'm Adam Wolfe, *New York Post.* I recognized you from the papers." He points to the reverend standing in front of the chanting crowd. "He's on a roll because the TV cameras are here."

The security guard gently pushes Raffi along through the crowd. "Get moving, Doc. It's dangerous out here."

Wolfe grabs Raffi's arm. "I'm an expert at this, Officer. I'll get him through."

"Good," the guard answers, gesturing with his thumb to the podium. "I need to get back to the barricade."

Instead of moving ahead, Raffi pulls away from Wolfe and stands, listening to the reverend bellow into the loudspeaker.

"Did Tommie Jackson deserve second class care because of his color? Did that rich white girl deserve more than Tommie?"

The crowd shouts its approval as Sanders presses on. "Now that our brother is dead, are we going to stand by and have our rights trampled?"

The crowd screams repeatedly in unison. "Justice for blacks!"

A gang of white teenagers gathers at the periphery, waving fists. "Niggers go home!"

Sanders roars back. "We can't allow racial profiling in our hospitals!"

Raffi fists his hand, looking to Wolfe. "Dammit, there was no racial profiling. Tommie Jackson reached the hospital the same time as Traci Doss, and they were both treated appropriately."

Wolfe shakes his head. "Makes no difference, Doc. It's all staged for the TV cameras."

A sudden scuffle breaks out between white and black youths. Police whistles blow and clouds from a smoke bomb fill the atmosphere as a swarm of police rush into the melee.

Wolfe nudges Raffi. "Doc, let's get out of here."

Raffi follows the reporter into the hospital building where they watch the battle unfold through the glass doors. Young white males appear from nowhere, charging into the fray. The police are losing control. His pager suddenly sounds.

"Dr. Sarkissian, STAT to the ER."

Raffi turns to the reporter, taking in his rumpled suit and black framed glasses. *A typical pushy newspaper reporter.* "Gotta go. They need me in ER."

Wolfe's dark eyes light up with excitement. Despite his slight frame, his dynamic energy exudes confidence. "Doc, what you're witnessing out there will become a national issue. That's how it works. One demonstration leads to another. Before you know it, any incident will be used for the reverend's cause."

Raffi can't seem to shake off the reporter who keeps his pace as they head to the Emergency Room.

"Mr. Wolfe, you seem to know so much, so what's all this hatred about? Tommie Jackson's case will be settled in court."

Wolfe lets out a sarcastic laugh, following Raffi in a steady gait. "It's pure politics, Doc. Anything to destabilize the system."

Raffi grumbles. "Where's Martin Luther King to keep the peace?"

Wolfe's right beside him, still following. "We're past that, Doc. These kids have no idea what made this country great. With rights come responsibilities."

Raffi stops to face the reporter, his voice shaking with anger. "We've a diverse patient load here at Manhattan Medical. Each patient gets the best care we can give. Put that in your paper, Mr. Wolfe."

"Don't take it personal, Doc. Like I said, it's just political. Here's my card. Call if you want to talk."

Raffi gives a hesitant nod, puts the card in his pocket, and heads to the Emergency Room, dwelling on the reporter's message. Everything happening outside the building has *nothing to do* with patient care. It's all about using innocent people to gain political power.

The ER nurse directs Raffi to a stall. "In here, Doctor. They just rolled the kid in. He's in coma and looks pretty serious. Name's Wendell Wilson."

A black teenager lies on the gurney, breathing heavily, accented by soft gurgles. Bright blood oozes from his head, staining the sheet. A nurse holds out the boy's arm as a technician draws blood.

Raffi slips on disposable gloves, circles the cart, and checks the patient's airway. The recognition is instant. Wendell Wilson is the kid he sent breakfast to just hours ago.

The nurse's brow knits with concern. "We can't wake him. His neck is stiff and his pressure's rising."

Raffi lifts the blood-soaked dressing, exposing a large scalp wound with a raised flap. *What the hell?* The depression in a sizable portion of open skull makes his stomach turn. Only a short time ago, Wendell was a healthy kid, and now this. *Why?*

He shoots an order to the charge nurse. "Stabilize his neck with a collar, call neurosurgery and order a STAT CT scan."

The collar is placed, the patient carefully repositioned onto his back and rushed to X-ray.

Raffi steps out of the stall, seething with anger over the useless fighting. "Where's the surgical intern?" he calls out.

The nurse at the desk replies, "He's sewing up another demonstrator in stall five. But we've got a kid here with a deep leg laceration needing attention. Name is Kevin."

Raffi follows her into the adjacent stall to find a white teenage boy lying quietly on the gurney. A bulky dressing saturated with blood covers his right thigh.

The boy frowns suspiciously as Raffi approaches. "You gonna hurt me?"

"Not as much as you hurt yourself," Raffi says, slipping on a new set of gloves. He removes the soaked dressing, which reveals a deep slash in the muscle, exposing sheared tendons. Blood clots fill the cavity, obscuring a complete view.

Raffi turns to the nurse. "Call OR—this has to be repaired in surgery."

The youth's eyes widen. "You gonna operate on me?"

"Yeah," Raffi answers in a firm voice, fighting his smoldering anger. He looks to the nurse. "Call the family. We need a signed surgical consent."

"He's nineteen and can sign his own consent," she replies.

Raffi faces the young man. The pale flesh on the boy's arms is covered with multiple tattoos. "Call his family anyway and let them know."

Kevin's lips curve into a smirk. "Yeah, if you can find them."

Raffi faces the nurse. "Get him to OR and call the neurosurgical resident for the kid with the head trauma." Annoyed, he leaves the stall, feeling he's on a pointless mission. *I can heal a sick body but not a sick mind.* Defiant demonstrations like the one outside can cause life-threatening injuries without solving anything.

~ * ~

It's seven o'clock when Raffi leaves the OR and finds Kevin's girlfriend in the waiting room. A bleached blonde teenager in washed-out jeans with holes in the knees sits hunched over, her legs crossed revealing a bracelet tattoo on her left ankle.

She jumps up as Raffi enters. "Is Kevin all right?"

"He'll be fine," Raffi says, "but he has to stay off that leg for a while."

She lowers her eyes, at a loss for words.

Raffi continues with instructions. "After discharge, he'll need physical therapy."

"For how long?" Her voice trembles.

"At least a month and then some."

The teenager closes her eyes, releasing a deep sigh. "I told him not to get involved with that gang."

"Then why did he?"

She stares back, shaking her head.

The anger that Raffi has tried to control finally erupts. "Right now one of those young kids who demonstrated with Sanders is having brain surgery because someone was mean enough to swing a club to his head. The kid could be mentally damaged for life. Tell me, is it worth it?"

Fear followed by tears fills her widening eyes.

*Christ, I'm shouting at the wrong person.* His voice softens. "I'm sorry, it's not your fault."

She jumps up; her lips purse in anger. "It's those gangs. They're always at war with each other." She rubs her eyes with the back of her hand. "I've tried to stop Kevin, but he won't listen. Thinks he has to be a big shot to get along with the guys."

Raffi pats her shoulder, trying to calm her. "Kevin's lucky. He'll be fine and hopefully he learns from this experience. I'll take you to recovery so you can see him."

The girl nods, wiping her tears with her sleeve.

Within fifteen minutes, he's paged for the third time and reaches for the hall phone. It's Dr. Noonan, the neurosurgical resident.

"Raffi, it's about Wendell Wilson, the kid with the blow to his head."

"What did you find?"

"A severe depressed skull fracture. He had a lot of intracranial bleeding."

Raffi leans against the wall, breathing a heavy sigh, hoping Noonan's surgical skill will give Wendell a chance. "Do you think he'll be OK?"

"Can't tell. Too soon to know what permanent brain damage he'll end up with. I did my best; the rest is up to God."

~ * ~

Several days later, Raffi sits at the dictation desk waiting for his next surgery. He's not spoken to Lorig since their dinner date, and with all the ER admissions, he hasn't had a quiet moment without interruption. Frustrated, he takes one last sip of coffee and angrily tosses the Styrofoam cup into the wastebasket. Other matters are clouding his thoughts. His residency ends in a week, and he'll have more control over his schedule—hopefully.

He sighs heavily, a cloud of doubt revisiting him. Even after five years of training, contacts with Flint were few and distant. Treating wealthy and prominent patients accustomed to pampered VIP services could be difficult, and cutting corners a formula for disaster. After all, didn't Elvis Presley, Michael Jackson and Marilyn Monroe prove that? Their doctors probably wrote overdosing drug prescriptions to stay in their celebrity patients' good favor. No matter what, he promises himself, he'll never indulge in a patient's irresponsible demands.

The overhead page calls out his name and he dials the extension.

Flint's voice is intense, demanding. "Raffi, keep your distance from Sanders! Tabloids are screaming racial discrimination with that Jackson boy, and now we face more shit with the brain-damaged kid...what's his name?

"Wendell Wilson."

"Yeah, the one who needed brain surgery on your shift. What are you, a magnet for racial wars?"

Raffi's cheeks heat as he listens to Flint vent. "Excuse me, Harold, I was on call when that boy came in. Not my fault."

Flint can't be contained. "The DA is a friend of mine, and he says Reverend Sanders is pushing for a Federal investigation."

Raffi suddenly feels he's slipping into political quicksand, but challenges Flint anyway. "Harold, let them investigate. The facts are clear. There's no racial discrimination at Manhattan Medical."

Flint roars through the receiver. "An investigation is what you *don't* want!"

In a calming tone, Raffi asks, "Why are you so concerned? None of this has anything to do with you."

Flint presses on. "It sure does. With Traci and the senator in the line of fire, that'll open Pandora's box. The press will jump on any unsubstantiated fact. Every kook, malcontent and racist action group will be parked outside our office building holding signs with angry slogans."

Raffi's aware the ripple effect of a Federal probe will do nothing to help Tommie Jackson or Wendell Wilson. It'll only stir up rumor and innuendo, raising another question. *Is Senator Davis involved in any way with that woman's death at Traci's party?*

Trying not to feed into Flint's fears, he calmly replies, "I hear you, Harold. I have only five working days left at Manhattan

Medical and I promise to do everything possible to avoid any racial issues."

Flint's voice carries the sound of finality. "Enough said. I'll see you in the office next week."

Raffi ends the call with an unsettled feeling. *Who is Flint trying to protect? Me or Senator Davis?*

~ * ~

On his first day, Raffi sits in his new office, reflecting on how his relationship with Flint will work out. *Life sends us in unexpected directions.* Despite his vision of a practice in a small ocean-side community, here he is in a posh Fifth Avenue office. While the affiliation with Flint is somewhat intimidating, he has to admit it's also exciting. Cheryl, the receptionist and office nurse, welcomed him with eagerness, indicating a favorable start.

This morning Flint is in surgery at the hospital and his own schedule is light, with only several patient postoperative wound checks. With little else to do, he's about to go to the hospital when the intercom on the desk crackles. "Dr. Sarkissian, Miss Doss is here to see you."

Surprised, he says, "Send her in."

Traci appears in the doorway, leaning seductively against the frame. It's the first time he's seen her outside the hospital and she looks smoking hot. A red sheath dress clings to her curvaceous body; her silky blonde hair falls to her shoulders.

"Hi, Doc, thought I'd stop by. Is that all right?"

He tries to maintain a sense of professionalism. "You look well, Miss Doss. I see you've fully recovered."

She glides in, seats herself before him, and critically scrutinizes the space. "This is a rather modest office, Doctor. I'll speak to Harold about giving you a more impressive consultation room."

Raffi returns a sheepish smile. "This suits me fine, Miss Doss."

Her eyes focus on him as she leans back in the chair. "It's about time you call me Traci. After all, you saved my life."

He clears his throat to keep control. "So, Traci, what brings you into the city? Weren't you flying to your ranch in Hawaii?"

"Yes, I was. I planned to spend a few days at my home in Beverly Hills and rest up before traveling to the islands." She shifts in the chair, shaking her head. "Instead I had to meet with the district attorney this morning."

Raffi's chest tightens, recalling Flint's concerns. Would the investigation pull in everyone involved with the car accident that night? For sure Flint's protecting Senator Davis, and as his new associate, he too could be involved. He asks, "Did they question you about Senator Davis and the woman who died in your apartment?"

Casually, she flips her hand toward Raffi. "I'd rather not talk about it."

His gaze meets hers. "Traci, what I'm asking—was the senator involved with that woman?"

Traci's voice rises. "I have lots of guests at my parties. I don't require FBI reports on whoever attends. Stop pestering me like a policeman."

He leans forward over the desk; their eyes lock. "Aren't you aware of what's going on? Reverend Sanders is telling everyone you're the rich girl who got preferential treatment over the black kid who died. They'll find anything to discredit you."

She raises her hand, checking the polished red fingernails. "Doctor, I have lawyers who take care of these things. What in the world does that have to do with Senator Davis?"

*What is she hiding? And why did she leave her party? Did something happen that upset her?* "Traci, you might be in danger. There's a mysterious death in a penthouse of a wealthy heiress involving a powerful senator. The press already is having a field day with the story. You have to protect yourself with the truth."

She crosses her legs in the chair and folds her hands in her lap. "I am telling the truth!"

"Are you? What condition were you in the night you crashed into Tommie's car?"

DR. RICHARD A. BERJIAN

Lines etch her brow, her lips tighten. "Why are you asking these questions?"

"Because the cops are asking why I didn't do a drug screen on you that night." His gaze fixes on her. "What was it? Alcohol? Drugs?" He knows by the anger on her face he's gone too far.

Abruptly, she jumps up, hands on her hips. "I came here as a friend and you're grilling me like a criminal!"

He persists, not letting up. "Believe me, Traci, don't take this too lightly. You're a very appealing target. Even with your battery of lawyers, Reverend Sanders' accusations are blowing everything out of proportion. I just want to help."

"How?"

He rises from the desk, approaches her, placing his hand on her arm. "I already did. I neglected to do an alcohol or drug screen on you."

~ * ~

The news breaks in TV sound bites as well as a front page lead in the *New York Times*. Senator Olin Davis is to be questioned by the New York District Attorney regarding his attendance at Traci's party.

The article infers any possible association by Olin Davis with the woman's death will create tremors throughout Washington's political community. As chairman of the powerful Foreign Relations Committee, the senator is responsible for US global interests, and any scandal will become a national bombshell of a story, causing potential international repercussions.

With newspaper in hand, Raffi sits in the doctors' lounge waiting for his next case. He studies an old campaign photo of the senator standing with his wife, and beside it, a picture of Nancy Wood posing seductively in a skimpy bikini. Mrs. Davis's white hair styled in a prim page boy makes her appear like the senator's mother, in contrast to the sexy image of Nancy Wood's flaming youth. Raffi only imagines what Davis and his wife are discussing behind closed doors.

His stomach tightens, visualizing Flint's angry description of TV cameramen and reporters camping outside his office building. As soon as Senator Davis's deposition goes public, even more speculation and rumor will hit the talk shows and scandal sheets.

A nurse sticks her head into the room. "OR is ready, Dr. Sarkissian."

"Coming," he answers, determined to ignore the media frenzy. His case, a laparoscopic removal of the gallbladder, is on a mid-level city official, and he doesn't want to screw up.

Standing at the scrub sink, he gazes through the glass window into the operating room, studying the familiar routine. A nurse places sterile drapes on the patient lying on the operating table while another nurse moves a stand carrying instruments next to the table. Kicking open the water valve of the scrub sink with his knee, he tears the plastic wrap from the soap-laden brush and scrubs his hands and arms vigorously. His reality is here in the OR, and no racial politics will keep him from fulfilling his years of training.

After scrubbing, he shoves open the swinging doors with his shoulder and enters the surgical suite. All distractions vanish. It's time to operate.

# *Twelve*

The following week, Raffi approaches the front entrance to Manhattan Medical close to 9 o'clock. A large group of angry demonstrators has already gathered, marching, holding signs. TV cameramen capture the event, focusing on the printed slogans that have become all too familiar. *How long can the hospital survive the ongoing protests?*

The usual signs are displayed. 'WHERE'S RACIAL JUSTICE FOR TOMMIE AND WENDELL?' 'NO JUSTICE, NO PEACE' 'WE STAND BY OUR BROTHERS.' Police stand in a tight barrier for crowd control, keeping a close watch on Reverend Sanders who walks through the crowd, his lieutenants beside him.

"Keep moving, Doc," the hospital guard urges. "The brain-damaged kid is getting discharged today."

He frowns, and guilt tracks his face. He hasn't kept current on Wendell Wilson's condition. The startup of his new practice and the change in schedule isn't enough of an excuse.

Once inside the building, he checks on Wendell's whereabouts and heads directly to his room. A hospital guard sits outside the door as three black youths loiter close by. Raffi flashes his identity badge, and the guard allows him to enter.

Raffi flinches on seeing Wendell in a wheelchair, dressed in a polo shirt and basketball shorts. The naïve kid he had sent breakfast to that Sunday morning is now staring vacantly into space, oblivious to his surroundings. The effects of his brain damage are evident—drooped head and a flat, spaced-out expression.

Dr. Bob Noonan, the neurosurgical resident, is giving discharge instructions to what appears to be Wendell's family. A heavy-set black woman in her mid-forties twists a tissue in her hands, tears in her eyes. A tall, muscular man too young to be the father stands by listening. Two teenage girls stand at Wendell's side.

As Raffi approaches, Noonan greets him. "Doctor, this is Wendell's family. Rufus, his older brother, his mother and two sisters."

Raffi nods to the family who appears to be close knit. "You should be aware Dr. Noonan did his best for Wendell. I'm glad he's going home to be with his family today."

Rufus reaches for the handle of the wheelchair, his face a mask of anger. "And who's gonna pay to take care of him?"

"I told you, Mr. Wilson," Noonan says, "Social services is arranging for his care."

The younger sister dries tears on her sleeve. "Wendell followed the reverend around like a puppy dog. Thought he was the greatest, and I warned him, but—"

"It's not your fault, Tamarin," Dr. Noonan tells the sister in a compassionate tone, while the older girl comfortingly rubs her back.

Noonan turns to Raffi. "The girls are in high school, and Mrs. Wilson and Rufus work. They're concerned who will care for him."

Rufus's face is tight with seething anger. "Those troublemakers caused the damage, and now who's taking responsibility?"

Noonan tries to put the family at ease. "Since Wendell is a minor, Medicaid will pay for visiting nurse support and rehabilitation. I'll direct you to our social services for assistance on that."

Rufus raises a defiant chin. "Then what happens when he ain't a minor no more, and the money runs out?"

Noonan uses the calmest voice he can muster. "He won't be abandoned, Rufus. He'll be followed in the clinic and cared for."

Raffi watches Wendell's mother sniffling into her handkerchief, her eyes red with grief.

Noonan's expression is earnest. "Please, Mrs. Wilson, give it some time. Social services won't abandon you."

"I pray not," the woman answers, hugging her son.

Raffi reads the hopelessness written on their faces. It's naïve young Wendell who pays the price for injustice, not perpetrators like Reverend Sanders.

~ * ~

Later, Adam Wolfe unexpectedly catches Raffi in the cafeteria and slips across from him at the lunch table.

Raffi looks up from his tray; his first instinct is caution. "What's up, Mr. Wolfe?"

The reporter sets his Coke can on the table and leans close, his tie dangling from an open collared shirt. He lowers his voice. "Just heard the DA questioned Senator Davis about the Doss party."

"I've seen nothing reported in the press." Raffi keeps eating.

"That's because the senator is an influential figure and the DA has to be careful."

Raffi puts down his sandwich. "Why bring up the subject? I have no connection to the senator."

"True, but you do have a connection to Miss Doss."

"As her physician, nothing more."

Wolfe's eyes track him. "Are you aware she's a major donor to Senator Davis's foundation, The American Way?"

Raffi pushes his tray away, rising from the table. "Excuse me, Mr. Wolfe. I've got a clinic full of patients waiting. What does this have to do with me?"

"Right now nothing, but there's an issue that'll interest you." Wolfe looks over his heavy dark-framed glasses that slipped down the bridge of his nose. "I know your mother's photographer friend, David Frohman, who works for *People* magazine."

Surprised, Raffi replies, "Yes, I've met him."

"He says you're Armenian."

"So?" Raffi throws him a questioning glance.

Wolfe straightens his glasses, peering through the thick lenses. "I stumbled onto something I think could go directly to elected officials—even the White House—that might concern you."

Raffi returns to his seat, curiosity getting the better of him.

"Let me tell you what I know." Wolfe pauses to lend weight to his next words. "An Armenian, Arthur Bedekian, is running for a congressional seat in Ohio as a Democrat. The seat is currently held by Republican Patsy Sweet. He claims the congresswoman received what he terms 'blood money' from the Turkish lobby to deny passage of the Armenian Genocide Bill. Congresswoman Sweet repeatedly insists the 1915 massacre wasn't genocide, only a civil uprising."

Raffi shakes his head. "Mr. Wolfe, it's no secret, over a million and a half Armenians were systematically killed by the Turks during World War One. It was called a massacre at the time, which we now call genocide. The least Congress can do is to admit to the systematic extermination of a race by passing the resolution."

Wolfe nods, leaning over the table to speak softly. "All across the world, including the United Nations, historians have confirmed the massacre as ethnic cleansing. Unfortunately the Turkish government has never acknowledged it, even *writes it out* of their history books. At present, well-funded Turkish lobbyists pay out big bucks to influence our congressmen to vote against the resolution. The State Department refuses to hurt Turkey's image because of its strategic position in the Middle East."

Raffi sits stunned, impressed by Wolfe's knowledge of the tragedy of which most Americans know nothing. His demeanor toward Wolfe softens. "How do you know so much about the Turkish lobby?"

Wolfe pulls a pamphlet out from his inside pocket and hands it to Raffi. "It's all in there. Sweet filed a complaint against Bedekian for accusing her of selling out to the Turks."

Raffi grabs the pamphlet, flipping through the pages as Wolfe drinks from his Coke can, watching.

"Read the article on page four, the one about the low level FBI translator who uncovered the facts. Her name's Jasmine Battia. She alerted her superiors and ended up getting the can. FBI fired her and the State Department placed a gag order prohibiting her from talking."

Raffi sits spellbound, absorbing this little known information. "It doesn't pay to be a whistleblower, does it, Mr. Wolfe? It's no secret the Armenian Genocide Resolution fails each year even though many in Congress claim to support it."

Wolfe is quick to reply. "That's because of the millions Turkey spends to persuade our congressional legislators and squash any mention of it in the news. Do you realize their influence has prevented the production of several Hollywood films relating to Turkey's atrocities during World War One?"

Raffi's interest is piqued. "So what's happening to the FBI agent...Battia?"

Wolfe takes another drink. "A whistleblower organization called The Legal Defense Fund, demands the attorney general review her case. But the AG's office stalled, claiming they couldn't find the request. So Battia's still under the gag order until her case is resolved."

The lines in Raffi's brow deepen. *I wonder if Mom knows about it.* "Sounds like some lowlife bureaucrat dropped the ball."

Wolfe's bushy eyebrows arch. "I doubt that. Not when it goes as high as the attorney general."

Raffi shrugs. "Politics is a dirty game, but what can I do?"

Wolfe lowers his voice, as if revealing a dark secret. "Be aware, Doc. Traci will also be in the line of fire."

That comment catches Raffi off guard.

The reporter presses on. "She's a major donor to Senator Davis's foundation. It's legally registered as a charitable organization, receiving millions in donations from the Turks and covertly used to attack the senator's political enemies. Who knows how much money he's milking from it?"

Raffi's jaw tightens; he fists his hand, pounding the table. "Turkey has gotten away with legalized murder for too long!"

Wolfe knows he's locked into Raffi's confidence, and persists. "As long as senators like Olin Davis use their underhanded pay-for-play tactics, the Armenian Genocide Bill will never get passed in Congress."

Raffi recalls Davis's duplicity the day they met at Flint's private club. "Are other congressmen on the Turkish dole?"

Wolfe nods, a slight grin crossing his face. "Quite a few. The past Speaker of the House repeatedly blocked the Genocide Bill and now receives thousands a month to push the Turkish agenda. A whole host of congressmen are receiving similar donations."

Raffi runs his fingers through his thick hair. He hates to think Traci could be tarred by the senator's black brush. She's vulnerable and has to be told. His eyes squint with suspicion. "Traci's innocent and I hate to see her hurt."

"Doc, if it's proven her foundation is supporting a lobby that bribes government officials, she could be in real trouble."

Raffi leans back in his chair trying to comprehend the ramifications of Wolfe's information. Dealing with powerful government officials and the Turkish nation is beyond his field of vision. "Look, Mr. Wolfe—"

"Adam."

"Okay, Adam, what do you want from me?"

"I'd like you to find out if Miss Doss is aware of the senator's unsavory lobbying and election activities. Don't scare her, but her name has attracted many wealthy friends who also donate to The American Way, which appears to be involved in illegal activities."

Raffi, overwhelmed, shakes his head. "You're really going to print all this?"

Wolfe removes his glasses and rubs the bridge of his nose. "Raffi, if I may call you that," he hesitates, and then presses on after Raffi nods. "For sure it'll make great press, but I also have my personal reasons."

He stops to drain the rest of the soda. "Most of my mother's family died in the Nazi Holocaust. Many, as well as myself, believe if the world had paid attention to the 1915 Armenian Genocide, maybe the Holocaust would never have happened twenty-four years later."

Raffi suddenly feels a shared link with Wolfe. He remembers Ani quoting Hitler's statement as a premonition for the Holocaust. *After all, who remembers the Armenians?* Following which the Nazi dictator proceeded to disenfranchise, imprison and gas millions of innocent men, women and children, merely because they were Jews.

Wolfe picks up the empty can and rises from the table. "Read the pamphlet. Jasmine Battia's testimony is all in there. And by the way, you'll find out the name Nancy Wood is only a cover for the woman who died in Traci's penthouse."

Raffi watches Wolfe toss the can into the trash and walk out the room. The reporter's ethical compass touches his moral sensitivity. Has he just found an honest friend in the brash reporter?

# *Thirteen*

Raffi remains seated and picks up the publication Adam gave him. He skims the front page headline. *IS CONGRESS FOR SALE?* A cartoon photo of a sparkling gold-domed Capitol building with dollars floating above angers him. Were congressmen using their elected positions to profit personally? Surely Traci isn't involved in Senator Davis's cover-up. She's just an over-indulged rich woman, oblivious to what her contributions support.

He abruptly picks up his phone and dials his office. "Cheryl, please track down Miss Doss. I need to speak to her."

"I'll try, Dr. Sarkissian, but she's not easy to find."

"Tell her to reach me on my cell phone."

"Will do," Cheryl responds.

His stomach muscles tighten into a queasy knot. He has no control over the Jackson family lawsuit or the reverend's constant media coverage pounding its racist message, but maybe he can save Traci from Senator Davis's deceit. He discards the lunch tray and leaves the cafeteria, heading to the men's room. Once inside, he draws in a heavy breath and peers at his reflection in the mirror, wondering if he's playing in a high stakes poker game, uncertain where the cards will fall.

His life is already entwined with Traci's. Why didn't he do a drug screen on her? Jeremy followed procedure and ordered one on the Jackson boy, which was negative. What if Traci was drunk and responsible for the accident? He'd eventually have to answer that question in court.

He leaves the men's room, wanting to do something positive. He still hasn't spoken to Lorig since the dinner date at Casa Luna. It's lunchtime and she'll be out of the classroom. He dials, waiting for her to pick up.

Her greeting sounds genuine. "Raffi, what a nice surprise!"

Her voice lifts his spirits. "Hi, glad you picked up. Can you talk?"

"Got five minutes before class starts. What's up?"

He hesitates, then continues. "Sorry for not calling sooner. Just wanted to hear your voice."

"Raffi, you sound preoccupied. I read about the lawsuit in the newspaper."

Despite all his concerns, his reply is flippant. "It's nothing. The hospital attorney says not to worry. Are you free Saturday night?"

"You're asking for a date?"

"I'm not asking, I'm begging."

She gives a teasing giggle. "You realize this is Thursday already."

"You're not going to turn down this overworked surgeon, are you?"

A pause follows until she answers, "OK, Saturday night it is. Six?"

"See you then." He smiles, and clicks off. Despite his casual fascination with Traci Doss, he senses Lorig could be the one to provide some sanity in his confusing life.

~ * ~

It's not often Ani visits Raffi in his bachelor apartment so he's both concerned and curious when she calls.

"I need to talk to you, Raffi—is tonight OK? I'll drop by after work."

Jasmine Battia's firing enters his thoughts. After Wolf's conversation, he's disturbed it might have something to do with his mother's recent position at the FBI.

Punctually at seven, he greets her at the door, hangs up her raincoat, and ushers her into the living room. "Sit down, Mom, you have me on edge. What is it you couldn't tell me over the phone?"

Ani folds hands in her lap; her face flushes. "It's very personal."

Raffi's eyes widen, waiting for an answer.

She leans forward. "There's a decision I can't make without you."

Raffi feels a twinge of panic. Why is this independent woman looking to him? *She's the one I relied on all my life.* Nervously, he sits on the edge of the couch, waiting for her to speak.

Her tight lips break into a rushed smile. "David Frohman has asked to marry me. We've known each other for over a year, and I've grown to respect and care for him. I haven't answered him yet, but I need your blessing if I accept."

Raffi releases a long sigh, sinking back against the cushions. "Mom, I thought it was something serious!" He pauses momentarily, then adds, "You know I like David. Why do you need my blessing?"

Ani's eyes mist, her voice turns mellow. "Raffi, you're the only one I can confide in and with the mistakes I've made, I don't want to make another."

"Mom, you never made any mistakes!"

Ani lowers her gaze; her voice softens. "Don't you think raising a child without a father is a mistake?"

A lump lodges in Raffi's throat, and he moves to her side. "Mom, listen. You've given me everything—love, guidance, my future. I never suffered not having a father."

Ani places a hand on her son's. "I tried to find him, to tell him I was pregnant but to no avail. After several attempts, I gave up, realizing his life had taken another direction." Her brow wrinkles, pained at the thought of losing the only man she'd loved. She sits silent a few moments and then says, "You do know David is Jewish, and I don't want that to pose any problems."

Raffi laughs jokingly. "You're planning to have children? Of course I approve."

Ani brings both hands to her cheeks, smiling. "Thank you. I'm blessed having you in my life." She gazes at her son's square jaw, his dark eyes, imagining Haig in him. "Your father would be very proud of you," she whispers.

Raffi takes a hard swallow, feeling a tremor in his voice. "There's so much I want to know about him."

"Darling, I've told you all I know. He just disappeared and is possibly dead."

Raffi hesitates, trying to keep his emotions in check. "Mom, when I was a kid, every time I asked about him, your eyes filled with tears. You'd look so sad, so I stopped asking. What did he look like? What attracted you to him?"

The fine lines on her face deepen; her eyes remain steady, focusing on her son. "His name was Haig Sarian, a tall, dashing dark-haired captain. I fell in love with him the first time we met. He loved me too, if only for a short time."

"Did he have any family?"

"His grandparents were Armenians living in Turkey at the time of the genocide. They were fortunate enough to escape to Georgia with their only daughter where they raised her. In Georgia, she married and had a son, and that son is your father."

Raffi gently touches his mother's arm. "Thanks for the history, Mom. What was he like?"

"He was bright, a romantic. He loved music and was gifted in languages. The military pursued him for that reason."

"You mentioned he was a captain."

A smile crosses her face. "With all his expertise, I imagine he stood out enough to become an officer in the Russian military. Remember, at that time Georgia was under Soviet domination."

"Did he have any brothers or sisters?"

"No, although I met his cousin, Berj. They were as close as brothers."

Raffi chokes back a swallow, wanting to know more. "How did you meet?"

Ani's gaze wanders into the distance, her voice soft as a whisper. "We both were translators working in Ankara. I had a position in the Turkish government and he worked in the Russian embassy. I fell in love with him the first time he came into the office for a meeting with my superior, Captain Orzan."

Raffi frowns, leaning both hands on his knees. "I never told you this, but when I was little, I hated him. I'd lie awake at night thinking, why did he leave? Why didn't he love us enough to stay?"

Tears fill Ani's eyes; her voice cracks. "Son, he never knew I was pregnant. I planned to tell him that evening but something drastic must have happened. I don't know if he was taken away by the Russians, or had to run from something dangerous. Years later I tried to find him on the Internet." She shrugs. "But to no avail."

Angry, Raffi raises his voice. "But why didn't he tell you he was leaving?"

Her eyes glaze with tears. "The Communists were still in power. I suspect he might have been involved with some type of undercover work. Later I heard his cousin Berj was apprehended as a spy. Everything was hush-hush then. We didn't have the freedoms you enjoy today."

Her slender figure appears to age as she rises to get a tissue from her purse. She dries her eyes and returns to sit next to him.

"Son, I trusted him and I don't know why he never got in touch with me. But in my heart, I know he loved me."

Raffi leans over and embraces her. "Sorry Mom, I didn't mean to open old wounds."

She pats his arm. "I'm glad we had this talk, darling. I've relived what happened over and over, but after thirty-one years, I'm not bitter. Only good memories remain."

Tears sting Raffi's eyes, and he kisses her cheek. "I love you, Mom. It's time you share your life with someone other than me. Tell David I heartily agree with the marriage. You both have my blessing."

She checks her watch. "I love you too, son, I better get going."

"Mom, let me drive you home."

"That's not necessary. It's a beautiful evening so I don't mind waiting for the bus. It's only a fifteen minute ride to my apartment."

He rises to get her shawl and places it on her shoulders. "How do you like your new job at the FBI?" *Has she heard anything about Jasmine Battia?*

Ani takes in a deep breath, securing the wrap around her. "I must say it's very different from what I had been doing at the UN."

He knows his mom learns quickly and in no time she'll figure things out. "Do you find it more challenging?"

Ani hesitates. "Let's just say, I'm discovering some unusual things that bother me."

He immediately thinks of Jasmine Battia's situation, but doesn't want to alarm her. "Have you consulted with your superiors?"

"I'm afraid to make waves since I've only been there a short time."

He hesitates bringing up the article in the publication Wolfe had given him. For all he knows, Ani might be Battia's replacement.

He ends the visit with a positive note and says, "Mom, don't sweat it. It's only a job. And it's your decision if you accept David's proposal. He's a good guy."

He stands at the door, watching Ani wave good bye. She has his blessings, but in his heart he wonders if she'll say yes to David.

# *Fourteen*

Raffi checks his watch as he rides the elevator to Manhattan Medical's executive suite. Hospital attorney, Barry Gold called a morning meeting with Reverend Sanders and his attorney, hoping to reach an out of court settlement. He insisted Raffi be present.

Raffi objected. "Dammit, Mr. Gold, I'm not guilty so why should I consent to any payment?"

But the attorney warned that without his cooperation, the hospital's insurance company won't cover his legal bills. All deposition costs, transcripts and attorney conferences would become his responsibility. With those words of caution, a reluctant Raffi enters the executive offices punctually at nine, facing a room full of men in business attire.

Reverend Sanders and his African-American attorney, Darren Hamilton, sit at the conference table, each wearing finely tailored suits. Gold introduces Raffi and then gestures to the gentleman next to him. "Dr. Sarkissian, this is our insurance adjuster, Philip Brock."

Raffi, dressed in greens, takes his place at the long mahogany table and nods. "Good morning."

Gold wastes no time opening the meeting and clears his throat before turning to the reverend's attorney. "Mr. Hamilton, your client has consented to discuss an out of court settlement with the Jackson family, but your figure of twenty million is out of line."

The figure stuns Raffi. He studies the thin, angular chin on Hamilton's face. The attorney's hardened, inscrutable expression demonstrates his determination.

Hamilton leans on the table, clasping his hands. "Tommie Jackson died and wealthy Traci Doss lives. No jury will have sympathy with your position."

Gold remains calm and persists. "Medical facts show no signs of negligence. Even a state investigation has cleared the hospital."

Hamilton's eyes narrow into slits. "Mr. Gold, it's up to the courts to decide if the hospital and its employees met the standard of care."

Gold clears his throat again; moisture beads on his upper lip. "The hospital proposes a one-time payment of two hundred fifty thousand to settle the claim."

Reverend Sanders bolts from his chair. "Ridiculous! That amount is an insult!"

Hamilton restrains Sanders with his hand. "Easy, Reverend. I'm sure Mr. Gold has another offer in his bag."

Raffi's gaze tracks both attorneys, astonished by the figures so glibly thrown out.

Gold hesitates, straining to keep his composure. "I see that doesn't please you. Just to see if we're in the same ballpark, I've been authorized to raise the settlement to five hundred thousand. Can we agree on that number?"

Hamilton exchanges a quick glance with Sanders, who vigorously shakes his head. "You're not even close, Counselor," he replies.

Sanders rises abruptly and grabs Hamilton's arm, prepared to drag his attorney from the room with him. "You're wasting our time, Mr. Gold."

Gold waves his hand, signaling them to remain seated. "Gentlemen, this is the hospital's final offer." He opens his brief case, shuffles to retrieve a paper, and holds it up. "Seven hundred thousand dollars—which is a lot of money, considering the medical aspects of this case were handled properly."

The insurance adjuster's eyes widen in astonishment as he looks to Sanders. "Let's be reasonable, Reverend. The hospital is medically without fault. We're prepared to contribute to Tommie's family and even consider donating to your organization. But in turn, you must agree to meet the hospital's demands to withdraw any claims of racism against Manhattan Medical and its employees."

Sanders pounds the arm of his chair, anger contorting his face. "No way! Paying the Jackson family what they have coming to them is one thing, but stopping me from fighting racial profiling and injustice? No, never!" Again he jumps up from his seat and moves toward the door. "Forget it. Let's go, Hamilton."

Hamilton returns papers to his briefcase, rises and faces Gold. "You're not even close, Counselor. Call when you figure things out." The two leave, closing the door behind them.

Dumbfounded, Raffi turns to Gold. "That's a bucket load of money. Isn't it best we prove our case in court?"

"Not quite," Gold replies, smoothing the few strands left on his almost-bald head. "Chances are we'll win in court but we'll lose the publicity war. Sanders knows that, and when the NAACP, the new Black Panthers and the reverend's organization get together, we'll be fighting a racial battle, a war no one wins."

The insurance agent breaks in. "Except Reverend Sanders. I just learned he filed to run for Congress in a heavily black district of Harlem. He'll push his racial agenda to turn out the black vote, and he'll use Tommie's death to do it."

Silence sweeps over the room until Raffi says, "Someone once told me, if you're searching for justice, don't go into a courtroom."

~ * ~

Raffi finally hears from Traci after a week of multiple calls. "Traci, I need to talk to you. When can you come to the office?"

Her voice is stiff. "Why? So you can pummel me with more annoying questions?"

Trying to protect her, he says, "I admit I came on too strong, but your wealth makes you a target. Forgive me, but you're more than a patient to me. I consider you a friend." Hearing no response, he pauses. "Traci, there's something you should know about Senator Davis."

Her voice softens, cautious. "Like what?"

"I don't want to discuss it over the phone. When can we meet?"

"God, you are persistent. No matter what you have to say, it always ends up with questions. I have no time for that."

"Please, just give me a few minutes. You might change your mind after I tell you what I've learned."

"What? Some tidbit you picked up from the tabloids?"

"Don't joke about this, Traci. The DA is still investigating Tommie's death along with the woman who died in your apartment."

A few seconds of silence pass before Traci speaks. "Jackson's death was an accident, and my lawyers have assured me I have nothing to do with what happened to Nancy Wood."

Raffi raises his voice in frustration. "A reporter friend from the *Post* revealed something you should know but it's too sensitive to discuss over the phone."

She releases a long dramatic sigh. "If you're so bugged about telling me, then come to the Marquis Club tomorrow night, but get there after nine."

"What's the Marquis Club?"

"It's a dance club, silly."

"I can't talk serious business at a dance club."

"You want to talk? Meet me there. I'm not changing my plans."

Raffi gazes at the ceiling, frustrated. "OK, what's the address?"

"Check the Internet. Goodbye."

Raffi ends the call with a sense of uncertainty. *Why am I meddling into her affairs?* He admits she's sexy hot, and despite her quirky faults, he's obviously attracted to her. No question, he'll meet her at the Marquis Club tomorrow night, and he Googles the address.

~ * ~

To meld into the disco scene, Raffi dresses in designer jeans and an open collared shirt. He exits the cab in front of the blaring lights of the Marquis Club, facing a long line queued up waiting to get in on a Thursday night. He approaches the muscular guard posing with arms crossed over a barrel chest. "Miss Traci Doss is expecting me at nine."

The guard lets out a sarcastic laugh. "Sure she is. You'll have to wait like everyone else."

Raffi steps out of the way of a young man built like a Sumo wrestler who lunges forward, pulling a curvy brunette by the hand.

The burly guard holds him back. "Wait your turn, buddy—get back in line."

The Sumo patron stands his ground. "We've been here for almost an hour. How much longer?"

Annoyed, Raffi looks past the man and waves, getting the guard's attention. "Would you tell Miss Doss that Dr. Sarkissian is waiting outside?"

Without saying a word, the guard knocks on the door and a clean-shaven head with a long ponytail appears in the shadow. "Ask Miss Doss if she's waiting to see a Dr. Sarkissian."

"Not fair!" Sumo complains.

The head disappears and Raffi grinds his back teeth, frustrated by the delay.

The guard jerks a thumb to the Sumo and his girlfriend. "Get back in line or you'll lose your place." They go, grumbling.

Raffi stands patiently waiting until the door opens again and the ponytail head reappears. "You can let him in."

Raffi's eyes smart from the smoke as he follows the bouncer alongside a lengthy winding bar at one end of the room. His nostrils catch the sweet aroma of marijuana as he walks past couples drinking and smoking. Colorful sparkling chandeliers light up the highly polished dance floor filled with dancers with flailing arms bouncing to the deafening disco music.

Raffi follows the man up a long, curved, double-wishbone staircase to the second floor, and looks over the balcony at the mob of humanity gyrating to the primitive beat of drums. Even at twenty feet, he smells the odor of marijuana floating upward. For a moment he wonders what he missed with all his years of training.

The music fades once he passes through double doors into a private room with booths and tables located opposite a bar. Without a single word, the attendant departs, closing the door behind him.

Raffi searches the dimly lit room until he finds Traci sitting with a sharp-featured man sporting a full head of black wavy hair and a trim mustache. He has a possessive arm around her back. Their table is littered with empty glasses along a trail of cigarette ashes.

Traci gestures with her hands as Raffi approaches, slurring her words. "You came! Order what you like, my dear doctor, and let's see how you party."

Raffi faces her, avoiding the companion's icy stare. It's obvious she's already had a few too many and he wonders if coming was a good idea. "Traci, give me a few minutes, and then I'll be off."

She frowns; her lips pucker in a pout. "At least one drink *and* one dance. Then we'll talk."

Raffi taps his foot, losing his patience. "Not tonight—I have a long day in surgery tomorrow."

Traci springs up from the booth, straightening her short skirt. "You're so square, Raffi." She points to a door labeled *Management*. "We can talk in there."

A slender, good-looking man wearing a gray business suit appears as they enter. The man nods politely. "Good evening, Miss Doss."

Traci responds with a giggle. "Jared, I need some privacy. Please keep the door closed."

"Of course, Miss Doss," he replies, unlocking the door to allow them entrance into what appears to be an executive office. The room contains a comfortable sofa and two club chairs separated by a cocktail table. A narrow bar runs along the back wall.

Traci sits on the sofa and crosses her legs, gesturing Raffi to sit next to her. "Now, what's this all about?"

*I hope she's sober enough to understand what I have to say.* He leans close to make his point. "Traci, there's information about Senator Davis you should know."

She scoffs and draws back. "What is it with you? Are you playing detective again?"

Raffi grabs her arm. "Listen, Traci. What I'm telling you is for your own good. What do you know about Senator Davis's involvement with the Wood woman?"

She gives him a menacing look, pulling away. Without answering, she rises and goes to the bar, pouring herself a drink—but doesn't offer him one.

He tries to get her attention once she returns and squarely faces her. "An investigative reporter told me things about the senator that could get you into trouble with the IRS and the government."

She takes a sip from the glass and places it on the table before them. "Don't worry, Raffi. I have plenty of lawyers protecting me."

*What can I do to make her listen?* He loses control and blurts out. "Maybe so, but even the most powerful firm can't protect you from the charge of murder."

Traci bolts upright in the chair. "Are you accusing me of murder?"

"No, but when the DA finishes investigating that woman's death in your apartment, you're going to get dragged into a big mess."

"My lawyers reviewed the facts and they claim I'm completely innocent."

Raffi wonders if she's too drunk to remember what happened that night. "I know you're innocent, but the tabloids are another problem. After they sift through the records, they'll print stuff that might influence a jury against you."

Her face turns red and she jumps up from the sofa. "Enough! I don't want to hear any of this!"

Raffi places a restraining hand on her arm and pulls her down next to him. Her skirt rises, baring her toned, tanned thighs.

He plants both hands on her shoulders to focus her attention. "A case is working its way through the courts that'll show Senator Davis is taking big bucks from the Turkish lobby to block passage of the Armenian Genocide Bill."

Incensed, Traci pulls away. "What in the hell is the Genocide Bill?"

"It's complicated, but in a nutshell, Congress has tried to pass a bill recognizing the 1915 massacre of over a million innocent Armenians by Turkey. It's called ethnic cleansing and Turkey's powerful lobby is in the business of bribing our senators and congressmen to vote against the bill."

Traci's eyes widen, her head cocks to one side. "Are you high? I'm not connected to anything like that. I don't do politics."

*Do I have to spell it out to her?* "Traci, whether you know it or not, you are involved. You donate to Senator Davis's American Way Foundation, don't you?"

"That's just one of many. I donate to a lot of causes. You're wasting my time, Raffi."

He slides his hand on her knee, forcing her to stay seated. "Understand, Traci, this is big stuff. Nancy Wood was a Turkish undercover agent sent by her government as a call girl to spy on the senator. I don't know her real name but read about it in the *Insider* magazine. This is going to blow up into an international incident."

Her head tilts suspiciously. "I don't give a damn about the *Insider*. Just how do you think you're helping with this salacious gossip?"

Raffi's quick to answer. "You have a reputation as a humanitarian—people support your causes because of *you*. If word gets out that you're backing a man that's milking the system, who'll trust you? And once word gets out about the senator's affair with the undercover agent, everything he touches will be tainted."

Traci sits speechless, staring back at Raffi.

The pitch of Raffi's voice surges. "Traci, you've got to stop donating to Davis's foundation! Tell the DA everything you know about the senator and his girlfriend."

Her body shakes with anger. "But I already have! So, you're concerned about my reputation?" She laughs sarcastically. "It's Grant's job to take care of those things." She softens and adds, "Don't worry, Raffi, I'll talk to him tomorrow, okay?"

Before he can say anything, she puts her empty glass down at her feet and gets up, throwing her arms up in frustration. Tears slide down her cheeks, and she wipes them with the back of her hand. Her voice cracks. "You say you care about me, but all you do is cause me aggravation!"

What he said was hurtful and he breathes a heavy sigh, watching her cover her face with her hands. He stands and gently brushes a strand of silky blonde hair from her forehead.

His voice softens. "Would I be warning you if I didn't care about you? Please distance yourself from Senator Davis. His girlfriend died under mysterious circumstances in *your* apartment."

He catches the slight quiver of her lips before she abruptly pulls away and runs out of the room.

# Fifteen

Raffi makes a quick exit from the Marquis Club, fighting mixed emotions. He just spoiled Traci's evening, but sometimes doing the right thing sucks.

Waiting for a cab at the curb, he questions why he's driven to get involved. She certainly doesn't want for legal advice. *Is my concern merely a mask for my attraction to her?* He pushes that thought out of his mind as Lorig's smile flashes before him.

He waves to the passing cabs but they all drive by carrying passengers. Frustrated by the night in general, he turns to walk to the Eighth Avenue subway. Taking brisk steps, he leaves the club's brightly lit entrance to enter the unfamiliar back streets. The sudden yowl of an alley cat jumping off a garbage can shoots a bolt of fear through him, and the eerie sound of his own steps forces him to quicken his pace. No longer in a residential area, he tracks the shadows cast by darkened commercial lofts dimly lit by a few street lamps. In the five years he's lived in the city, this is the first time he's strayed so far west at night.

Two figures emerge from the darkness, walking toward him. The taller one in a khaki jacket blocks Raffi's path while his companion, sporting a long leather coat, stands behind.

A bolt of adrenalin races through Raffi. *I'm going to get mugged.* Trapped between the two men, he scrutinizes the face of the guy blocking him. How can he describe him to the police? The only significant feature on the black face is the high forehead and warlock hair.

The guy places a vise-like hold on Raffi's shoulder. "Hey, bro, can you spare some cash?"

Raffi fumbles to remove his wallet, willing to give up money but not his credit cards. "I'll give you what I have," he answers.

"Don't take all day," the deep voice shouts from behind.

Raffi's hands shake, struggling to flip open the wallet and remove the bills.

The man facing him grabs the money and counts. "Forty-seven bucks. That's fuckin' bullshit! Give me that wallet."

Raffi pulls back the wallet to protect the credit cards, and the mugger catches a glimpse of the Rolex Traci had gifted him.

"Gimme that watch!" the mugger demands, grabbing Raffi's arm.

"You have my money," Raffi replies. The switchblade snaps close to his ear and he feels the cold knife press against his throat.

The man in the coat comes up from behind. "You're a dead man."

The sudden sharp pain of a hard object across the back of his head is the last thing Raffi remembers.

~ * ~

Harold Flint stands over Raffi's hospital bed, shaking his head. "You must be crazy walking the streets at night in such a dangerous area."

Raffi's propped up in bed, his head wrapped in white gauze bandages, his face swollen with stitches at the base of his throat. "It's a long story, Harold. Let's just say I was stupid."

"Stupid is an understatement. Christ, you're supposed to be helping me. Now I have to pick up your surgical load."

Raffi sighs, knowing whatever explanation he gives, Flint won't be satisfied. "I was just trying to do someone a favor."

Flint roars back. "Who could be that important to make you risk your life?"

"That might be me," a voice replies from the doorway. Traci Doss strolls into the room dressed in a smartly tailored emerald green suit jacket and pencil thin skirt. "Raffi was there because of me. I asked him to meet me at the Marquis Club."

Flint's voice softens. "Hi, Traci."

Raffi can see the anger on Flint's face melt away. Traci's wealth, beauty and social position have a definite influence on his partner.

She approaches the bed, focusing on Raffi's bruises and bandaged head. "You poor thing. You could have been killed!"

"Exactly what I told him," Flint adds, giving Raffi a fatherly smile. "Have the police interviewed you?"

"Not yet," Raffi replies, shifting uncomfortably with all the attention.

Flint frowns, directing his gaze at Traci. "How are you doing? I saw your name in today's paper. The DA requested a grand jury inquiry into the deaths of Tommie Jackson and Nancy Wood."

Traci sighs and avoids looking at Raffi. "It's a mess, but I had nothing to do with that girl's death, or Tommie's."

"How can I help?" Flint asks with a touch of sincerity.

Traci strokes Raffi's arm. "You can't, Harold, but thank you. Only my lawyers can do that. First, let's get this poor boy well."

Traci's open familiarity in front of Flint makes Raffi flinch. "I'll be OK. Probably get discharged tomorrow."

Traci's quick to reply. "No you won't. My attorney spoke to the ER physician and he said you had a serious concussion. You need rest and time to heal."

Flint's brow wrinkles in amazement. "They won't tell me a blessed thing. How did he get that privileged information?"

Traci lets out a satisfied chuckle. "Harold, don't you know lawyers have their ways?" She moves and sits on the edge of the bed, placing an arm over Raffi's shoulder just as Lorig walks into the room.

Lorig stands at the door; her eyes widen, taking in the scene. "Excuse me. I hope I'm not interrupting anything."

"Lorig," Raffi calls out, his cheeks flaming as if he'd done something wrong. "What a surprise!"

Awkwardly, she remains stationed at the threshold, as if afraid to enter. "I was so worried, Raffi. The paper said you were admitted to the hospital, and you didn't answer your phone, well, how could you? They probably stole it."

Lorig keeps hold of the door, avoiding Traci. "I had to see what happened to you."

Traci, still seated on the bed, eyes Lorig like a playful cat tracking a mouse. "I don't blame you for being concerned. You must be very close to the doctor."

Lorig blushes. "We're just friends. I'm Lorig."

Traci doesn't budge. Harold wears an amused smile.

Raffi asks in a strained voice. "Aren't you teaching school today?"

Lorig fumbles for words as she steps further into the room, her sneakers squeaking against the tile floor. She's dressed for comfort in jeans, a gray sweater, her chestnut hair in a ponytail. She crosses her arms. "When I read you were mugged, I called in for a personal day. The report didn't mention your condition and the hospital switchboard refused to give me any information."

Traci rises from the bed, straightening her skirt. "Lorig, how sweet of you to skip school just to visit the good doctor. Are you *sure* you're not more than friends?"

Raffi catches Lorig's discomfort and comes to her defense. "It's nothing like that, Traci."

Pleased she's made her point, Traci extends her hand. "I'm happy to meet you, Lorig. I'm the infamous Traci Doss, and this is Dr. Harold Flint, Raffi's partner."

Lorig shakes her hand, gives Flint a weak smile and moves to Raffi's bedside, studying his injuries with concern. "Do you mind that I came to see you, Raffi?"

"Of course not—I'm really touched you did." He wishes it were just the two of them, so he could explain—but explain what? He hasn't done anything wrong.

An awkward silence fills the room until Flint rises and clears his throat. "Should I go get some coffee from the nurse's station?"

Lorig quickly interjects. "I was just about to leave." She places a hand on Raffi's shoulder, gazing into his eyes. "I'm glad you're okay." She gives Flint and Traci a forced smile. "It was nice meeting both of you."

Before Raffi can say anything, she turns and rushes out of the room.

Flint buttons his blazer and moves to the door. "Gotta go. No need to come to the office until you're ready, Raffi."

"I'll make sure he gets his rest, Harold," Traci calls out. Once again alone in the room, she bends over to kiss Raffi's cheek, her blue eyes sparkling. "Now that I've met your special friend, I know who my competition is."

~ * ~

After two days' mending in the hospital, Raffi returns to his apartment, suffering the occasional headache. Flint insists he take the rest of the week to convalesce. He hasn't heard a word from Lorig and puts off calling her, hoping things will cool down. But Traci keeps in touch, texting, calling several times a day from her home in Palm Beach, checking on him. She finally persuades him to join her in Florida for several days of rest.

Raffi rationalizes it would be the perfect time to take a short break from the practice. Flint has warned him that cases are already scheduled for his return the following week, so what will it hurt if he takes a short vacation since he has never been to Florida.

At seven the next morning, Traci's limousine waits for him outside his apartment. The chauffer holds open the limo door.

"Let me help, Doctor. Miss Doss mentioned you're recovering from a recent injury and we don't want you to hurt yourself."

"Thanks, I'm fine," Raffi replies, slipping effortlessly onto the slick leather back seat.

With luggage in the trunk and doors closed, the long black sedan heads to the West Side Highway and the airport.

Raffi's mind wanders as they travel north. Yesterday, the district attorney officially cleared Traci of any wrongdoing in Jackson's death. The police investigation showed a blown-out tire on her car had caused the accident. But the malpractice suit against the hospital filed by Tommie's family is still working its way through the courts. In addition, Reverend Sanders' civil rights action against Manhattan Medical sits on the court docket.

The limo crosses over the George Washington Bridge into New Jersey, traveling Route 46 to reach Teterboro Airport. On arrival, two pilots escort Raffi to a waiting Lear 60 jet as soon as he steps out of the limo.

The young captain, wearing a smartly tailored blue uniform, greets Raffi and accompanies him up the metal stairway into the aircraft. "Welcome aboard, Doctor. You'll be traveling alone in the cabin this morning. Since we don't have a flight attendant, may I get you a cocktail?"

"A Coke will be fine," Raffi replies as he settles comfortably into the roomy bucket seat. *So this is what luxury feels like.*

After the pilot leaves for the galley, Raffi inspects the cabin, enjoying the ambiance of a private corporate jet. Within minutes, the pilot returns with a cold can, and Raffi thanks him, scanning the six empty chairs. "Is it common to have only one passenger?" he asks.

The captain smiles, placing a copy of the *Wall Street Journal* on the seat next to him. "Teterboro is one of the nation's busiest executive airports. We fly groups or just a single passenger on short notice. Businessmen need to get to where they're going quickly. Press the call button if you need anything." He leaves to join his co-pilot in the cockpit.

Raffi skims through the newspaper as the plane taxis to the tarmac, waiting to receive clearance from the tower. Within minutes, the jet is airborne, cutting through misty clouds until it enters the clear blue sky.

He sips his drink, surrounded by the luxury reserved for corporate wealth, a universe quite foreign from his medical world. He tells himself that accepting Traci's invitation puts him in a doctor-patient relationship far removed from his original intentions. Something draws him into her space, but he hasn't quite figured out if it's more than friendship. *Go with the flow.* He's never had a real vacation, and deserves time away from his daily challenges.

After two and a half hours, the jet lands at Palm Beach International Airport. A private limo waits to drive him to the Five Star Breakers Hotel. He stops at the reception desk to discover he's already checked in. No sooner does he unpack and change into a casual shirt and slacks when the phone rings.

It's Traci. "Are you settled and ready for lunch?"

"Yes, on both counts." His stomach rumbles in agreement.

"Then meet me at the cabana pool. The concierge will direct you."

Raffi spots Traci sitting at a table shaded by a large green and white umbrella. Palm trees sway in the background and the bright blue of the ocean reflects the sunlight. He makes his way around swimmers and sunbathers to approach her. "Well, I made it," he announces.

She looks casual-chic, wearing white slacks and a blue striped polo shirt, tailored to accentuate her seductive figure. She rises to kiss his cheek, holding down her wide-brim hat in the breeze. "Was the flight comfortable?"

"Couldn't be better," he says, taking a chair. Her beauty takes his breath away. A gentle breeze blows through her long blonde hair; her warm pink glow matches the colorful fresh flowers on the table.

He slides his hand across the table and gives her hand a friendly pat. "This is beautiful. Thanks for the invitation, Traci."

She focuses on his bare wrist. "Why aren't you wearing the Rolex I gave you?"

Raffi frowns. "The muggers stole it."

She smiles; dimples rise on her cheeks. "Now I know what I can get you for your birthday."

Raffi flushes. *Am I a kept man?*

She waves to a waiter, who quickly approaches and hands them each a menu. "Would you care to order, Miss Doss?"

"Thank you, Pierre. Just give us a minute. "

Raffi assumes Traci is a frequent guest, friendly with the staff, and wonders how it would feel to spend your life being catered to.

It's close to one o' clock and Raffi is famished, but he's careful not to rush his meal as he's accustomed to in the hospital cafeteria. Their conversation is light and chatty as they lunch on shrimp salad stuffed in avocado.

"It's a luxury to eat at a slower pace," Raffi comments, wiping his mouth on the cloth napkin. "Everything tastes so much better."

She drops her napkin over her plate. "I find the company helps too," she teases. "That was delicious." She stands up, her silk scarf whipping in the breeze. "Ready for some exercise? We can swim here," she gestures to the blue expanse of ocean, "or go to the beach at my house. It's just down the road."

Raffi shakes his head in disbelief. Traci owns a penthouse in New York, a huge farm estate in New Jersey and homes in LA and Hawaii, not to mention Europe, and this one. How does she manage to spend time at all these places?

She gives him a coy smile. "You look surprised."

"I am," he answers with honesty. "How do you keep up with all your homes?"

Her laugh turns flirty. "Darling, it comes in handy when the seasons change. Shall we go to my place?"

Raffi reaches for her hand. "There's no rush. Why don't we just sit and talk?"

"Ahh, there you are!" comes a voice from behind a potted palm. The words carry the hint of a Spanish accent.

A tall, trim young man sporting a mustache approaches and Raffi knows he's seen him before. *Was it at The Marquis Club?* His casual linen slacks and open silk shirt reflect his designer tastes.

Traci snaps harshly. "Carlos, I thought you were still in New York."

"I left because you never called. Your staff said you went to Palm Beach." His accusatory gaze turns to Raffi.

"Carlos, this is my friend, Dr. Raffi Sarkissian. He's my guest for the weekend."

Carlos's eyes shift warily. "He's staying at your home?"

Traci's reply is curt. "He's staying at the hotel. We have a busy weekend planned," she adds.

The man's jaw tightens, his body stiffens. "I'll wait for your call when you're *not* busy." He turns on his heels and walks away.

Raffi watches the exchange with interest. "Carlos doesn't seem very happy with you."

Traci waves a hand, annoyed. "He'll get over it."

It's clear Carlos, and who knows how many others, are romantically interested in her. *Have I become one of the crowd?* Once more Lorig comes into his thoughts, and he wonders if he's done right accepting Traci's invitation.

An ocean breeze suddenly erupts, and Traci holds a hand to keep her hat from blowing away. Raffi catches the light reflecting on the multiple gold bangles on her wrist, seduced by her elegant beauty. *Slender, beautiful and rich.* He wonders if a man can be attracted to two women at the same time and have each of them meaningful in his life.

# *Sixteen*

Traci's imposing Palm Beach home stands across from a clean, sandy and very private beach. She explains that all Florida beaches are open to the public, but the tunnel access connecting the mansions to the beach make it unlikely any strangers will appear. They change into their swimsuits in the pool house and then walk through the tunnel. Traci, in an itty-bitty bikini, grabs Raffi's hand as soon as they reach the sand and pulls him into the crashing surf.

As they swim against the powerful currents, he watches her smooth, efficient strokes, forcing him to increase his pace. They enter into the still waters beyond the rushing waves, and he grabs her waist, drawing her close. Her skin feels smooth and firm.

He catches his breath. "Where did you learn to swim like that?"

She lets out a hearty laugh and responds by wrapping her arms and legs around him as they float.

He enjoys the sensation of her body against his and kisses the nape of her neck, tasting the salty ocean water.

She responds by placing a gentle kiss on his lips, gazing into his eyes. "Raffi, I wanted to do that for a long time," she says, then dives back into the waves and shouts, "Catch me if you can!" laughing like a schoolgirl.

After a play of water tag, Raffi follows her strong strokes heading back to shore. He runs through the fine white sand following her, and drops onto the blanket, pulling her down by his side. He kisses her again, tasting her. They each pull back for a breath.

"We should do this all the time," she says, reaching for a towel.

"If only I could with my crazy schedule." He lies down on his towel, watching as she dries herself. Her voluptuous curves in the tiny bikini cloud his mind. *What does she see in me?*

She throws him a tender glance and gets on her knees, bending over him. Stroking the wet hair away from his face, her voice becomes sober. "Raffi, I'm serious. We can easily change your busy schedule, if you like."

He banters back, not wanting to get serious. "Are you bribing me?"

"All's fair in love and war," she replies, caressing his cheek with her hand.

He draws her close, not caring about damp suits or wet hair and seeks her parted lips, kissing her deeply. "You little devil. Are you seducing me?"

She rolls over and grabs a comb from her beach bag, running it through her hair. "I hope you like being seduced."

He plays into her game. "You fly me down to Palm Beach in a jet, book me into a five star hotel and here I am on a private beach with a beautiful woman. What's not to like?"

Her gaze teases, her voice still somber. "Raffi, be honest. You think you can get used to this?"

He has to keep it light. "Who couldn't? But I'm curious. When you're not playing, what does a multimillionaire-heiress do with her free time?"

Her brow creases into a frown. "Believe it or not, I don't have very much of that. I'm busy with my charities, financial consultants, not to mention all my so-called friends."

He rolls over on the blanket to face her. "Truthfully, I'd like to know you better, Traci. The real you."

Her tone's still serious. "You know me better than anyone." Suddenly she bursts out laughing. "Do you realize you're the only one who's seen the inside of me?"

He raises himself up on his elbows, locking eyes with her. "All kidding aside. Have you ever been in love?" From what he's read, she's never been married, or linked to any man for a long period of time. He can't judge—he hasn't been serious either.

She holds his gaze. "I don't know. Have you?"

He hesitates a moment, guilty that Lorig has drifted far from his thoughts. "Been too busy with my career to think about getting involved."

She nudges him playfully. "That's no answer. I've seen some of the nurses at the hospital. How could you fight off temptation?"

He laughs, stroking her arm, undeniably attracted. "Looks aren't everything. It's important to get to know each other."

She rises on one elbow and gives him a long kiss. Breathless, she says, "I think this is a good start."

~ * ~

Later in the day, a refreshed Raffi moves through the spacious mansion to reach the dining room. After a warm shower, short nap and fresh clothes, he feels renewed.

A young maid dressed in a pale turquoise uniform welcomes him. "Miss Doss will be down shortly. May I get you a drink?"

"No thank you, I'll wait," he replies, moving to the TV in the sitting room. He turns to the six o'clock news on CNN just as the commentator reports the actions of the House Foreign Affairs Committee. By a vote of 23 to 22, they approved bringing the Armenian Genocide Bill to a floor vote. While the news lifts his spirits, his optimism is guarded. The Turkish lobby continues spending mega millions to block Congressional recognition of the twentieth century's first government-mandated genocide. However, like previous votes, this resolution will fail as usual due to politics.

Hearing Traci's footsteps, he quickly turns off the TV. This is not the time to discuss his personal views, especially on the Turkish lobby.

She enters the room wearing a bright tangerine shift contrasting against her tanned skin. Her firm body shows she's serious about working out. She gives Raffi a warm smile. "I feel much better now. What would you like to drink?"

"Scotch on the rocks would be perfect," he says, studying her sensual beauty as she mixes the drinks.

She hands him a Scotch and takes one for herself before leading him through the open French doors onto the covered veranda. Silently, they sit on cushioned club chairs surrounded by potted palms, nursing their drinks, watching the sun drop below the horizon.

Raffi breathes in the cool evening breeze, capturing the sensuous beauty of the evening. He rises and approaches the balustrade to gaze out to the ocean. His voice is low, gentle. "I never realized how peaceful sundown on the beach could be."

She joins him, placing her hand on his. "Even more beautiful when it's shared with someone special. Raffi, can you get used to this?"

Before he can answer, the ring of the dinner bell saves him. He holds her elbow and escorts her inside. Manhattan Medical, Sanders and lawsuits, quickly vanish from his mind.

Traci brings her wine glass to a toast with a broad smile, revealing two dimples on her sun-freckled face. "After dinner, we'll celebrate at Club Collette."

He senses her eyes linger on him, searching to read his thoughts. He's pulled into a dreamlike paradise, a world without demands or responsibilities, something unlike he's ever known. Intrigued and besotted, he replies, "How can I say no?"

~ * ~

Raffi and Traci enter a packed Club Colette, the favorite private watering hole for Palm Beachers. Well-dressed couples sit at tables or the bar while others dance to the trio playing swing in the bright light.

The greeter at the door nods with a smile. "Good evening, Miss Doss. We have your table ready. Please follow me."

As they walk through the crowd, several people approach to chat with Traci. Raffi waits patiently to be introduced and shakes hands, knowing all too well his name means nothing to this elite social set. Despite his credentials, in Traci's world, he doesn't count to those present.

"Everyone seems to know you," he remarks, holding a chair out for her to sit at their table.

Her reply is matter of fact. "I've spent most of my winters in Palm Beach since childhood and grew up with these people."

There was innocent truth to her statement. In the world of social affluence, Palm Beach is only one of the winter havens where the wealthy congregate before moving on to other exclusive playgrounds. From the Hamptons to the French Riviera, Monte Carlo or the Costa del Sol, their migration is dictated by whatever the season demands.

The music starts up again, and Traci grabs his hand. "Let's dance," she says, pulling him onto the floor. Within seconds they're part of the scene, swinging to the raw rhythm.

She giggles as he spins her around. "Where'd you learn to dance like that, Doctor?"

"My mom insisted I learn the basics." Armenian summer camp had been his first dance, and his first kiss.

A sudden sharp blow of an elbow crushes into his spine, and he stumbles forward to get his balance. He turns to see the mustached man he met at the cabana earlier in the day.

Traci throws Carlos a frown, keeping her hand on Raffi's waist. "Watch it!"

Carlos nods deferentially. "Excuse me, so sorry."

DR. RICHARD A. BERJIAN

Raffi straightens up, catching Carlos's smug grin. *A real character trying to get Traci's attention.*

Carolos's dance partner, a matronly woman in a black lace dress, stares at Raffi with concern. "I hope you're all right, young man," she says.

Raffi keeps his composure. "Guess the floor's too crowded."

Traci hugs the heavy-set woman. "Elsie Dodge, it's so good to see you."

The woman fingers the multiple strands of pearls draped over her chest. "Traci, dear, I've been meaning to call you."

The music grows louder, the rhythm faster as dancers jostle against them. Traci pulls Raffi's arm. "Let's get off the floor before we get trampled."

The two couples stand to the side and the older woman turns to Traci. "I'm chairing this year's Red Cross Ball. May I count on you as a chief sponsor?"

"Of course, Elsie," Traci replies. "Sign me up for platinum or gold, whatever you wish. I'm happy to help."

Raffi hears Carlos whisper to Elsie. "I told you we'd bump into her."

Traci's face hardens and she steps back from the couple. "Stop hounding me, Carlos! Find another meal ticket."

Carlos's jaw tightens as he leans into Elsie. "We had a small disagreement in New York. Traci doesn't mean that."

"Yes, I do, Carlos," Traci insists. "Like the song says, *it was just one of those things.*"

Elsie touches Traci's arm. "Dear, don't take Carlos seriously. You know how playful he is."

"No, Elsie. What he did to Raffi was on purpose and mean, not playful. I'll support your ball, but not your friend." She takes Raffi's hand and says, "Let's get a drink."

Raffi's already pegged Carlos as a lowlife, serving wealthy widows like Elsie. But the Dodge name catches his interest. Seated before their cocktails, he asks, "Is Elsie Dodge related to the auto company?"

Traci takes the cherry pierced on a pick from her Manhattan and sticks it in her mouth. "Yes, she's the last grandchild. Though the company no longer exits, the family has managed to preserve its wealth."

Raffi's gaze wanders around the room, observing diamonds, gold and platinum on women, young and old. "Is everyone here, pardon the expression, filthy rich?"

Traci lets loose a hearty laugh. "Most likely, not including leeches like Carlos."

Curious, Raffi asks. "Is there something between you two?"

Traci puts down her drink. "Carlos thinks so, but I don't."

"You told him to get another meal ticket." Raffi shouldn't press, but his curiosity gets the better of good manners.

Traci leans back and sighs. "I did a friend a favor. A wealthy Mexican couple introduced him to me at one of their parties. At the time, Carlos was attending medical school in Mexico City with their son, and he wanted to transfer to the States on the Fifth Pathway program. I pulled some strings and got him in."

Raffi recognized the program immediately. A few northeastern medical schools created the project to help Americans studying offshore finish their training in the U.S.

"You supported him financially?"

"At first I did, but he never completed the program. Now he floats around wealthy Palm Beachers, squiring widows to functions, acting as a social companion."

"Well, he seems to think you're more than a friend."

"Let him think what he wants. He's just a nuisance."

A young smiling couple rushes to the table and Traci rises to embrace the woman. "Janet, show me the ring!"

Janet isn't more than twenty-five, and her eyes dance as she holds out her hand. The glittering stone is the size of a large cherry pit.

"Gorgeous," Traci squeals, and turns to Raffi. "Meet the newly married Jonathan and Janet Bennett. And this is the doctor who saved my life, Raffi Sarkissian."

The new bride gushes in delight. "We just returned from our European honeymoon last week, and we're having an impromptu dinner party at our home tomorrow night. Please do come."

Traci looks to Raffi who nods his agreement.

"We'll see you both at six," Janet says, leading her husband back to the dance floor.

Traci throws Raffi a smug glance. "You asked what I do with my free time. There are days I have none."

Raffi tugs at his collar, a bit overwhelmed. "The Bennetts look like a friendly couple. By chance would they be related to any captains of industry?"

Traci laughs quietly. "Jonathan's heir to the founder of the international computer company, Savoy Electronics. Janet's a granddaughter in a family that controls the global corporation Tyler Foods."

Humbled by the affluence in the room, Raffi's thoughts wander. *Could I fit into this world?* He answers his own question. *More important, do I want to?*

# Seventeen

Raffi works hard to keep up with Traci, but after three Manhattans, it's time to return to the hotel. Traci insists on driving, and takes the wheel of her Porsche. With the wind whipping through her hair and Raffi at her side, she speeds the convertible toward the Breakers Hotel. Her eyes glow as she turns to look at him. "I had an amazing time tonight, Raffi."

"So did I,' he replies and slides his hand on her thigh, feeling her muscle contract beneath the tangerine fabric. His head spins, all of his reserve abandoned. "Traci, you were the most beautiful woman in the club tonight."

She leans over and gives him a breathy kiss on his cheek, speeding faster than she should.

The cool salty breeze blows across his flushed face, and with the ocean just several yards from the narrow two-lane road, he listens to the sound of surf lapping onto the sandy beach. So many generations of Palm Beachers enjoyed this very same view, he reminds himself; maybe now it's his turn.

Traci grips the wheel, pushing up her speed and shouts to be heard over the noisy rush of wind. "Raffi, let's not go back to the hotel. Why don't we head to my place for a nightcap?"

The smell of the ocean, the drinks at Colette's, make him reckless. "It's your show tonight, Traci. I'm game." The sensation of careless abandon is something new to him. Unburdened by the pressures at Manhattan Medical, for the first time, he feels free, just letting go.

Without warning, Traci jams her foot on the brake, causing a spine-tingling screech. Swerving the car around on the narrow road, she turns and races in the opposite direction toward her house.

The abrupt move quickly sobers him. "God, Traci, take it easy! You nearly ran us off the road."

Her full red lips break into a wide grin. "Trust me, dear boy. I'm an excellent driver."

He catches the flicker of lighthearted joy on her face and laughs, pointing ahead. "As one drunk to another, lead on."

Together, they sing "Show Me the Way to Go Home" interrupted by raucous laughter until they pull into the mansion's oversized garage.

As Traci stumbles out of the car, she trips and Raffi rushes to her side, holding her close. "Are you OK?"

She bends over with laughter, trying to catch her breath. "Raffi, I haven't had such a wonderful time like this for eons." She takes a firm grip of his hand. "Come, the night is *very, very* young."

She leads him into the living room, removes two crystal snifters from an elegant mirrored bar and fills cognac into the glasses. Her tone is teasing. "A little schnapps for my personal physician?" She hands him the drink and toasts. "Here's to my hero of a doctor, my new-found friend."

He admits to himself it feels good being appreciated, and raises his glass. "To a fabulous evening. No hospital, no emergencies, even if it's only for a weekend."

She points to the open French doors leading to the veranda. "Look Raffi, a beautiful full moon tonight."

They walk out to lean on the balustrade, facing the sea. Moonlight shimmers across the surface of the ocean.

"God, Traci, this is paradise."

"That's because you're here." She takes his drink and places it on the table along with hers, and then wraps her arms around him in an embrace, brushing his ear with a kiss.

Her scent sends shivers down his spine, and he turns, kissing her deeply. His hand caresses the curve of her back, down to the fullness of her butt.

She offers no resistance and flips off her heels. In a throaty voice, she whispers, "Let's go upstairs."

They stagger up the staircase together, laughing, holding each other to keep from falling. At the landing, she leads him into a darkened bedroom, only partially lit by a small bedside lamp.

In spite of the alcohol rush, his senses have never been keener. He wants her with a driving lust that has to be satisfied. He unzips the back of her dress as she fumbles to unbutton his shirt. His body quivers when she runs her hand across his abdomen, pressing against tightened muscles. She gropes lower, finding his hardness.

Sweat beads on his brow; he searches for release. He drops his pants and shorts, watching her slip out of her dress. In the dim light, she stands before him in a racy thong and flimsy bra. He releases the clasps and slides each strap from her shoulders, exposing the soft curves of her full breasts.

In the midst of all the passion, it hits him like a bolt of lightning. He's about to bed one of the world's wealthiest women—one who controls everything and *everyone* in her life. But at this moment, he's the one who sets the pace.

Without saying a word, he leads her to the bed and turns off the light, slowly releasing her onto the mattress. He takes her; her soft moans encouraging him until they both climax. They sleep soundly, oblivious to the tropical lightning and thunder rumbling across the sky.

~ * ~

Raffi spends the flight home to New York thinking about work. Refreshed and energized, he's ready to tackle the heavy case load Flint has set up for the new week. He enters the apartment, and the message light flashing on his answering machine calls him back to the real world.

Five calls from Ani. He quickly dials her number. "Mom?"

Ani's voice is frantic. "Raffi, where have you been? I called your office, apartment, and cell phone with no answer."

"Sorry, Mom. I spent the weekend in Florida."

"Florida? What in the world were you doing in Florida, especially after being in the hospital?"

"I flew to Palm Beach as a guest of Traci Doss—with Flint's approval."

"You have to be joking." His mom's worried voice turns cool.

He puts the phone on speaker and begins flipping through the accumulated mail on his desk. "No joke, Mom. I flew down in a private jet and will go back to work tomorrow."

A frustrating silence ensues before Ani speaks. "Tell me, Raffi, are you getting involved with that woman?"

Annoyed, he wishes he hadn't told her. "Of course not. Just needed some time away, that's all."

There's a pause, and then, "You're playing with dynamite. She lives in a different world than you, son."

How can he tell Ani he no longer needs her guidance? "Don't worry, Mom, I know how to drive this boat."

Her laugh is strained. "You've come a long way—don't do anything foolish." She clears her throat and asks, "What about the nice Armenian school teacher? Are you giving up on her?"

"Mom, I quit telling you about my girlfriends after sixth grade. As far as Lorig is concerned, yes, I really like her. She even visited me in the hospital. But we're just friends." His emotions are still in a whirl after the weekend with Traci.

"Friends is a good start. Have you called her?"

"I was planning to until this Palm Beach trip came up. Now, I don't know." He flips the advertisements in the trash, and turns off the speaker to talk into the receiver.

His voice lowers. "While I have you on the line, I want to give you a warning. Be cautious about what you say to your superiors at the FBI when you translate secret Turkish government communications."

"Raffi, you're scaring me." Despite her words, her tone hardens. "What's your point?"

"Have you heard anything about Jasmine Battia? She's an FBI translator fired for blowing the whistle on some congressmen. She claims they're taking bribes from the Turkish government to vote against the Armenian Genocide Resolution. "

Raffi hears Ani's heavy breaths over the phone, until she confesses, "Yes, I was afraid to tell you. I've heard about the payoffs. It disturbed me but I haven't said anything."

"Good," Raffi replies. "Just do your job and hold your tongue."

"I will, son, but I don't know for how long. It isn't right."

Raffi ends the call, conflicted. He admires his mother's sense of justice but fears for her safety dealing with international criminality.

# *Eighteen*

It's well past nine in the evening when a tired Jeremy walks out of Manhattan Medical. After an exhausting day in surgery followed by an emergency bowel resection that came in after six, the work day never seemed to end. Now that Raffi joined Flint's practice, as chief resident, he's on call for all surgical emergencies.

He walks the dark streets crossing over Eighth Avenue to reach his apartment on Ninth. While most of the married interns and residents live in apartments provided by the hospital, Jeremy opts to live in his old quarters with his girlfriend.

He climbs the steps of the brownstone to the first landing, unlocks the door and enters, leaving behind the scarred walls of a hallway desperately needing a fresh coat of paint. He breathes a contented sigh of relief once inside what he calls *my love nest sanctuary* that he and Rachel worked on so furiously, scrubbing, painting and refurbishing.

He calls out. "I'm home, honey."

A cheerful voice answers from the depths of the apartment. "You finally made it, did you?"

"Your one and only," he replies, entering the bedroom. "It was one hell of a day."

Rachel lounges in bed and looks up from the book she's reading. "I thought you'd never get home."

He loves the way her large brown eyes sparkle, the warmth of her satin smooth skin. He sits on the edge of the bed and kisses her cheek. "The Civil Rights Commission interviewed me and asked the same questions over and over."

She wrinkles her tapered nose. "Face it, sugar, you got a big problem. There's a whole lot of talk at the beauty salon about how your hospital looks down on us blacks."

"Rachel, you know that's not true!" Defensive, he peels off his clothes, flinging them into the wicker laundry basket in the corner. "Where do people pick up all this crap? The commission's investigation is supposed to be secret." Annoyed, he enters the bathroom to shower.

Rachel presses on, shouting to him through the open door. "Look, the commission may be secret but the reverend's lips are spurting poison about Traci Doss. They say poor Tommie got shafted."

Jeremy returns to the bedroom with a bath towel wrapped around his hips. "Shafted? Nobody's listening to the facts! Tommie Jackson was a dead man even before he reached the hospital. He collapsed in x-ray, and died in the operating room before we could do surgery." He angrily tosses the towel on the chair, standing stark naked. "Are they saying the black man was shafted—by another black man?"

Rachel puts aside her book with a frown. "Don't go ballistic, Jeremy. I know you did your best, but I'm only telling you what I hear."

He lets out a frustrated sigh. "Sorry for shouting but I feel like a target. Even the blacks working hospital maintenance give me funny looks when they pass by."

"Don't beat up on yourself, Jeremy. There's nothing more you can do." She eyes him with a wink. "Now let me tell you some *real* gossip."

He looks at her, questioning. "More dirt you picked up at the hair salon?"

"Just calm down, big boy. Go shower and I'll tell you once you're in bed."

After cleansing off the day's sweat, Jeremy is more refreshed and returns to the bedroom.

A waiting Rachel draws back the covers, exposing her naked body. "Enter and I will spill the beans on what I heard today."

Jeremy loves Rachel's flare for drama. Her dynamic personality wins her many friends, and has stolen his heart. "What's so important?"

With a twinkle in her eye, she leans toward him, her breath sweet. "What if I told you the honorable and righteous Reverend Sanders keeps a mistress in a Harlem apartment? Her name is Twila Barnett."

~ * ~

Friday evening Raffi opens the door to his apartment, wrestling gloomy thoughts over Jeremy's interview with the Civil Rights Commission. He's scheduled to be questioned the following Tuesday. Trying to cheer himself up, he recounts what he knows...nothing. So what's he worried about? He has nothing to hide.

Entering the kitchen, he sees the light on the answering machine blinking, but he's in no mood to be distracted. Reverend Sanders' successful rally courting interested parties to lend support to the commission's investigation lingers in his thoughts. As spokesman for the Harlem black community, Sanders carries influence with Black Panthers, Black Muslims, and NAACP. Even the ACLU appears to be involved, despite the medical facts that support the hospital.

His fear the panel will make a decision based on politics rather than medicine is confirmed when he Googles the eight members serving on the committee. All lawyers or politicians, not one with a medical background. It's a sure bet none of them ever faced an emergency like the one he and Jeremy experienced that Saturday night.

Hungry and frustrated, he removes a frozen dinner from the freezer. As a bachelor, he always has a backup at home in case he doesn't eat at the hospital. As he prepares the meal in the microwave, his gaze turns to the blinking light on the answering machine. What if it's his mom?

The first two messages are solicitations but the third is from Traci, and he winces hearing her voice.

"I miss you, Raffi. Why haven't you answered my calls? I know you're very busy, but at least reach me on my cell. I'm leaving for my foundation board meeting at the university and after that, I might have to fly to LA. I don't have my whole schedule, but please call. We had fun together. I miss you."

He hears the click, feeling a rush of guilt. She deserves more, especially after that incredible weekend and yes, sex. Amazing sex, and a surprising amount of laughter. But if there's a real heart connection, should he still be thinking of Lorig's shy smile? With everything exploding around him, he can't plan that far ahead.

Sill trying to make sense of his thoughts, he removes the hot tray from the microwave and places the food on a dish before clicking on the next message.

"Raffi, this is Adam Wolfe, *New York Post*. Before you give your statement to the Civil Rights commission, call me. Your career might be in great danger."

A cold sweat breaks out on his brow; his brain goes numb. All the suppressed fears flood back into his head. Too tired to eat, he grabs a power bar and throws the microwave dinner in the trash. It's time to get some sleep.

~ * ~

Raffi awakes to Monday morning's explosive headline news. Senator Olin Davis is indicted by the New York District Attorney for the death of Turkish Agent Saya Origlu, alias Nancy Wood.

After Adam Wolfe's troublesome message, Raffi calls the reporter and arranges to meet him for breakfast in the hospital cafeteria. In a corner, away from the bustle of people carrying cafeteria trays, Raffi faces Wolfe with an untouched breakfast before him.

"I appreciate your interest in my case, Adam. Tell me why my testimony to the commission will target me?"

Wolfe's bushy eyebrows rise into peaks. "Good question, Doctor. With only the civil rights issue facing you, there's little risk. But the senator's indictment opens up a whole new can of worms."

"How?"

"While the senator's trial will deal with the death of Nancy Wood, there's another side to this story. The tabloids will identify her role as an agent for the Turkish government arranging payments to Davis's Foundation in exchange for his vote against the Armenian Genocide Bill."

Raffi darts an irritated gaze at the reporter. "But what does that have to do with me?"

Wolfe leans over the table, lowering his voice. "Let me give you some background. Tommie Jackson was a Black Muslim. Before joining the Nation of Islam, he was a drug addict and had a record of several misdemeanor convictions. The Nation converted him into an upright moral and responsible citizen."

Raffi shakes his head. "If you're trying to make me feel worse about Jackson's death, you've succeeded."

Wolfe gestures Raffi to begin eating his breakfast and presses on. "That's not my point. The fact that a foreign country lobbies our congressmen with money to manipulate their votes is red meat for the news media. That'll give Armenian organizations ammunition to publicize and criticize the Turkish government's policy of denying the genocide."

Raffi puts down his fork. "Look, Adam. How can I deal with all these issues? I'm just a physician doing what I trained for. "

"Doc, I'm not trying to worry you, just to inform." Wolfe taps the Coke can in front of him with his finger. "As an Islamic nation, Turkey believes in the Quran. The Nation of Islam also believes in the Quran, so any attack on Islam will appear to be an attack on Black Muslims."

"Look, Adam, you're going beyond my political vision. Connect the dots."

Wolfe removes his glasses, wiping them with a napkin. "I've spent time studying the Black Muslim movement. It was started by an African American in 1930 and espouses principles to improve the spiritual, mental, social and economic condition of African Americans in the US and all humanity. But unfortunately it's become anti-Semitic and racist. All you need to do is to read the writings or Malcom X, Elijah Muhammad and Farrakhan who don't deny these allegations.

"Many of the new recruits don't understand the difference. Traditional Islamic ideology espoused by the Islamic prophet, Mohammed, in the Quran is one hundred eighty degrees opposite the doctrine of the blacks' belief in the Nation of Islam which rejects violence. But that fact could get lost in the heat of this trial."

"Well, you're a reporter. Why don't you explain that when you write your news reports?"

"I will, but the black community's sentiment will be against you. As chief resident, you saved the rich white girl's life while ordering Jeremy, a lesser trained surgeon, to operate on Jackson, a Black Muslim. Jackson died, and Traci Doss lives."

"So what can I do about it?"

"Be very careful what you say to the Commission."

"All I can do is tell the truth."

"Get real, Doc. This is a great story for me, but I like you, and don't want you to become an innocent victim. The commission is going to grill why you didn't operate on Tommie instead of Jeremy. They're going to question if bias of race or religion had anything to do with that decision."

Raffi's jaw hardens. "Absolutely not! I don't consider those issues when I treat patients."

"You don't have to convince me, Doc, but you did have a choice. That question hangs out there."

Raffi's voice bristles; he pounds the table. "Look, I did what I had to do and I make no apologies!"

"Slow down, Doc. What you don't want to do during your interview is to get heated. Stay calm, stick to the facts, and show no emotion."

"That's hard to do when you've being unfairly accused."

"I agree, but if the Civil Rights Commission decides to support the reverend's charges, you and Jeremy will be the fall guys. Jeremy's black, but that won't satisfy some people. Impoverished African-Americans often harbor grudges against those who seem to have made it in white society."

Raffi shoves his plate away, his eyes dark with anger. "The hospital can prove I've never demonstrated any form of racial bias."

"They can, but it won't mean much. Manhattan Medical will survive, but who knows if the Justice Department will decide to prosecute both you and Jeremy? Remember, a civil rights prosecution has nothing to do with money."

The penetrating look in Wolfe's eyes gives Raffi a chill. With Tommie's case going to court, his as well as Jeremy's name will be plastered across the headlines. Any adverse action by the Justice Department will reinforce the impression they're racists. Adam Wolfe's analysis finally sinks in.

He abruptly rises from the table, thanks Wolfe for his advice, ending the conversation. Confused thoughts swirl in his head. Although he'd planned to call Traci, he's in no mood to make small talk. Maybe it's time to tell Ani what is happening before it hits the newspapers.

~ * ~

A matronly receptionist leads Raffi into a dimly lit room in the downtown Federal Building furnished with a desk and two metal office chairs. A narrow beam of sunlight crosses the space, lending the only warmth. Her tone is as flat as her expression.

"Please wait. Investigator Benson will be with you shortly." She turns and leaves, closing the door behind her.

Raffi sits, reflecting on Jeremy's view of the investigation. He's required to relate what occurred the night of the accident. Nothing more.

Within minutes, an African-American man dressed in a navy blue suit and red striped tie enters the room. He's clean shaven with close-cropped hair, conveying a corporate image. He nods to Raffi before taking a seat behind the desk. Abruptly, he opens his attaché case and removes a few papers, placing them before him.

"Good morning, Dr. Sarkissian. As an investigator for the Civil Rights Commission, I must ask if you're aware of the ramifications if this complaint should go forward."

Raffi remains calm and sits erect in his chair. "I would appreciate an explanation, Mr. Benson."

The investigator skims his notes. "I'll give you a brief outline. This interview is being conducted in hopes to intervene and resolve issues generated by the civil rights complaint against you and the hospital. As the investigator, my role is to mediate disputes between an individual or individuals, and to inform them of their legal rights before the complaint advances to a civil rights action committee."

Raffi tugs at his collar, feeling heat on the back of his neck. "What happens after the facts are reviewed?"

"If the complainant decides there is no fault, the process stops here." Benson pauses momentarily, shuffling papers. "However, if the complainant decides to go forward to a formal hearing, then you must appear before an administrative judge."

It's clear to Raffi a detailed explanation is urgent to avoid facing a formal hearing. "Sir, I will do my best to give you the facts as I see them."

Benson smiles, leaning back in his chair. "Good." He presses on to ask about time lines, Raffi's and Jeremy's location when the emergencies arrived, and Tommie Jackson's condition on admission. A good deal of time is spent on how Raffi made the decision to assign Jeremy to Tommie.

Raffi answers in depth, surprised by Benson's grasp of medical details, as the investigator scratches notes on a yellow pad. After close to an hour of questions, Raffi sits back, relieved the session is near completion.

Benson suddenly leans forward and taps his pencil on the desk, shooting a piercing gaze at Raffi. "Dr. Sarkissian, I understand you were told Dr. Flint's patient was also in need of surgery."

"That's correct," Raffi answers, feeling moisture gather under his arms. He has to justify why he tended to Traci before Tommie.

Benson's brow wrinkles, a wave of doubt crosses his face. "Did the fact that Dr. Flint's primarily white patients from a higher economic level influence your decision? Is that why you intervened with Miss Doss, and left a less qualified surgeon to care for the black boy, Tommie Jackson?"

Raffi's aware Benson is setting a trap and exudes a calm posture. "I wasn't aware the patient was Traci Doss."

"But you did know she was Dr. Flint's patient and probably a very important person."

Careful to maintain his composure, Raffi replies, "I don't choose patients on political priorities or wealth."

Benson persists, holding two fingers up. "You and Dr. Flint, two experienced surgeons, operated on Traci Doss, leaving Jackson in the hands of a junior resident with no senior attending surgeon. That decision demands an explanation, Doctor."

Raffi feels his heart pound and tightens his grip on the arms of his chair. He has to set Benson straight. "At the time, both Jeremy and I were surgical residents with comparable training. Who's to say I was the better trained resident?"

"Yes, but you were *chief resident in charge*. Tommie might have been saved if you had helped Jeremy."

Raffi catches Benson's underlying bias. How can he make the man realize the truth? "I stand by my decision. Both patients came to the ER at the same time. Unfortunately, Tommie's injuries were too severe to save him, no matter who operated."

Benson nods, returning to a more pleasant demeanor. "Thank you for your time, Dr. Sarkissian. Is there anything you want to say before we end this session?"

"Yes, Mr. Benson, there is. I am not a racist. Please judge my actions in this case on the medical facts."

# Nineteen

In the evening, Raffi unwinds on his couch waiting for the lasagna he picked up from the hospital cafeteria to warm in the microwave. He flicks on the TV just as Reverend Sanders' contorted expression fills the screen. Suddenly his appetite vanishes.

Sanders' booming voice comes across. "Racism, that's what killed Tommie Jackson!"

The female Asian news reporter breaks into Sanders' rambling. "What makes you think the hospital would support such a discriminatory policy?"

The reverend snarls. "Money! Tommie had none but the Doss lady donates millions to the hospital. It's the same old story. The poor black man gets inferior treatment because of his color."

"Bullshit!" Raffi shouts angrily at the TV screen. It's obvious Sanders intends to infect public opinion in preparation for the Jackson family civil suit.

But Raffi has his own problems on the legal horizon. In addition to the civil rights interview that morning, he received a subpoena as a witness for the Jackson family civil trial. To add to his ongoing headaches, he has to testify at Senator Davis's homicide trial. What information can he offer the court about people he doesn't know? Never met the woman who died in Traci's apartment and as far as his relationship with the senator, his only encounter was casually at Flint's club. His stomach gurgles, and he enters the kitchen, grabs a Coke from the fridge, aware he has no control over those conflicts

He drains half the can as his thoughts transfer to Lorig. He hasn't talked to her since the hospital episode with Traci and frowns, guilt tracking his face. *I don't have to be a rocket scientist to know why she doesn't answer my calls.* Tired of getting the cold shoulder, he picks up the phone and dials Traci.

Traci's voice is welcoming. "Raffi, hon! I thought you fell off the planet."

He leans against the kitchen sink while the beep of the microwave sounds. "*Mea culpa,*" he answers. "Between work and my legal problems, I wish I could do just that, fall off this damn planet and hide."

"Darling, I'm still in LA for another week. Why don't you join me? I'll make the arrangements."

"Love to, but it's impossible. Harold's away and I'm literally swamped."

Traci pauses, taking on a somber tone. "We have to talk, Raffi. I prefer not over the phone, but—"

Raffi flinches, fully aware where the conversation is leading.

Her voice is subdued. "Did that weekend in Palm Beach mean anything to you? It did to me."

He tries to evade the question. "You know I had a great time."

"Then why wait so long to call? Was I just a weekend hookup? Tell me, I'm a big girl."

He has to take control, something he has trouble doing with her. "Look Traci, I just can't fly to LA at the drop of a hat. I have people who depend upon me. I'm busy."

"I hope it's not with another girl."

"What girl?"

"The pretty one who came to your hospital room."

He feels a twinge of guilt, not wanting to open the topic and gives a sharp reply. "With my workload? I have no time to fool around."

"Don't get in a huff, darling. I'll take your word for it. I have to be in Frisco and return to New York in two weeks. " Her voice lowers. "I want to see you again, Raffi."

Raffi's spirits lift—he has more time to figure out how to handle the relationship. "Same here, Traci." He bites his lip. Why does he always give in to her?

"What's that beeping I hear?" she asks.

Raffi laughs. "My microwave is calling me to dinner."

"A microwave dinner? We'll take care of that when I see you."

Raffi muffles a yawn. "You're three hours behind me. I'm bushed and have a long day tomorrow. I'll keep in touch."

He hangs up; his brow furrows deep in thought while the microwave keeps buzzing. Traci wants to get serious, but does he? He takes out his dinner and places it on the table along with the Coke, convinced he has to decide whether to continue with Traci.

*Lorig is a different matter.* He definitely feels comfortable in her world, and wants to see her again. But after the hospital incident, he's uncertain she feels the same way.

Still in no mood to eat, he opens the Coke and quenches his thirst before dialing Lorig's number. *What the hell, there's no time like the present.*

His heart races, waiting to hear her voice. Even though he spent the wild weekend with Traci, Lorig still occupies his thoughts.

She picks up after the fourth ring. A chilly, "Hello."

The caller ID has clued her it's him. *At least she picked up.*

"I've been thinking of you, Lorig. You have a few minutes?"

Silence follows until she answers, "Just a few."

He hesitates, fearful she'll hang up on him, and all he can say is "Thanks for visiting me in the hospital."

"Is that what you called about?"

*That didn't work.* "No, I meant it was good seeing you."

"Thank you, but if that's all—"

He takes in a deep breath "Lorig, why did you walk out of the hospital so abruptly? I hoped to spend more time with you."

"I'm afraid this conversation has nowhere to go, Raffi."

*Now or never.* "Yes it does—I want to know."

"Raffi, I don't think you'll be satisfied with what I have to say. Why don't we just say goodbye like two adults."

"Not until we talk face to face."

Her reply is curt. "I'm too busy."

"Please, Lorig, don't leave me dangling. Pick a time when I can see you."

She has an edge to her voice. "Look, Raffi, this conversation is pointless. Haven't you gotten the message yet? I don't want to go out with you."

His heart sinks like a drowning ship. He can't let her get away so easily. "I know you don't owe me anything, but I'd love an explanation. I thought we were friends."

She let out a sarcastic laugh. "All right, I'll tell you. After your romantic escapade in Palm Beach with Traci Doss, what possible interest could you have in me?"

He hears the sound of betrayal in her voice. "So that's what this is all about? Don't believe anything you read in the shiny sheets."

"Do you deny being there?"

"Of course not."

"I saw photos of you two in the papers. The paparazzi follow her like hound dogs. By the way, you and Traci make quite a pair."

"I give up, Lorig. If I can't convince you the trip meant nothing meaningful, why am I calling for a date?"

"Maybe you enjoy conquering different women. I watch *Grey's Anatomy* and I see what some of you doctors are like."

Her comment catches Raffi off guard. It's almost humorous but he holds in his chuckle. Granted, he'd gone overboard with

Traci. But now, removed from all the glitz and glamour, he needs to connect with someone more grounded. He hesitates a moment, taking another swallow of Coke. "What if I told you the frivolous Palm Beach lifestyle made me feel *very* uncomfortable?"

"I'd say you're either lying or naive."

He lowers his voice. "Yeah, maybe. I keep thinking about something you said on our first date."

She hesitates. "What is that?"

"About givers and takers."

"Have you classified yourself yet? Are you a giver or a taker?"

"Don't know. Maybe I'm a little of both."

"Sorry, Raffi, you can't be just a little bit pregnant."

"Then I want to be a giver. We gotta talk."

"About Traci Doss? I don't want to be the other woman, just another notch on your belt."

Her blunt honesty shakes him and his voice softens. "Believe me, Lorig, there's no competition between you and Traci. Any personal relationship I have with her will be over when the trials end. After that, she'll just be another patient." He hopes his words are true because he knows the connection with Lorig is from the heart. "When can we meet?"

After few seconds of delay, she answers. "I'm free on Saturday."

"Great! I'm taking you somewhere special so put on your best." His joy at seeing Lorig again answers his question about Traci. How does a man break up with an heiress?

# *Twenty*

Jeremy follows Rachel up the long row of steps leading into Harlem's Baptist Revivalist Church. He gazes at the architectural details of the time-blackened thick stone walls. A bronze plaque adjacent to the open doors proclaims the building was erected in 1890 by Presbyterians and sold in 1941 to African-American Baptists at a time when blacks and Hispanics were gradually replacing the white population.

The crisp morning air and a radiant sun brighten the day for Rachel's friend's wedding, which is to take place after Sunday's 11 o'clock service. Rachel, an active church member, stops to greet friends as Jeremy patiently waits beside her.

When they finally settle into a pew, he turns to her with a whisper. "I hope the sermon's short so we can get on with the wedding."

She pats his hand, her voice hushed. "Stop fussing. You may be a great doctor, but hearing the Lord's words will make you a better man."

The organist plays the opening chords with a grand flourish leading into the first hymn. The full choir, dressed in silver and blue robes, streams in front of the altar to their places. Elderly women in wide-brimmed flowered hats rush to take their seats and families dressed in their Sunday best follow.

The minister walks onto the podium and nods to the organist, who ends the lively hymn. Straightening his glasses, he reads the opening homily. When it ends, the choir and organist break into a fast-paced spiritual backed up by a rocking drummer pushing the rhythm.

The animated music lifts Jeremy's spirits as he witnesses the jubilant expressions of the singing parishioners. It reminds him of his childhood when he'd go to church with his mother. He long stopped attending services, but this day is special going with Rachel.

The music ends and the congregation settles down; silence permeates the voluminous dome. A burly thick-chested man dressed in a robe walks on to the dais, taking a seat in the ornately trimmed armchair positioned to the left.

Jeremy can't believe his eyes. The man in the place of honor is none other than Reverend Coleman Sanders.

The minister nods toward Sanders and then looks out to the congregation. "Today, in spite of civil rights legislation, our people still face challenges we must overcome." He pauses, his gaze touching each member sitting before him. "You all know what I'm saying 'cause y'all have been victims of racism."

Shouts of "Amen, brother," "That's right," and "I been there," follow from the audience. Jeremy grits his back teeth. What were the chances of the man making his life hell turning up here?

The minister waits for the responses to die down. "Today's sermon will be given by another man of the cloth. Reverend Coleman Sanders has labored not only to do the Lord's work, but to fight for justice for his people." He turns to Sanders. "Speak to us, Brother."

Sanders strides to the podium as voices cry out, "Let's hear the Lord's words."

Jeremy looks to Rachel, who sits attentively with hands folded in her lap. *Is she buying into this crap?*

Reverend Sanders clears his throat. "Sisters, brothers, we have struggled for justice for hundreds of years. We slaved in the cotton fields, broke our backs on farms and tobacco plantations, always sweating to serve the white man."

A voice from the crowd shouts, "Amen, you got dat right. Tell us, Brother."

Sanders waits for quiet, casting his eyes upward to the vaulted ceiling before continuing, "Even though they say we've won our civil rights, in truth, have we?"

Sharp outcries of "Say it again," "Amen," "Keep shinin' the light," echo in the room.

Jeremy studies the parishioners around him, their heads bobbing in agreement. He shifts uncomfortably on the wooden pew, wondering what Sanders is up to.

The reverend stares into the crowd with raised arms. "Brothers, sisters, I hear my calling from God. In humility, I will lead the way to our people's salvation by running for Congress. Politics is the best way to fight the racists who supposedly freed us only to labor under their yoke."

His voice rises to a higher pitch. "Today the black man has the highest unemployment rate, the highest number in prisons and we are the poorest. Wall Street, rich lawyers, politicians keep stealing from us, money that's rightfully ours."

Jeremy gazes around, watching people clap and cheer, interrupting the reverend's speech with enthusiasm.

Sanders holds out his palms, gesturing people to hush. He barks into the silence. "I support Tommie Jackson's lawsuit against Manhattan Medical. Their racist policy caused this young man's death, and that behavior has got to stop!"

Another booming outcry of cheers and shouts explodes with chants of, "Make them pay, make them pay."

Jeremy feels Rachel's hand clasp his, her attention focused on Sanders. Is she swayed by the reverend's emotional rhetoric, or is it just a comforting squeeze?

Sanders again waves his arms for quiet and the noise melts away. His voice intensifies; he sticks out a fist and shouts. "Friends, we gotta take control! That's the only way they'll listen."

Shouts of "Right on, Brother, let them know," ring out, encouraging Sanders to continue. "Only when we got the power will they listen!"

The sermon ends and the crowd rises shouting "Halleluiah," "The Lord be praised," and "You got it, Brother." Amid the raucous bellows, the organist begins playing "When the Saints Come Marching In." The choir joins with the congregation singing and swaying to the rhythm.

Rachel stands and claps with those around her, but Jeremy remains seated. She tugs at his sleeve. "You're not feelin' the spirit? Get up and praise the Lord."

Jeremy slowly rises to please her while Martin Luther King's message rings in his thoughts. *Judge a man by the content of his character and not by the color of his skin.* But Reverend Sanders' message condemns all whites. The smiling faces and bobbing heads surround him. Their approval of Sanders' sermon tells him how far his people have strayed from King's message. Instead of being spiritually moved, Jeremy feels manipulated and pandered to, witnessing a political movement.

Jeremy watches Sanders return to his seat amidst claps and cheers, eager to for the spectacle to end. He nudges Rachel's shoulder. "When does the wedding begin?"

She points to the rear where four men dressed in tuxedos stand in the narthex leading into the church. "Be patient, the ushers are already at the door."

The crowd calms, the minister gives the final blessing and people who don't want to stay for the nuptials begin leaving their pews. Sanders is nowhere to be seen.

With all the legal preparations by hospital attorneys, Jeremy thought Tommie's case hadn't a chance. But after today's voracious response to the reverend's speech, he's not so sure.

~ * ~

Jeremy sits at the table with other guests in the Rosa Parks Fellowship Hall located on the lower level of the church. The wedding reception follows the usual protocol. Toasting the couple, applauding their first dance and enjoying an elegant meal. He observes dancers enjoying themselves as the disc jockey switches beats from rock and roll to rap.

He finishes his drink, the only one after the champagne toast. The huge crowd stationed at the bar makes him decide against another. With all the noisy shouting and laughing, the party is in full swing. He tries to get into party mode, but can't.

Rachel sits at his side talking to friends across the table. Their conversation is interrupted with sporadic squeals and laughter. He touches her arm. "I'm going to the men's room. Be right back."

Her eyes dance; she's having a good time. "Okay, sugar, but before you go, say hello to my cousin, Clarice."

He extends his hand. "Hi, I'm Jeremy."

"Oh, I know," the pretty woman gushes. "So when are you two gonna tie the knot?"

Jeremy's not prepared for the question, and catches Rachel's questioning look. The topic of marriage has been laid to rest until he finishes his training. "You must be married, Clarice, if you recommend it."

Clarice giggles, slapping her thigh. "Not yet, darlin', but I'm working on it."

Rachel pushes Clarice's shoulder in jest. "You're all talk. Get out there, girl and snare one of those young studs on the dance floor."

Clarice says goodbye and leaves, still laughing.

Rachel raises an eyebrow. "You had a hard time finding an answer to Clarice's question."

"We've talked about this. Nothing's going to happen until I finish the residency."

Her mouth turns into a pout. "I knew you'd say that." She pushes his arm and says, "Go on, empty your bladder!"

He rises from the table and kisses her on the cheek. "I love you, Rach. Just be patient."

"Doctors!" She chuckles, giving him a private little smile to let him know she's forgiven his lack of enthusiasm.

Jeremy makes his way to the back of the room, walking between dancers and tables crowded with partying guests. On entering the narrow hallway leading to the restrooms, he's confronted by four angry looking men who block his entry. Ages range from teens to thirties, all wearing street clothes. Are they invited guests of the bride and groom?

The tallest of the four confronts him, arms crossed against his chest. "It's busy in there. Ya gotta wait."

Jeremy nods, not interested in making a scene. "OK, but for how long?"

"Makes no difference," the man replies. "Ya gotta wait."

Jeremy grins, shuffling his feet. ."Look man, I gotta go."

"Ya can't pass," a shorter, wider man repeats, standing in his way.

Jeremy catches the menacing look and raises his hands. "Calm down, I'm not looking for a fight."

The youngest of the four wears a frayed Army jacket. The kid steps forward, peering into Jeremy's face. "Hey, I seen you in the papers. You're the doc who let Tommie Jackson die."

Jeremy decides it's time to retreat as the four close in on him. He holds up both palms. "Let's not start something at the girl's wedding."

Just then, the door to the men's room swings open and to Jeremy's surprise, a stunning young black woman appears in the doorway. Her straight long dark hair falls to her shoulders in a precise cut; a red knit dress enhances her curvaceous figure. The dudes guarding the door push Jeremy aside so she can pass into the hall.

Jeremy watches, compelled by the shifting moves of her hips, until she's out of sight.

The kid snaps, "That ain't for you to see."

"Sorry!" He turns his attention to the bathroom. "Can I go in now? Come on, guys, I gotta go."

The tall man lets out a guttural snarl. "Hey dude, you're talking to the New Black Panthers, and when the Panthers say walk, you walk!"

Just then Reverend Sanders appears at the open door, adjusting his tie. "Okay boys, let's go." He comes to a halt on seeing Jeremy and points a finger. "I know you. You spyin' on me?"

Jeremy contains his anger as he puts two and two together. "Look, man, I just want to use the restroom."

Sanders tilts his head and nods to the tall man. "Let's get outta here." With that, the Panthers leave without saying another word.

Jeremy enters the restroom, trying to make sense of what had just taken place when Rachel's comment flashes into his mind. The stunning woman must be the reverend's secret mistress.

# *Twenty-one*

In his heart, Raffi knows this Saturday date with Lorig will determine if their relationship is to progress or if he'll fall flat on his face. As he accompanies her down her home's walkway, her stiff body language tells him it won't be easy to regain her trust. Since his arrival on her doorstep, he's endured many moments of uncertainty before coming to grips with the depth of her bitterness. In short, the girl is pissed.

But what does he expect after his wild weekend with Traci? The Doss name is a magnet for the paparazzi, and his photo was plastered all over the tabloids. He'd been having fun, and Lorig was left to wonder if their "friendship" was over.

He ushers her to the borrowed car, capturing the sight of her slender form gracefully slip into the seat. He comments, before closing the car door. "You look beautiful tonight, Lorig. Red becomes you." For a moment, he hopes he's not being too obvious.

Her lower lip quivers…she stares ahead, refusing to look at him. Her reply is curt. "Thank you."

To break the ice, he places a hand on her arm. "Lorig, let's make tonight special. I reserved a table at the Four Seasons."

She turns to him, poker-faced "That's a very famous restaurant and pretty pricey. Dinner for two can cost close to four hundred dollars. Guess money doesn't matter now that you have an heiress for a friend."

His intention to impress her doesn't do the trick and he has to think of a quick response. "It's kind of a special place for me. My mom hosted my graduation from med school there."

Her face flushes, embarrassed, and her voice softens. "Forgive me, Raffi. If it's special for you and your mother, it will be special for me too."

Raffi turns on the engine, beginning to feel more optimistic. Maybe he has a fighting chance to convince her. At the George Washington Bridge, he pays the toll, and travels across toward the West Side Highway. As he cruises along the Hudson River, he watches Lorig's gaze fix on the tall buildings dominating the New York skyline. In the silence, he casts a quick gaze at her. She's a natural beauty, honey-like hair framing a face smooth as porcelain.

She finally breaks the silence, tucking a strand of hair behind her ear. Diamonds glitter from her lobes. "Raffi, do you enjoy living in the city?"

He senses a genuine friendliness to her voice. She wants to know about him, and that's positive, so he speaks openly. "I know nothing else. When I arrived in this country as a child, Mom and I lived in a small Brooklyn apartment. Spent all my growing up years there while going to college and med school. Now that I'm earning some bucks, I rent a Manhattan pad close to the hospital, small but adequate."

Her body relaxes; she leans toward him. For the first time she smiles. "New York is exciting but it's always good to return to the tree-lined streets in the suburbs."

He ponders her comment as they exit the highway and drive east on 52nd toward the Seagram's Building located between Park and Lexington Avenues. He parks the car in the garage directly across from the restaurant and slips the parking ticket into his pocket. Taking her arm, he crosses the street, enters the lobby of the office building and they ride the elevator to the second floor.

As they enter, an attractive hostess greets them from behind an ornate reception desk. "Good evening, welcome to the Four Seasons. Do you have a reservation?"

"Yes, the name is Dr. Sarkissian."

She scans the list with her finger and stops halfway down the page. A glimmer of a smile crosses her face before she regains her professional poise.

Raffi suspects she recognizes his name, probably linked with Traci Doss in the tabloids. But none of that is important. Tonight he has to win Lorig back.

The hostess points with a flourish. "Right this way, Doctor."

Raffi holds onto Lorig's arm following the hostess between tables of diners, dodging busboys and waiters until reaching their destination.

They sit side by side on a cushioned bench leaning against the low room divider at their backs. A floor to ceiling glass wall facing the street dominates the room, revealing the star-like sparkle of lights from windows in buildings across the way.

After the waiter takes their orders and leaves, Lorig leans back comfortably on the seat. She folds her hands on her lap, her eyes locking into his. "Raffi, I truly appreciate your bringing me to your special place. Thank you."

Raffi feels a flush of excitement and gently grasps her hand. "You have no idea how much that pleases me. Even on my busiest days, you're constantly on my mind."

"I'll admit I spend a good bit of time thinking about you, too."

Her words thrill him and he raises her hand and kisses it.

She blushes, allowing him to keep his hold.

The waiter returns with a bottle of red wine, pours Raffi's goblet and waits to see if it's satisfactory. Raffi sips and nods, after which the waiter pours Lorig's glass, fills his and places the bottle in the ice bucket next to the table. "Enjoy your evening," he says and leaves.

Raffi raises his glass. "I toast that we get past what happened that weekend in Palm Beach."

Lorig's eyes mist. "Raffi, I believe you care for me. But seeing you in the newspapers with Traci really hurt me. And then in the hospital—"

He put down his glass, drying her tears with his napkin. "Traci means well, but she's all glitz and so are her friends. She has no understanding of what I'm all about." He persists, knowing he has to open up to her. "But when I'm with you, my life seems to fall in place. You're beautiful but real."

She lowers her gaze; a smile forms on her lips. "I appreciate the compliment, Raffi. Any girl would." She hesitates a moment and faces him. "What are you looking for in a woman?"

The question comes unexpectedly. Raffi clears his throat, thinking for a moment. "There are two loves a man can have for a woman. One is the physical love all men desire. The beautiful body, the gorgeous face, but there's another, even more important."

She leans closer. "Which is?"

"An inner beauty. A love that's sensitive, spiritual, reflecting joy from within. It lasts a lifetime, even when age defiles physical beauty. It's a graceful glow a woman radiates her entire life. Lorig, that's what I see in you."

Lorig caresses the glass with her fingers in a reflective mood. "Quite an observation. I must admit I'm flattered if you view me that way."

He holds up his wine. "I do, and offer a toast."

She does the same, smiling with him.

"To us. Lorig, whether you want to hear it or not, I'm falling in love with you. We haven't known each other long, but that's how I feel."

"You do say the right things, but how can I tell?"

Raffi clears his throat, his voice lowers. "I want to convince you the weekend with Traci was a mistake, a stupid fling. I haven't see her since and don't intend to again, socially."

Lorig takes a sip of wine, still gazing at him, and then sets down the glass. Her brow wrinkles, her face serious. "I think you're growing on me," she whispers.

The waiter arrives with the meal and as they begin eating, their conversation flows effortlessly; he explaining about his work, and she of the challenges at school. He admires her dedication and honesty of purpose, working with mentally challenged children to overcome their physical, personal and social problems.

Despite the constant flow of waiters and attractive high-fashion couples, they sit in their own world, gazing at each other, feeling the chemistry.

Suddenly a statuesque man with thick wavy blond hair stumbles against their table, trying to avoid running into one of the waiters. He stops and smiles at Lorig. "Excuse me, miss. This room is pretty crowded."

Lorig bursts out. "Are you from the TV show, *Empire*?"

A wide grin crosses the actor's face and he reaches for her hand. "Thank you for recognizing me. I hope I didn't disturb your dinner."

"Not at all," Lorig replies, shaking his hand. "It's nice meeting you."

"The pleasure is all mine," the celebrity adds. His companion, a young woman wearing a snug black sheath exposing most of her long legs, grabs his arm. "Bye!"

After they leave, Raffi chuckles. "See what I mean? You're so beautiful even a TV star had to stop at our table to greet you."

He watches her gaze follow the celebrity's entourage. While the evening is a success, he wonders if she still has doubts about his sincerity. Only time will tell, but tonight in his heart, he's convinced she's the right girl for him.

~ * ~

Ani's call is unexpected on a Sunday morning. "Raffi, I hope it's not too early?"

Raffi sits up in bed and rubs his eyes, detecting anxiety in her voice. "It's never too early for you, Mom. What's on your mind?" Last week she called to tell him that she decided not to marry David after all—there was too much love still in her heart for Raffi's dad. He's seen that to be true over the years.

"Can you come over? I prefer to see your face when I talk to you—nothing's wrong, Raffi, but I'd like to discuss a few things, like we used to do."

His self-reliant mother, who always knows the right thing to do, needs him. "Sure, I'm free this morning." He stretches his arms and climbs out of bed, feeling a bit anxious himself.

"Thank you—don't eat. I'll have breakfast ready."

It takes Raffi less than an hour to sit at his mother's table. "What's so troubling you couldn't discuss over the phone?"

Ani carries two plates filled with cheese omelets and biscuits, placing them on the table. "Let's eat before it gets cold. Then we'll talk."

Raffi can't contain his anger. "Mom, you call me at seven on a Sunday morning just to eat breakfast? I can tell something's bothering you."

Ani sits down, her voice dropping to a whisper as if the apartment is bugged. "I'm nervous about my job at the FBI."

Raffi frowns with concern. "You think you're getting fired?"

Her reply is noncommittal. "Yes and no."

Raffi persists, trying to understand what she means. "You can't divulge state secrets, I know that, but can't you be more specific?"

Ani straightens upright in her chair, her face ashen with apprehension. "I'm in charge of translating diplomatic conversations from Middle East nations, and see intelligence I can't believe."

"Like what?"

Ani frowns, her voice lowers. "Raffi, the Turkish government has intensified their lobbying efforts. I hate seeing how they're bribing Congress and sweeping justice under the rug."

He knows this is a heartfelt issue for Ani and for many Armenians. Almost one hundred years have passed since the genocide, but it still resonates in the hearts of his people.

He tries to calm his mother's fears. "Mom, you're aware the US policy is to do nothing to offend Turkey because *supposedly* they're our ally."

Ani's face flushes and she bursts out angrily. "Turkey's government imprisons journalists and anyone who exposes their underhanded tactics. When will the truth come out?"

Raffi remains silent, aware of his mother's desire for social justice. But her work at the FBI is too close to home and he has to protect her. "Understand this, Mom. You're dealing with powerful Washington elites." Recalling Wolfe's comment about Jasmine Battia, he adds, "Just close your eyes and do your job translating. That's it."

Ani bites her lip, her cheeks an angry red. "That's easier said than done." Her voice shakes with fury. "Do you know why the Speaker of the House killed the Genocide Recognition Bill at the very last minute?"

Raffi stares back without answering.

"I just found out. The Turkish lobby bought his vote with cash! They arranged junket trips to Turkey at a particular hotel." She pauses, her eyes wide with disgust. "There's more. The lobby sent him underage males for sexual favors and—"

Raffi raises his hand, interrupting her. "Please, I don't want to hear any of this. It's dangerous stuff."

"I know, Raffi, but it's keeping me awake at night."

"Mom, I hope you haven't discussed this with David." Even though Ani decided not to marry David, they still remain close friends.

Ani shakes her head. "You're the only one I can trust, son."

"Good," Raffi replies. "Let's keep this *our secret*."

Ani shakes her head in disbelief as she rises to carry the coffee carafe to the table. She seats herself, facing her son. "But how long can I keep mum on this?"

Raffi's uneasy, knowing his mother's sense of morality. "Mom, remember what happened to Jasmine Battia! For your own safety, you've got to keep this to yourself."

Ani's dark eyes sharpen. "Son, I love this country, but knowing what the Turks did to our people, how could anyone defend bribing our elected officials? That's a recipe for destroying our democracy. We must think beyond our own safety."

"Mother, be careful. I don't want to see you harmed." Frustrated with her determination, he eyes the meal before him, hoping to change the subject. "It's not often I share breakfast with you, so let's eat."

Ani picks up the basket of biscuits, offering him one. Resolute, she presses on. "I'll still do my job, but it's hard to ignore what's going on in a government in which we place our trust. There has to be another answer."

Raffi studies his mother's forlorn expression as she fills cups with coffee. "Mom, politics can get dirty, even dangerous. Don't do anything foolish."

"I hate to think you're right." She picks up her napkin and dabs the moisture from the corner of her mouth. "We've come a long way to this point in our lives. As a naturalized citizen, I have more faith in America than some of our elected officials."

Raffi's aware his mother's sense of justice will put her in a vulnerable position. If she blows the whistle, she'll face the same consequence as Jasmine Battia. He grasps her hand firmly to make his point. "Mom, this is bigger than you or me. We're talking international intrigue and there's nothing you can do with this information but keep it to yourself."

He reads the sadness in her eyes as she pulls her hand away. Feeling helpless, he picks up his fork and says, "The eggs look great. I'm starving, so let's eat."

# Twenty-two

It's only two days after Raffi's breakfast conversation with Ani when he dials Adam Wolfe's private cell. His message is urgent and he's relieved when the reporter immediately picks up.

"Adam, Raffi Sarkissian here. Believe it or not, I have Jasmine Battia in the ER and I think you should speak to her before the police arrive."

Wolfe cuts in before Raffi can explain. "You've got to be kidding! The FBI analyst?"

"Yes, the one under a gag order. Someone shot at her car, but luckily missed—although she crashed into a telephone pole. She's here in Manhattan Medical and I just finished sewing her up."

Raffi feels stares from personnel eavesdropping on his conversation and lowers his voice. "She might have a mild concussion but she's lucid and responds to questions. She's scared, Adam. If you don't come now, I'm afraid she'll clam up."

"Thanks, Doc, give me some time. I have a deadline to meet and my editor's waiting for my story as we speak."

"No deadline will compare to this scoop. If you don't question her now, you might not have another chance."

Wolfe pauses, calls out to someone in the background, and then returns. "I'll be there in twenty minutes."

Raffi sighs with relief. "Thanks, Adam. I'll have Security clear you for the ER."

He ends the call, convinced the threat is linked to payoffs to key elected officials like Senator Olin Davis. If Wolfe can get her to talk, then possibly characters like Davis can be exposed for their underhanded schemes.

His thoughts race like wildfire. Who, other than the Turkish lobby, would want to do away with Battia? The circumstance of her termination at the FBI is murky, and he knows the State Department's gag order effectively blocks any public disclosure. There has to be someone, some organization determined to silence her.

For a moment, a cold chill sweeps over him. Has he done right by calling the reporter? This spy thing is not his forte and only an investigative sleuth like Wolfe can dig out the details.

Shrugging, he snaps on the recording machine, dictates the operative report and writes Jasmine's admitting orders into her chart just as a surgical resident approaches. "Nice job repairing those facial cuts, Dr. Sarkissian. Should I send her up to the floor?"

"Not yet. The police are on the way to complete the accident report. I'll stay with her until they arrive."

After the resident departs, Raffi calls his office. Traci has left a message but he doesn't have the finesse to chat with her at the moment.

No sooner does he hang up than Wolfe approaches, accompanied by a guard. The reporter's rumpled suit jacket has a sticky visitor's pass plastered onto the lapel. His loose collar and tie reinforce the typical image of a workaholic newsman.

Raffi leads Wolfe through the hanging curtains into Jasmine's stall. She's trembling on the gurney, her dark deep-set eyes staring toward the ceiling. A bandage covers her left cheek, and fresh abrasions cross her forehead. Her right leg and left arm are also bandaged, and her body shakes with each gentle sob.

The attending nurse taking Jasmine's blood pressure looks up as the men enter. "Her pressure's slightly elevated, but I'll check again in a few minutes."

"That won't be necessary," Raffi replies. "Thanks. I'll take it myself. You can leave now."

The nurse nods and departs through the curtains.

Raffi hands Jasmine a tissue to wipe her tears. "I know how frightened you are, Miss Battia. Let me repeat, I have a special interest in what you uncovered, and I'm here to help."

Jasmine's brow wrinkles, her face ashen. "This isn't the first time they've threatened me. How can you help?"

Raffi gestures to the reporter. "This is Adam Wolfe with the *New York Post*. I've asked him to see you because he's aware of all the hard-handed tactics of the Turkish lobbyists."

Jasmine's eyes fill with terror, her lips quiver. "Please, I can't talk."

"Miss Battia, trust him. He can help."

"I can't!" she repeats. "By law, I must remain silent."

Wolfe approaches the gurney. "That's true, Miss Battia, but you don't have to stay silent about the car accident. Tell me what happened."

She lets out a resigned sigh. "What difference can it make? How can I be sure it won't happen again?"

Wolfe uses his most calming demeanor. "If this isn't exposed, you can be sure it *will* happen again until they succeed. Your life is on the line."

Jasmine remains silent for a few seconds before she replies. "What do you want to know?"

Wolfe removes a pencil and pad from his pocket and pulls up a chair. "Is this the first time you were attacked?"

"Yes, but I always feel I'm being followed. That's all I can say."

Wolfe scribbles on his pad, determined to press on. "Did you know Nancy Wood?"

"We met a few years ago. I'm Persian and she's Turkish and we kept meeting socially at different Mid-East gatherings."

"Did you know she was a Turkish agent and the name Nancy Wood was just her cover?"

"Not at first, but when the FBI files showed her name repeatedly connected with elected officials opposed to the Armenian Genocide, it all finally sank in."

Wolfe continues writing, his eyes darting with excitement. "Did the FBI file identify her as a Turkish agent?"

Jasmine frowns and turns to Raffi. "I'm saying too much."

Wolfe shoots back, anxious to get as much information as possible. "So the FBI files did identify her as an agent? Senator Davis is getting big payments from the Turkish lobby. Was that before or after he got involved with Nancy Wood?"

Jasmine grips the edge of the hospital sheet, releasing a heavy sigh. "I'm afraid to talk."

Raffi looks to Wolfe. "If Jasmine is muzzled by presidential order because of national security, what would be the point of doing away with her?"

Wolfe's eyes lock onto Jasmine. "You must know something that others beside the State Department want to hide. I know you're suing the FBI, claiming you were fired for improper reasons. Where does your case stand today?"

Her voice is raspy, her fingers still tight on the sheet. "The motions have been filed. I have to respect the gag order."

A deep voice calls out from behind the curtains. "May we enter?"

Raffi parts the drapes to see Detective Daley and a uniformed policeman. "Come in," he replies.

The detective's large figure enters through the thin fabric drapes. "I believe we've met before, Doctor."

"Yes, I remember," Raffi answers.

Daley nods as he approaches Jasmine. "Sorry to bother you, but we confirmed someone shot at your car while you were driving, Miss Battia. The bullet holes in the auto's body and glass show that. Luckily they missed you, but to prevent it from happening again, could you give us some clues? Are you able to describe a person or car following you? Who would want to do this?"

Jasmine shakes her head in the negative, without answering.

Raffi reads the distrust in her eyes, the fear for her life. He looks to Daley. "She's still pretty shook up, Detective. Maybe you can interview her later."

Daley's eyes narrow. "This is serious, Miss Battia. Someone wanted to kill you. Why?"

"I don't know," Jasmine answers meekly.

Daley looks to Raffi. "Are you going to admit her?"

"Yes, for a few days."

The detective writes notes on his pad, and then faces Raffi. "We're running a background check. If we learn more about her situation, we may need a police guard outside her room."

Raffi agrees. "That's a very good idea, Detective. The sooner the better."

Daley nods and leads the officer out of the stall.

Wolfe looks at Jasmine, eager to get more information. "Are there other women acting as Turkish agents sent to influence congressmen?"

Jasmine flinches without answering. Raffi puts his hand on Adam's shoulder. "Enough, she's tired."

This is Wolfe's signal to leave. "Thank you for the interview, Miss Battia. I will be in touch before I print anything. I don't want to say anything that will injure your case."

Jasmine sighs, pulling the sheet over her shoulders. "I appreciate that, Mr. Wolfe. I just want all this to be over."

"We do too, Miss Battia," Raffi adds.

Outside the stall, Wolfe's gaze locks onto Raffi. "Somewhere there has to be a trail, and it always ends the same. Sex and money."

# Twenty-three

Raffi stands on the terrace of Traci's Manhattan penthouse, looking out into the distance. The city's skyscrapers glow, their glittering diamond lights pierce the night's darkness.

Leaning on the stone-edged balustrade, he sighs. "It's so peaceful and serene up here. It's hard to believe the hectic activity on the streets below."

A gentle breeze catches the skirt of Traci's chiffon dress, exposing her shapely legs. "Yes, this is my getaway when I'm in the city."

He studies her beauty as she gracefully removes the champagne bottle from a silver ice holder and fills two crystal goblets. She holds hers out and touches it to his glass. Her eyes sparkle with pleasure. "To us, Raffi, it's been too long."

Raffi focuses on the mission ahead of him; his jaw tightens with guilt. Before entering her apartment, he vowed to dispel any of her romantic illusions. The weekend in Palm Beach definitely caught him off guard, a big mistake and he has to tell her. But how?

She takes a few sips, sets both glasses on the table and holds out her arms, drawing him close. Her warm body presses against his and the familiar scent of her perfume reminds him of their sensuous encounter in Palm Beach. She encircles his neck in an embrace, sending her erotic message. But this time he'll decline, and he pulls away, promising to be true to Lorig.

"Traci, there's something I must tell you."

She touches his lips with her fingertips. "Nothing negative tonight, dear heart. I reserved this evening for us."

Just then the maid, dressed in a black uniform and starched white apron, approaches through the sliding door. "Dinner is ready, Miss Doss."

Raffi welcomes the interruption, uncertain when to deliver his unpleasant message. The right moment hasn't arrived, so he extends his hand and says, "Shall we?"

"Why not," Traci replies, locking her arm onto his.

Dinner is set at an intimate circular table in the mahogany paneled library rather than in the formal dining room. Throughout the meal, Traci's eyes glisten as she chats about her university board meetings and favorite charities. He listens with interest, giving her his full attention. Two flickering candles floating in a small crystal bowl reflect the warm glow on her face, making it difficult for him to broach what he has to say.

Traci looks up when the maid enters with a dessert tray. "Don't bother cleaning up tonight, Mattie. You can go home now."

"Thank you, Miss Doss, I'll finish tomorrow," the maid answers and leaves.

Traci puts down her fork, continuing her conversation. "In two weeks I'll be free of all my obligations. Then we'll get away." She pauses to look into Raffi's eyes. "How does Hawaii sound?"

Raffi's heart pounds as he searches for the right words. "There's something I must tell you, Traci."

She places her hand on his, taking a firm hold. "Raffi, I know you're a very busy doctor, but darling, you don't have to work. I have more money than you can ever make. I just want us be together all the time."

His gaze drops; he pulls away from her grip. "I can't do that, Traci."

"Darling, why not? You've proven yourself as a fine surgeon. After all, you saved my life."

His brow furrows and he searches her eyes. "Traci, medicine is my life's challenge. Like you, I have commitments. I signed a contract with Dr. Flint who is good enough to give me the opportunity to join his practice. He's depending on me; I can't let him down."

He pauses, drawing in a breath. "Then there's the issue of our legal problems."

A frown crosses Traci's brow. "We have no legal problems. My lawyers told me I have nothing to worry about and neither do you."

He scoffs, fiddling with his dessert fork, stalling. "Don't believe everything lawyers tell you. They're paid to do that, no matter the outcome."

Traci's eyes narrow with suspicion. "Something else is bothering you, Raffi. You have a strange look on your face."

It's clear the time has come. "Yes there is," he whispers, lowering his head to avoid her censure. "There's another woman in my life." Not hearing any response, he looks up to see her stunned expression. "I had to tell you, Traci. You've been so very good to me, but you had to know."

In an instant, anger contorts her face and she shouts. "Who is this woman? How long has this been going on?"

Raffi straightens up in his chair like a schoolboy being reprimanded by his teacher. "Not very long. We met recently."

Her lips curl with fury, her hands fist with anger. "Is she the little sweetie who visited you in the hospital?"

"Yes."

"A hottie looking for her knight in shining armor?"

Raffi's guilt makes him defensive. "No, she's nothing like that. She's actually a school teacher."

Traci lets out a hearty laugh. "A teacher! My God, can't you do better than that?"

"Please, don't judge her that way."

She glares back in fury. "I'll judge her any way I want! You spring this on me from out of nowhere? What do you want me to say?"

But what more can he say? "I know this comes as a shock, but believe me, I'm still very fond of you." As soon as the words fall from his lips, he knows the word *fond* is not what she wants to hear.

Her eyes well with tears and her mouth pouts. "We had something real going on together. How could you give that up?"

His voice cracks; he clears his throat. "You had to know the truth." He rises to kiss her cheek, but she turns away, her gaze fixed on the dessert of melting ice cream dripping over strawberries.

In an unexpected move, she pushes the dish aside and looks up. Her voice shakes with anger. "I opened my heart to you, and you trashed it. I was so happy finally meeting someone who loved me for me and not my money."

"Please, Traci, I can't change what's in my heart. I don't want us to end it this way. I still want to be your friend."

She bursts out with a biting laugh. "Some friend! I may not know who my real friends are, but I do know you're not one of them." She leaps up and throws her napkin at his face. "You'll pay for this, Dr. Sarkissian. You can leave now!"

Helpless, Raffi backs away, hating himself for the pain he just inflicted. With nothing more to say, he slowly turns and leaves the room.

On entering the private elevator, he hears her explosive sobs. It's a bitter ending with no answer for all the sorrow he just dumped on her.

~ * ~

Raffi has no further contact with Traci over the following two weeks, although the memory of the breakup that evening still haunts him. At least he's in Lorig's good graces. He sits in the doctors' OR lounge sipping hot coffee from a Styrofoam cup, waiting for his surgical case and flicks on the TV. The screen lights up with stock market gurus expounding on financial numbers, jobless rates and rising mortgage defaults. The reporter questions whether summer vacations will entice consumers to spend more, despite the recession.

Preoccupied with his thoughts, the news holds no interest for him. He swallows the last of his coffee, and sits slumped on the sofa, his legs stretched out on the low coffee table before him. With the forthcoming trials, for good or bad, his life is still entangled with Traci's. As her surgeon the night of the accident, he'll have to testify in the Jackson family civil suit brought against her and Manhattan Medical.

Then there's Senator Olin Davis's homicide trial. Traci will also be subpoenaed, since Nancy Wood's body was found in her apartment. He expects to be interrogated at the trial regarding any relevant information Traci might have divulged during her stay in the hospital. Due to the sexual overtones surrounding Nancy Wood's death, he knows a publicity feeding frenzy waits in the wings.

Despite Traci's bitter feelings, he wants to help her. Emotionally drained, he picks up the newspaper lying on the table. Traci's photo appears on the social page, partying with some handsome wannabe at the Cannes Film Festival on the French Riviera. His heart sinks. That's not the kind of publicity she needs.

His face heats up with anger and he grabs the remote, shutting off the TV. Why doesn't she lie low before the trials? The only help he can give now is to convince both juries she's not the airhead conjured up by the tabloids. He needs to paint Traci's image as one of a generous benefactor dedicated to supporting worthwhile charities. Yes, that's what he'll do to protect her.

# Twenty-four

Ani perches on the edge of the bed, her grip tight on the phone. Anger creases her brow. "Raffi, this is worse than I thought. The exposure of Turkey's illegal pay for play is being shut down by someone high in the State Department. They're covering up, shoving it under national security."

Raffi roars into the phone. "Mom, remember they tried to kill Jasmine Battia. Someone's lurking out there to do whatever it takes to hide Turkey's dirty laundry. If you even hint about the bribes, you'll be the next one targeted."

Ani's heart pounds, but how can she stay silent? The Jews had their Nuremberg, but after a century where was the justice for her people? Not wanting to burden her son, her reply is cautious. "Let me think about it."

"No, Mom! Don't think about it. Just close your eyes and keep your mouth shut."

Never before has Raffi spoken to her with that tone of voice. Her face flushes, hurt by his hostility. Though angered, she has to quell his fears and says, "Raffi, I understand your concern."

But what should she do? Before hanging up, she whispers, "Don't worry, son. Love you."

She sits in the silence of her room, deliberating her next move. How can she stand by and allow such evil acts to continue? The country she has come to love as the beacon of hope is allowing Turkey to get away with murder, merely because of its politically strategic location. American foreign aid taxes are supporting a country where journalists find themselves in prison if they don't follow the party line. Turkey's democracy is only on paper. She knows that as a fact because she has lived it.

After painful deliberation, for the first time she decides to go against her son's wishes and dials the hospital, asking for Jasmine Battia's room. She has much to share with this brave woman who stood up for principles she believed in.

A timid voice answers on the third ring. "Hello?"

Ani's delivery is direct. "Miss Battia, I'm Ani Sarkissian, your doctor's mother, and I just learned what happened to you. Before you say anything, you should know I'm also an FBI translator and I might be your replacement."

A prolonged silence follows, and to Ani it appears Jasmine may refuse to talk to her.

Jasmine finally responds. "What do you want?"

Ani's pulse races, her spirit determined. "I'd like to visit you, Miss Battia. I've seen evidence of Turkey's payoffs and feel we need to talk. May I come to the hospital tomorrow?" Ani's heart races, waiting for an answer.

A pause, and then the woman answers. "Tomorrow will be fine."

"Thank you, Miss Battia. I'll come after work. Is that OK?"

Her reply sounds flat. "I'll be here."

"Take care."

Despite Raffi's warning, she concludes she's doing the right thing. Hadn't her life taken many unexpected turns? The bold steps she bravely took brought her to the present where she might be able to right some wrongs in life. Her mission is not only to comfort this woman, but to connect with a brave individual who seeks justice. In good conscience, she can't let the woman stand alone.

~ * ~

Just after six o'clock the next day, Ani's cleared by the police guard to enter Battia's room. Jasmine sits in bed wearing a hospital gown, her dark hair in a ponytail, light makeup on her face in an attempt to mask the bruising from the accident. An uneaten dinner cools on the bedside table.

Jasmine speaks first. "I was surprised by your call, Miss Sarkissian."

Ani approaches the bed. It's easy to empathize with this woman who has endured so much. She studies her face, noting their similarities. Warm olive skin, hazel eyes. Close in age. She extends her hand. "Please call me Ani. When Raffi told me what happened, I had to talk to you about my work at the FBI. I've had my share of sleepless nights over what I'm uncovering."

Jasmine nods slightly, her face fused with apprehension. "You know I'm under a gag order until my lawsuit is over."

Ani slips onto the bedside chair, leaning close. "Raffi told me. I came to share what I know and show my support."

Jasmine smiles for the first time. "We may have many things in common, Ani...your Middle Eastern background, your work."

Ani takes an instant liking to this woman. Her melancholy eyes send a message of sadness, gentility. Perhaps they could have been sisters in another life.

"Yes, that's true, Jasmine. I was born in Ankara of Armenian parents, and migrated to the States for work when Raffi was only a child. This country has been very good to me."

Jasmine brushes back a strand of hair from her forehead, focusing on Ani. "Your son has been especially kind to me. After meeting you, I know why. It must run in the family."

Ani looks down, twisting the strap of her purse. "He doesn't know I'm here. Doesn't want me to get involved, especially after the shooting."

"I'm sure he wants to protect you." Jasmine sighs and averts her gaze. "I have enough evidence to prove the corruption and cover-up extends to the highest levels."

That's exactly what Ani fears. The documentation she transcribed confirmed the corruption went to the top. She clasps her hands in her lap in an effort to remain focused. "According to Raffi, your hearing will come soon."

Jasmine grabs a tissue, and dabs her eyes. "That's probably why someone shot at me. To stop me from talking."

"What can I do to help?" Ani asks.

"There's nothing you can do. It's in the hands of my lawyers." Jasmine smiles and her face softens. "I can see you're a decent woman and what you're uncovering at work is tearing you apart."

Ani nods, tears fill her eyes. "Yes, it's a heavy burden to carry—as you know."

Jasmine leans forward, touching Ani's arm. "For your safety, stay quiet. Let's see how my complaint advances. Ani, it's kind to offer your help, and now I know I've made a new friend."

At that moment, the nurse enters the room. "You haven't eaten your dinner yet, Miss Battia."

"Just leave it, and I'll finish later."

Ani rises and scribbles her phone number on a piece of hospital stationery. "Call me after you're discharged and then we can visit over coffee and Armenian *choregs*."

Jasmine tracks Ani as she moves to the door, and calls out. "Wait, Ani! Can you spare a few more minutes?"

Ani returns to her bedside. "I don't want you to say anything that can endanger you."

Jasmine hesitates, then says, "On second thought, I'll let you go since I know you've had a long day. My story can be told another time."

Ani bends over and hugs Jasmine. "I look forward to our next visit when you're well and in the privacy of your home." She says goodbye and leaves the room, sensing a strong connection to this woman. Despite her reservations about the visit, there's a bounce to her step as she leaves the hospital, thrilled to support a friend in need.

# Twenty-five

Adam Wolfe sits on the oak pew bench in Harlem's Redeemer's Baptist Church, a recorder hidden in his pocket. He's listening to Reverend Sanders deliver a campaign speech, anticipating it to be newsworthy. The congressional slot had opened when the incumbent was forced out due to illegal use of campaign funds. Polls show Sanders is already favored to win in the midyear special election.

The reverend's voice echoes throughout the large domed cathedral. "Brothers, sisters, political power's our road to salvation. Jesus said, 'Do unto others as you want done to you!'"

Six men in makeshift Army khakis stand behind the podium armed with bat-like clubs hanging at their sides. Sanders points a finger toward them. "This, my good people, is our strength—the power of the New Black Panthers. We're here to fight the oppressors of all people of color. That's why I'm running for Congress to address the injustices our communities face not only here, but across the world."

In unison, the audience cheers and whistles, breaking into explosive applause. Sanders pauses, allowing parishioners to respond to his message. He takes a sip from the glass before him and wipes his brow. "We didn't get justice at Duke University. We didn't get it from Canada when they blocked Black Panther Chairman Shabaz from entering the country. Thank you, Anti-Defamation League and Jewish Defense League, for telling Canada not to let him in to speak at a Toronto rally. Does this mean Canada is now being run by Israel?"

Shouts erupt, fists shoot up in the air. "Right on, brother," "Shoot the pigs," "We demand equal rights."

Wolfe shifts in his seat, uncomfortable with the rising tension. As the only white person in the audience, he checks for the nearest exit should a riot break out.

Sanders waves his arms for calm, stopping to take another sip of water and then gazes into the crowd, waiting for the uproar to die down.

"Good people, I stand before you to tell you of my commitment to fight the daily battle we blacks face. I promise to keep us all on a level playing field. I promise to expose police brutality, to fight for our rights in the voting booth. To do this, we must band together to accomplish our goals."

Beads of sweat trickle down his forehead as he removes the mike from the stand and grasps it, walking to the edge of the platform. "How, you ask?" He turns, pointing to the six men behind him. "By supporting black nationalism." He raises his arm, the pitch of his voice resonating throughout the cavernous temple. "A vote for Sanders is a vote for all blacks. Run, my friends, to the polls. Don't walk, run and vote!"

Raucous shouts and whistles echo to the rafters as the reverend waves the victory sign with his fingers. Black Panthers circle him, discouraging followers from asking questions.

Wolfe shifts uneasily on the pew as Sanders descends the stage in the midst of noisy chatter. His attention is drawn to a Panther who approaches a gorgeous young black woman and hands her an envelope. She immediately slips it into her leather shoulder bag, and once secured, makes a quick exit from the church.

Wolfe's investigative DNA smells a story, taking in the furtive scene. He decides to follow the woman out of the hall into the empty vestibule, keeping his distance. She's easy to spot—about 5'6" with latte-colored skin, black straightened hair to the center of her back. Her snug purple dress rises to her thigh, accentuating her shapely legs. Wolfe guesses she's in her mid-twenties. Dancing down the church steps in high heels, she waves to a cab at the street corner, slips in and disappears.

Wolfe waits on the top step as the taxi drives away. Who is she? And what does the envelope contain? He senses something covert, a story worth investigating.

His stomach growls and he checks his watch. It's six o'clock. He descends the stone steps, surveying the small mom and pop stores on the street. Searching for a sandwich shop, he comes upon a quaint eatery with a striped awning and Wendell's Diner printed on the window and enters.

The few tables are occupied by diners, and at the counter, two men in khakis sit on bar stools. Wolfe instantly recognizes the lead Panther by his distinctive goatee and the stud in his ear.

A tall, heavy-set black man wearing an apron stands behind the counter. Still unnoticed, Wolfe catches sight of a wad of bills poorly hidden under a napkin. The bearded Panther grabs the stash and tucks it into his pocket, giving the aproned man a nod. With their mission accomplished, the Panthers rush out of the diner past Wolfe, who steps aside to keep from being knocked to the floor.

Wolfe slips onto a counter stool, reading the server's name tag. "Nice little place you have here, Wendell."

The owner, thick around the middle, appears haggard and worn, wearing several days of whiskers. He looks to Wolfe with an apathetic expression. "What'll you have?"

"A turkey sandwich on rye and coffee, black," Wolfe replies.

The man fills a mug from the coffee urn, and then goes about making up the sandwich. Wolfe hears him mumble under his breath, as if upset. He places the sandwich before Wolfe without saying a word and adds a dish of coleslaw and half pickle.

The turkey is moist, the bread home-baked, and Wolfe takes a few delicious bites before trying conversation. Wendell ignores him, cleaning up behind the counter.

"I'm Adam Wolfe, reporter for the *New York Post*," he says, after swallowing a bite.

Wendell looks up from wiping the counter, his gaze guarded.

"Could I ask you a question?"

Wendell tosses the towel into a bucket below the sink. "Depends."

Adam knows he has to tread softly. Strangers don't like nosy reporters, but he gambles that the diner owner's irritation might make him chatty. "Just came from listening to Reverend Sanders speak—looks like he's going to win his election, big time."

Wendell's jowls sag and he answers with a grunt. "Guess so."

"But he's a guest preacher, right? I'm trying to figure out where the reverend's church is based."

"Don't know," Wendell answers. "Don't think he has a church."

"Then how does he support himself?"

"Ask him," Wendell answers harshly. He reaches for a wood-handled broom and dustpan.

Wolfe chuckles. "Believe it or not, I tried, but can't get close to him."

Wendell sweeps behind the counter without looking at Wolfe. "Sounds like you got yo' answer." He uses short, angry strokes to clean the floor.

Wolfe's inquisitive instincts tell him this story is too good to pass—what if the good reverend is using the Panthers to extort money? Wolfe puts his cup down and looks at the careworn shopkeeper. "Just one more question, Wendell. I couldn't help notice you handed money to those two guys."

Wendell's eyes widen, his jaw clenches and he stops sweeping. "Ain't none of yo' business."

Wolfe presses on, keeping his cool. "Aren't they members of the New Black Panthers? Was that protection money you paid?"

Wendell throws him a piercing glance, spins around without answering, and storms into the kitchen, slamming the door behind him.

Wolfe finishes his coffee as a waitress moves around narrow tables clearing dishes. Slender, her black curls cropped short, she heads to the kitchen, ignoring him as the door closes behind her. From the other side, Wolfe hears Wendell's harsh voice and the waitress's muffled response engaged in an apparent argument. He knows he's struck a chord and eagerly waits for her to come out. Will she talk to him about the Panthers?

When she appears, he approaches the register to pay. "Look miss, I don't want to offend you, but may I ask a question?" He catches her attention. "That man with the goatee who was just in here? I saw him give a very attractive young woman, about this tall," Wolfe uses his hand to demonstrate, "with long black hair, an envelope. Then she dashes out of the church." He smiles encouragingly. "Do you know who she is?"

The girl freezes, her hand on the register keys, and then mumbles under her breath, "That bitch!"

"Could you tell me her name?" he persists.

The waitress adopts a flat expression and says, "That'll be six dollars and seventy-eight cents."

With no other information, he pays, leaves the restaurant, and walks the streets of Harlem convinced the light-skinned beauty is somehow connected to Sanders. Despite the difference in age, Sanders wouldn't be the first politician to dabble with a little hanky-panky outside of marriage.

Those thoughts run through Wolfe's mind as he walks by store fronts operated by small shopkeepers. A fruit market, a dry cleaning store, and a beauty salon all servicing the neighborhood. How many of those establishments pay protection money to Sanders' syndicate?

"Hey mister, wanna buy a wallet?" a voice calls out. A teenager stands next to a table covered with trinkets and small leather goods. The boy, wearing a Yankees sweatshirt and baggy pants cut off at the calf, motions him toward the table set out in front of a pawn shop. A frail old man in a gray baseball cap dozes in a chair by the barber shop next door.

Wolfe saunters over and picks up a wallet, checking it out.

"Give you a good price," the black youngster offers with a wide grin.

Wolfe figures the kid isn't more than thirteen years old. "How much do you want?" Wolfe asks blandly.

"Made from alligator skin, best one on the table. How 'bout twenty bucks?"

Wolfe places the wallet back on the table. "I don't need a wallet, but I'll give you a twenty if you can help me."

The boy's body tenses, his eyes narrow, staring back. "What kinda help?"

"I'll bet you know this neighborhood better than anyone."

"Yeah, I know it," the boy answers suspiciously.

Wolfe reaches for a key case on the table, fingering it as he speaks. "I need to talk with Reverend Sanders and hope you can tell me where he lives."

A frown crosses the boy's face. "Are you a cop?"

Wolfe shakes his head. "No. I want to ask him about appearing at a veterans' rally."

"Why don't you go to his election headquarters? It's on a hundred twenty-fifth street."

"I did, but they said he left for his apartment in Harlem. Thought I'd catch him there." Wolfe remains silent as the boy searches his face for a possible scam. He's treading on dangerous territory, but he needs a lead.

The boy makes a sudden turn and calls out to the elderly man, waking him up. "Hey, Damon, com-mere."

The man rises, leaning on a cane, his spine severely bent. "Watchu want, boy?" he asks, shuffling to the table.

The teenager points to Wolfe. "This dude wants to know where Reverend Sanders has his Harlem apartment."

The man sneers, wrinkles etching his face. "You da the police?"

"No," Wolfe replies, but before he can say more, the man breaks in. "What you pokin' around for? You best be gone before you gets in trouble."

"I'm not looking for trouble," Wolfe answers. "We want the reverend to speak at a veterans' rally next week. I've got to get to him quick." He pulls out his wallet. "Fifty bucks if you can take me to his apartment."

The boy looks up to the older man, who keeps his shrewd gaze on Wolfe.

The man finally answers. "OK, but it'll take a hundred bucks. Fifty for me and fifty for the kid."

"You got it," Wolfe replies, taking out the bills. He counts fifty and hands it to the man. "The kid gets the last fifty after he takes me there."

The man nods to the boy. "You take him and I'll watch the table."

The boy's face breaks out in a broad grin. "Follow me," he says and leads Wolfe down the street.

To break the silence, Wolfe asks, "How old are you?"

"Makes no difference," the boy says. They walk by shops and move around groups of black youths who exchange high fives with him as he passes by. They all look at Wolfe suspiciously...an outsider...one who doesn't belong.

Wolfe, in pursuit of a story, ignores the risk. "You go to school here?"

"Half days," the boy replies, walking faster to avoid questions.

They turn to a side street, go another block and stop before a brick apartment building.

The boy holds out his hand, palm up. "In there," he says.

Wolfe chuckles. "Where in there? This is a big building, son." At least five stories tall, and who knows how many apartments per floor?

"Second floor."

"If you want the fifty, the deal is to get me to the door. For all I know, the apartment's not listed in his name."

The boy keeps his hand extended, waiting for his money.

Wolfe can see he needs some enticing. "What if I give you an extra ten to lead me to the door?"

The boy relents with a shrug and leads Wolfe up the stairs into the dark narrow hallway. Cooking odors fill the air although the corridors appear clean and the building fairly well-maintained.

They stop in front of the apartment with brass numbers 211 nailed to the door. "This is it," the boy says. "Where's the money?"

Wolfe hands him sixty dollars and watches the youngster fly down the stairs. He waits to hear the front entrance door slam shut before ringing the bell. He'll check the name listed on the lobby mailbox later when he leaves.

When no one answers, he rings the doorbell again and waits. One the third ring, he hears footsteps approach and the door suddenly opens. There she stands, the same beauty from church. African-American heritage shows in the texture of her hair, the shape of her nose and the fullness of her mouth. She clutches her terry cloth robe; her exposed bare shoulder suggests she's naked underneath.

With a startled look, she closes the door halfway. "Who are you? What do you want?"

"I'm Adam Wolfe, a reporter with the *Post*. I'm looking to talk to the reverend about—"

"Go away!" she shouts, shutting the door.

He keeps it from closing with his foot when a bare-chested Sanders, clad in underwear, shuffles to the door. His portly abdomen hangs over tight black briefs.

"Get the hell outta here," the reverend shouts, slamming the door in Wolfe's face.

The reporter stands in the dimly lit hallway, chuckling to himself. The connection is evident. Not only is Sanders in an extramarital relationship, but he most likely supports his sexual appetite with protection money from Harlem's small shopkeepers. His nose hasn't let him down.

Excitedly, he moves toward the staircase to exit as muffled shouts come through the door of 211. He has just pierced the reverend's religious cover and finally has his scoop.

# Twenty-six

For three days Adam Wolfe sits patiently in the tension-filled court room observing the Senator Davis trial unfold. Since no evidence of premeditation or malice is found by the Grand Jury indictment in the death of Nancy Wood, the district attorney charges Davis with the lesser felony of criminally negligent homicide. Media publicity causes a volcanic explosion both in Washington and around the world. Domestic and international reporters fight for seats in the crowded courtroom. Wolfe has a front row seat, witnessing political history. How often does a trial center on a nationally known senator?

Tables reserved for the prosecution and defense are positioned across from the judge. Jonathan Gaylord, Davis's attorney, is stationed at the defense table shuffling papers, while next to him, Senator Davis stares aimlessly into space. In contrast, the stern-face prosecutors at another table huddle like a football team receiving instructions from their coach.

For several days, Wolfe listens attentively to the prosecutors describe the circumstances leading to Nancy Wood's death. The defense team counters by outlining the senator's distinguished public record and reputation. But Wolfe knows in the end, the decision of guilt or innocence rests in the hands of twelve jurors.

It's late morning when Traci is called to testify. Wolfe studies her confident walk to the witness box. She's wearing a smartly tailored suit, and her blonde hair is pulled back in a loose bun. She swears the oath before taking her seat.

Fredrick Marshall rises from the prosecutor's table and approaches the witness box. Wolfe knows Marshall to be a sharp and experienced prosecuting attorney. A man in his early fifties, his tall, slim frame gives him an athletic appearance. His dark hair is seasoned with silver at the temples. Dressed in the classic lawyer's blue suit, he addresses Traci.

"Miss Doss, when was the last time you saw Nancy Wood on the night of her death?"

She responds in a firm and clear voice. "I'm not certain. Possibly around nine or so. With so many guests present, I didn't take notice."

Marshall gives her a casual nod and leans over, resting his hand on the rail of the witness box. "Did you invite Miss Wood to your party?"

Traci shakes her head adamantly. "No! She was a guest of Senator Davis."

Her answer opens up a series of questions ranging from the occasion for the party to how often she invited the senator, and if Nancy Wood accompanied him when he attended.

Traci's responses are general and vague, until prosecutor Marshall asks the crucial question. "Miss Doss, your maid testified the senator and Miss Wood disappeared into a bedroom the night of the party. Had you seen that occur at other times and were you aware of this pattern in their relationship?"

Traci replies without hesitation. "No, I don't spy on my guests."

Marshall persists. "Weren't you at least a bit curious about the absence of the senator? Did you have many drinks that night?"

Davis's attorney calls out, "The prosecutor is badgering the witness."

The judge states, "Please answer the question, Miss Doss."

Traci casts a defiant glare at Marshall. "I was perfectly sober."

Marshall pushes on. "Your maid testified you abruptly left your party and ran out of your apartment in a fury. Why?"

Wolfe knows Traci's blood alcohol level hadn't been taken the night of her accident—Dr. Sarkissian had confided in him that he'd acted on Traci's immediate need for surgery. No doubt, the prosecutor's intention is to influence the jury to believe Traci was inebriated that night. If the charge of drunk driving succeeds, Traci will face the penalty of vehicular homicide for Tommie. He drums his fingers on his knee, waiting for her answer.

Traci leans back in the chair and crosses her legs, appearing in control of her emotions. "My actions had nothing to do with alcohol. It was a personal matter. I had an argument with my one of my guests. I was angry and left."

"So you say you were perfectly sober when you left your penthouse?"

Wolfe notices the prosecutor stresses the word *penthouse*. Is it to reinforce the chasm between her lifestyle and that of the jury? Marshall stands poker-faced, waiting for an answer.

The pitch of Traci's voice abruptly drops. "As I told you, I did not drink that night."

"Miss Doss, are you aware that Nancy Wood's body was found on the bed in your guest room? Evidence from the crime scene as well as the coroner's report shows that, although drugs were present in her blood, her death was caused by asphyxiation."

Traci clenches her fist in her lap. "I know nothing about that."

The prosecutor's voice rises. "The woman was naked when the police found her. The coroner's report shows evidence of sexual intercourse and death by erotic asphyxiation."

Traci raises the palm of her hand toward him; her voice trembles. "I don't know what you're talking about."

"Then let me explain, Miss Doss. A plastic bag was found on the bed. Most likely it was used to cover her face and head. By depriving oxygen to the brain at the time of orgasm, the victim gets a heightened rush more powerful and addictive than cocaine. Miss Wood died in your apartment and you say you know nothing about the senator's sexual conduct? You say you've known nothing about the senator's relationship with Nancy Wood, even though they were frequent guests at your home?"

Wolfe watches Traci's body stiffen, her composure falter. Is it possible she hadn't known? She gazes at the judge as though pleading to put a halt to the prosecutor's relentless questioning.

The defense attorney jumps from his seat, coming to her rescue. "I object! The prosecution is badgering this witness. She answered his questions, and now he's leading her."

"Objection sustained," the judge orders. "The jury will disregard the question regarding knowledge of the senator's sexual activity. Those questions will be stricken from the record."

The prosecutor pauses, a smirk crossing his face, aware he's made his point. "Your Honor, let me put the question another way." He faces Traci and presses on. "Miss Doss, are you aware that Senator Davis is a married man?"

Traci's brow wrinkles, her delivery sharp. "Yes."

"When Senator Davis brought Miss Wood to your home, weren't you curious why he wasn't with his wife for a social occasion? Did you ever ask about his wife?"

Marshall waits for an answer but Traci remains unmoved, staring into her lap. "I'll take your silence for a no, Miss Doss."

She locks eyes with Marshall. "I didn't say no! I'm not responsible for the senator's personal activities."

The prosecutor shrugs, turning to give the jury a smug grin. "That will be all, Miss Doss." Looking to the judge, he adds, "The State reserves the right to recall this witness if needed."

"The court agrees," the judge responds, and then turns to Traci. "You may step down, Miss Doss, but you must be available if called again." Banging the gavel, he announces, "This court will recess and resume at two this afternoon."

Wolfe observes Traci step down from the witness box and stare straight ahead, making no eye contact as she returns to her chair. A ripple of high-pitched conversation breaks out in the room, and she throws Marshall a fierce look.

After the morning's interrogation, Wolfe's convinced her ordeal is just beginning. He prides himself as a sharp judge of character but he can't put a label on Traci. Spoiled heiress, or wronged society princess?

~ * ~

The court resumes at two o'clock with a packed room of spectators. Raffi is called to the witness box, and waits for the prosecutor to finish sorting papers. The senator's defense counsel informs him that Traci has testified in the morning session but makes no comment on her testimony.

He glances toward the twelve jurors, intent on ensuring nothing in his testimony will put Traci in a bad light. As for the senator, there's nothing he can do to alter his situation.

Prosecutor Marshall approaches the witness box. "Dr. Sarkissian, the record shows you were the surgeon on call when Miss Doss was brought to the emergency room." He pauses for a moment. "When you examined her, did you suspect she was under the influence of drugs or alcohol?"

Raffi's response is swift. "No, I saw no evidence of either. She was in pain and her physical findings suggested intra-abdominal injury."

Marshall tilts his head in a slight nod, and turns to the jurors. He paces in front of them, rubbing his chin, then suddenly turns toward the witness stand. "Then you decided to take her to surgery?"

"Yes," Raffi replies without hesitation.

"You were willing to subject her to an anesthetic without first drawing a blood alcohol level? Even if it risked her life?"

It's obvious where Marshall is going. "She had internal bleeding that had to be stopped to save her life. The risk of delaying surgery was greater than any other issues."

Marshall approaches the witness stand, leaning into Raffi. "Now Doctor, had you met Miss Doss before the night of her accident?"

"No," Raffi replies.

"Is the reason you didn't draw her blood level because she's a prominent socialite? And you were protecting her from a charge of vehicular homicide?"

Gaylord, the defense attorney calls out. "Objection! The prosecutor is leading the witness, concluding medical bias in Dr. Sarkissian's treatment without the basis of fact."

"Objection sustained," the judge answers.

"Yes, Your Honor," comes Marshall's sharp reply. The smile on his face leads Raffi to believe he has succeeded in planting a seed of doubt in the minds of the jurors.

The prosecutor tents his fingers thoughtfully and continues. "But since the accident, has not your relationship with Miss Doss become more personal, in fact, intimate?" He walks to the prosecutor's table, picks up a tabloid and holds out the photo of Traci and Raffi at Colette's in Palm Beach.

Once more Gaylord calls out, "Objection. The implication in that article is of no medical importance regarding Miss Doss's condition at the time of her admission to the ER."

Raffi's sighs with relief, hearing defense attorney raise the objection.

Marshall keeps his cool and persists. "Your Honor, I merely want to show the court that the witness's response might be affected by his relationship with Miss Doss."

"I will allow the question," the judge answers.

Marshall's smug smile reveals he's won his point. "Then, Doctor, have you maintained a personal relationship with Miss Doss since her accident?"

Raffi knows he's under oath and has to be careful. He glances at the jurors focusing on him, eagerly waiting his response. "I was

Miss Doss's guest for a weekend in Palm Beach, but I have no meaningful relationship with her."

Marshall lets out a snide chuckle. "But that begs the question, Doctor. Why would you accept a personal invitation to spend time alone at the home of a woman who is your patient? Wouldn't that put you in the position of compromising your medical opinion about Miss Doss's sobriety?"

Raffi leans forward in his chair, angry. "No! My medical assessment stands. Miss Doss presented with the classic signs of intra-abdominal injury, which required immediate surgery or she could have died." He pauses, taking a calming breath. "As far as my personal life, my interest lies with another woman."

"But, Doctor, if you state Miss Doss was not inebriated, did she mention what happened to Miss Wood that night?"

"No, she made no such reference."

"Are you certain of that?"

"Yes—she was in pain and barely speaking."

"Then what was she referring to when your anesthesiologist reported in her deposition that Miss Doss kept repeating, 'No, not again, not again'."

"I have no idea what that refers to—I didn't hear it." Raffi suspects if she did say anything, it had to be when he was out of the OR, scrubbing at the sink.

"Could Miss Doss have possibly been referring to the senator's repeated sexual misconduct in her apartment? She must have known this was going on before."

Davis's counsel blares out. "Objection! The prosecution is leading the witness on informational supposition."

"Objection sustained," the judge replies.

"No further questions, Your Honor. The prosecution rests," Marshall announces, returning to the table.

Raffi sits frozen, attempting to read the jurors. Have his answers been convincing? Lawyers ask questions with built-in implications, so he's just another innocent victim of the legal system.

# Twenty-seven

Raffi sits in the OR lounge and reads the morning paper, waiting for his scheduled surgery. Adam Wolfe's account of the senator's trial the previous day is featured on the front page. He reports Dr. Sarkissian has no personal relationship with Traci Doss, but he goes on to write, "...the surgeon admits he is involved with another woman." Who the woman is, Wolfe leaves to speculation. Raffi can only imagine what Lorig is thinking when she sees the article.

Amidst the hubbub of doctors floating in and out of the room, he puts the paper down. Clearly, he has to see Lorig again. Not this weekend, but tonight, to assure her Traci is out of his life.

The OR circulating nurse pokes her head through the door, interrupting his thoughts. "Your case is on the table, Dr. Sarkissian."

"In a minute," he replies, picking up the phone to dial his office. "Cheryl, please do me a favor. Order two dozen red roses from the florist around the corner and have them sent to Miss Lorig Balian."

"Hmm, sounds wonderfully romantic, Doctor. What address should they be delivered to, and how do you want the card signed?"

"You'll find her address in my rolodex and—" he pauses for a moment and then adds, "Write this. *Want to see you tonight. Love, Raffi.*"

"I'll take care of it right away," Cheryl replies with a musical lilt to her voice.

He ends the call, satisfied with his decision. Lorig is the right girl for him—now to convince her.

Suddenly the door opens and Flint appears, dressed in green scrubs. He approaches, his voice bristles. "Raffi, we gotta talk."

"I have a case waiting for me, Harold. Could we meet later?"

"I checked your schedule. You should be free by late afternoon. See me in the office around four."

Flint's menacing tone can only spell trouble. "I'll be there," Raffi replies, and heads to the OR. As usual, when in surgery, there's no room for anything else.

At exactly four o'clock, he enters the office suite and tells Cheryl to alert Flint that he's returned. He proceeds to his consultation room and sits at his desk sifting through the mail when a knock announces the senior surgeon's arrival. Flint walks in, out of scrubs and in slacks and a polo, closing the door behind him.

Raffi reads the hard lines etched on his brow, signaling a problem. "What's up, Harold?" he asks.

"I need a favor."

Flint always demands, never asks, no less a favor. "Sure, what can I do?"

Flint leans over the desk, his expression determined. "We can't allow the senator take the stand. With all the damning DNA evidence against him, along with eyewitness accounts at the party, he'll be found guilty whether he testifies or not."

Raffi hesitates, shuffling the envelopes on his desk. "How can you help him?"

"*We.*" Flint's eyes narrow and he shoves his hand into his pocket. "*We've* got to put a halt to the trial by admitting him to the hospital with the diagnosis of a massive stroke."

Raffi's jaw drops "Did I hear you correctly? Fake a stroke? That's impossible! It won't fly."

Flint's lip curls in a sneer, his face worn and gaunt. "It will work, it must work! He needs time to let public opinion die down—we check him in, with only select private nurses who will *care* for him twenty-four hours around the clock. I've already arranged it, without the director's knowledge. Just for a few days—nobody will know."

Stunned, Raffi draws in a sharp breath. "This sounds too preposterous to work."

"It will work," Flint persists. "The senator's a close friend and too important to waste away in a prison."

Raffi can't believe what Flint is asking of him. "But Harold, remember the girl *died* that night—"

Flint cuts him off. "She knew what she was doing. For all I know, she sucked him into that type of kinky sex."

Raffi's face flushes, and he bolts up from his chair. "I want no part of this—it's medically dishonest, illegal, and wrong on every level."

Flint's face reddens with anger. "It's all arranged, so be prepared to do exactly what I ask. You owe me."

Raffi looks around the upscale office and swallows hard. "This is madness, Harold. You'll never get away with it."

Flint paces the room as he talks. "Yes, we will. A special ambulance will transport Olin from his hotel to the hospital, right before he's called in to testify."

"Why do you need me?"

"I'm too close a friend, and there might be questions if I admit him."

Just like the night he operated on Traci—there still ramifications. Raffi sinks back in his chair, crossing his arms. "I won't do it."

Flint comes to a halt and thrusts a finger toward Raffi. "You can't stop the show! I've arranged everything so there won't be any slipups. A neurologist friend will report that Senator Davis is paralyzed and unable to speak after sustaining a massive stroke." Flint shrugs. "It's out of your control."

Raffi's thoughts scatter. *How can I protect myself from Flint's crazy plan? I have no pony in this race!* He angrily pounds the desk. "Count me out!"

Flint lowers himself in a chair facing Raffi and casually crosses his legs. He throws his young associate a sly leer, his voice cold as ice. "The plan is already set in action. Raffi, mark my words. If you don't follow the formula, I'll destroy you." With that, he rises and walks out of the room.

~ * ~

The earlier scene with Flint continues to rattle in his thoughts on the drive to Lorig's home. The risk of losing her makes him nervously drum his fingers on the steering wheel as he tosses about how to approach the subject. *What can I tell her? That I'm part of an immoral scheme?* That Lorig accepted his invitation to dinner is the only good and decent part of his confusing life.

The evening progresses without a hitch as they chat casually on the drive to the restaurant. She looks sophisticated in a simple black sheath that clings to her slender, shapely figure. Her silky hair falls to her shoulders, swaying in rhythm as she moves gracefully to their table in the chic, dimly lit dining room of Bella Roma. Couples sit in cubicles, lending an atmosphere of intimacy. It's just what Raffi wants.

Tonight he'll put his conflict with Flint on the back burner until he reveals his true feelings for her. Only then will he know if they're meant to be. He faces her across the table, studying the warm candle glow casting a shadow on her high cheekbones. *God, she's perfect!*

Her expressive green eyes meet his. "Raffi, the flowers you sent are truly beautiful and much too extravagant." She hesitates, facing him with an earnest look. Her hands slide across the table to touch his. "I wanted to call but with all your work, the trial—I didn't want to bother you."

His heart pounds, and he takes in a deep breath, hearing Lorig expose her feelings for the first time. He reaches across the table and folds her hand in his. It all comes out so naturally. "Lorig, can't you tell? I've fallen in love with you."

She lowers her head, then lifts her gaze. "What about—?"

"Please believe me. Traci means nothing to me."

She lets out a satisfied chuckle. "I read *that* article in the *Post* *twice*, hoping I was the other woman." She squeezes his hand, her smile fading. "Raffi, I do believe you, and don't want to ever doubt you. I care for you, too."

Now that he knows he has a chance for a real relationship, he has to be honest with her, about everything. "Lorig, there's something that might make you feel you want no part of me."

Her eyes widen in puzzlement.

Before he can continue, the waiter approaches, breaking their physical connection as he places bread on the table, takes orders, and finally leaves.

She holds his hand again. "What is it, Raffi? No secrets between us, promise?"

His gut twists with shame—he hasn't been raised to be dishonest, but he's in a no-win situation. Will Lorig judge him? Good or bad, he has to let it all out. "I have to make a decision."

Lorig leans forward in her chair, her hand still in his, ready to listen. "Tell me, what is it?"

He explains Flint's scheme to hospitalize the senator with a phony diagnosis, and waits for her reaction. At first there's none, but after another short pause, he goes on to relate Flint's threat to destroy him if he doesn't participate in the scheme. When she still doesn't reply, he says, "I hope I wasn't wrong to burden you with my dilemma."

She breaks her silence. "What are your choices?"

"I can go along, and if the scheme is exposed, get professionally destroyed and end up hating myself." He rubs his thumb along hers. "Or get fired and become *persona non grata* at the hospital or at any other credible institution in this city. With Flint's political power, either way, I'm screwed."

"Why do you have to write the admitting orders?"

"Because he has a strong relationship with the senator, and wants to distance himself. That makes me responsible for the case."

Anger flashes in her eyes. "Flint is dumping his ruse on you. Can you get him to write the admitting orders?"

Raffi thinks for a moment. "Only if he writes them under my name, but countersigns."

"Countersigns? What does that mean?"

"It's done all the time. Nurses take verbal orders over the phone and countersign for the doctor. Or doctors write orders given to them by consultants and countersign."

Lorig cocks her head, her honey chestnut hair sliding over her shoulder. "In essence, if you get Flint to physically write the orders, you can claim he wrote them without your knowledge should the scheme get exposed."

"I don't like any part of this, but you have a point." *But can I live with my conscience?*

As if reading his mind, Lorig withdraws one hand, holding his other. "This is garbage, Raffi! Just walk away. Don't put your name to anything!"

"It's not that easy, Lorig. The politics of medicine are no different than the politics of Washington. Sometimes you're forced to do what's politically expedient. If I don't do what Flint wants, I'll be committing career suicide and I've worked too hard for so long. Can you understand?"

They stare at each other across the candle light, when the waiter returns with a bottle of red wine, interrupting the intensity of the moment. He pours the merlot, places the bottle on the table, and leaves.

Solemnly, Raffi raises his glass. "I have no idea what we're toasting tonight, but I had to share this with you—no secrets between us, if you wish to continue a relationship with me."

"I do." She smiles and takes a drink. "But I think you've got to avoid any involvement with Flint's lie—I watched your expression when you were talking just now, and it's not you. He'll eventually be exposed, so let him make his own bed."

Raffi shrugs. "I might as well say goodbye to my career in Manhattan, or anywhere else, for that matter."

"Better to stay true to your own moral code," Lorig persists. "Raffi, your days are numbered with Flint. I don't care how powerful he is. There's an old Armenian saying: *know when to step away, no matter the cost.*"

"I thought I'd heard them all from my mother." He gives her a sheepish look, shaking his head. "That's a big order, challenging Flint with all his clout."

She sips her wine. "I can't imagine all of the intrigue in your profession, but that's the philosophy guiding my decisions. In the end, I want a life partner who plays it straight, and I want you, Raffi."

~ * ~

The reports of Senator Davis's massive stroke hits the airwaves and print media like an avalanche the following morning. Raffi hears the news on TV as he climbs out of bed, relieved he convinced Flint to countersign the admitting orders. At first the senior surgeon balked, threatening Raffi with his usual aspersions. The only positive thing in the negotiation is that if Flint tries to screw him, Raffi will claim he never wrote the orders. It's not a satisfactory deal and for now he still has his job, but at what price?

Still in pajamas, he stands before the TV listening intently to the commentator's report. No questions are raised concerning the senator's diagnosis. The media and public believe that the stress of the trial caused his stroke. Excitedly, he flips to other news channels and again, hears nothing to doubt the senator's bogus misfortune.

He shaves, dresses and drains a tall glass of orange juice before leaving for the hospital. Hungry for a story, the media will be ready to pounce on all medical personnel coming through the doors of Manhattan Medical.

Now that he's earning a salary in private practice—thanks to Flint—he has bought his own car, the least expensive Lexus model on the floor, parking it in the garage across from the hospital, which is an additional expense. He pulls into his reserved spot, prepared to face any possible assault by a reporter waving a mike at his face.

As expected, reporters and television cameras gather in front of the hospital approaching employees entering the building. He makes his way through the mob, hoping to go unrecognized, but in the clamor of confusion, a voice calls out, "Look, there's Sarkissian, the senator's physician!"

A swarm of reporters surround him like honey bees zeroing in for nectar. Three security guards break through the crowd and escort him into the building. Once inside, he heads to the doctors' locker room to change into scrubs when Jeremy comes in.

"Hey Raffi, since when do you take care of stroke patients? The senator needs a neurologist, not a surgeon."

Raffi speaks as he pulls the scrub shirt over his head. "He came in late last night as an emergency. A neuro consult is scheduled for this morning." A sour taste forms in his mouth, his brow wrinkles with shame. He and Jeremy have trained together as trusted colleagues, depending on each other in and out of surgery. But this ominous secret can't be shared, no matter how close the friendship.

Jeremy's nod suggests he accepts the answer.

Raffi forces a smile and changes the topic. "You've been seeing Rachel for how long now? Looks serious?"

Jeremy slips his shoes off as he speaks. "She's the one, Raffi. I don't know what I'd do without her." He opens his locker.

"Sounds like you two are headed for the altar."

"Wish we could walk that walk," Jeremy replies. "But we decided to wait until the Jackson civil rights complaint is settled. Hopefully by that time, my residency will be completed and I can earn a decent living. Like you—nice car, by the way."

"Thanks." Raffi knots the tie around the waist of his scrub pants, throwing Jeremy a questioning gaze. "Why wait? Even if the court finds the hospital guilty of a violation, you won't have to pay the settlement. The hospital does."

Just then an African-American in a hospital maintenance uniform enters, making a half-hearted attempt to empty the wastebaskets. He pauses, giving Jeremy a hateful glance before leaving.

Raffi raises an eyebrow. "What's that all about?"

Jeremy pulls on scrub pants and a shirt without answering.

Raffi persists. "Is Sanders *stalking* you?"

Jeremy slams the locker door shut. "He reminds me that I can be reached anytime and anywhere. Our apartment, church, wherever."

Raffi puts a firm hand on his friend's shoulder. "This is serious! Are we talking physical violence?"

"So far, no. Just vague threats. The reverend regards himself as the community organizer. Wants all blacks to walk in step with him." Jeremy scowls and slides his feet into leather clogs. "Unfortunately, I won't march to his drumbeat. His message isn't unity…it's separation, and I'm not about that."

"You can't let this ride, my friend. Do the hospital attorneys know about this?"

"No."

"Jeremy! You've got to tell them." Raffi shakes his head. "If you don't, I will."

Jeremy bites his lip, his deep brown eyes locking onto Raffi. "This is *my* war with *my* people, and I don't want you getting involved." Angrily, he slams the locker door with a bang. "I can't marry Rachel until things settle down, otherwise she'll be exposed to the same scrutiny, and I don't want that for her."

"This really sucks," Raffi mumbles. "Your people should be proud of your achievements, not condemn you."

"I'm a grown man, Raffi. I can handle it."

Raffi lowers his head. Does he lack Jeremy's integrity by covering up for the senator? His colleague is man enough to stick to his principles, accepting the risks. *Why didn't I walk away?*

The overhead page crackles, "Dr. Sarkissian, urgent call to room ten-fourteen." Senator Davis's Penthouse. Just then, the whirring noise of a helicopter sounds and both men look out the window of the doctors' locker room. To their surprise, the copter flies close, barely missing the hospital.

Raffi's smart phone flashes a Breaking News logo and he reads the alert. "The ABC Helicopter Sky Team has just obtained a video of Senator Davis in his room at Manhattan Medical. Despite reports the senator is on death's door following a massive stroke, pictures show him out of his hospital bed, walking with a newspaper under his arm."

Blood drains from Raffi's face and he staggers onto the bench.

"What the hell is going on?" Jeremy questions.

An irate Harold Flint bursts into the OR locker room, his fury directed at Raffi. "You gotta go out and talk to those reporters. Explain the man in the video is another patient, not Senator Davis."

Raffi holds up his phone. "I don't know, Harold. It sure looks like the senator."

The tip of Flint's nose grows beet red, and he curses. "I don't give a God damn! Get out there and do damage control!"

Raffi winks at Jeremy, tilting his head toward the door. This argument's not going to be pretty and doesn't need witnesses.

Jeremy takes the cue. "Excuse me. Got a patient waiting in OR." He darts out of the room, closing the door tightly behind him.

Raffi clears his throat, mustering the courage to speak his mind. "Harold, let's not get any deeper into this sinkhole. I'll go tell the senator to stay in bed until this entire farce blows over. We'll have to think of something to get out of this mess."

"Are you crazy? We've got to kill this in the bud." Flint snaps his fingers. "You've got to make a statement claiming mistaken identity. Insist the senator is in another penthouse hospital room, still in coma."

Raffi studies the age spots dotting the old surgeon's saggy cheeks, the desperation in Flint's stance. He can't play this political game any longer—even if he has to return the Lexus. "Sorry, Harold. I won't lie for you."

"You're disobeying my order?"

"Yes." Raffi immediately straightens up, the weight gone from his shoulders.

Flint wags his finger at Raffi, his lips trembling with anger. "I warn you! I'll ruin you if you don't come on board."

Raffi folds his arms across his chest, prepared to take the consequences. "I won't lie, Harold."

Flint turns crimson, fisting his hand. "You had your chance, Sarkissian. You're fired!"

At that moment, Raffi lets out a sigh, relieved from Flint's suffocating manipulation. Lorig is right. It's been a matter of time, and the time has come.

"If that's what you want, Harold, I'll leave as soon as my cases are discharged." He heads toward the door. "Right now I have a patient waiting for me on the OR table."

As he turns to leave, Flint calls out. "Don't bother. You're finished taking care of my patients."

Raffi comes to a halt and angrily faces the aging surgeon. "The patient lying on the OR table signed a surgical consent for *me* to operate, and that's what I'm going to do."

Flint pulls his phone from his pocket and dials. "Cheryl, Dr. Flint here. Cancel all of Dr. Sarkissian's scheduled appointments and work them into my caseload." His face contorts scornfully, listening to Cheryl's response. "No!" he shouts. "The doctor is no longer connected with us."

# Twenty-eight

Adam Wolfe waits in front of Manhattan Medical amid TV cameramen and reporters, all demanding access to Senator Davis's doctors. Hospital security summons police for help, a move that momentarily calms the restless mob. But the hungry media is unsatisfied, wanting visual proof of the senator's condition.

New York's finest in SWAT garb blocks the hospital entrance as an overhead loudspeaker blares. "Please stand aside. Only patients and visitors with proper identification will be allowed to enter."

After standing for almost an hour, Wolfe tires of the constant shoving and colliding of elbows and shoulders, and decides to call Raffi to get the inside scoop. He's gathered information for the doctor, and possibly, they could help each other.

A glance at his watch tells him it's already 11 o'clock, and he dials Raffi's office, hoping to catch him. "Good morning, Cheryl." "This is Adam Wolfe, reporter for the *New York Post*. Remember me? I came to your office a while back to interview Dr. Sarkissian."

"Yes, Mr. Wolfe. How can I help you?"

"I'd like an appointment with the doctor to give him information he's requested."

"He's not in the office."

"Could you please tell him it's urgent? My cell number is—"

"Thank you, I have it," she replies and hangs up.

Wolfe pockets his cell, attributing the hollow sound in Cheryl's voice to the media clamor. Certainly the senator's condition has to be impacting office routine—it's no secret that Senator Davis and Doctor Flint are tight friends.

Shrugging, he returns to his office to await Raffi's call. The announced explanation that Davis isn't the patient on the video is not convincing. Years of investigative reporting leads him to suspect a big lie hides beneath all the medical dialogue. *Yes, I definitely have to speak with Raffi.*

~ * ~

Raffi takes Cheryl's call on his cell as he walks out of the operating room past the nurse's desk. "Adam Wolfe? What information did he say I requested?"

"He didn't say but I have his cell number."

Raffi stops to grab a pen from the nursing station and writes Wolfe's number on his green scrub suit over his thigh. "Thanks, Cheryl, I got it."

Her voice wavers. "Before you go, Doctor, are you leaving us?"

Raffi's voice lowers. "Not by choice, Cheryl."

"I see. I'm sorry," she answers meekly.

"Please don't concern yourself—everything will be okay. I enjoyed working with you, Cheryl." He clears his throat. "I'll call Mr. Wolfe."

Entering the doctors' lounge, he feels a twinge of anguish. Over the weeks, Cheryl has offered help and concern for his success. While they never speak about it, he senses her respect for him and feels the same about her.

He sits at the dictation desk in the doctors' lounge, prepared to record his operative report, when his attention is diverted to the TV. Replays of the viral YouTube video fill the screen. He watches in dismay as a healthy Senator Davis paces around the private penthouse room, interrupted by scenes of reporters gathered outside the hospital building. Flipping on the dictation machine, he's still preoccupied with Flint and Davis. No way can the truth be silenced. Possibly a talk with Adam Wolfe will help buffer the coming tsunami.

He completes his report but remains seated, pondering his future professional direction. After this last case, he'll be out on the streets looking for a position. If he remains at Manhattan Medical, he'll be competing for surgical referrals and face a political enemy in Flint—an unsavory situation. *Maybe it's wise to leave all this crap behind. Why not locate to the Jersey shore with a fresh start?* He slumps back in his chair, his eyes dark with worry. *Will Lorig go with me?* The vision of her walking the beach the day he first saw her rushes into his thoughts.

Mulling over career choices, he casts his gaze downward and spots Wolf's cell number scrawled across his pant leg. He forgot about the reporter's message, and calls.

"Raffi Sarkissian here, Adam."

Wolfe's gravelly voice comes over the line. "Raffi, glad you returned my call. I discovered vital information about the Turkish lobby that might be of interest to you. Can we get together?"

Raffi sighs, smoothing back his thick hair. "I have enough on my plate right now." *Like finding employment.*

"Aren't you the doc treating Senator Davis?"

"That's debatable." Tempted to tell Adam the real scoop, he dismisses the idea.

"Doc, be aware the Turkish lobby knows you talked to Jasmine Battia when you admitted her to the hospital. Who knows what extent those agents will go to squelch the senator's involvement?"

Wolfe's words cut through Raffi like a knife. Any link to Davis's imaginary stroke not only would discredit his reputation, but even worse, he would be a sitting duck for the Turkish lobby.

Wolfe presses on, not hearing an answer. "We have to talk, Raffi, but not on the phone. Could we meet at your office?"

"Adam, meet me at the hospital entrance. I'll have security clear you. The last I checked it was still a madhouse out there."

"Thanks. I'll be right over."

Raffi waits and within twenty minutes, the hospital security guards usher Wolfe through the swinging doors. The audible sound of media clamor outside disappears when the doors close behind them.

"This better be good, Adam," Raffi says, leading the reporter toward the elevators. He frowns, pushing the button. "I'm in no mood to play with the press."

Wolfe carries a leather attaché case over the shoulder of his shapeless jacket and follows Raffi into the lift. "I promise you won't be disappointed, Doc."

The elevator stops at the floor of the executive office, and Wolfe trails Raffi into the reception area. The secretary points to an empty boardroom. "As you requested, Doctor, the room's free for the rest of the day."

With the doors shut, Wolfe takes a seat across from Raffi, placing his briefcase on the table. "I have information regarding Senator Davis's dealings with the Turkish lobby but first, I need to know the truth about his medical condition."

Raffi lets out a smug chuckle. "You, along with the entire media." His grin turns to a frown. "Adam, I'm just a mere physician. What can I do about Davis's underhanded bribes?" *I've already taken a stand against Flint and got fired for it.* Frustrated, he rises to end the conversation.

Wolfe motions him to return to his seat. "Raffi, I'm worried there might be serious reprisal against you by the Turks." He pauses, his dark eyes intensifying. "Especially since you're Armenian."

A sense of unease overcomes Raffi. *I refuse to get drawn into Wolfe's world.* He extends his hand. "Sorry, Adam, this meeting is over."

Instead of shaking Raffi's hand, Wolfe snaps open the attaché case and slides a printed flyer across the table. "Take a minute to read this."

Raffi scans the header of the newsletter. *The Turkish Coalition of America.* "Never heard of them."

Wolfe's bushy eyebrows peak. "It's a foreign political action group, a front organization for Turkish deniers of the genocide. As we speak, they're backing a lawsuit against the president of the University of Minnesota filed by a twenty-one-year-old Turkish student enrolled there. Do you know why?"

Raffi shakes his head, returning a curious look.

Wolfe grins. He's finally captured Raffi's attention. "Because the university's website, *Center for Holocaust and Genocide Denial,* lists the *Turkish Coalition* as an unreliable source for information concerning the Armenian Genocide."

Raffi shrugs and taps the paper. "So what's new? The Turks have always denied the genocide."

"But this is different, Doc. They've now gotten the audacity to threaten free speech on our university campuses."

Raffi remains silent, reading the headline. *Fostering Understanding of Turkish- American Issues through Public Education.* He fists his hand, skimming the words. Conversations with his mom about his roots come back in a rush.

"Adam, this article is pure and simple propaganda! As a nation, when are the Turks going to admit what happened? Germany admitted its guilt and made reparations to the Holocaust victims' families after World War Two. Unlike the Armenian Genocide, what Hitler did is well documented in history. Despite original sources describing *our* tragedy, we're still searching for justice."

Wolfe removes his glasses, rubbing his eyes. "Now you're getting closer to the truth. Turkey can't admit the genocide ever happened because reparations would cost them a fortune, and the ruling party could lose its control."

Raffi leans his elbows on the table, drawn in despite his intentions. "So they bribe elected officials like Senator Davis to block the Genocide Bill. It comes up every year for a vote, but gets turned down."

Wolfe pats the briefcase. "Exactly! And when FBI translator Jasmine Battia discovered the truth and blew the whistle, her life was threatened." He leans back in his chair, a scowl crossing his face. "And now the lobby might decide that with the senator alive, they also could be threatened if his link to them is exposed."

Raffi draws in a heavy breath. "This kind of dirty politics makes me sick."

"Look, Doc. It's time to take a stand. Protecting the likes of Davis will bring more harm than good. Remember, he's supporting Turkey's interests, not America's. You've seen the YouTube clip of him strolling around his penthouse suite like he's on vacation. If the guy experienced a massive stroke, he sure made a miraculous recovery."

It seems this is the day for Raffi to choose sides—right or wrong. Davis deserves to face the consequences for his actions. Uncomfortable in the role of judge, he bristles with rage. "I'll tell you this. I haven't stepped one foot in the senator's room since his admission. Flint wrote the orders and he's in charge."

Wolfe's dark eyes gleam with satisfaction. "I'm glad to hear you're no longer involved in his care."

Raffi straightens up in his seat, aware the reporter's hunting for a story to confirm Davis's medical condition. Wolfe's an honest investigative reporter and so he clarifies his relationship with Flint.

"Adam, circumstances have changed over the last number of hours. I'm no longer working with Flint."

Wolfe slaps his knee. "I smelled something fishy when I spoke to Cheryl at your office—she wasn't her usual cheerful self. I want that scoop, Doc." He hesitates, his eyes grave. "I imagine your break with Flint wasn't amicable?"

"Not exactly. I was fired for standing up for my beliefs."

Wolfe breaks out in a grin. "Raffi, help me find a hospital maintenance uniform. I need to do some sleuthing." He presses on when Raffi doesn't immediately agree. "Come on, Doc. The truth will eventually come out. You very well might end up at the short end of the stick."

Raffi ponders Wolfe's request. He's not going to lie about Davis's condition. And what loyalty does he have to Flint?

"Maybe this will sway you." Adam withdraws another booklet from his attaché case and holds it up for Raffi. "The propaganda against the Genocide Bill is heating up. The Turkish American Defense Fund, The Turkish Coalition among others, claim Armenian American organizations pushing for the Resolution bill are merely propaganda tools, falsifying what happened."

Bewildered, Raffi opens the folder. "I never heard of them."

"Doc, you're not alone. When the senator's homicide trial resumes, political action groups supporting the bill will try to expose the Turkish payoffs. If you get called to testify, well, you don't seem the kind to lie."

Raffi lifts his head a little higher as Wolfe persists. "So the Turks will do anything to discredit you, even threaten you. And because Flint fired you, they will try to trash you personally and professionally."

Raffi pales at the thought; his pulse races. He can't imagine what dangers lurk ahead because of choices already made. *Why is Wolfe intent on putting him in such a situation? Is it just for a story?*

He looks squarely at the reporter. "I'm puzzled by your intensity in pursuing this issue about the Turkish lobby."

An amicable smile creeps over Wolfe's face. "Are you asking me for a motive?"

"Yes, I am, Adam. Israel has close ties with Turkey. As a Jew, why would you chase a story that could harm Israel's only Muslim ally?"

Wolfe pounds the conference table. "Israel's ally? That's a myth! Turkey proclaims itself a democracy but in reality, it's not. It doesn't allow freedom of speech or press. If you say or write anything against '*Turkishness*,' you're thrown into prison, or slaughtered on the street like the Armenian Turkish journalist, Herant Dink. There's no real freedom of religion. I see Turkey as a fundamentalist Islamic regime and honestly, I worry about Israel's future. I don't want to see Israel destroyed."

Raffi reads the fierce intensity on Wolfe's face, seeing passion for the truth. Maybe he does need Adam to report the story in the press. As a Jew, Wolfe's people endured extermination, just like the Armenians. Dedicated people like Adam are in a position to document world history.

Raffi runs anxious fingers through his hair. *What a day.* "Okay, Adam. It's after five and most of the maintenance crew should be gone. Let's find you a tool belt and a uniform in the basement. After that, you're on your own."

# *Twenty-nine*

Raffi leads Wolfe to the elevator and presses the button to the underground level. The only time he's visited the bowels of the hospital's basement was during the first year of his surgical residency when he needed an awl to punch holes in the strap of his new camera case.

After exiting, the two men walk along a drab concrete-walled corridor illuminated by bare fluorescent lights. Metallic screened panels separate the darkened empty work stations. As Raffi suspects, the maintenance crew has gone home by this time of day.

Going to the end of the passageway, they enter a room with a long row of metal lockers standing against the back wall. Wolfe points to a leather tool belt hanging from a hook in a locker with an open door. "There! That'll come in handy."

Raffi grabs the blue denim jacket hanging beside the tool belt, eyes the reporter and tosses it to him. "Put it on for size and take off your tie. It's a dead giveaway."

Wolfe chuckles, slips on the oversize jacket, and then buckles the leather belt holding a hammer and various tools around his waist. He removes his tie, folds it neatly and carefully puts it into his coat pocket, giving Raffi a wry grin. "Don't want to mess up one of my favorites."

Raffi stands, nodding his head, watching Wolfe transition from reporter to expert mechanic. *I can't believe I've fallen for this scheme.* "Be careful, Adam, and don't tell me what you're up to! I don't want to be discovered 'borrowing' tools. Wonder if I can get fired twice in one day?" Pointing to the tool belt, he gives a final order. "One more thing, Adam. Make sure those get back where they belong."

~ * ~

After Raffi leaves, Wolfe explores the room. He picks up an electric cord lying on the workbench and slings it over his shoulder. A workman's cap on the bench catches his eye and he wears it before moving into the elevator. Taking a deep breath, he pushes the red penthouse button—he doesn't have much of a plan, but hopes to wing it.

The elevator finally comes to a stop at the top floor. The doors open, and he spots a man in a security uniform slumped on a chair in the hallway, dozing. Four doors line the corridor, and he deduces the senator's room is the one with protection.

The guard suddenly snaps to attention at the sound of Wolfe's footsteps.

"Is this the suite that has the TV power flickering?" Wolfe asks innocently.

"I have no idea," the guard answers, taking in Adam's tool belt and the extension cord. He picks up the newspaper that has fallen to the floor and holds it up to continue reading.

Wolfe knocks on the door, and after a short wait, he opens it slightly and shouts, "Maintenance. Need to check an electrical problem." Hearing no answer, he opens the door wide and recognizes Senator Davis sitting on a lounge chair in crimson silk pajamas.

He enters, his tool belt snug to his waist. "We don't want to start a fire, sir," he chuckles. "I'll only take a minute." Wolfe has gotten that far without any suspicion. The senator ignores him, and continues reading a book on golf.

He moves to the large TV sitting on a dresser, acting as though there's nothing unusual about the work ahead of him. Shoving one end of the dresser away from the wall, he kneels, hidden from the senator and proceeds to grab the TV cable from the power source. He pulls out plugs and puts them back, deliberately making noise with his tools. Patiently, he waits for his chance, peeking at the senator with a sideway glance. Yanking at cables with one hand, he carefully raises his cell phone and snaps multiple photos of the all too healthy senator who remains in the chair, reading and eating cashews.

"All finished," he calls out, and rises to shove the dresser back against the wall. "Sorry to disturb you, sir. Everything is fine now," he reports, nodding to the senator. His pulse races as he walks out of the room and passes the guard whose chin rests on his chest, asleep in his chair.

It's an eternity waiting for the elevator doors to open. Once inside, an adrenaline rush comes over him. He brushes the sweat from his face with his sleeve and presses the button to the basement. There he'll discard the workmen's garb and hopefully leave without being discovered. What a scoop! Now, what to do with it?

The cool breeze refreshes him when he finally steps out of the building into the evening air. Patting the cell phone with the damaging evidence in his pocket, he laughs to himself. If Senator Davis had a stroke, he must have gone to Lourdes for the quickest damned recovery known to man.

~ * ~

It takes less than twelve hours for Adam Wolfe's front page exposure of Senator Olin Davis's illusionary stroke to dominate the media. Raffi anticipated the article would cause shock waves, but visualizing the photos of a healthy Davis contradicting the hospital's public statement sickens him. As the doctor of record, he definitely will get drawn into the inevitable political quagmire, despite Wolfe's assurances that he would help.

DR. RICHARD A. BERJIAN

He falls back to sleep after a restless night, wakes up later than usual to read the news on his iPhone. "Dammit," he mutters, hitting the nightstand in anger at himself for getting involved with the seasoned reporter. Since there's nothing he can do about it, he quickly shaves, dresses and leaves for the hospital to see his last patient.

Instead of driving the short distance, he walks, working off his pent up frustration. For sure his name will surface again in the press, and the only wise thing he's done is to tell Lorig about Flint's crazy scheme. Hopefully she'll be prepared for the onslaught coming from the morning's media blitz. In his heart, he's convinced she cares for him. She's been supportive and her goodnight kiss after dinner still lingers with him.

He walks the street, not responding to the usual waves from the few local shopkeepers who recognize him as they sweep the front sidewalks and polish windows. This is not the time to explain—he has to get to the hospital unnoticed and avoid the media which will surely be gathered outside.

The usual crowd of reporters and satellite TV trucks are already camped out in front of the hospital. To avoid them, he quickly turns the corner and trots to the rear delivery ramp. He flashes his plastic ID tag; the security guard nods, giving him clearance.

This day, like any other at Manhattan Medical, is active with a full patient load. He presses the up button for the sixth floor, impatiently tapping a foot as he waits for the elevator door to open. His mood turns somber, aware his hours at Manhattan Medical are numbered. After discharging his last patient, he'll probably no longer walk these halls.

As the elevator doors open, a quick glance at the nursing station tells him something is amiss. The usually friendly nurses avoid eye contact, their faces glued to charts. The desk secretary quickly picks up a phone, cupping her hand over the mouthpiece. Her panicked expression convinces him her call is to alert someone, probably Flint, about his arrival.

He shakes off his paranoia and enters the nursing station, removing his patient's chart from the rack. At the desk, he flips through it and looks to the charge nurse.

"Flo, I'm planning to discharge Miss Smith today, but the pathology report is missing."

Her body stiffens, and without answering him directly, she turns to the desk secretary. "Jane, call the lab and have them send the printout the doctor needs." She then returns to her computer screen, avoiding further conversation.

Although her cool reception surprises him, he responds with a hesitant, "Thank you." Placing the chart back into the rack, he goes to the patient's room, changes the dressing and returns to the desk. The clerk informs him the path report still has not arrived.

With no other patient to see, he walks down the flight of stairs to the surgical lounge for coffee. He fills his cup from the coffeepot and sits on the empty sofa to watch the news. Surgeons enter and leave, change into scrub suits and head for the OR. In spite of the activity behind him, he sits alone, unnoticed and undisturbed.

Reports of the senator's condition continue on the news channels. Suddenly the newscaster announces, "The senator's admitting doctor of record is Dr. Raffi Sarkissian, who could not be reached for comment."

His chest tightens, and his hands shake as he places the cup on the table before him. His name has finally emerged, and now he's party to Flint's devious scheme.

Taking a deep breath, he rises from the sofa and makes his way back to the sixth floor to check on the pathology report. To his surprise, the hospital administrator and Harold Flint stand at the nursing station, as flat-faced nurses continue carrying on their duties.

Flint jumps forward, shaking a finger at him. "You son of a bitch! You fuckin' Judas! I'm going to ruin you!"

"Easy, Harold," Administrator Mays cautions, placing a restraining hand on the surgeon's shoulder. His gaze darts to Raffi. "Dr. Sarkissian, please come with us to my office."

Despite Flint's influence with administration, Raffi stands his ground, and answers sharply. "What for?"

Flint roars back. "To cut off your balls, that's what!"

The nurses and aides stand frozen in place, witnessing the drama unfold. Even Flo turns from her screen.

"To my office!" Mays gestures Flint toward the elevator and Raffi follows. On entering the executive offices, Mays walks directly to his desk, grabs the front page of the *Post* picturing Senator Davis, and holds it in front of Raffi. "Dr. Sarkissian, if you're responsible for this article, you put our medical center's reputation at great risk."

"Yeah!" Flint growls, staring at Raffi. "Where else would Wolfe come up with that information? Only from you."

Raffi stands unmoved. *Am I responsible? Not exactly.* Since Wolfe didn't name his source, Raffi remains silent, given the anger facing him.

Mays tosses the newspaper on his desk. "With the release of these new pictures showing the senator appearing vital, the hospital is forced to permit reporters to interview him. If this investigation proves—"

"God dammit," Flint interrupts, pointing to Raffi. "No question he's the culprit. Kick the son of a bitch off staff!"

Mays replies in a matter-of-fact tone. "We can't do that, Harold. We have staff by-laws and rules we need to follow."

Flint's eyes bulge, his arms swing wildly. "Fuck the rules! I want him out immediately!"

Raffi continues with a firm stance, glaring at Flint. "I didn't take those pictures nor did I write the article. My hands are clean. If I were you, Harold, I'd be more concerned about explaining the senator's incredible recovery to the judge!"

Flint's face turns beet red. His stare pierces through Raffi like an arrow. "I know your scheme! You're undermining me to take over my practice! Is that what you're doing?"

"I don't want—"

The ring of Mays' phone brings the heated argument to a halt. The administrator holds the receiver to his ear, listens for a moment and turns a ghostly white. Ending the call, he drops into his chair and stares at the two surgeons before him. "Gold, our hospital attorney, just received a call from the district attorney. The judge presiding over the senator's court case has ordered the Chairman of Columbia University's Department of Neurology to examine him."

"I can't take any more of this shit!" Flint shouts, turning to leave when a knock on the door stops him.

The assistant administrator enters, his hair disheveled, his expression worn, and faces Mays. "Calls are pouring in from loads of our charitable donors! They don't like what they're hearing."

Mays throws the assistant a pitiful scowl and rises from his desk, exchanging glances with Flint and Raffi. "Gentlemen, before Columbia's Chief of Neurology examines Senator Davis, I propose we all ride up to the penthouse and visit our most popular patient together. Don't argue, Harold, Raffi is the admitting doctor."

~ * ~

Raffi rides the elevator to the penthouse floor with the two men; the consequences will be dire once the senator's good health is confirmed. His professional credibility is rapidly running down the drain like dirty bath water.

As they approach the senator's room, Mays flashes his ID and instructs the security guard sitting outside the door. "No one is to enter the senator's room while we're inside. That includes nursing, pharmacy and food service. No one, understand?"

The guard nods, and returns to reading his magazine.

Mays knocks on the door, and without hesitation, enters the room with the entourage following. Before them sits Senator Olin Davis lounging in a recliner, his legs outstretched, watching TV. He's wearing a plaid flannel bathrobe and hospital scuffs. A couple of days' of unshaven whiskers appear on his face.

Scowling, he turns toward his unexpected visitors. "What the hell is going on, Harold? You promised I'd be protected!"

Mays looks from Flint to Davis and breaks in. "Senator, as administrator of the hospital, I must inform you that the chief neurologist from Columbia University's Medical Center is scheduled to examine you tomorrow. The examination is ordered by the DA."

The senator's widened eyes focus on Flint. "You said I'd be safe here, Harold."

Flint doesn't answer, dropping his gaze to the floor.

Davis's cheeks flush crimson as the implication hits home. "Hell! No one's going to touch me! What's happened to doctor-patient privacy, Harold? Tell them!"

Flint shakes his head, avoiding face contact. "Olin, there's nothing I can do about it. It's court ordered."

Davis angrily snaps the back of his recliner to the upright position and thrusts forward. "I'm a sick man! No court has the right to order me to do anything."

Mays cuts him off. "You don't look sick, Senator, and you will have that exam."

Davis realizes Flint isn't coming to his defense. He bolts up from the chair and pokes a finger into the administrator's chest. "I've crushed bigger men than you, Mays. There will be no examination!"

In his wildest dreams, Raffi could never have imagined a more vividly evolving scene. Here stands a powerful US senator and a highly respected surgeon. Two influential men, destined to be destroyed by the truth.

Suddenly, Davis stumbles backward and grips the arm of the recliner. His entire body shakes with tremors as he rocks back and forth. "Oh, shit! The pain, the pain!" he cries, holding his hands to his head. He falls into his chair, shaking and moaning. His coloring goes from red to white.

Mays and Flint freeze, looking at each other. Mays asks, "Is he faking?"

Raffi immediately rushes to the senator's side as the man's eyes roll back, showing only the whites. *Nobody could be that good an actor.* "Harold, help me get him into bed."

Both men struggle to raise Davis, who continues to twitch and shake, and finally drag him onto the mattress of the hospital bed.

Flint's eyes bulge with fear as he stares down at the senator's shaking body. "Shit! Olin, can you hear me?"

The senator continues convulsing, and Raffi slips a hand under his neck, flexing the head forward. He feels the stiff resistance of nuchal rigidity, confirming a stroke. The senator's knee begins to bend, the classic sign of Brudzinski Reflex. "He's having a stroke and going into a coma," Raffi loudly announces.

Mays begs, his voice shaky. "Do something, Harold."

Flint leans against the bed, his expression one of incredible disbelief. "There's nothing we can do but wait. If he stays in coma, he's a goner."

Panicked, Raffi shouts, "There's a crash cart in the hall!"

Flint doesn't move. Raffi rushes out to grab it.

Mays pleads with Flint. "Isn't there anything you can do?"

"No, he's too far gone. Coma following a stroke spells death." He pauses, giving the administrator a steely-eyed look. "If the press learns the senator did have a stroke, won't that be the proof Manhattan Medical needs?"

Raffi returns to the room, sick at hearing Flint's words. "There's no airway tube in the cart!"

Flint stands composed, witnessing the senator in distress without placing a helpful hand. Smacking his lips, he states, "Too late, he's finished."

Raffi doesn't give up, still working to revive the senator. "Call for the code, Harold. He needs an airway. Maybe we can save him."

Flint doesn't move.

Raffi mumbles to himself. *If he treats a friend like this, I feel safer as an enemy.* He struggles to place a plastic oxygen mask over the senator's face, and lets out a yell. "Harold, I said to put out a call for Code Blue."

Flint finally picks up the phone and calls, but out of the corner of his eye, Raffi notices the surgeon presses a finger on the disconnect button. He waits to hear the Code blare over the intercom, but it never comes as Davis slips further away.

Flint hangs up and turns to Mays. "There's nothing else we can do."

Precious minutes are passing and still no Code Blue announcement. "Call the operator again, Harold! The Code didn't come through!"

Flint dials again, asking for the Code.

This time the announcement finally rings from the intercom, minutes too late.

Flint stands by with a smirk on his face watching Raffi intent on pushing the oxygen. He clears his throat and announces, "Mr. Mays, I believe we've just solved Manhattan Medical's legal problem."

# *Thirty*

Raffi dodges a shooting bullet when the head of Columbia Neurology confirms Senator Olin Davis has indeed suffered a cerebral hemorrhage. With the senator comatose at death's door, the DA promptly issues a statement cancelling the homicide trial.

Ironically, although the senator's stroke saves Manhattan Medical's credibility, it reflects poorly on Wolfe's journalistic reliability—not that Raffi has heard from the reporter. He still faces his own problems—Tommie Jackson's impending civil rights case as well as his professional future. He spends Saturday with his mom and David, going to dinner to celebrate Ani's birthday—it isn't the time to bring up bad news. Sunday, he and Lorig discuss various possibilities, but then decide to forget their troubles and go to the movies.

He rises early Monday morning. Over the weekend, Mays leaves word on the answering machine asking to meet with him as soon as possible. He suspects the hospital administrator wants to discuss the senator's on again, off again stroke and its uncertain effect on the hospital's reputation. With that in mind, he will stand his ground and insist the scheme is Flint's doing.

He calls Mays at 9 o'clock and by 9:30 rides the elevator to the executive suite where the receptionist ushers him quickly into the administrator's office. On entering, Raffi's greeted with a warm welcome by Mays who rises from his desk, shakes his hand, and offers him a chair beside the desk. Raffi guesses the discussion will focus on the senator's "medical problem."

Mays takes his seat behind the desk, gesturing for Raffi to be seated. "Glad you could make it this morning, Dr. Sarkissian. Hospital administration considers you a strong asset to this institution."

*They do? This is not what I expected.*

"To encourage you to remain on staff, we are offering six months' rent-free office space located in the Medical Arts Building close to the hospital."

The proposal takes Raffi by surprise. "But Flint—"

The administrator continues, waving Raffi's words away. "We realize many of Flint's referring physicians may not want to send you cases since the split. But between cases from the emergency room and our younger doctors, you should do quite well."

"Thank you." Raffi tries to regain his composure and gives Mays a questioning look. "I'd like to have a few days to think it over, Mr. Mays."

The administrator holds his hands out, palms up. "What's to think about?"

Raffi rubs his chin. He and Lorig had discussed many different outcomes yesterday, but this hadn't been one of them. "This may sound corny but there's a special person in my life I need to talk to."

Mays smiles like a benevolent parent. "By all means. If you take our offer, we want you to feel convinced it's right for you."

Thoughts scatter through Raffi's brain. Wherever he opens a practice, he'll face the same costs. Malpractice insurance, rent, receptionist, nursing assistant. At least he's known at Manhattan Medical, which gives him an edge. "I'd like to see the office first, Mr. Mays, and I'll get back to you."

"Fine," Mays nods. "But there is something else."

Raffi cringes inwardly. Here comes the hook.

"Our hospital attorney, Mr. Gold, raised a question you might have to face at the Jackson trial. Why wasn't a senior attending called in on the Jackson boy?"

"I'm glad you asked. It's no secret that we're short-staffed with senior attendings. That's why Jeremy had to manage without one." Raffi could say more but doesn't. Although he has continually asked for additional senior surgeons to be available, no one in administration has done anything about it.

Mays replies with a frown. "I'll have to look into that, but I won't hold you any longer. Get back to me after you've seen the office."

Raffi rises to leave. Is the hospital gifting him office space to cover up for his multiple unanswered requests for more senior staff coverage? Jeremy would have been covered and not face the situation he's in.

As Raffi prepares to leave, Mays asks, "Are you planning to attend Senator Davis's funeral in Washington?"

It never crossed Raffi's mind to attend. Flint would have a coronary. "I haven't considered it."

Mays rises, leaning on the desk. "A word of advice. We feel it would be good PR to be seen at the memorial and burial service."

"Why?" Raffi questions.

"To confirm how concerned the hospital is over the senator's death. You realize he was well respected in Congress and the press will play it up. We want to leave the public with a positive image about the hospital."

Of course the request is politically driven. Acknowledging the senator's death is of lesser concern than the hospital's reputation. "When is the funeral?"

"The day after tomorrow."

"Tell Mr. Gold I'll be there," Raffi replies, his hand on the knob.

"Thank you, Dr. Sarkissian, and thanks for coming."

Riding the elevator, conflicting thoughts run through Raffi's mind. Flint is sure to be at the service, and it's possible an ugly confrontation might ensue. By the time the doors open, he has the solution. Lorig will accompany him as a buffer. More than ever, he needs her.

~ * ~

Raffi, with Lorig at his side, speeds along I-95 past Baltimore, heading to Washington in the Lexus he can still afford. He discusses the pros and cons of accepting the hospital's offer, and is pleased she agrees he should. But the raging question he wants to ask has to wait. This is not the time or place to pop a proposal of marriage. While reasonably certain she cares for him, blind faith and crushing disappointment are legendary companions, and he can't take that chance. He'll wait for the right moment.

As he drives, he shoots her a glance. Dressed in a fitted black skirt and suit jacket, her hair in a bun, she's class personified.

She teasingly kisses his fingers, and then leans across the console to kiss his cheek. "That's all you get—for now."

With the help of the GPS, they finally arrive at the National Cathedral. Due to the large number of mourners, they have to drive a distance to find space in a parking lot which leads to a longer than expected walk to the church. Under the watchful eyes of uniformed police, they follow the parade of mourners into the cathedral and sit in the next to last pew, far removed from the altar.

The service begins with the majestic sound of the pipe organ followed by a large choir rendering the hymn, "Oh God, Our Help in Ages Past." Given the senator's extramarital affairs and pay-for-play politics, Raffi isn't quite sure if Davis deserves all the pomp and circumstance.

The pastor gives the opening homily and then introduces two of the senator's congressional colleagues to speak. When they finish, he invites Harold Flint as the senator's intimate friend.

Raffi holds Lorig's hand as Flint strides to the altar and approaches the podium. The man's head of full, white hair glistens in the beam of light directed on the speaker's stand. His face appears ten years younger, possibly due to an expert makeup job.

Flint clears his throat, places his hands on the pedestal stand and looks into the audience. "My friendship with the senator stems back to our early days at Yale. When he decided to run for political office, I was at his side, assisting any way I could." He continues to praise Davis's trustworthy character, his dedication in serving his country, both as a war veteran and statesman, and concludes with a flourish of his arms. "In his long years of service, my dear friend never lost sight of his purpose—his devotion to the American people."

A TV camera spots the senator's wife on the large screen placed in view of the audience. An attractive matronly woman dressed in a black tailored suit, she sits stoically in the first pew, her hands crossed on her lap. Raffi wonders what she's thinking, considering her husband's many years of chronic infidelity.

With Flint's tribute concluded, the organ pipes fill the voluminous cathedral with the opening chords to "Amazing Grace." The choir sings a stirring rendition, finally ending the service.

Lorig and Raffi wait as the senator's family, followed by pall bearers carrying the casket, walk out of the building. They're one of the first to pass outside the doors, only to face a host of clicking cameras.

A reporter recognizes Raffi and pushes a mike toward him. "Dr. Sarkissian, what could you tell us about the confusion over the senator's illness?"

Raffi keeps a firm hold on Lorig's hand. "What confusion? Senator Davis suffered a stroke—period."

Once in their car, they follow the procession stretching over a quarter of a mile. Motorcycle police lead the way, straddling the parade of automobiles and the hearse right up to the front gates of Arlington Cemetery.

Raffi and Lorig remain in the car while the hearse, followed by the limousine holding the family, pulls up to the burial plot. In the distance, he sees the canopy covering the gravesite as Mrs. Davis and loved ones walk the path leading to the site.

"Why are we waiting?" Lorig asks, hesitating to unbuckle her seatbelt.

Raffi scans the grounds for white hair. "Just checking to stay clear of Flint."

"Sooner or later you two will have to deal with each other."

"You're right," he answers, shaking his head. "Let's go."

The moment they leave the car, the same reporter, followed by several others, appears, poking a microphone at him, asking a barrage of questions. "Could you comment about the senator's health when he first reached the hospital, Doctor? What about Dr. Flint? Was he aware of the senator's condition?"

Raffi forges straight ahead, gripping Lorig's hand without responding.

A reporter walks up to Lorig, thrusting a microphone in her face. "Could you please give us your name, miss?"

Raffi pulls her aside, astounded at the number of media present as they move closer to the gravesite. He keeps apologizing, "Excuse me, please move," as they make their way through the crowd. The media thins out as the pastor begins reading from the prayer book.

Lorig abruptly comes to a halt and points ahead. "Isn't that Traci Doss standing with Dr. Flint?"

Raffi takes a minute to search the distance. "It sure is." Traci looks sexy even in mourning clothes. The elegant black full-skirted dress lends her a classy image, and the lacy wide brimmed hat shades her beautiful face. But Lorig has something more that can't be bought.

He fidgets, realizing Traci's caught sight of him. Now he has to deal with her as well as Flint.

Lorig whispers. "Look, Dr. Flint sees you. There's no way you're going to avoid him now. You should make the first move—by taking the job at the hospital, you've won."

He nudges Lorig. "You're right. But after the service, do you mind waiting in the car? Who knows, fists might fly and I don't want you involved."

Her voice hitches. "Are you sure?"

He doesn't want to talk to Flint and Traci in front of Lorig—what they have to say won't be pretty—so he hands her the keys. "I won't be long, just a few minutes."

At the conclusion of the pastor's eulogy, Lorig squeezes his hand and retreats from the crowd as people wander along walkways toward their vehicles.

Raffi walks up to Flint and Traci, breaking into their conversation. "Excuse me. Harold, I'd like to talk to you." He has to soothe things over if he's to continue at Manhattan Medical.

Flint's mouth contorts into a sneer. Before he's able to speak, Traci interrupts. "Raffi! I hoped to see you here."

Raffi's gaze focuses on Flint—he'll do as Lorig suggested—offer the olive branch, and then leave. "It's good to see you too, Traci, but I have to speak to Harold."

Traci's lips curl into a pout. "Let's not talk business now." Her voice softens. "Harold, could you please spare me a few minutes with Raffi?"

Flint ignores her request, pointing a finger at the young surgeon. "You son of a bitch! If you stay at Manhattan Medical, you better not cross my path!"

Raffi catches flashes from cameras snapping photos of Flint's angry gestures and speaks without rancor. "I'm not here to argue, Harold."

Traci cuts him off. "Enough of that!" She links arms with Raffi, leading him away from the crowd to a secluded area under an oak tree, speaking softly into his ear. "Please Raffi, we need time together to work things out. I miss you."

Raffi lowers his head. "I'm sorry, Traci, that's not going to happen."

She throws her arms around him and kisses him on the lips. "I still think about how good we were together that weekend."

"This isn't a good idea," he mutters, attempting to pull away.

She holds onto him, ignoring people walking by, glancing at them. Her voice is breathy, determined. "How can you refuse me?"

He steps away, aware of people passing by. "Things are different now. You know I'm serious with someone."

Traci's lips tighten and she flips the brim of her hat back in anger. "Oh, you mean that sweet little school teacher?"

"Understand, Traci. You and I live in two different worlds." His voice lowers. "I never meant to hurt you. We're still friends, right?"

"Friends!" Her eyes flash anger. "You honestly believe the crap about different worlds? You looked damned comfortable in my world that weekend in Palm Beach."

He takes a long, painful look at her. The poor little rich girl demanding her share of happiness. He turns toward the sound of snapping cameras as reporters press close, taking in the unfolding drama for the next day's shiny sheets' headlines.

Before Raffi can say anything, Flint approaches, his face flushed in anger. He's not ready to make peace as Raffi hoped. "Dump this guy, Traci. He's a loser."

Raffi catches Lorig standing close by and wonders how long she's been watching. She covers her mouth with her fingers, turns and runs away. "Lorig, wait! I can explain!"

Flint chuckles cruelly. "Don't even try."

Raffi dashes after her, leaving Traci behind, standing with her hands on her hips.

"Lorig, it's not what you think!" Raffi shouts, but she keeps running. He elbows his way through clusters of mourners until he reaches the car where he finds her leaning against the fender, crying. He moves to her side and holds her, raising her chin. "She means nothing to me."

Lorig looks up at him, tears clouding her eyes. "I'm not to believe what I just saw?"

Dammit, he has to convince her. "What you saw was Traci's show, not mine. Honest, hon, there's nothing between me and that woman."

She gazes into his eyes, searching for the truth. "I want to believe you, but how can I? She has her grip on you."

He wraps his arms around her and kisses her. "Believe me when I say I love you."

The clicking of cameras catches his attention as they stand in each other's arms. He quickly turns to shield Lorig but the sporadic flashes of cameras tell him those images will soon be fodder for the gossip columns.

"Let's get out of here," he says, pulling away to open the car door.

They travel in silence but after ten minutes into the drive, he reaches across the console and takes her hand. "Don't be surprised if your students see you in the paper tomorrow. I'm afraid you're a celebrity now."

# Thirty-one

With Raffi's residency over, Jeremy easily slips into the role of chief surgical resident at Manhattan Medical, quickly gaining the approval of staff surgeons who specifically ask him to assist on their cases. Busy with the heavy surgical load, Jeremy favors working with certain surgeons more than others. At the bottom of his priority list is Harold Flint, and he shudders each time he's called to operate with the man.

The Monday after Davis' memorial service, Flint walks into the operating room, his ruddy complexion signaling signs of alcoholism. This time the senior surgeon is prompt, and Jeremy prays the case will go smoothly. With Flint's social agenda, Jeremy purposely scheduled the first case for midmorning to give him time to recover from any weekend binge.

From experience, Jeremy knows of Flint's laxity in reviewing pre-op data and has already performed that task. He addresses the senior surgeon as the scrub nurse gloves him. "Dr. Flint, this sixty-two-year-old gentleman's scheduled to undergo a laparoscopic cholecystectomy, and his labs are in order."

The lines on Flint's forehead deepen and he holds up his gloved hand. "God dammit, son! I know my own patients!"

Jeremy bites his lip. "Yes, sir. Just to remind you, he's experienced multiple gallbladder attacks which can cause severe scarring." Jeremy worries Flint's careless moves might be problematic in this case. If he doesn't properly identify the cystic artery and duct, clipping them before removing the gallbladder, a surgical nightmare will follow.

As anticipated, Jeremy stands across from Flint at the OR table watching him search for the artery lost in a maze of adhesions. The room is eerily quiet as the surgical team waits. Jeremy catches the stony glare from Gail, the anesthesiologist, who nods to the young surgeon, pleading for him to take control.

After twenty minutes of struggle, Jeremy breaks the silence. "Dr. Flint, can I help find the artery?"

The senior surgeon ignores him, continuing to probe the surgical site with a long pointed dissector, magnified on the television screen and witnessed by all.

Moisture forms on Jeremy's brow, studying Flint's pointless moves. He speaks again. "Can I help, Dr. Flint?" Fearful Flint will injure the common bile duct, he places a hand on the elder surgeon's wrist. "I think I see it, let me try."

Flint's eyes widen over his mask, but he finally hands the dissector to his assistant.

Jeremy works cautiously to find the surgical landmarks. Without comment, he begins dissecting above the scarred area, peeling the adhesions from known areas to the unknown. With all eyes focused on the surgical field visualized on the television screen, Jeremy continues dissecting until he identifies both the cystic artery and duct. He clips the artery and then cuts the vessel, freeing the duct. Everyone in the room sighs in relief, aware Jeremy saved the day by preventing Flint's dangerous probing.

With all the vital structures identified and secured, Flint finally growls, "I'll take over now."

Jeremy relinquishes the instruments to Flint who dissects the gallbladder away from the liver, removing it from the abdomen. With the procedure completed, Jeremy steps away, his nerves frayed. He enters the doctor's lounge, tears off his mask and splashes cold water on his face, realizing how close he came to witnessing a horrific event. He knows one day something serious is going to happen, and he hopes it won't be on his watch.

He has just enough time before the next case to fill a cup of strong coffee when Raffi comes into the lounge—gray scrubs, thick dark hair recently cut short, clean-shaven. Jeremy worried for his friend during the Flint blow-up, and is glad to see Raffi has weathered the storm. "Yo' brother, you got a case?"

Raffi heads to the coffee urn—the doctors' life-blood. "Have a few minutes before I meet with Administrator Mays. What's up?"

Jeremy moves to his side, lowering his voice. "I can't take this shit anymore. Operating with Flint's a nightmare. Mays has to be warned."

Raffi blows on the hot brew in his Styrofoam cup. "You know how many times we've discussed this? Now that I've split from the bastard, whatever I say will sound like sour grapes."

Jeremy takes one last swallow of coffee and flips his empty cup into the trash can. "Hey man, somebody has to say something. That guy is dangerous."

Raffi shrugs his shoulder. "Administration is in Flint's pocket. With all the uninsured patients flooding the ER, the hospital is losing money. Without Flint's wealthy donors, Manhattan Medical would be bankrupt."

Jeremy smirks. "So you're falling for that bullshit? Flint shouldn't be operating without supervision and meanwhile the training staff needs more senior staff attendings to cover the residents for night and weekend call." He throws Raffi a hard glare. "Look, you know we're short of help. How do you think we both got sucked into the Jackson lawsuit? I don't mind telling that to the judge."

Raffi agrees. "You're right, but it's not like we haven't tried."

Jeremy lets out an exasperated huff. "Nothing's gonna change around here." He places a friendly pat on Raffi's shoulder and leaves the lounge to get back to work. If the Davis scare hasn't shaken the higher-ups, then nothing will change the politics of medicine at Manhattan Medical.

~ * ~

The next morning Raffi's mission is to rent and furnish his new office. Jeremy's comments bothered him all night, but he knows from experience, nothing will change. He quickly shaves, dresses, tosses down his usual glass of orange juice and heads for the hospital. As he walks the street, his thoughts turn to a more positive vein. Even after the incident with Traci at the senator's funeral, Lorig is still committed to him. He whistles as the crisp morning breeze brushes his face, determined to have a successful practice and future at Manhattan Medical.

He enters the hospital, rides the elevator to the surgical floor, and searches for Nurse Supervisor Martin, who keeps abreast of all activities in the department. He spots her at the reception desk.

She looks up from her chart as he approaches, giving him a nod. "Good morning, Doctor. Need to schedule a case?"

"Not today," Raffi replies, "but maybe you could help. I need to hire a nurse for my new office. Is there anyone you recommend?"

The nursing supervisor returns a broad smile from her seated position behind the desk. "Why yes, Doctor. Mary Brewster works the night shift in ICU. She told me she's looking for a day job with no weekends."

"Thanks, Flo. I know her, she's top notch. Could you please ask if she's interested?"

"Sure thing, Doctor. I'll speak to her tonight."

As Raffi turns to leave, Jeremy approaches in mint green scrubs. "You're my ER attending today, pal." He claps a hand on Raffi's shoulder. "Are you here scheduling a case?"

Raffi groans, touching his forehead. "Geez, I completely forgot I'm on call. Can you fill in for me? I'm heading to the medical supply house to order equipment for the new office. I shouldn't be long, so keep things quiet until I get back."

Jeremy grins. "No problem, man. Make sure to say a good word for me when my residency is done—I'd like to be in at the Medical Arts Building."

"Sure thing, pal. We'll share an office." Raffi respects Jeremy's work ethic, and they get along well as a team.

A young intern fumbling to tie his face mask approaches. "Dr. Jenkins, which room do I scrub in?"

"Room Four," Jeremy replies. "You're scheduled to assist with the colon resection."

The intern nods and heads down the corridor.

Jeremy's name blares over the intercom requesting that he return to OR room six. He winks at Raffi. "I meant to ask earlier. Who is the cute chick with you at Senator Davis's funeral?"

Raffi grins. "Lorig—the teacher I told you about. We've been seeing more of each other lately."

"If she's so special, why don't we go out some night? I'm sure Rachel would love to meet her."

"You pick the time and place. A night out sounds great."

"I'll get back to you," Jeremy replies, hustling down the hall.

An exciting thought quickly flashes in Raffi's mind. The moment he can afford it, he'll ask Jeremy to be his future partner in practice.

~ * ~

It's two o'clock when Jeremy walks out of operating room six. His team finished the last scheduled case with a second year resident closing the abdomen. He heads to the reception desk to check his messages before making rounds on the next day's surgical cases when his cell phone rings.

"It's Rachel, Jeremy. I need your help!"

He hears panic in her voice. "Hey, you okay?"

"It's not me. It's about my friend, Twila Barnett. Jeremy, she's in big trouble and needs your help."

He comes to a halt, phone to his ear. "Who's Twila Barnett?"

"Don't you remember? She's Reverend Sanders' girlfriend. We work out at the same gym."

Jeremy recalls Rachel commenting the reverend had a mistress. She was the beauty at the wedding reception in Rosa Parks Hall who walked out of the men's room right before the good reverend. "What kind of trouble is she in?"

Rachel's cries jump an octave. "Sanders beat her bad! She's all bloody, in serious shape."

"Honey, keep it together. Take her to an emergency room."

"She won't go, that's why she called me. She knows you're a doctor. You should see what he did to her! She's soaked through a whole roll of paper towels with the cut on her head."

"This makes no sense, Rachel. Call nine-one-one and get her to the nearest hospital."

"She won't go to any hospital in Harlem. With Sanders' political connections, she's afraid what his henchmen will do if she tells anyone he beat her."

*That son of a bitch Sanders!* He clenches the phone and asks, "What does she want?"

"She asked me to drive her to Manhattan Medical so you can examine her with no questions asked. Wants to avoid any publicity."

Jeremy heaves a desperate sigh. "Rachel, how could you put me in this position? You know my problems with the reverend."

"I do and I'm sorry, but you should see how horrible she looks. Please, honey, I know I can count on you."

Jeremy searches his brain for other options he could suggest, but finds none. The woman needs to be seen at an acute care facility.

"Okay, Rach, I'll see her. When did this happen?"

"Not even an hour ago."

Jeremy shakes his head, realizing he has no way out. "You owe me, Rachel. Get her to the ER and ask for me."

He hears the smack of her lips throwing a kiss. "Love you, sugar," she says.

Within the hour, Jeremy hears his name paged for the ER and sprints to the elevator. With the Jackson lawsuit hovering over his head, he doesn't need another run-in with the reverend. As soon as Twila's patched up, he'll transfer her to the medical service.

He enters the brightly lit ER, spotting Rachel pacing outside a curtained stall and moves toward her.

She stops, relief clear on her pretty face and puts her hand on his forearm with a squeeze. "She's really hurting, Jeremy."

He slips through the drapes and faces the same attractive woman at the wedding reception. A nurse at the bedside is busy taking Twila's blood pressure.

The nurse releases the cuff and looks up at Jeremy. "Her pressure's okay but her pulse is racing at ninety-eight, Doctor. I cleaned her up so you could see the injury."

Jeremy studies Twila's swollen face and heavily bruised left eye. Even with her injuries, her high cheekbones and long dark hair remind him of the beautiful Halle Berry. She can't be more than twenty-five. *What the hell is Sanders doing involved with such a young thing?*

He takes his stethoscope from around his neck and places it on her belly. She releases a soft moan. A press on the upper abdomen produces a more excruciating cry.

He looks to the nurse. "Let's get moving. I need STAT labs and a CT scan of the head and abdomen."

Exiting the stall, he faces a wide-eyed Rachel. "Looks like she has internal injuries and might need surgery."

Fear sparks her eyes and she grabs his arm again. "Jeremy, her life is in danger! She needs protection, so you must be the one to operate."

Jeremy frowns, uncomfortable getting involved with anyone connected to the reverend. "Raffi's my attending today. She'll be safe with him, though he won't be happy about this either."

Rachel bites her lip, worry on her face. "As long as word doesn't get out in the streets. Who knows what his hoods will do to her?"

Jeremy lets out a relenting sigh. "I'll call Raffi now. Twila's scared, Rach, so stay with her until I come back."

Rachel enters the cubicle to comfort Twila and Jeremy dials Raffi who quickly answers. "Man, you're not going to believe who we're taking to surgery today."

"What's up?" Raffi asks.

"The good Reverend Sanders just beat up his mistress and I think she's bleeding internally." Jeremy waits for Raffi's response but none is forthcoming. "Hey man, did you hear what I said?"

Raffi's voice drops. "Yeah, but I wish I hadn't."

# *Thirty-two*

Raffi leaves the medical supply house and grabs a cab back to Manhattan Medical. Jeremy calls again, telling him Twila Barnett's pressure is dropping so he's rushing her to surgery. The ultrasound study shows abnormal fluid collection below her liver, which he suspects to be blood from internal bleeding.

The abdomen is open when Raffi enters the OR. "She has a tear in the liver," Jeremy announces.

With arms still dripping water, Raffi approaches the OR table, surveying the open wound. "The portal triad, was it injured?"

Without looking up from the operative field, Jeremy replies, "Haven't checked yet, but I've done a Pringle maneuver. I think the bleeding's slowed down."

Raffi smiles inwardly. Jeremy has trained well. Compressing the portal triad will stop any arterial bleeding from the injured organ.

The intern assisting Jeremy steps aside as Raffi takes his place at the table. Jeremy has already packed the liver with lap pads to tamp the bleeding from the torn surface.

The two surgeons focus intently on exploring the abdomen, ruling out any other injuries. None are found. After cauterizing, clamping, suturing and debriding the fragmented segment of the liver, bleeding is controlled.

"Slick job, Jeremy," Raffi comments as they leave the operating room. "You did good."

Jeremy lets out a caustic laugh. "No pressure like operating on the lover of the man who's suing you." They both chuckle and head to the surgical lounge where Rachel is waiting, anxiously clasping her hands.

She jumps up as they enter. "Is she all right?"

Jeremy tears off his mask, his green scrubs stained with blood. "She's not out of the woods yet and needs close watching. She might bleed again or develop a bile collection that could get infected."

Sudden tears fill Rachel's eyes. "I never realized—"

Raffi places a comforting hand on her shoulder. "You saved her life, Rachel. Did she say what happened?"

"I asked, but she wouldn't tell me at first. Then when her pain got so bad, she finally admitted Sanders did it."

"Did she say why?"

Rachel takes a tissue from her pocket and blows her nose. "The usual. He promised to divorce his wife but after two years when it still hasn't happened, she confronted him, threatening to expose their relationship."

Jeremy nods sympathetically. "So she pushed his button so hard, he exploded?"

Rachel's eyes narrow as she slips the tissue back into her pocket. "He sure did! Put his fist right into her face."

Raffi presses on. "From all her injuries, he must have done more than that. What about her belly?"

Rachel shakes her head, anxious to tell the complete story. "After he socks her, she throws a heavy ashtray at him and nails him on the forehead. He gets so mad, he starts to come on to her with the meanest look, ready to belt her again. That's when she grabs a kitchen knife lying on the counter to fend him off."

Jeremy runs his fingers through his hair, shocked at the violence. "Holy shit!"

Rachel closes her eyes, pausing for a moment. "That's why he slammed her belly with a kitchen chair."

Raffi rubs his chin, listening. "That explains the fractured liver."

Jeremy looks to Raffi. "Sanders' face must have taken a beating. He better get himself a good cosmetic makeover to hide the bruises. With only two weeks before the election, he still has campaigning to do."

Raffi answers with a raised eyebrow. "That won't be a problem. He's got the congressional seat locked up unless—"

Jeremy throws him a questioning look. "Unless what?"

"Unless Twila Barnett leaks what happened to the press."

~ * ~

Raffi exits the hospital elevator just as Adam Wolfe heads toward him. It's 8:30 the following morning, and Twila Barnett is his only patient. After quick rounds with Jeremy's team, he's left with two pressing needs: breakfast and waiting for equipment deliveries to his office.

Adam appears tidier than usual. His beard is groomed to a fuzz, his pants creased. "Morning, Doc. I hoped to catch you here."

Raffi picks up on the reporter's somber demeanor. They hadn't talked since the Davis stroke fiasco. "What's up, Adam? It can't be a social call this early."

"You're right," Adam agrees. "Could you spare some time for a quiet chat?"

Raffi doesn't want to hear any more negative news, but relents. Wolfe's breaking news article on the senator ended up like a sideshow. "Join me, just heading to the dining room for breakfast. My treat."

They fill their trays, and after finding a quiet corner of the cafeteria, Raffi faces Wolf from across the table. "Adam, what're you sniffing for today?"

"I guess that's fair." Wolfe takes a bite of his toast, wiping the jam from his mouth. "I believe you just operated on Twila Barnett, Sanders' *secret* mistress."

"You don't miss a trick, do you?"

Wolfe smirks with a shrug. "That's what an investigative reporter does."

Raffi puts down his coffee cup. "Are you asking about her medical condition? You know I can't release anything that isn't public record."

"What's the story? The word is she got beat up real bad."

"Look Adam, if you want to know, you'll have to ask her yourself."

"When do you think I can talk to her?"

"When she's physically and mentally prepared, but only if she agrees."

Wolfe puts down his cup and tips back in his chair. "If I confirm what my sources tell me, I'll have a dynamite story."

"Don't you ever sleep, Adam?"

"Not when I have a mission."

Raffi turns serious. "Speaking of missions, have you learned anything more about Jasmine Battia? She hasn't come into the ER again, so hopefully no more attempts on her life."

"Yeah, the case is still languishing, bound by that presidential gag order. It doesn't pay to be a whistleblower. No way will the FBI hire her back."

Annoyed, Raffi stabs at his bacon. "It's typical bureaucratic bullshit. Claiming she risked national security? That's a cover, if there ever was one." His brow deepens with concern. "She's scared, Adam. It must be hell being a target."

Wolfe wipes his mouth, and tosses the napkin on his empty plate. "At least she's alive. Nancy Wood and the senator are dead. The Turkish lobby dodged a bullet when those two people bit the dust."

Raffi drinks the last of his coffee, then shoves his tray away. "Besides all this international shit, I still have to face Reverend Sanders in court. Keeps me up at night."

"Hang in there, buddy, and thanks for breakfast." Wolfe pushes his chair back and gets up to leave, then stops. "Have you spoken to Traci lately?"

"Not since the senator's burial."

Wolfe leans his hands on the table, lowering his voice. "Don't want to send up any warning flares, but she's heading for trouble."

Raffi picks up his tray and says, "Look Adam, she's a big girl."

Wolfe remains standing at the table, waiting to alert Raffi on the facts. "Since returning from Europe, she's been hitting the club circuit, partying. I caught a glimpse of her the other night at the Marquis Club and she didn't look good. Slurred her speech and all."

"You think she's on drugs?"

Adam brushes his chin, looking concerned. "Most likely. She was with this guy, a typical wanabee rock star who keeps company with big time pushers."

Raffi's heart drops, but he can't get sucked in again with her erratic behavior. "Sorry to hear that, Adam. There's nothing I can do or say about her conduct."

"Come on, she still claims you're her doctor. Talk to her. She needs help."

"Thanks for telling me, Adam. "I'll see what I can do." A shard of guilt pierces his psyche, remembering how he had turned her off. Could he be the reason for her downward spiral?

# Thirty-three

Raffi sits at the desk in his new office with a comforting satisfaction. In the past two days, he's seen four new consults, two of which are scheduled for surgery.

His nurse, Mary Brewster, a 47-year-old RN, is a well-trained graduate from a South Dakota nursing school. Her practical hands-on experience includes multiple functions like organizing the office, arranging furniture and stocking shelves with medical and surgical supplies. She also serves as receptionist, answering the phone until they get busy enough to hire a secretary.

Mary's voice suddenly comes over the intercom. "Were you expecting Adam Wolfe, Doctor? He's at my desk asking to see you."

"No, I wasn't, but send him in." Twila's interview must be the reason for the surprise visit.

Wolfe enters the office, takes a quick glance around, giving an approving nod and settles in the chair in front of the desk. "Pretty classy, Doc, and thanks for seeing me."

"Let me guess why you're here, Adam."

Wolfe grins. "You're psychic. It's common knowledge that Twila Barnett is the reverend's mistress. I'll officially break the news in my column tomorrow but first I need to interview her."

"You're ruthless! Why the interview?"

"Because I feel she's the injured party and needs to be protected."

Raffi raises an eyebrow, showing his surprise by the gruff reporter's play at concern for the victim. "But her relationship with Sanders was consensual."

"True, but men of power can be very convincing and persuasive with their promises."

"You're referring to the reverend's promise of marriage?"

"Yes, and I want to show the hypocrisy of this so-called 'man of the cloth.' He stands in front of people ranting religious and moral values, but all he wants is power—political or otherwise. I'm afraid this news is hurting Twila, not Sanders. Voters don't want to see the weakness of their leader exposed. There's a good chance Twila will be seen as the tramp, the seducer."

"Don't bullshit me with your suppositions, Adam. What you really want is a hot story." Raffi leans forward on his desk, demanding nothing but the truth from the newsman.

Adam chuckles. "That's my job, Doc. Will she see me?"

Raffi shrugs. "I already asked, and she's willing as long as Jeremy's in the room as a witness."

~ * ~

Later that day, Raffi leads Wolfe and Jeremy into Twila's hospital room. She's been transferred out of ICU an hour earlier. A single IV solution hangs from the bedpost dripping fluid into a vein. Wearing no makeup, her dark long hair spreads out on the white pillow as she dozes.

Jeremy gently touches her shoulder. "Hi, Twila, sorry to wake you, but there's someone I want you to meet. He's the reporter we talked about. Raffi and I think he can help you."

Twila, now fully awake, rubs her forehead, trying to focus. "Jeremy, I changed my mind. I don't think it's a good idea to discuss this with anyone. I'm afraid what I say might end up hurting *me*."

The reporter moves to the bedside. "Twila, I'm Adam Wolfe. If I get the story, I promise you will be seen as the injured party when I write the article. You gotta get your story out first, before Sanders' followers paint you as the wayward woman chasing after a man of the cloth. The reverend has a whole lot of influence in Harlem."

Twila studies Wolfe's face, analyzing the full weight of her decision. "I'm scared. He's hot tempered and can erupt when least expected." She touches the bruise on her cheekbone.

Raffi breaks in to offer his opinion. "Twila, it's your choice, but you have the power to expose him for the fraud he is before anyone else is hurt. You can't go back to him."

She sighs, pulling the sheet over her shoulders. "I know. Look, I'll tell you what you want as long as I see what's written before it goes into print."

Wolfe responds with an outstretched hand. "That's a promise, Twila."

Despite her bruised face, she smiles and shakes his hand in agreement. "Where do you want to start?"

~ * ~

Wolfe's expose about the reverend's abused mistress hits the front page of the *Post*, selling record copies. The photo and graphic description of Twila's injuries produce an explosive outrage, especially among women's organizations. Even Sanders' alleged promise of marriage takes a back seat to the moral indignation over physical violence. Candidates competing with Sanders for the Harlem congressional seat fuel the flames of societal outrage. The polls reflect it with the reverend's voter approval plummeting.

~ * ~

Raffi awakes to a cloudy morning and flicks on the TV remote before rising from bed. Summer has raced by and Sanders' special election results are counted. The news comes as a pleasant surprise. Reverend Sanders loses the election to a young black political science professor from New York's City College by only a slim margin.

While the news sends shock waves throughout the black community, comments by reporters show the expected mixture of joy and dissatisfaction from various groups. However, no demonstrations or violence are reported. Raffi is certain that whichever church the reverend speaks at this Sunday, the press will be sure to follow.

Raffi dresses at a leisurely pace, listening to classical music on the local NPR radio station. Beethoven's genius floats through his apartment, lifting up his mood as he fills a tall glass of orange juice to quench his thirst.

Fortunately, Twila recovered quickly after her liver surgery as well as her subsequent facial re-construction to straighten her broken nose. At his and Wolfe's insistence, a police report is filed to prevent Sanders' henchmen from stalking her again. With the story public, nothing Sanders does will remove that stain from his reputation.

On his usual walk to the hospital, Raffi's mind turns to Wolfe's comments about Traci. In the past month he's come to accept the reporter's description is on target. Traci is a drug addict. Photos of her in the scandal sheets show unbecoming glimpses of her at clubs, getting in and out of cabs, wearing dark sunglasses—most likely to hide the puffy face and circles under her sunken eyes. One photo shows her with a glazed startled expression staring into a paparazzo's camera, confirming drug use. Traci is heading for trouble, if not there already. But he's no longer her doctor, and no longer her friend.

For a moment, his gut tightens, feeling lousy writing Traci off. But how can he help? His cell phone rings and he stops walking to answer it.

"Dr. Sarkissian, Barry Gold here, the hospital attorney."

Raffi feels a pang of fear, questioning what's ahead. "Yes, Mr. Gold?"

"I'd like to meet with you at Administrator Mays' office this morning if possible."

"Certainly. When?"

"Could you come now?"

Caught off guard, Raffi hesitates. "Yes, I have no surgery—I'm already on my way into the hospital."

"Fifteen minutes OK?"

Suddenly his attention is diverted from Traci's problems. "I'll be there," Raffi replies. Apprehension follows the unexpected request and he ends the call, stepping up his pace. Whatever reason for the meeting, he wants to get it over with, the sooner the better.

Mays rises from his desk, and gestures Raffi to take a seat. "Thanks for coming on such short notice, Dr. Sarkissian."

Gold sits in a leather chair next to May's desk. The attorney's lean stature and dark frame eye glasses lend him an elder statesman appearance. But his blue eyes exude wisdom and calm that comes from years of experience. He rises, shakes Raffi's hand and gestures him to take a seat.

He levels his gaze at Raffi and clears his voice. "The court has finally set a date for the Tommie Jackson lawsuit against the hospital. You and Dr. Jeremy Jenkins will be called to testify, so you both need to be prepared."

"When will the trial begin?"

"The judge figures within two to three weeks, depending on the pace of the court calendar."

"Any idea how long it will take?"

Gold shakes his head. "Hard to predict. My associate, Devon Smith, will be the lead trial attorney defending you and the hospital. Give us a time when you can meet with Devon so he can coach you."

Raffi squelches his anger; his hands tighten on the arms of the chair. The timing couldn't be worse. Just starting his practice, he knows this burdensome interruption will prove costly in time and energy. "The medical facts are clear, Mr. Gold. Why do we have to prepare?"

The attorney lowers his glasses, his shrew eyes directed at Raffi. "Despite your sincere intentions, Doctor, a plaintiff's attorney can make any honest answer sound as though mistakes were made. You and Dr. Jenkins must be advised so you can be legally astute."

Raffi shifts restlessly, unsettled by Gold's answer. "I hope you're not telling me the hospital is going to lose, are you?"

Gold shakes his head. "No, nothing like that. But this case will not be simply about a medical issue. Reverend Sanders has publicized the incident with racist charges. The question of injustice in rationing good medical care based upon race will dominate this trial. Despite the medical facts, you need to be primed about an ugly truth—it's called racial politics."

~ * ~

It's a quarter past noon and Ani checks the antique clock on her mantle waiting for the arrival of Jasmine Battia, her luncheon guest. The woman, emotionally distraught after the shooting incident, repeatedly refused Ani's invitation, fearing to leave her apartment, and Ani worries Jasmine might not show up.

The ring of the doorbell relieves her apprehension and she rushes to welcome her guest. Jasmine stands at the entry wearing a lemon yellow dress with a matching cardigan sweater and colorful rhinestone-studded sandals. Her dark hair falls gracefully to her shoulders. Ani thinks the woman can't be much older than herself. "Welcome! I'm so glad you came."

Jasmine leans over and kisses both Ani's cheeks. "It's my pleasure. I feel as though we've been friends forever. "

Struck by the woman's openness, Ani embraces her. "Jasmine, you can feel safe with me. I will not impose on you in any way, or endanger you. Let's just share these moments together as friends."

Jasmine's voice cracks. "It's been so hard, but I'm trying my best to get over my paranoia. I worry someone's lurking in the background, watching me. That's why I remain at home most of the time." Her eyes dart around the apartment. "I feel safe here," she confides.

Ani takes her arm, leading her to the dining room table.

Jasmine gushes with delight. "Oh, Ani, your table is fit for a queen! I love the gold-trimmed dishes, the crystal goblets. It's all so welcoming."

"Thank you. I used to go antique hunting in consignment shops. Surely they're worth more today than the few dollars I spent years ago." Ani smiles, inwardly proud of the vintage bone china and silverware. She loves using these possessions whenever she hosts, bringing back memories of the old world.

She offers Jasmine a seat at the table, and pours wine in the crystal goblets, toasting their first social occasion. After watching her guest sit back in her chair, relaxed, she excuses herself to the kitchen. Within minutes she returns with a tray holding several platters.

Jasmine feasts her eyes on the banquet of food. "Ani, the *lahmajunes* look and smell delicious. They remind me of Persia. Did you make them?"

Ani places one of the round flat breads covered with chopped vegetables and ground lamb on Jasmine's plate. "Yes," she says with a chuckle. "I call them Armenian pizzas."

The two women chat as they dine and end the meal with demitasse coffee when Ani gently touches her arm. "Have you had any more threats since leaving the hospital?"

There's a prolonged silence until Jasmine replies. "Thankfully no, although I can't stop feeling I'm being watched."

Ani returns her gaze. "Have you reported this to the police?"

Jasmine shakes her head. "Why should I? They give me no protection. It seems I'm *persona non grata* until my lawsuit challenging my dismissal is cleared. And with the gag order, there's nothing I can do to protect myself."

Ani hears the unmistakable despair in her voice. The woman conscientiously performed her job by reporting the illegal Turkish payoffs and now she's treated like a traitor by the government. She has to convince Jasmine she's not alone in this battle, and speaks out firmly. "I respect what you did, Jasmine. Especially since you are an Iranian Muslim. That took a lot of guts."

Jasmine's eyes light up, her voice lowers to a whisper. "Ani, I wanted to tell you the day you visited me in the hospital. My great-grandmother was born into a Christian Armenian family."

Ani gasps, bringing a hand to her face. "You say you're not Muslim?"

Jasmine clasps her hands prayer-like, resting them on the table. "I was in my early twenties when my grandmother told me." She takes in a deep breath, her voice shaking with emotion. "At the time of the Genocide, my great-grandmother was ten years old. Her entire family was killed and she was the only one to survive because a Muslim family saved her, taking her in as one of their own."

Fascinated, Ani leans closer. "How did you learn about this?"

Jasmine opens her purse and removes a small gold cross on a chain. "Shortly before my grandmother died, she told me her mother's story and passed this on to me as a remembrance."

Her fingers fumble as she brings the cross to her lips and kisses it before returning it to her purse.

Ani reflects on how many stories like Jasmine's are out there. "In spite of this, I take it you're a practicing Muslim?"

"Yes, because my father was a Muslim. I was raised that way."

Ani's brow wrinkles with curiosity. "Did your grandmother know what happened to her family?"

Jasmine's gaze lowers, her voice falters. "My grandmother said her mother's father was conscripted into the Turkish army and marched off, never to return. Later, hundreds of bodies of young men were found in open ditches, their flesh preyed on by animals." She bows her head, and then continues. "Stories circulated that these young Armenian men were used as slave labor to build the government's railroad and then done away with."

Ani gently places a hand on Jasmine's. "What happened to the rest of her family?"

Jasmine's eyes well with tears. "My grandmother wept as she related what her own mother told her. Turkish soldiers broke into the family home, and even though her mother was only ten, she clearly remembered everything that happened on that horrible day."

Ani hands her a napkin to wipe her tears. "You don't have to go on with this, Jasmine."

Battia's eyebrows arch in anger. "No, I need to tell you." After composing herself, she presses on. "When the soldiers pushed open the door of the cottage, my great-grandmother got so frightened, she dashed into the nearby closet and hid. Through an opening no larger than a slit, she watched them grab her mother and two aunts. The men ripped off their clothes and jumped all over them. She never forgot how fiercely the women kicked and fought to defend themselves. Through that slight opening, this ten year old child watched the soldiers beat and rape her mother and two aunts."

Jasmine takes the napkin and again dabs her sad brown eyes. "Ani, I still see the pain in my grandmother's eyes as she struggled to tell her mother's story. It was as though she were reliving the trauma herself."

Ani's tone is gentle. "What happened to them?"

"It's believed her mother and two sisters were marched away into the desert and never heard from again. Like many other Armenians, they most likely died from hunger and fatigue under the severe conditions."

Ani's eyes fill with sympathy. "Then your great-grandmother was lucky to survive by hiding in the closet."

"Yes. Muslim neighbors took her in and raised her. She eventually married a Muslim and had two children—my mother and uncle. My mother was only two when her father took the family to Persia to join a cousin in business."

"So that's how you ended up in Iran?"

Jasmine's brow wrinkles into a frown. "Please don't refer to my country as Iran. Call it Persia. It might not make a difference to most people, but Persia's rich culture has been overshadowed by the Islamic revolution."

Ani's voice drops. "Forgive me. I didn't realize how sensitive an issue it is." She pauses, her voice questioning. "But if your grandmother was happily raised as a Muslim, why did she want to tell you this?"

Moisture glazes Jasmine's dark eyes. "I knew I was very special to her. She was close to death when she confided that she felt a part of her was still a Christian Armenian. The gold cross is the one she wore as a child and kept hidden all those years. Though she outwardly professed being a Muslim, she never stopped reciting the Armenian prayers at night that her mother had taught her as a child. She said that was the only way she wouldn't forget who she really was."

A lump lodges in the back of Ani's throat, keeping the words from coming out. Her heart aches for all the Armenian families separated during the Genocide. She watches Jasmine's forlorn gaze as if reliving her great-grandmother's tragic experience.

Jasmine collects herself, clearing her throat. "My grandmother told me she felt fortunate to have been cared for by a kind family, but others were not. Many orphaned children taken in were treated as servants at best, or even slaves. Some were even sold into prostitution."

Ani sits numb without speaking, her heart heavy with pain. She gets up and places a hand on Jasmine's shoulder. "Thank you for telling me your family's story. Was there a reason you wanted me to know?"

Jasmine nods. "I have mixed feelings about identifying myself as a Muslim or a Christian. But witnessing how successful Turkey has been in denying the extermination of my ancestors, I had to tell you. I knew you'd understand."

Ani understands very well. Hadn't she heard similar stories? She hugs her guest. "You are a brave woman, Jasmine. Thank you for sharing it with me."

Suddenly Jasmine smiles, dismissing the sad events she just described. "Funny, I had a horrible headache all day, but now it's gone. Talking to you makes me feel so much better."

"I'm so glad you let it all out, Jasmine." But Ani has her own concerns and decides to reopen the subject that's been keeping her up at night. "Did you realize the danger you'd face exposing the Turkish payoffs?"

Jasmine sits quietly thinking for a moment before answering. "No, I didn't. I guess I had more faith in the U.S. government than it deserves."

# *Thirty-four*

By nine o'clock, the annual Manhattan Medical Auxiliary Ball is in full swing with dancers crowding the floor. Raffi and Lorig sit across from Jeremy and Rachel in the Plaza Hotel ballroom listening to a male singer belt out, "New York, New York."

Rachel taps her feet to the rhythm, nursing her drink. "Nothing beats the classic Sinatra songs."

"Even sounds like him," Jeremy adds, tugging at his tuxedo shirt collar.

The orchestra breaks into a slow ballad, and Raffi rises, takes Lorig's hand, and leads her through the crowd to an opening on the dance floor. He twirls her with the flourish of a ballroom performer, catching the glow on her face.

She giggles lightheartedly. "You took lessons from Fred Astaire?"

He grins back. "You think I'm that good?"

Whether it's the drinks or just being with her, all his troubles seem to melt away. The music slows, and he holds her close, brushing his lips across her bare shoulder. "I'm glad you finally met Rachel and Jeremy," he says.

"They're a wonderful couple. Jeremy's pretty special, and I can see why he's such a good friend to you."

"And the best surgical resident at Manhattan Medical," Raffi adds. He shared his idea with her about Jeremy joining his practice, though he hasn't asked him yet.

The music stops, the crowd claps and they return to Jeremy and Rachel still seated at the table.

"I saw that move, Raffi," Jeremy teases. He throws a friendly smile at Lorig. "I guess you know what a show-off this guy is."

Lorig's enjoying Jeremy's humor and laughs. "I can live with that, but where did he learn to dance so well?"

Sweat peppers Raffi's face and he takes out a handkerchief, wiping his brow. "It's damned hard work," he chuckles, "but I'll show you more of my moves when the dance floor clears."

The ring of his cell brings the banter to a halt. Just as he answers, the music resumes, forcing him to raise his voice to a shout. "I can't hear. Wait 'til I find a quiet spot." He stands, looking to his friends. "I'll take it outside. Be right back."

The outer lobby is quiet and he presses the phone to his ear. "Sorry. Who did you say is calling?"

"Doctor, I'm Candice Baker, Traci's friend. We met the night you operated on her."

*Candice Baker...anchorwoman.* "Yes, I remember. What can I do for you?"

"It's about Traci. She needs your help."

Raffi stiffens, loosening his tie. "What kind of help?"

"I'm at the Marquis Club with her and I'm afraid she's in bad shape. She's more than drunk and needs medical attention."

Raffi hesitates and cringes inwardly, recalling Wolfe's comments about Traci's drug problem.

"Doctor, are you there?"

"Yes. What do you want me to do?"

"Please come to the club and talk to her. No matter what I do, she refuses to go to the hospital."

He searches for an excuse, not wanting to leave his own party. "I know she won't listen to me. Take her home and let her sleep it off."

Candice's voice is loud and clear. "Look, Doctor. You were the topic of conversation all night while she smoked and drank herself silly. Who knows what else she took, but if she doesn't get to the hospital, I don't think she'll make it until morning."

Her ominous words and emphatic tone convince Raffi he can't refuse. "I'm at the Plaza Hotel. I'll grab a cab and be there in twenty minutes—but I can't stay." He catches the relief in Candice's voice.

"Thank you, Doctor. I'll alert the club manager and the guards. Come to the Red Room."

Raffi ends the call and stands, contemplating a discreet way to tell Lorig he has to leave. Starting back to the ballroom, he questions how to break the news. Tell the truth, he decides and instantly picks up his pace. If she's ever to be a doctor's wife, these intrusions are part of the package.

Questioning looks greet him at the table. "That was Candice Baker, the TV reporter, Traci's friend. She claims Traci's in bad shape, possibly overdosed and wants me to go see her."

A frown crosses Lorig's brow. "I can't believe she called you. Why didn't she call nine-one-one?"

Raffi shakes his head. "Traci refuses to go to the hospital. She has a stubborn streak and unless she agrees, Emergency Medical Services won't take her to the ER against her will."

Jeremy faces Lorig, watching the anger flash in her eyes. "What Raffi says is true, Lorig. He's a physician and he'll never forgive himself if something happens to Traci." He looks to Raffi. "Don't worry, Chief, we'll take Lorig home."

Before leaving, Raffi bends down and kisses Lorig's cheek. "Are you sure you want to marry a doctor?" he whispers.

She smiles, her anger vanishing. "As long as you always come home to me."

~ * ~

"The Marquis Club," Raffi orders on entering the taxi. "Step on it, it's an emergency."

The driver trips the meter's flag and obliges by racing through New York's lower West Side, apparently hitting every pothole in sight. He finally pulls up to the brightly lit entrance to the club with a sudden stop, collects his fare and waits for a jostled Raffi to climb out of the cab.

Raffi walks to the door where two burly men stand guard, holding back the line of waiting guests. "I'm Doctor Sarkissian here to see Traci Doss."

"We're expecting you," one replies. "Come with me."

Raffi's eardrums vibrate from the deafening blare of music. At first, squinting in the dark, he can't see, but his eyes finally adjust to the dimly lit room. He follows the guard pushing through mobs of youthful bodies swaying and jumping to the repetitive beat of rap until they reach the double doors to the Red Room.

"Over here!" Candice shouts as Raffi enters.

He sees Traci slumped in a chair, her head face-down on the table.

Candice sits next to her, fear in her eyes. "She keeps saying to leave her alone. She's asleep now but I'm afraid she won't wake up."

Raffi leans close to Traci's ear, raising his voice. "It's Raffi! Open your eyes." He can see she's in a deep stupor and grips her shoulders, shaking her. She's unresponsive and he grabs her wrist, checking her pulse. *Too damned fast.* He finally gives her a hard pinch...still no reaction.

"Candice, how much did she drink?"

"Too many to count."

"Did you see her take any drugs?"

"No, but her friendly pusher was at the apartment when I got there."

"Where is he now?"

"I don't know. He ran out the moment I arrived. He knows I loathe him."

"There's no time to waste. She's overdosed and has to get to the hospital real fast." He pulls the cell phone from his tuxedo pocket and dials 911.

"Dr. Sarkissian here. A woman overdosed at the Marquis Club on West Tenth Avenue and has to be rushed to Manhattan Medical." He listens a moment and replies, "Thanks for your help. It's urgent."

He pockets his phone and looks to the guard. "Keep her in the chair and we'll carry her to the front door."

"Good idea," the guard answers.

Together they lift the chair holding Traci's limp body and carry her to the front entrance with Candice following. A few onlookers stop to stare as they walk through the crowd, but most are absorbed in their dancing, oblivious to their surroundings.

When they reach the entrance, Candice checks her watch. "Thanks so very much, Dr. Sarkissian, but I've got to get to the studio for my eleven o'clock newscast."

"Candice, before you go, you said Traci kept talking about me. What did she say? Is there anything I need to know to help her?"

Candice releases a hesitant sigh. "Traci has a habit of spouting off when she's drunk. I've known her since college and I don't usually take what she says seriously." She lowers her voice, her words sad. "She said she could buy anything in this world except you."

Raffi's heart hardens. They had one weekend months ago. An addict will find any reason to use. "So it's the poor little rich girl story again, is it?"

"I guess, but I hate to judge her. She's one of my closest friends."

Raffi respects Candice's loyalty. "You're a true friend, and you probably saved her life by calling me."

"She'll be all right, won't she, Doctor?"

"I'll take care of her from here. You better get going if you're going to make that newscast."

Candice gives a tense nod and quickly slips out the door.

Raffi's mind wanders, looking at Traci, numb to the world. Why can't he be more sympathetic? Maybe because she's not a victim like so many others. Like Jasmine Battia, fighting for justice and getting none. Or the kid who suffered brain damage in front of Manhattan Medical. And what about all the Armenian Genocide victims silenced because of their religion? Sure, Traci might be trapped by her wealth, but everyone is trapped by something, even if it isn't money.

The ambulance pulls up to the curb, Traci is placed on a stretcher and carried into the vehicle. Raffi sits next to her, studying her pale beautiful face as the siren blares in the background. *Traci is no victim. She's her own enemy.* His Armenian heritage has taught him a hard reality. Real victims know that justice doesn't fall from the sky like rain. You have to fight for it.

# Thirty-five

It's well after midnight when Raffi walks out of Traci's ER stall. A urine drug screen identifies heroin in addition to a high blood alcohol level. Due to depressed breathing caused by the overdose, she's immediately placed on a respirator. Satisfied everything is under control, he heads to the lounge for a cup of coffee, and to call Lorig for an update.

A sudden outburst of shouts fill the air as the emergency team rolls in a black teenager on a gurney, crying in pain. Two policemen follow.

The ER doc calls out, "Glad you're here, Dr. Sarkissian. Could you take a look at this guy?"

Raffi follows the gurney and police into a stall, closing the curtain behind him where the nursing team is already cutting away the blood-stained clothing. They take the victim's pressure, put in an I.V. drip and draw blood for labs, a mandatory protocol.

The stout police officer stands watching and removes his hat, wiping moisture from his hairless scalp. "Kid got shot over by Eighth Avenue. Name's Jimmy and it's not our first run-in with him. He's one of the captains in the turf battle brewing out there."

Raffi places his stethoscope on the boy's chest and stomach, hearing no bowel sounds and looks to the nurse. "Kid's bleeding internally. Get him to X-ray for an abdominal series, chest x-ray and once the tests are done, to OR. Make sure lab puts a rush on blood. This kid needs surgery."

Once the patient is rolled away, Raffi takes a moment to complete his notes in the ER record when another series of shouts pierce the room. A gurney holding another teenager crying out in pain rolls past him as two policemen follow.

One of the officers looks to Raffi. "This kid got shot in the leg. Bleeding big time."

The other officer adds, "They're going wild out there, Doc. There must be a new stash of drugs, and things are heating up." He points to the boy on the stretcher, holding his thigh. "Marcellus is lead honcho of the gang that shot Jimmy. Someday they'll end up killing each other."

Raffi shakes his head, aware the leg on Marcellus will also need surgery. His attention is abruptly directed to a third teenager in handcuffs being dragged along by an officer. A tall heavyset youth in jeans hanging below his butt shouts wildly at Marcellus on the cart ahead of him. "Yo ass is mine, nigger."

"Shut up and keep moving," the officer growls, struggling to restrain the boy pulling loose from the handcuffs. The officer catches Raffi's attention. "Jimmy, the kid shot in the gut, is his brother. He demands to see him."

Raffi faces the heavy set boy in handcuffs. "You'll have to wait. Your brother's in bad shape and on his way to surgery."

The wild-eyed youngster faces Raffi. "You da doc gonna operate on Jimmy?"

"Yes," Raffi answers.

"What's yo' name?" he demands.

Raffi decides the sooner he cooperates, the sooner the kid will calm down. "I'm Dr. Sarkissian."

The boy stares, squinting. "Ain't you the one dat let Tommie Jackson die?"

The officer cuts in. "Hey, kid. If Doc says your brother needs surgery, he needs surgery."

The boy frowns at the officer. "And let him kill my bro, just like Tommie?"

Raffi reads the anger on his face, but says nothing.

The teenager yanks his arm from the policeman's grip, locking eyes on Raffi. "That ain't what Reverend Sanders sez. Last I heard, Tommie's family is suing you."

The black population is feasting on the Tommie Jackson civil rights case, and Raffi hesitates taking the kid's brother to surgery. *What if Jimmy doesn't make it?* He doesn't need more bad press, and how will it affect the upcoming trial? Thankfully Jeremy's at the party, so they both don't get dragged down.

The nurse at the desk alerts Raffi. "OR called and said Jimmy's pressure dropped to below ninety. Better get moving."

As Raffi turns to leave, he throws a sharp glare at the heavy set boy. "Instead of sniping, kid, your job is to pray for your brother Jimmy. My job is to save him."

The boy's face turns somber, his attitude mellows. "Den do yo' best, Doc."

Before Raffi leaves, he turns to the policeman holding the handcuffed kid. "Have him wait in the visitor waiting area outside OR. I'll talk to him after Jimmy's surgery. The kid's really concerned about his brother."

The policeman smirks. "He's involved in the shooting, too, so he'll be booked. But out of the kindness of our hearts, we'll wait with him until he knows his brother's outcome."

"Good enough," Raffi replies. As he rides the elevator up to the surgical floor, he thinks it ironic his weekend with Lorig is ruined by trying to save the life of a kid whose brother wants to sue him.

~ * ~

Raffi rises from the leather couch in the doctors' lounge, exhaling a weary yawn, and checks his watch. It's eight in the morning, and with only four hours of sleep, he still has a full day ahead. In the bathroom, he splashes cold water on his face and feels the stubble on his chin. It's over 24 hours since his last shave.

Returning to the lounge, he fills a cup of coffee and dials the Intensive Care Unit. The teenager he operated in the wee hours of the morning is doing well. Thankfully, Jimmy's brother has no grounds to sue.

He then calls the ER and one of his favorite nurses answers. "Hi, Dory, how's the kid who came in last night with the gunshot to the leg?"

"Marcellus? Doing fine. The surgical resident sewed him up and transferred him to room two-twenty-three."

Raffi puts his cup down, annoyed. "Fine, huh? From what the officers said last night, Marcellus is seriously involved in the narcotics battle rampaging the streets. These gangs stop at nothing to protect their turf in this senseless drug war."

Dory replies, "It's been pretty bad, Doc. We've had several deaths this past month because of drugs."

Frustrated, Raffi runs his fingers through his cropped wavy hair. "I've got to talk to that kid, Marcellus. Maybe I can drill some sense into him."

The nurse lets out a discouraged sigh. "Good luck. Most of them won't listen and only end up in an early grave."

"Probably true, but I have to try." He hangs up, tosses his cup and rides the elevator down to the second floor patient rooms to knock some sense into Marcellus when his cell phone rings. It's Lorig.

"Raffi, are you all right?"

*Crap, I meant to call.* "I'm fine, just a little tired."

"Didn't you get my message?"

"Sorry, hon. Been a bit busy." He exits the elevator, heading toward Marcellus' room as he speaks. "Got held up operating a kid shot in a turf war. Ended up sleeping at the hospital."

"Is Traci okay?"

"Haven't checked on her, but she was admitted to ICU and should be fine. I would have called, but the emergency surgery held me up."

"That's fine, and I won't keep you, but I wanted to remind you of our plans for tonight. Dinner at six, my house. Can you still make it?"

"I'll be there after some shuteye."

"Perfect, see you then."

As he approaches Marcellus' room, explosive shots ring out, echoing down the corridor. Within seconds, four youths dart out of Room 223 and race down the hall, disappearing through a door leading to the stairwell. One of the kids brandishing a gun stops for a moment and glares at Raffi, before dashing off.

Raffi runs into Marcellus' room, his pulse quickening. "Holy shit!" he shouts, shuddering as he studies the scene. Marcellus lies in bed, blood trickling down his face. A closer view shows the bullet entered the boy's brain, causing instant death. Raffi checks for a pulse and heartbeat but finds none.

A nurse rushes in, witnessing the bloody scene and shrieks before darting out for help.

Raffi grabs his phone and dials the switchboard operator. "Dr. Sarkissian, here. Alert security four black kids just ran down the second floor stairwell heading to the lobby. They must be stopped but warn that they're armed."

"Right away, Doctor," comes her breathless reply.

Raffi hangs up, his gaze fixed on the lifeless body lying in a pool of blood. Dory's prediction was right. The kid never stood a chance.

The angry look of the youth Raffi faced in the hallway remains fixed in his mind. With a diamond stud in his left ear lobe, a scar on his right cheek and a tattoo on his neck, the kid won't be hard to identify. This is one issue he has no problem taking a side on—right after work, he'll speak to the police.

~ * ~

Raffi stands outside Room 223 watching the coroner's team roll away the dead boy on a stretcher. Police remove yellow-taped barriers and the last of the crime team follows the entourage to the elevator.

Detective Daley approaches Raffi. "Thanks for the great description of the kid who ran out of the room. You'll have to come to the station to go through our rogue's gallery to identify him."

Raffi's voice trembles, still numb after the cold-blooded incident. "I just wanted to talk to him. Thought I could convince him to stop dealing, but I guess I was too late."

"Nice try, Doc, but don't beat up on yourself. These kids are programmed long before they get into their teens. Could you come to the station now?"

"Christ, I'm tired. Can it wait?"

"You do look bushed. Go home and get some rest, but call me. Here's my card."

"I promise."

"The sooner the better—while the kid's face is fresh in your memory." Daley pauses. "I must admit you sure lead an exciting life, Doc."

"Not by choice," Raffi replies. "All I wanted to do was to talk to Marcellus and then head home to sleep."

"Come on, I'll walk you out."

They move to the elevator and when the doors open, he hears his name.

"Raffi, just the man I want to see."

It's the ICU doctor caring for Traci. "Chris, I hope Miss Doss hasn't taken a turn for the worse." He holds the elevator door open, one foot inside the car, the other out in case he needs to check on Traci.

"No, her airway's removed and she's breathing on her own."

*Good.* "Is she awake?"

"Not yet. She's hallucinating but that's to be expected."

"You're a pal, Chris. I'm too tired to see her today, but call if you need me."

Raffi and Daley descend to the lobby and when the elevator doors open, Reverend Sanders stands facing them with Jimmy's older brother next to him.

Raffi stiffens as two men with New Black Panther Party insignias on their shirts approach behind the reverend.

Sanders glares at Raffi. "Hey, I know you!"

The stone-faced boy points his finger at Raffi. "Yeah, he the doc who fixed Jimmy. We come to see my brother. Is he OK?"

The reverend casts a suspicious glance toward Raffi. "He better be."

Daley steps forward, holding out his badge. "OK, take it easy. Official business."

Raffi shrugs, following Daley through the lobby. *It's black on black violence. Why all the anger?*

As they walk out into the sunlight, Raffi turns to Daley. "With the looks Sanders threw me, I feel like I'm the next target."

"With no evidence of a crime, there's nothing the police can do—just watch your back."

"Does that mean I have to get killed before the law can act?"

Daley cautions. "Don't blame the police, Doc. We can't be all things to all people. There are only so many of us, compared to them."

The hairs on Raffi's arm stand up with Daley's comment. He pushes the point. "So you're telling me I should pack a gun?"

# Thirty-six

Promptly at six, Raffi stands at Lorig's front door and presses the bell. The glow from coach lanterns mounted on both sides of the entrance break the darkness of the crisp evening. Waiting, he studies the stately white pillars anchoring the wraparound porch, a charm newer homes fail to capture.

The door opens and Lorig's excited smile greets him. "You made it! My brothers are at a basketball game so it's only my parents and us tonight." She takes his coat and leads him through the spacious black and white marble foyer into the study. Albert Balian, in white shirt and tie, rises from his club chair when they enter and greets Raffi with a friendly nod, gesturing him to the cushioned chair facing his. "Good to see you again, Raffi. What can I get you to drink?"

"Thank you, Mr. Balian, red wine would be perfect."

Lorig interrupts. "Raffi, I'll be in the kitchen helping my mother. Make yourself comfortable."

Lorig leaves as Balian fills merlot at the bar for his guest, and then fixes himself a scotch on the rocks. His scrutinizing eyes focus on Raffi as he hands him the wine. "I heard there was a shooting at your hospital today."

Raffi catches a hint of a frown on Balian's brow. *Is the man harboring reservations about me?* Surely the media publicity hasn't helped his image, and he hesitates before answering. "Yes, it was an unfortunate incident—a revenge killing by a drug gang."

"I see," Balian replies, placing his glass on the side table. He strokes his chin, tilting his head to the side. "When Lorig told me she was dating a doctor, I never believed you could be involved with so much violence."

Hesitating to answer, Raffi's relieved when Alice Balian enters. Her coloring, fair as Lorig's, her hair much darker with streaks of white. She smiles, warm, inviting. "We're so pleased you were able to come tonight, Raffi. Thank you for taking time from your busy schedule." She then turns to her husband. "Dinner is on the table," she announces.

Raffi follows Mr. Balian into the dining room, impressed by the glistening sparkle of the crystal chandelier hanging over the elegantly set table. A fireplace anchors one side of the room, and above it, a finely carved mantle. A stained glass clerestory window is centered on the back wall, and below it, a French provincial breakfront, lending further opulence to the room.

Lorig smiles, welcoming him to the table, and sits next to him. Balian fills the crystal goblets with wine before sitting at the head of the table. Alice Balian glows, her eyes focused on Raffi. "I decided to make some of the Armenian recipes I learned from my mother. I hope you enjoy them." She begins assisting filling dishes for everyone.

Raffi's mouth waters at the stuffed cabbage and freshly baked bread on his plate. Alice passes a bowl of homemade yogurt, a daily staple on the Armenian table.

"The *dolma* looks delicious," Raffi comments as he places a tablespoon of yogurt on the cabbage rolls. "Looks just like my mother's," he chuckles, which leads the conversation to a polite and friendly exchange about their favorite Armenian foods. *Nothing dangerous in that.*

Once the main course is over, Lorig helps her mom clear the table and carries out a tray of small walnut-filled finger desserts cut into triangles. As Mrs. Balian pours the coffee, her husband's expression turns serious.

"Raffi, you've mentioned your mother works for the FBI as a translator. Is she acquainted with the Iranian woman who was fired for exposing Turkish lobby payoffs?"

Raffi sips his coffee, aware he's into issues of interest to Armenians. Before he can reply, Lorig puts down her fork. "Dad, her name is Jasmine Battia and she's Raffi's patient."

Balian's eyes widen, surprised by the connection. "What can you tell us about her, Raffi?"

"She's a courageous woman, but can't talk. She's been muzzled by a presidential court order."

Balian raises an eyebrow. "For what reason?"

Thanks to Adam Wolfe, he knows enough to add to the conversation. "The State Department regards leaking classified information to the press as a threat to national security. Turkey is considered our ally in the Middle East."

Lorig interrupts, having shared the incident with Raffi. "Someone shot at her car and tried to kill her. What's horrible, no one's been held responsible."

Balian leans back in his chair as his wife pours another cup of coffee. "I didn't catch that in the news. So her life's in danger?"

Raffi hesitates to say too much. "She's single and lives alone. I'm sure she worries it might happen again."

Balian remains silent, sipping his coffee, and then places his cup on the saucer with a contemplative gaze. "Raffi, I'd like to meet Miss Battia. If she's at risk as you say, possibly she could stay with someone until this blows over."

As with all Armenians, Raffi senses Balian has strong anti-Turkish feelings. "That's a thought, sir. My mother and she have become good friends. Maybe something can be arranged." The vibration of his phone in his pocket cuts the conversation short, and he excuses himself from the room to answer. He hears panic in the nurse's voice.

"Dr. Sarkissian, Miss Doss is in a terrible state, asking for you. Nothing we do will calm her and she's refusing medication. Can you come in?"

*Oh shit.* He hesitates a moment, not wanting to be rude to the Balians, but relents—Traci is his patient—his responsibility. "I'm on the other side of the river in New Jersey. Give me about thirty minutes."

He returns to the dining room and the expectant faces before him. "That was the hospital. I'm sorry, but I have to go. Thank you, Mrs. Balian, Mr. Balian. Dinner was delicious, the conversation interesting."

Alice shakes her head, still smiling. "How disappointing, Raffi! We thank you for coming and enjoyed getting to know you."

Albert rises from the table, extending his hand. "Raffi, a pleasure conversing with you. I can see why Lorig speaks highly of you."

Raffi returns Balian's grip. "The pleasure is mine," and then turns to Lorig. "I'll call you tomorrow."

Lorig drops her napkin on the table and rises from her chair. "Let me walk you to the door."

Raffi reads frustration on her face as she hands him his coat from the foyer closet. "I'm really sorry—"

There's an edge to her voice as she helps him into his coat. "I thought you weren't on call. Is it a surgical emergency?"

Raffi decides to tell the truth, knowing it will come out sooner or later. "It's Traci. She's in a state, asking for me."

Lorig bites her lip, anger in her voice. "That woman again? Why must she always haunt you?"

"Please hon, try to understand. She's come out of her coma crying and shouting she has to speak to me—I am her doctor since I admitted her after the overdose."

Lorig's tone is heavy with sarcasm. "And you think you can cure a druggie?"

"Don't know, but something's driving her erratic behavior. I have to find out what triggered this episode."

Lorig scoffs. "Get serious, Raffi. She's knows she can control you. If you ask me, she's just a rich spoiled brat!"

Raffi's heart melts, seeing the hurt in Lorig's face. He takes her hand into his. "I think her problems are deep-seated. Something's going on in her head and maybe she'll tell me."

She pouts, pulling her hands away. "Raffi, tonight was supposed to be special."

"Lorig, it was special, and your parents are fine people. They must be 'cause they raised a daughter like you, didn't they?"

Her expression softens. "I'm being such a crab. It's just that we don't see enough of each other."

Emotion coloring his voice, Raffi tries to make her understand his world. "Lorig, I can't help the kids I'm losing to drugs on the street. I get them after they've been shot—I heal them and they go out again. With Traci, maybe I can reach her. Save her from drugs."

"Save her from the unseen enemy?" She draws her arms around his neck, embracing him. "I know how much you care and I'm sorry I got so upset."

He holds her close, whispering in her ear. "Don't ever question my love for you," and kisses her before leaving.

~ * ~

Raffi hears shouts coming from Traci's room as he enters the ICU. Lorig's taunt about curing Traci's addiction lingers with him. But despite the heiress's spirited lifestyle, he'd never witnessed her taking drugs that weekend in Palm Beach or ever. *What's causing her emotional breakdown?* He has to find out.

A man in his late twenties suddenly dashes from the curtained stall of her room, his beady eyes darting toward Raffi. He wears tight jeans, a flaming red shirt, and mousy brown hair down to his thin shoulders.

Startled by the man's suspicious demeanor, Raffi rushes to Traci's side, followed by a nurse. She's thrashing relentlessly in bed, like a frightened trapped animal trying to escape.

Raffi turns to the nurse. "Who is that man?"

As they both restrain the delirious patient, she throws him a bewildered look. "He said he's her stepbrother."

Raffi's not convinced. *Must be the drug dealer Wolfe was talking about.* Was he checking to make sure Traci wasn't on death's door?

The nurse holds Traci by the shoulders. "She's ready for her next dose of sedation. She's been fighting us and calling for you."

Raffi leans over Traci's bed and gently strokes her arm, calming her. The gaunt colorless face makes his heart sink. *Is this the happy confident woman he got to know that weekend?*

He brushes away strands of hair clinging to her moist forehead and caresses her arm. "I'm here, Traci. It's Raffi. Speak to me."

Traci looks up, dark circles under her eyes, signs of sleepless nights. She blinks, trying to focus on his face and draws in a deep sigh. Her voice is weak, subdued. "I knew you'd come, Raffi."

He stares at her, heartbroken for this lost person he once cared for. As she struggles to raise herself, her hospital gown is drenched with sweat. He sits by her side, patting her hand.

Finally she speaks in a clear matter of fact tone, her voice weary. "We need to talk, Raffi."

The nurse discreetly leaves and Raffi asks, "Traci, what is it?"

She grabs his arm, pulling him close. "I'm pregnant, and I don't know who the father is."

"Christ," he mumbles, stunned. *What can he say?*

She rests a finger on his lips. "You're the only one who knows because you're the only one I can trust."

Raffi studies the wild look in her eyes, a train wreck in progress. Whether it's panic or drug withdrawal, he can't in good conscience walk away. He gathers strength, hoping to help her. "We'll work this out, Traci. Right now get your rest. We'll talk tomorrow."

Her grip tightens. "Don't go."

"I'll be back, I promise. Get some sleep."

She releases him and falls back onto the pillow, murmuring to herself. "Raffi, you're the only one I can count on."

Just then the nurse enters with a full syringe and administers the medication into the IV tubing. She nods to Raffi. "I'm glad you came. She'll be able to sleep now."

Raffi remains in the room, watching Traci's eyes gradually close. "Rest and we'll talk in the morning."

Sleep comes heavy, but Traci fights it like a defiant child. "I knew you'd come, I knew you'd come," she repeats before drifting off.

Raffi quietly slips out of the room and heads to the parking lot, paralyzed by his thoughts. *Who is the father?* He calculates the months since their nefarious escapade. Biologically it's not him. Who, then? Even she doesn't know.

Unlocking the car door, he sits and turns on the ignition; troublesome questions cloud his mind. If she raises this child, will she find the love she's looking for? Possibly cure her? Or should she get an abortion and be done with it? Then there's the legal question of paternity. Most crucial, will she agree to go through drug rehab? But even if she does, will she have the guts to stick it out?

There's only one other person he'll trust who will protect her. First thing in the morning, he'll call Traci's personal attorney, Grant Perry.

# Thirty-seven

Raffi accompanies Grant Perry to Traci's room late the following morning. They find her in bed, dressed in a revealing nightgown, the TV volume raised. With a touch of blush on her cheeks and color on her lips, she appears visibly in control, gradually weaning off heroin.

Raffi smiles, remembering the lipstick theory he first mentioned the night of the car accident months ago. "You look great, Traci. Hope you're rested enough to talk."

She frowns, pushing her breakfast tray away. "I feel much better now that I'm out of the pathetic hospital gown. Candice stopped by early and dropped off some clothes."

Her attention zeroes in on Perry. "More papers to sign?"

Raffi clears his throat, interrupting. "Traci, I asked Grant to come. It's time you fill him in on your situation."

She ignores Raffi's comment and turns to the TV, focusing on the *Good Morning* news show.

Raffi persists, touching her arm. "Be assured, whatever you say will be confidential. You can trust us. He's your attorney and I'm your physician."

She mutes the TV. "Latest breaking news, Grant," she quips sarcastically. "I'm pregnant and only God knows who the father is."

Raffi sees Perry maintain a flat face. No shock, no emotion.

The lawyer asks, "How far along are you?"

She picks up a hand mirror from the nightstand, checking her reflection. Before answering, she applies more coloring to her mouth and smacks her lips. "I missed two periods so it must have happened in Europe."

Perry's tone carries the slightest edge. "And the father, you have any idea?"

"No," she replies, emphatically.

Perry's eyes narrow, he rubs his chin. "We must take protective steps."

Raffi wonders what Perry means. With Traci high on drugs and booze, most likely she's slept with more than one man. "What kind of protective steps?" he asks.

The timbre of Perry's voice is flat, methodical. "The age of the fetus must be determined by ultrasound, followed by a DNA test."

Traci's eyes spark in anger. "Why the DNA test?"

Perry is one hundred percent lawyer as he explains. "Traci, you are a wealthy woman. When this news comes out, you'll face an avalanche of fraudulent paternity suits. We need evidence to block all dishonest claims."

Traci's lips tighten into a thin line. "That won't be necessary, Grant. I'm getting an abortion."

"So you're ready to make that decision?" Perry asks.

Raffi interrupts. "It's too early to discuss this. She's just recovering from a rough night."

Fire lights Traci's eyes and she leans forward, the strap of her nightgown falling off her shoulder. "My mind's made up! When do I get out of here?"

"It depends," Raffi replies. "Are you willing to go to drug rehab?"

She turns her head, gazing out the window. "No need for that. I'll manage fine without the hand-holding."

Raffi stands resolute, his hands in his pockets. *Rehab's her only chance.* "Traci, it's your best way to kick the habit. There's an excellent facility close by—we've had many patients come through the program."

She bites her lip, tapping her fingers on the hand-held mirror, not answering.

Raffi presses, "Please Traci. If you don't nip this in the bud right now, things will only get worse."

Perry agrees. "Listen to him. You're young with too much on the line. You've got to break the habit."

Traci answers with a trace of sarcasm. "Who really cares as long as they still get their checks?" She releases a deep sigh, focusing on Raffi. "I'll go, on only one condition."

"What's that?" Raffi asks.

"You visit me each and every day."

Guilt crosses Raffi's his face, and he hesitates a moment thinking of the heavy strain it'll put on his relationship with Lorig. But he also knows that drug dependent people need all the support they can get.

Perry looks to Raffi, doubt on his face. "Are you willing to do that, Doctor?"

Raffi finally answers. "Yes, I'll do it."

"Good," Perry replies, somewhat surprised. "I'll take care of the legal stuff and you can manage the medical. OK?"

"You've got it," Raffi replies. *Now how to justify this to Lorig.*

Perry returns his focus to the heiress. "You can do this, Traci—you're stronger than you know. I'll be in touch."

"I'll walk you out, Mr. Perry," Raffi says. He gives Traci's arm a reassuring squeeze. "Get some rest. I'll try to stop in later."

She ignores both of them, staring aimlessly out the window.

The two men leave the room and approach the elevator, when Perry stops to face Raffi. "Do you have a few minutes?"

"Yes," Raffi replies. "Why don't you join me for breakfast?"

Perry nods. "A cup of coffee will be fine."

As they sit across from each other in the doctors' dining room, the lawyer speaks in his usual sober manner. "Doctor, I talked to your hospital attorney, Mr. Gold. He informed me the upcoming Tommie Jackson trial is being fast-forwarded."

Raffi pokes at his scrambled eggs. "Yes, he's told me."

The lawyer continues, leaning forward across the dining table. "Reverend Sanders is pushing the envelope. There's major unrest in the black community with persistent demonstrations, and the judge hopes to calm things down by expediting the trial."

Raffi takes a bite of his toast, shaking his head. "Either way, it looks bad for me and Jeremy as well as the hospital."

"You're right on that issue. The media's coverage is very sympathetic to the black community. After all, they're considered the underdogs."

Raffi tosses his toast down in frustration. "Exactly! Should the hospital win, Sanders will say it's a cover-up. But if a jury decides there was racial profiling, it only adds fuel to the fire. Either way, it's a no-win in our multi-cultural society."

"I regret hearing that, Dr. Sarkissian, but no matter, my job is to protect Traci's interests. The hard fact is that the accident was caused by her tire blowout, not her sobriety status. No way will I allow her to appear at trial."

Raffi senses his vulnerability by neglecting to order a blood alcohol level on Traci that night. "You're telling me I'm on my own?"

"Don't worry—the hospital has your back," the lawyer replies, rising from the table. "Got matters to attend to, but thanks for the conversation." His eyes suddenly narrow. "Do you think Traci has the stamina to get clean?"

Raffi considers the past few months of bad press she's gotten, but then recalls the glimpse into the real person he met in Palm Beach. A woman hungry for love.

"Yes, Mr. Perry I think she can make it." He hesitates, and then asks, "What do you think?"

DR. RICHARD A. BERJIAN

The lawyer replies, no doubt in his voice. "I don't think so."

Raffi's dismayed by his hardened answer. *Now I understand why Traci feels so alone.*

~ * ~

Two weeks later, Raffi heads to the locker room to change into scrubs for his eleven o'clock case. With twenty minutes to spare, he enters the lounge, draws a cup of water from the cooler and sits to watch TV.

As commercials flash by, his thoughts return to Traci. He promised to visit, but the facility's policy is to restrict all visitors for a certain period, giving patients the necessary time to address their dependency. Despite her calls to his office every day demanding to be discharged, he convinces her to stay the course.

Each time the subject comes up, Lorig insists Traci's manipulative ways are strictly done for attention. As far as she's concerned, Traci is the typical spoiled immature female who uses her wealth to get whatever she wants.

But Raffi knows better. Traci's psychological flaws are rooted in her childhood, a more realistic cause for her dependency. But the last thing he wants is to jeopardize his relationship with Lorig.

His attention turns to Jeremy, who enters wearing a wide friendly grin.

"Hey Raffi, I'm scrubbing with you on your eleven o'clock case."

Raffi smiles back. "Cool! Surgery always moves faster when you assist."

Just then Reverend Sanders flashes on the TV screen, larger than life, casually sitting with two guests.

Jeremy curses and stalks toward the television for a better look. "Son of a bitch! They reward that fuckin' wife-cheating philanderer with a TV show?"

Raffi picks up the remote, prepared to turn it off when Jeremy grabs it away from him. "Wait, I want to hear this."

The two men stand side by side, watching Sanders introduce his guests sitting around a circular table. Michael Haines from the

*New York Times* wears an open collared shirt, rubbing his scruffy beard with his fingers. Beside him, the attractive blue-eye blonde, Michele Molari, from *Newsday* peers across the table from host Sanders. Her low cut blouse exposes slight cleavage, lending her a seductive appearance.

The reverend sports an expensive tailored suit, and his wavy thick hair is professionally groomed. He opens the show with a broad smile, revealing white capped teeth. "Good morning to all friends and *foes*. Welcome to *The Reverend Sanders Show*, an hour exposing what drives the policies of our nation. Today's topic will be the racial prejudice built into our immigration laws."

Jeremy elbows Raffi in disbelief. "Sanders landed a talk show to push his agenda. What next?"

After a short discussion, the *Times* reporter interjects. "It's time we pass an amnesty law for illegals living in our country. They work, pay taxes, and deserve to be a part of our economy."

Molari's voice is firm. "Not until we secure our borders."

Sanders cuts in. "And how's that gonna happen?"

The two guests begin talking over one another with Sanders joining in. Annoyed, Raffi turns off the TV just as the OR nurse sticks her head in the room. *Perfect timing.*

"Doctors, your case is ready."

The two physicians scrub at the sink together, lathering their hands and arms in preparation for surgery.

Jeremy nods at Raffi. "Looks like Sanders is warming up for the Tommie Jackson trial."

Raffi hears the concern in his friend's voice and hopes to share his confidence. "I'm not worried about the trial, Jeremy. I'm prepared for anything those lawyers throw at me."

Jeremy stops scrubbing. "You sound awfully confident, my friend."

"I am." He'll tell the truth, and nothing but.

Jeremy flips his scrub brush into the sink. "Easy for you to say, Raffi. You don't live in the black community like I do."

"Are you still getting harassed?"

"Yes, and Sanders' bullshit is even getting to my own friends."

Raffi kicks off the water valve with his knee. "Sorry to hear that, but as chief resident, you're living proof America has overcome its racial prejudice. You're a terrific surgeon, period. So let's get in there and do something positive."

~ * ~

Raffi quickly finishes office hours on the following Friday with one thing in mind. Traci's pregnancy has progressed past ten weeks and time is running out. Whether she keeps the baby or decides to abort, it's her choice. After weeks of drying out at the Cornwall Rehabilitation Center, her mental status appears clear enough to make a decision.

He's refrained from discussing the pregnancy issue, but can't put it off any longer. His visit this weekend will force a decision, and he wants Lorig with him to discuss such a delicate issue.

Removing his lab coat, he slips on a blue blazer when the message *ding* sounds on his phone. The text is from Lorig. "Call when you're free. I have a great plan for tomorrow."

He gets her on the first ring. "Hi hon, what's up?"

"How about doing something cultural for a change?" she suggests excitedly. "The Guggenheim Museum is showing their Van Gogh collection, and I think we should go."

Not his cup of tea, but the timing for a favor is perfect. "Okay! Sounds interesting—but, Lorig, I need a favor."

"Sure, what is it?"

"I'd like you to come with me to visit Traci at the rehab center."

There's a long pause and Raffi frowns, worrying she'll say hell, no.

Her reply is curt. "Why?"

"There's something I have to discuss and it'll help if you're with me." He still senses having the baby will be a positive thing in Traci's life. But what does he know about being a mother? Possibly a single mother.

"Discuss what? Why are you so evasive?"

"I can't say right now." He'll have to clear it with Traci before telling Lorig about the pregnancy. "Will you go with me?"

He hears her usual sigh and holds his breath, waiting for an answer.

"You know, Raffi, it's not that I don't like the woman. At times, I really feel sorry for her."

He lightens up, laughing. "Why do you feel sorry for one of the richest women in the world?"

Catching his sarcasm, she replies in a quiet voice. "Because she doesn't have you."

He breaks out in a smile. "So, tomorrow, okay? I'll make you a deal. After we visit Traci, we'll take in the Guggenheim and I'll spring for dinner too."

"How can I say no to that?"

Raffi sighs with relief, lowering his voice. "You see what a good fit we are together?"

She chuckles, cynically. "It's better I go than have you face that conniving woman without me!"

~ * ~

Because of parking problems in midtown Manhattan, Lorig takes the bus from New Jersey across the George Washington Bridge to the terminal on the New York side where Raffi meets her. Together they ride the subway to West 57th and walk the rest of the way.

"This is it," Raffi says, pointing. The outer façade of the Cornwell Rehabilitation building carries an ornate stone architecture popular in the 1920s and 1930s, indistinguishable from the residential apartments lining West 57th Street.

A stale odor greets them as they enter the worn marble floor lobby and Raffi asks the matronly receptionist for Traci's room.

Without so much as a smile, the woman says, "Miss Doss is in room six-o-three, sign here." She shoves a visitors' guest list toward Raffi, and then points to the narrow corridor. "Take the elevator to the sixth floor and turn right."

They sign the ledger, ride the elevator, and find the door to Traci's room slightly ajar. She's sitting in a lounge chair facing a large window. A woman in a white uniform sits next to her. The room is large enough for a bed and a pleasant adjoining sitting area with windows offering a clear view of the city.

They enter and approach Traci, whose expression remains flat on seeing them. Despite her gaunt appearance, Raffi is encouraged by the sobriety in her eyes.

"Do you remember Lorig?" he asks.

Traci focuses on Lorig's face—if she remembers, she shows no evidence.

The aide rises, adjusting her uniform. "Miss Doss, I'll leave you to your guests."

Raffi gestures Lorig to the sofa, and takes a seat beside the two women. "You're looking well, Traci. Has Grant been in to see you?"

"He came yesterday with papers to sign for my foundation." She focuses for a few moments, studying Lorig and then turns to Raffi. "I told him in no uncertain terms, I'm hell bent ready to leave this place. They can't keep me against my will any longer."

"You've come a long way, Traci. Listen to your therapists. They know how detoxing works. The physical, as well as the mental. In the meantime, have you made a decision?"

Traci tilts her head toward Lorig. "Does she know?"

"I left it up to you, if you wanted to share. Lorig can be trusted—I wouldn't have brought her here otherwise."

Traci's gaze fixes on Lorig, her fingers tremble in her lap. "It's no secret now that I'm throwing up every morning. What the hell, I'm pregnant and I want an abortion."

Lorig sits quietly, observing, not answering. She's calm as he'd hoped.

Not getting a reaction, Traci leans forward, determined to be on her worst behavior. "Single and knocked up. What would *you* do without a man in the picture?"

Lorig's brow knits, her gaze sympathetic. "I really can't say without being in your shoes."

Traci's lips tighten; her eyes glaze as she drums her fingers on the arm of the chair.

Lorig rises from the sofa, placing an empathetic hand on the woman's shoulder. "Traci, abortion isn't an easy decision for any woman. You have to be convinced of your decision."

Annoyed, Traci pulls away, determined. "I've made up my mind, and it's final."

Lorig is quick to answer. "And that's your right! It's your decision and no one else's." Looking to Raffi, she adds, "Can you take care of that?"

Raffi's stunned, surprised how readily Lorig supports Traci's decision to undergo abortion. "I'll set it up," he answers.

Lorig removes a tissue from the box on the lamp table and hands it to Traci. "Who'll be with you when you go to the hospital?"

Traci sniffs, wiping her tears. "I'll go alone."

Lorig's nose wrinkles. "You shouldn't—isn't there someone you're close to, someone you can trust to be with you?"

"I have no one."

"What about your friend, Candice Baker?" Raffi asks.

"I don't want to ask her. She's a news reporter, and that would put her in a very difficult position." Traci lowers her head, balling up the tissue. "I have many so-called friends, but no one I can really trust." She gazes at Raffi with defeat. "I've learned to live with my loneliness."

Lorig swallows hard, studying the sad soul sitting before her. She rises, embracing Traci. "You're not going alone. I'll be with you."

# *Thirty-eight*

Two weeks later, Lorig sits alone in Raffi's apartment waiting for him to return from the hospital. Their movie date, interrupted by an unexpected call from the ER an hour earlier, tells her that life with a doctor is full of unexpected intrusions. But she's also learned that Raffi's professional dedication makes him great at what he does.

She sits comfortably on the leather sofa and picks up one of his medical journals from a stack piled high on the table. Flipping through pages, she's amazed at the abundance of information physicians have to absorb to keep up with the latest medical developments. Finding it difficult to understand the technical jargon, she deposits the journal back on the table and picks up the TV remote. Before she turns on the set, the phone rings and lets the answering machine record the message. She hears Traci's panicked voice.

"Raffi, I have to speak to you. You're not picking up on your cell phone."

Irked by Traci's tone, Lorig instantly grabs the receiver. "Raffi's not here," she says. *This woman's high maintenance.*

"Who is this? Where's Raffi?"

"This is Lorig." *You know, the one that sat in the hospital with you?* "Raffi's at the hospital."

"I need to speak to him right away."

She hears an undertone to Traci's words, snapping her from her petty thoughts. *Is she having complications from the abortion?* But the surgery was ten days ago, and she asks, "What's wrong, Traci?"

Traci screams into the phone. "Stop with all your silly questions. I need Raffi now!"

Lorig speaks firmly, as if talking with one of her students. "Calm down, and tell me your problem."

There's a long silence before Traci speaks again. "You don't like me, do you?"

Lorig lets out a sigh of resignation. "It's not that I don't like you, Traci. I don't understand you."

"I know that," comes her quick reply.

Lorig shifts on the couch, holding the receiver. "No you don't. Tell me, why are you always calling Raffi? Are you bleeding, cramping? Are you in pain? What is it?"

After a long interval, Traci responds, her tone distant. "I'm scared. I feel so alone."

Lorig sits up, more attentive. She's seen for herself how alone. The woman has a giant house and servants—no friends or family. "Isn't your maid with you?"

"I need Raffi. I'm afraid I might do something." A pause, then a whisper. "What's the point?"

Lorig catches the hollow echo in her voice, but feels unprepared to talk sense to an emotionally unstable woman. The sudden thought that Traci might attempt suicide turns her ghost white. If it happens, she'll never forgive herself.

The pitch of her voice jumps an octave. "Don't do anything foolish, Traci. Raffi will call you when he's free." She hangs up, rises from the sofa and paces the floor, debating whether to call

Raffi. Just then her cell phone rings, displaying Raffi's number. "Hey," she says.

"Sorry, Lorig, but our plans have to change. I'm taking the emergency to surgery so don't expect me until late tonight."

Lorig laughs nervously. "That's convenient—because I had Traci on the phone demanding to see you."

"What's her problem?"

"I don't know, but she sounds suicidal. Do you want to speak to her?" *Maybe he'll call, and talk the heiress down.*

"My patient's already on the table." He clears his throat. "Can you try to calm her? See what you can do."

*How do I handle a female like Traci?* "Thanks, darling, for trusting me. I'll grab a cab and check on her—but you owe me, Raffi. Goodbye."

She clicks off and redials Traci from Raffi's house phone. Her maid answers, and then Traci comes on the line. "Raffi?"

Lorig grits her back teeth. "Look Traci, this is Lorig. Raffi's in surgery. Don't do anything stupid. I'll be there in less than a half hour."

"Thanks," Traci answers in a soft whimper.

Within minutes, Lorig is on the street, vigorously waving for a cab. While she doesn't approve of Traci's lifestyle, she can't ignore the woman's cry for help. Is this how she keeps pulling Raffi into her drama?

During the taxi ride, she ponders how to help Traci out of her depression. As a school teacher, she's experienced in helping young people solve their problems, but she's no psychologist. She quickly Google-searches depression, drugs and alcohol. What if Traci's slipped back into her old patterns?

As the cab pulls in front of Traci's Central Park West apartment, Lorig's pulse races, her chest grows tight. What in the world is she doing, taking care of a suicidal female who hates her for breaking up the fling she had with Raffi?

The driver parks in front of the penthouse address. "That'll be twelve bucks," he says.

"Right!" Lorig fumbles in her purse for cash to pay the fare. Getting up her courage, she walks through the ornate mahogany doors to enter the lobby.

The night doorman sitting behind a marble reception desk greets her. "May I help you, ma'am?"

"Yes, I'm Lorig Balian, here to see Miss Doss."

He nods. "Yes, Miss Doss is expecting you."

Lorig takes a quick elevator ride to the penthouse and rings the bell. The uniformed maid ushers her into a spacious glass-walled living room, offering a dramatic view of the New York skyline.

Shimmering street lamps brighten the darkness, and lights from apartment windows cast a glow in the night. Central Park lies as a buffer between the bordering high rise apartments. She stares at the breathtaking view, wondering how anyone could be depressed living in such luxury.

She finds Traci dressed in a silk robe, her hair disheveled, sprawled across a long white sectional. She asks, looking to the maid. "How long has she been this way?"

"Since I've been here," the maid replies in a fearful tone. "I tried to get her to eat, but she refuses. I'm new here. The service called me this afternoon. Miss Doss had a falling out with her regular caregiver."

Lorig picks up the plastic pill bottle on the cocktail table and reads the OxyContin label. The half-filled bottle of scotch next to it tells her that Traci has combined the pills with alcohol. *So much for rehab.*

She rocks Traci's shoulder gently, and then more vigorously, waiting for her to respond. "Wake up, Traci. This is Lorig. I'm here."

The limp figure turns and opens her eyes, making a feeble attempt to sit up. Lorig grabs an arm to help but Traci resists, pushing her away and flops back down on the couch.

"Get up, Traci, you need to eat something."

Traci mumbles, "Let me sleep."

"Sit up," Lorig repeats, "or else I'll throw you into a cold shower." One of the suggestions she found on the Internet.

Traci shakes her head and closes her eyes.

Lorig turns to the maid. "Make a pot of strong coffee right away! Bring dry toast, too."

The maid nods and leaves quickly for the kitchen.

Lorig knows she has to keep Traci awake and talking until the narcotic and alcohol wear off. She grabs her by the shoulders, rolls her onto her side and holds her arm, getting her in an upright position.

"You're hurting me!" Traci cries out.

"Good," Lorig answers, gently slapping the woman's cheeks to rouse her temper. "Talk to me."

"About what?" Traci mumbles.

"About anything, your life, anything."

Traci moans. "Just let me sleep."

"You can't sleep! I meant it when I threatened the cold shower."

Traci's eyes open slightly, focusing on Lorig's face.

Lorig studies the woman lost in the wretched depth of despair. Whether or not she walked in those designer shoes, she can't deny that Traci is hurting.

Lorig keeps shaking her shoulder. "Coffee's coming, keep talking. Tell me about your first date, anything, just talk to me."

Traci brushes back her hair, appearing more lucid. "My first date? God, I can't think."

"Okay, what about your first car?" Lorig recalls her parents wouldn't let her have a car until she'd saved a down payment.

"BMW," Traci murmurs in a daze. "Dad gave it to me for my sixteenth birthday."

*Different worlds.*

The maid returns and places the coffee on the table. "Is there anything else I can do, Miss Balian? Miss Doss is very private and reluctant to have staff involved in her personal life."

"I understand," Lorig replies. "Let me see if I can keep her awake. If I need to throw her in the shower, I'll call for help."

After the maid leaves, Lorig pours strong black coffee into a large mug. "Sugar, cream?"

Traci doesn't answer.

Lorig pinches her arm and Traci cries out. "That hurts!"

Lorig persists. "Do you want sugar or cream?"

"Black," Traci answers.

Lorig raises the cup to Traci's lips, forcing her to take a sip. "You have to drink more than that because I'm not giving up." *We're different, yes, but in the end, we're both human, and that's enough.* "Drink!"

~ * ~

It's five in the morning when Traci finally comes out of her trance-like state and returns to a normal weariness. Lorig works all night plying her with coffee, toast and talk until effects of the pills and scotch wear off.

She takes the cup from Traci's hand. "Popping oxy and drinking is not what your therapists at Cornwell ordered. After all you've been through, why did you do it?"

Traci's shoulders sag and she shakes her head. "You know why."

*The baby? Raffi?* "But you have so much to live for."

She stares back. "Really? Like what? Another trip? Another party?"

"Come on, Traci. Stop feeling sorry for yourself. With your position and influence, you can make a difference in this world."

"I do that with my foundation and charities, but it does nothing for *me*." She brings her hand to her heart.

Lorig has no advice and wonders about her family. What's missing in this woman's life? Bone-tired, she props her feet on the coffee table and tilts her head back on the sofa. "Where's your mom? Are you close to her?"

Traci's slow to answer. "No. She's dead now."

"What about your father?"

Traci slumps back next to Lorig, fully sober. "Didn't see much of him, although the little I did was good. His life was busy developing the Doss corporate empire. Never married until he was much older. He's gone, too."

"Are you an only child?"

"By my father? Yes. But I have a stepsister. Mother was widowed with a daughter from her first marriage when she hooked up with Father." She stops to rub her eyes, letting out a deep yawn.

"Are you close to her, your stepsister, I mean?"

"No, never keep in touch. She's married, living in Oregon."

"Sorry to hear that."

Traci stares into the distance as though trying to pull memories from her past. "I always felt a lot of distrust and tension in my parents' marriage. I guess it was Father's money and social standing that Mother loved—and he knew it. After he died, I had nothing to do with her or my step-sister."

"What about friendships growing up?"

"As a child? Never had any. Private tutors most of the time—either a book or a nanny. No kids to hang out with."

"So you were raised as a little adult?"

Traci yawns again, drowsy with sleep. "I guess you could say that."

Lorig knows she has to keep her talking to keep awake. "Were you ever in love?"

A faint smile crosses Traci's face, her eyes more alert. "I thought I was."

"What happened?"

Traci's lethargic trance suddenly disappears as anger takes hold. "I loved him, but he loved my money!"

Delighted by the energetic response, Lorig pushes on. "Why do you say that?"

Traci sighs, sitting up and cupping her head in her hands as if in pain. "It's a long story and I don't want to go into it."

Lorig feels she's making progress and nudges Traci's shoulder. "This is important—get it off your chest."

Traci raises her head, her blurred eyes tracking her challenger. "I was twenty and so crazy in love. We were running away to get married in Europe."

"What happened?"

"You don't want to know."

"Yes, I do."

Traci takes in a heavy breath, more alert now. "We checked into Hotel Pierre in the city, preparing to fly to Paris to get married the next day." She pauses, wrinkling her brow.

"And?"

"I don't feel like talking about this."

"Well I do, so don't cut me off."

Traci continues, her tone flat. "It was all too good to be true. The guy I fell in love with, this gorgeous hunk who said all the right things. He lied and poisoned me about trusting men."

Lorig's aware she's hitting a hot button and persists. "Why is that?"

Traci frowns, looking for a cigarette on the table before her. She lights one, taking in a long drag before speaking. "In Paris, we checked into a three room bridal suite with plans to marry the next morning. That very night, I walked out of the shower wrapped in a towel, excited to celebrate and picked up the phone to call room service for champagne. I heard my husband-to-be talking to a woman on the extension, telling her he couldn't wait to see her."

Lorig brings a hand to her mouth. *Oh, no.*

A spark of anger clouds Traci's face as she continues. "He gave her the name of a Paris bistro near La Place de Concorde where they were to meet later that night. I was shocked, paralyzed. The man who was going to marry me was nothing but a rotten womanizer."

"And you confronted him?"

315

Traci shrugs, taking another drag from her cigarette. "I didn't know what to say. I was young and in love, and very confused. So I decided to wait until the champagne arrived."

"You actually held in your anger until then? I'm impressed, Traci."

She waves away smoke. "Yes, I needed time to think."

"And then what?"

Traci's eyes narrow, speaking with a false bravado. "I told him to pour the champagne. He did exactly that and gave me a sheepish grin as he raised his glass. That's when I proposed the toast and said, 'Who should we drink to tonight? Marlene or me?'"

Lorig stifles her laugh. "What did he do?"

"I watched the damned fool freeze and nearly shit in his pants, trying to think of an answer. The only thing he could say was 'Who's Marlene?'"

Traci gets up from the sofa, fully awake, and paces, wobbling around the room. She drops her cigarette to the ashtray and faces Lorig.

"It hit me all at once. My father's warning rang in my ears telling me to be careful who I trusted. Especially men! And I failed."

"So what did you do?"

"I told the bastard what I heard and got him kicked out of the hotel that very night!"

Lorig's smoldering resentment softens, watching the despair on Traci's face. For the first time, she understands the prison the heiress lives in. *Who could she trust? Everybody wanted something from her.*

Traci drops back onto the sofa, her smile cold and assertive. "Don't feel sorry for me. I was damned lucky I didn't marry the bum."

"What did your parents say about all this?"

She gives her head a vigorous shake. "Never told them. I knew what my father would say."

"So you were all alone with your decision?"

"Yes, all alone." She lets out a sarcastic snicker, brushing the hurt off with humor. "Oh, I got over it quickly. And that's the hidden story of my wonderful youth. Empty and isolated."

Lorig pauses and holds her firmly by the shoulders. "That's all in the past. You're young; you can do anything you want. You have a future."

Traci's voice hardens; wet tears glaze her eyes. "What kind of future? I aborted the only life I ever had in my body. The rest of me's garbage, a waste."

"Listen, what you've done can't be undone, but that doesn't mean you never can have children—when the time is right for you."

"Where do I start? How do I find a man who isn't attracted to me because of what I represent? Someone like Raffi—he never cared about all that."

Compassion overtakes Lorig as she listens to Traci's frustrating tale. She leans over and hugs her. "You can't change who you are, Traci. You'll always be expected to use your wealth for others—to fund charities and interact with people in high places. That's good; it gives you a purpose. But somewhere in this universe there has to be a man for you who's equally rich and sensitive to your same problems."

Traci exhales a yearnful sigh. "I hope so," she says, her voice drifting off.

Lorig sees the faraway look in her eyes. One thing is certain: Traci will never connect with anyone until she recovers from every ounce of her self-pity.

# *Thirty-nine*

The day for Tommie Jackson's civil trial finally arrives. Raffi's primed for two hours by Manhattan Medical's defense counsel, Devon Smith, preparing him with questions the prosecutor will throw at him. The topic of racial discrimination is top on the list, even though Raffi feels more confident sticking to the medical facts. He listens attentively to Smith's advice, finally deciding the best he can do is tell the truth as he sees it.

He eats a quick breakfast at the kitchen table, reviewing the notes taken in Smith's office. *Keep your answers short and direct. Watch for the pitfalls the prosecuting attorney will present.*

TV camera crews are already capturing the scene of picketers carrying signs when he arrives at the courthouse. He forges his way past a young African-American teenager lifting a placard in bold print, "RACISM IN AMERICA AIN'T DEAD." The police hold back a crowd of male protestors dressed in khaki uniforms along with teenagers in jeans with similar signs. Women with children, some in strollers, gather in groups standing at the sidelines as older youngsters run about laughing and playing as if at a picnic. Raffi finds the scene surreal.

"Justice for Jackson" the crowd chants as they march behind police barriers set up in front of the courtroom steps.

Raffi catches sight of Reverend Sanders among the crowd, gesturing to the people, rallying them to keep up the protest. He approaches the roped off area when a shrill voice cries out. "There's the doctor!" A heavy-set woman in bright purple lunges toward him, her brown eyes filled with hate. "Killer!" she shouts.

Two policemen shield Raffi and ask for his identity and court appearance documents. Once produced, he's allowed to pass. Inside the building, he follows a guard to the designated courtroom and is instructed to wait outside until called. He sits on the bench adjacent to the courtroom door, watching an assortment of people pass by. Tall, short, thin, stout, all ages and shades of color from all parts of the world. It seems no one is immune from the risk of litigation.

Raffi knows Jeremy's questioning is scheduled before his and hopes to see him when he exits the courtroom. He sits patiently, looks at his watch and drums his fingers on his thigh, waiting to be called.

Fifteen minutes go by when Jeremy exits the courtroom, his face tight with anger. Instead of his usual scrubs, he wears a somber gray suit matching his mood.

Raffi jumps up and approaches. "Jeremy, how did your testimony go?"

Annoyed, he shakes his head. "Who knows? Shifty is too kind a word to describe Jackson's attorney. He actually tried to convince the jury *I'm biased* against my own people!"

Raffi holds his temper, and whispers under his breath. "That son of a bitch! Even when you said Tommie was practically dead before he reached the ER?"

Jeremy frowns, raising fingers to his temple. "Whenever I tried to bring up Jackson's medical condition, the bastard cut me off. Faced the jurors, telling them it was *my inexperience t*hat led to Tommie's death. He made me look like a stupid shit. And then he turns to me and asks, *how many patients have you lost, Dr. Jenkins?"*

Raffi shivers with apprehension. "And you said?"

Jeremy grits his teeth. "Only Tommie Jackson, I said. Then he tears into me with a vengeance. Blamed me for not taking the right precautions."

"What precautions?"

Jeremy smirks, shaking his head. "Like checking for metabolic acidosis causing the drop in his blood pressure."

Raffi loses control and shouts. "That's bullshit! Tommie hemorrhaged to death. He had a tear in his aorta."

Jeremy's worried eyes focus on his friend. "No matter how I tried to explain the medical facts, he kept hammering that I was negligent because I didn't do special tests."

Raffi's body shakes with anger—how is he supposed to stick to the truth if he's not allowed to tell it? "Jeremy, the guy doesn't know shit! So the medical facts be damned to confuse the jury."

Frustrated, Jeremy drops his head, lowering his voice. "I'm afraid so. He kept pounding the same mantra—we didn't do everything in our power to save Tommie because he's black."

"Did the jury buy it?"

"Don't know, but he sure left enough doubt in their minds."

Raffi grasps Jeremy's shoulder. "I'm sure you did fine. You look bushed, so go home and crash."

Jeremy eyes light up. "No way. I'll be in there when you testify—moral support. At least you'll have one person on your side."

Just then the door swings open and the bailiff announces, "Raffi Sarkissian to the witness box."

"That's me," Raffi calls out, rising from the bench. "Is it okay for Dr. Jenkins to be in there again?" Raffi hadn't been allowed in for Jeremy.

The guard nods and lets them pass into the courtroom.

Guided by an officer to the witness stand, Raffi sits, preoccupied, scanning the serious-faced jury. *Where do their sympathies lie?* It's hard to tell. There's an even split of black and white with a few murmuring in Spanish in the mix. The elderly judge directs a kindly smile toward him, making him feel he might have a fighting chance. He remembers to project a confident image, assumes a relaxed posture, hands held in lap. If the facts don't sway the jury, maybe he can charm them, and raises his hand to take the oath. He deliberately smiles at each juror. It's his turn to tell the truth and he's ready.

~ * ~

Silence fills the courtroom as Tommie Jackson's malpractice attorney rises from his seat at the table and peers at Raffi over his half lenses. Daryl Murphy, a short stout man with a full head of wavy salt and pepper hair, wears a finely tailored suit. However, the bulge at his waistline suggests beer is his favorite beverage of choice. He has wisely, for good reason, chosen a black attorney as co-counsel, aware race will be the cornerstone for his arguments during the trial.

The attorney moves in slow, deliberate steps and approaches the witness box, resting both hands on the oak rail. He focuses on Raffi. "Dr. Sarkissian, you were chief resident on call when Tommie Jackson reached the emergency room on the night of the accident. Were you not?"

"Yes, I was," Raffi replies.

Murphy takes a step back, giving the jury a clear view of Raffi. "And was it your decision to assign Dr. Jeremy Jenkins, a junior surgeon, less trained, to tend to Tommie Jackson?"

"Yes, and no. Yes, I assigned Dr. Jenkins to Jackson's case, but I disagree with your premise he's less trained. He was close to finishing his fourth year of surgical residency and equally qualified to operate major trauma cases."

"I see," Murphy counters. "But with your additional year of training, weren't you the more skilled surgeon?"

Raffi's aware the plaintiff's attorneys will try to establish doubt over Jeremy's credibility rather than address the medical issue. He calmly replies, "Dr. Jenkins' expertise is not in question here. The fact remains that the extent of Mr. Jackson's injuries were beyond repair."

Murphy's smirk turns into a smile. "That's very noble of you, Doctor. Complimenting your colleague is one thing, but isn't there a reason why surgeons are required to have that additional year of training?"

Raffi keeps a steady voice. "Despite your presumption, I repeat, Jeremy Jenkins was equally qualified to take care of Mr. Jackson."

Murphy's jaw tightens, his smile vanishes. "We'll let the facts speak for themselves, Doctor. There must be a reason why you chose to operate on a well-recognized billionaire heiress with less apparent injuries."

Raffi quickly responds, prepared for the question. "At the time I didn't know who the patient was or the full extent of injuries. Wealth never influenced my decision."

Murphy persists, tenting his fingers. "However, you as *chief resident* and Dr. Flint, who we all know as a seasoned and *highly regarded surgeon*, decided to save the life of a prominent woman rather than a poor black boy. Isn't that so?"

Raffi feels heat on the back of his neck, aware he has to keep control of his anger. "I disagree. Both Tommie Jackson and Traci Doss received the best medical care available. Unfortunately, Mr. Jackson's aortic tear caused him to hemorrhage. Neither I, nor anyone else, could have saved his life."

Murphy tilts his head, peering over his glasses. "Again, I must compliment you for your loyalty, Doctor, although there's another question that comes to mind. Dr. Flint is a successful surgeon, catering to the socially prominent. Did you not join his practice when your residency ended shortly after the incident?"

"Yes, I did."

"I should think there was incentive for you to curry Dr. Flint's favor by assisting him in saving the life of one of his wealthy patients."

Raffi's heart pounds; he tightens his grip on the arms of the chair. *Stay cool, keep a steady voice.* "Absolutely not! Dr. Flint never discussed partnership with me at any time before Miss Doss's surgery."

"That may be, Doctor, but isn't it true, following Miss Doss's surgery, he invited you to join his practice?" Murphy turns quickly to face the jury. "Even if Mr. Jackson was destined to die as you allege, didn't he deserve your services as the more experienced surgeon?"

Raffi contains his anger, maintaining a composed posture. His gaze floats toward the jury, settling on Murphy. He punctuates each word. "Sir, given the near-death situation Tommie Jackson faced, Dr. Jenkins's skills were equal to any contribution I could have made."

Murphy's dark eyes spit fire, fiercely scrutinizing Raffi. "The fact that you deliberately chose to operate on Miss Doss instead of tending to Tommie Jackson shows your bias against a poor black boy. It also questions Manhattan Medical's policy regarding ethnic minorities. What is evident, however, is that you chose to save a woman of prominence which would advance your career."

Devon Smith, the defense counsel, calls out to the judge. "Objection! Too many narrative questions with conclusions."

"Sustained," the judge replies.

Even though Murphy's accusations are stricken from the record, Raffi tells himself the prosecutor's plan to plant the seeds of discrimination into the minds of the jurors has succeeded.

Murphy removes his glasses and rubs the bridge of his nose. "Allow me to rephrase the question. Dr. Sarkissian, what made you decide to assign Dr. Jenkins to Mr. Jackson's care?"

Raffi clears his throat, remembering not to wander, but give direct responses. "When I was informed two serious accidents were in the emergency room, I realized there was little time for a senior attending surgeon to come to the hospital. Without any knowledge of the level of either patient's injuries, I decided to have Dr. Jenkins tend to Mr. Jackson while I checked on Miss Doss."

Murphy's smile returns and he directs his gaze to the jury again. "But why did you have Dr. Flint, a senior staff surgeon with you when you operated on Miss Doss while Dr. Jenkins had only house staff? Could you explain that to the jury?"

"Because Miss Doss is Dr. Flint's patient and he called saying he was on his way in and expected me to assist."

Murphy glances at Manhattan Medical's defense team, a triumphant grin crossing his face. "Your witness, Counselor Smith."

Raffi's focus shifts to the jurors but he can't read their thoughts. Has Murphy created enough doubt to obscure the facts? His shirt clings to his back with moisture as he debates that question.

Defense attorney Devon Smith approaches the witness box. In contrast to Murphy, Smith is tall and lean, appearing to be a man in his sixties. His dark suit looks crisp and neat, following the contour of his athletic frame. His voice is steady, his manner calm as he faces Raffi.

"Dr. Sarkissian, you testified Dr. Jenkins was qualified to care for Mr. Jackson's injuries. If you tended to Mr. Jackson instead of Miss Doss, what additional steps would you have taken to save his life?"

"None."

"And the reason is?"

"The tremendous amount of blood Mr. Jackson lost before reaching the hospital led to his death. Because of his dire condition, he crashed in radiology before repair of the thoracic aorta was possible."

Smith nods, returns to the defense table and clicks on a projector directed toward a screen facing the jury. An anatomic display of the thoracic aorta is demonstrated along with the heart and lungs.

He turns to Raffi. "Dr. Sarkissian, using this slide, could you please describe the type of injury Mr. Jackson sustained, and what, if any, operative steps were needed to repair Mr. Jackson's life-threatening injuries?"

Raffi rises from his chair, steps off the witness box and approaches the illuminated screen. He reaches for the laser pointer and directs the beam onto the aorta in the diagram. First he describes Jackson's injury, and then the necessary steps to control the bleeding. It's evident, he explains, Jackson bled out before any surgery could be performed. Sensing he's captured the jury's full attention, he returns to the witness box, allowing the jury to absorb the medical issues his fellow surgeon faced.

Smith lowers his voice. "So Dr. Sarkissian, in your opinion, Tommie Jackson would have died even if he had the most experienced surgeon Manhattan Medical could offer. The fact is the man could not sustain the overwhelming injuries, whether he made it to the OR or not."

Murphy calls out, "Objection! Counselor is leading the witness."

"Sustained," the judge answers.

"Then I'll rephrase the question," Smith replies. "Dr. Sarkissian, given Mr. Jackson's condition, as the senior surgeon, could you have saved Mr. Jackson?"

Raffi shakes his head, "No."

Smith smiles at the jury and then turns again to Raffi. "You testified Dr. Flint never spoke to you about joining his practice before you operated Miss Doss. Is that correct?"

"Yes, that's true."

"Then Doctor, did you choose to operate on Dr. Flint's patient because of the motivation to join his practice?"

"Absolutely not!"

"But the plaintiff's attorney suggests that was your motive, and why you discriminated against a person of color."

"Objection!" Murphy calls out. "Counselor's opinion is without merit. The fact is Dr. Sarkissian did join Dr. Flint's practice."

The judge answers, "Sustained."

Smith places a foot on the edge of the witness box, leaning in toward Raffi. "When did you hear the claim that Tommie Jackson died due to *racism*?"

Raffi's quick to answer. "At a rally outside Manhattan Medical immediately after the incident. Reverend Sanders and his supporters claimed racial discrimination caused Tommie's death."

Smith nods, pleased to have Raffi confirm the role of Sanders. "And do you have an opinion regarding the reverend's motives?"

Raffi looks to the judge who responds, "You may answer, Doctor."

Raffi decides it's time to express how he feels. "In my opinion, Manhattan Medical, Dr. Jenkins and I have all become targets of the reverend's agenda to advance his political objectives."

Murphy jumps up from his seat. "Objection! The witness's opinion is not relevant. Move to strike and instruct the jury to disregard the answer."

"Sustained," the judge answers.

Unable to contain himself, Raffi rises from his chair and points a finger at Murphy. "You're just camouflaging the facts by claiming racism. What do you or Reverend Sanders know about medical emergencies? Doctors work to save lives, not to make social policy!"

The judge slams his gavel as shouts from the courtroom gallery erupt. "Order in the courtroom," he demands. Quiet returns; the judge peers down at attorney Smith from his high bench. "The last statement by the witness will be struck from the record. Counselor, if you have any further questions for this witness, please stick to the facts or I'll hold you in contempt."

"Yes, Your Honor," Smith replies, and then turns once more to Raffi. "No further questions, Doctor."

Raffi glows inwardly, pleased Smith got his message across to the jury. *All the racism crap is just a phony cover.*

As Devon Smith steps away, an outburst of chatter rings through the courtroom. The judge raps his gavel. "Order in the court!" The commotion subsides, and he announces, "It's nearly noon. The court will adjourn and resume at two o'clock."

Engulfed in a background of inaudible conversation, Raffi steps away from the witness stand, mopping his brow with the back of his hand. He approaches Jeremy, sensing the juror's stares focus on them, and says, "Let's get out of here."

A sizable gathering of demonstrators confront them outside on the street, chanting, "Tommie! Tommie!" Someone cries out, "There they are!" The mob pushes toward them.

Jeremy's eyes widened with apprehension. "Where the hell are the guards? Maybe we should go back into the courthouse."

From out of the mob, a black youth dressed in a Mets baseball shirt pushes through, pointing a gun at Raffi. "You're the one who killed my cousin," he shouts.

Jeremy lunges forward to protect Raffi and raises his hands, shouting. "Hey bro', put that gun down!"

The youth turns the gun at Jeremy. "Outta my way!"

The crowd draws back while Jeremy moves closer to the teenager. "Drop the gun before someone gets hurt! No need for violence."

The boy cries out, his hand holding the weapon visibly shaking. "I said outta my way. It's him I want!" He points the gun toward Raffi.

Jeremy stands in front of the boy and reaches for the gun to stop the violence. "Drop it!" he shouts. The pistol fires in the scuffle, and Jeremy crumples to the ground.

Raffi kneels, holds Jeremy in his arms and lets out an anguished cry. Screams echo around him as the mob scatters—the boy runs off.

"Get an ambulance!" Raffi cries out, staring at the lifeless body of his friend. The bullet entered just above Jeremy's eyes and a small trickle of blood oozes from the open wound. He checks for a pulse, but it's too late. Jeremy died instantly.

# *Forty*

Mourning Jeremy's death, Raffi goes through the motions of operating and seeing patients, but the hope for his friend to join him in practice will never happen. Although Jeremy had no accumulated wealth living on a resident's salary, Raffi wants to honor his colleague with a proper burial. He decides to ask friends for donations when he receives an unexpected call.

"Dr. Sarkissian, I'm attorney Robert Tremble. I have instructions to contact you since you are Dr. Jeremy Jenkins' closest friend. An anonymous donor has offered to pay all funeral expenses including the burial site and wake for the doctor on the condition you make all the arrangements. This is my contact number and all bills should come to my office."

Raffi immediately dials Jeremy's girlfriend, Rachel.

"Who would do such a generous act?" Rachel questions through her tears.

"I don't know," Raffi replies, although he has his suspicions. "Jeremy was well liked and with all the publicity in the news, it could be anyone. Let's not look a gift horse in the mouth, Rachel. This is a generous deed, no matter who's behind it."

~ * ~

On the day of the funeral, Raffi sits in the front pew next to Rachel and Lorig, his eyes focused on the open bronze coffin. The small Harlem African Baptist Church choir opens the service with the singing of "Amazing Grace." Jeremy's two sisters from Atlanta are present, along with the mayor and city dignitaries. Every church pew is occupied, with an overflow crowd standing outside. While police security is visible everywhere, Reverend Coleman Sanders is notably absent.

Raffi remembers hearing Jeremy talk about his family one night while waiting for an emergency case. Jeremy's father abandoned the family soon after his birth. His mother, a religious woman, raised her three children with strict discipline tempered with love. It's fortunate, Raffi thinks, she isn't alive to see her son die at such a young age. Breast cancer took her from the family soon after Jeremy completed medical school and maybe that was a blessing.

He listens to the minister's simple eulogy. The pastor admits he didn't know Jeremy well, but praises him for his stellar academic achievements and service to the community during his brief life. Gentle sobs fill the modest church, as viewers approach the coffin to give their last goodbye.

The service ends, and Raffi leads Jeremy's two sisters, along with Rachel and Lorig, outside where the gifted limo awaits them. A small procession of cars follows the hearse over the George Washington Bridge into New Jersey to the burial site. Mourners who do not plan to go to the cemetery are invited to attend the Manhattan restaurant where the wake will be held. Many of the hospital's medical and nursing staff are present to honor their well-loved colleague.

On the return from the burial site, Raffi sits beside a mournful Rachel staring out the limo's window.

With her eyes red with tears, she turns to him. "What am I going to do now? Jeremy was my life. I should have made him marry me."

Raffi swallows hard, a lump lodges in his throat. Unable to answer, he remains quiet, as Lorig gently places a consoling arm around Rachel's shoulder.

His voice cracks when he finally speaks. "Rachel, you shouldn't be alone. Do you have someone to stay with you?"

Rachel fights back her tears, wiping her eyes with her fingers. "I'll be all right if I keep busy at the beauty salon."

"A very wise decision," Raffi says. Returning to her daily routine is better than sitting at home reliving the torture of losing Jeremy, the man she loved and planned to marry.

~ * ~

After the memorial dinner midtown, the chauffeur drops Raffi along with Lorig and Rachel at his apartment building where he picks up his car. He drives Lorig to the George Washington Bridge where her father meets her, and then heads back to Harlem to drop off Rachel.

He rides in silence with an exhausted Rachel dozing off in the passenger seat. Driving north along Park Avenue, her cell phone rings, breaking the quiet. She answers, listens and then abruptly sits up. Her eyes widen with fear.

"Twila, do as I say! Go to my apartment and wait for me in the lobby. Raffi's driving me home and we'll be there in fifteen minutes." She clicks off the phone, and turns to Raffi. "No need to worry about me being alone. Twila Barnett will stay with me."

"Is Twila OK?" *Is she seeing the reverend again?*

"A bit frightened, but she'll feel better once we get there." Rachel replies.

Speeding the car along Park Avenue, he drums his fingers on the steering wheel and sees Rachel sadly leaning her head against the glass window. "Funny how quickly Reverend Sanders recovered from the bad press about Twila. It's as though nothing ever happened."

She bites her lips, forcing back a sob. "Please Raffi, don't get me any more upset than I am at this moment. As far as I'm concerned, that man not only beat up Twila, but he killed my Jeremy. He stirred the hate in this city, and that's not godly."

Raffi keeps driving without saying a word until he turns onto 114th Street. Finding an open parking space, he pulls in. "We're in luck tonight."

He follows Rachel up her apartment steps to the outside landing, opens the door and sees Twila sitting pensively in the lobby. She's pale as a ghost, holding a large duffel bag close to her chest.

She jumps up, crying. "They're after me!"

"Twila, what happened?" Raffi asks, ushering the women up the steps to Rachel and Jeremy's first floor apartment.

Twila nervously glances behind her without speaking.

Once inside, Rachel leads Twila to the sofa, takes the duffel and places it on the floor. "Now tell us what this is all about," she demands.

Twila cups her hands over her face, her body shaking. "I'm in real trouble."

Rachel moves to her side, placing a comforting hand on her shoulder. "What kind of trouble?"

Twila's voice trembles. "Sanders is after the duffel bag. After the beating, I hid it, knowing he'd be coming for it."

Raffi reads pure panic in her eyes. "What's in the bag?"

Twila's lips quiver; she takes a deep breath. "About a hundred thousand in cash along with the black ledger recording protection money he collects from mom and pop shops in Harlem. He kept it in my apartment for safe keeping."

Raffi recalls Wolfe's conversation about Sanders' henchmen making a collection at a small Harlem diner.

Lines crease Twila's brow as she continues. "After he beat me, I didn't answer his calls—I knew he'd send his goons to break into my apartment. That's why I hid it in my basement locker."

"Did they come?"

A smirk crosses Twila's lips. "Yeah, they sure did and tore up my place. I wanted to file an assault and battery complaint but didn't 'cause I was scared as hell. Who knows what else he'll do?"

Raffi's eyes widen as if he had an epiphany. "Twila, the black book may be our answer to getting at this low life. Did he threaten you?"

She crosses her arms over her chest to stop shaking. "He called me, and in the sweetest voice he could muster, insisted I give him the bag. When I said go to hell, he went ballistic and screamed at me. Said his boys were coming and I'd better have the duffel ready for them or else."

Twila breaks into sobs again, and after blowing her nose into a tissue, she clears her throat. "That's when I went to the basement, grabbed the bag and ran out of the apartment to call Rachel from the alley."

A frightening thought suddenly grabs Raffi. For sure Sanders knows all about Rachel and anyone who has anything to do with Jeremy through his loyal Harlem followers. Not only was Twila in danger, but so was Rachel.

Twila jumps up and rushes to the window, nervously searching outside. "I feel someone's out there waiting for me," she murmurs.

"Stay away from there!" Raffi shouts.

As Twila reaches to pull down the window shade, a gunshot rings out, shattering the glass. Fragments fly through the air as Twila drops to the floor, crying in pain.

"My shoulder, my shoulder," she shouts.

Raffi gets on his knees, tosses his phone to Rachel and crawls to Twila's side. "Stay down, Rachel, call nine-one-one." The shoulder-high bloody stain on Twila's sweater assures him the bullet missed her chest. Trained for emergencies, Raffi's non-emotional side of his brain takes over—but the emotional vision of Jeremy dying in his arms still lingers.

Lying on the floor, Rachel hurriedly dials just as loud banging erupts on the lobby's front door. The pop of a gunshot followed by crashing metal echoes through Rachel's apartment door.

Rachel screams into the phone. "Help, someone's breaking in. Nineteen hundred Lexington Avenue, apartment one-o-two."

Raffi picks up Twila from the floor, looking to Rachel. "Take us to your back room."

Twila screams, "Get the duffel bag!"

Still holding Twila, Raffi grabs the bag and follows Rachel into the rear bedroom. He gently places Twila on the bed, props a chair against the knob of the door to block forced entry and grabs the phone from Rachel. Pounding on the front door persists, followed by the crashing sound of a door coming off its hinges.

Droplets of sweat bead on Raffi's brow as he punches in 911 on his phone. "This is Dr. Sarkissian. We have a major fire here at nineteen hundred Lexington Ave, first floor, number one-o-two. Come quickly!" He hears the rapid beating of his heart and ends the call as heavy footsteps pound the wooden parquet floors inside the apartment.

His eyes dart around the room, searching for an object that'll serve as a weapon. Perfume bottles sit on a vanity with a cushioned bench next to it. He picks up the bench, ready to strike, hoping the police will arrive before Sanders' hoods break into the bedroom.

Twila moans, quivering on the bed as Rachel tries to comfort her. Raffi stands ready to strike, still holding the bench, and listens to the unmistakable clatter of boots resonating on vintage hardwood floors.

"Where're they hiding?" a husky voice calls out.

"Check the bedrooms," another shouts, as a rush of heavy steps descends the hallway.

Raffi puts down the bench and leans firmly on the chair propped against the door. He looks to Rachel and nods toward the window. "That's the only way out of here."

Rachel's eyes widen in shock. "You mean through the window?"

Raffi nods. "It's either that or you know what—"

She cuts him off. "What about Twila? There's at least a ten-foot drop to the ground."

The sudden thud against the door causes Rachel to jump up, rush to the window and open it.

The rumble of a body ramming against the door makes Raffi press his full weight against the chair. He can't hold off the intruders much longer. "Get Twila out now!" he shouts.

Rachel helps Twila from the bed and says, "Come on, sweetie, you can do this." Despite Twila's moans, Rachel leads her to the window.

The pounding on the door continues and a raspy voice shouts. "We know you're in there. Open up!"

Raffi feels a tremendous force pushing against the door and leans the full weight of his body to keep it from opening, straining with all his might. "Rachel, you go first, and I'll hand Twila down to you."

Rachel climbs onto the ledge with the duffel bag and suddenly disappears from the window.

Raffi hears her scream as she hits the ground. He races to Twila's side, lifts her onto the ledge as she whimpers in pain. He looks down to see Rachel scramble to her feet on the soft patch of grass that cushioned her fall.

He sees the bedroom door bow inward, and urgently calls out to Rachel. "Grab her legs, I'm letting her go." He releases his hold from under Twila's arms. Rachel's outstretched arms catch Twila, blunting her fall.

Before Raffi has the chance to escape, a burly black man barrels through the door and grabs him by the collar, throwing him to the floor. "You ain't goin' nowhere."

Stunned, Raffi looks up to see the familiar scorpion tattoo on the invader's neck. The diamond in his right earlobe clinches it. The intruder is the same thug he witnessed running out of the hospital room the day the young drug dealer was shot in the head. The police hadn't caught the man, despite Raffi giving a detailed description.

Raffi winces in pain as a heavy boot on his chest forces him to the floor. Another two men enter wearing military fatigues with ankle high boots. One has a scar running down his cheek and stares at Raffi while the tattooed man continues to hold him to the floor with his boot.

"Where's the money?" a husky voice demands.

"Check the other rooms," another orders. "If it's not in Twila's apartment, it's got to be here."

"Checked all over, found nothing," scar-face answers, gesturing for his companion to check under the bed.

His crony kneels and looks, shaking his head. "Nothing here."

The man with the tattoo curses, kicking Raffi in the ribs. "You son of a bitch! You ain't gonna make it out of here if you don't tell us where you parked the cash."

Raffi grunts in pain, his pulse races, praying for 911 to hurry. He shouts, "What cash?"

The man snarls, kicking Raffi again. "Tell us where you parked the duffel bag, or you know what!"

Raffi grunts louder, trying to roll away from the man's foot.

Scar-face races to the window and looks out. "Twila and Rachel are outside at the curb!" he shouts.

"Jump out and grab them!" Tattoo orders.

His partner climbs out of the window and drops to the ground. Raffi hears a thud as he lands.

Tattoo leans down, wrapping his thick fingers around Raffi's neck. "OK, last chance, talk."

"Don't know," Raffi gasps, his throat burning.

The man raises his fist ready to strike but becomes distracted when swirling red lights flash through the open window followed by the sound of heavy truck engines and sirens. The disruption gives Raffi a split moment to jump up and lunge at his assailant, throwing him onto the floor. He pounds Tattoo with his fists, but to no avail. The thug grabs Raffi and pulls him back onto the floor.

"Help, over here!" Raffi shouts, hearing heavy boots approach.

A fireman holding an axe appears at the doorway. "Where's the fire?"

The tattoo man doesn't waste time and pushes Raffi away, scrambles to the open window and jumps out.

"Stop him!" Raffi shouts.

The fireman rushes to the window, looks out and shouts to the firefighters on the ground outside. "Stop that guy!"

Another fireman enters the bedroom. "What's going on here?"

Raffi rubs his neck, slowly getting up from the floor. He brushes the dust from his pants, and asks, "Did you see two women at the curb?"

"Yeah," he answers. "The one with the gunshot is on her way to Harlem Hospital."

"What about the other?"

"She went with her," the fireman answers.

A police officer walks through the door. "Are you Dr. Sarkissian?"

"Yes, I am," Raffi replies, straightening his jacket. Hard to believe he just came from Jeremy's funeral.

"Nine-one-one reported a fire, but where's the fire?"

Raffi confesses. "It was the fastest way to get you here to catch a murderer."

The officer's eyes narrows. "Murder?"

"They're the ones who shot Marcellus right in his hospital bed. It happened a few months ago."

The officer takes a hold of Raffi's arm. "We'll need to question you down at the stationhouse."

"No problem, Officer. But will the women be safe at the hospital? They need guards, just in case…"

"What's going on?"

"Those guys are after them, with guns. The women hold a duffel bag containing criminal evidence against Reverend Sanders."

The officer's eyes narrow as he snaps on the two-way radio clipped to his lapel. "Officer Hernandez calling in."

The radio crackled. "I read you."

Hernandez continues. "Were those two ladies holding a duffel bag?"

Raffi hears the response from the speaker. "No, no bags."

The policeman looks to Raffi. "Nothing about a duffel bag— let's go to the station."

Raffi tucks his shirt back into his trousers, facing the officer. "Did they capture those three hoods?" He has to safeguard Rachel and Twila for Jeremy's sake as well as his own.

The officer shakes his head, returning his pistol to his belt. "We got two. Were there three?"

"Yeah. What about the guy with the tattoo on his neck?"

The policeman returns a blank gaze. "I don't remember any tattoo."

# *Forty-one*

Raffi sits in the rear seat of the squad car, adrenaline coursing through his veins. While fresh in his memory, he consents to review the mug shots of convicted felons at the police station, though last time he'd done it, he hadn't found his man. Checking his phone, he sees Lorig's two texts.

*Where are you, Raffi? I'm worried.*

Despite the late hour, he dials and leaves a voice message. "Lorig, I can't explain right now, but I'm in a police squad car heading to the station house. Call me when you get this."

Within minutes, Lorig calls back. "My God, Raffi! What happened?"

He bites his lip, not wanting to upset her—but needing her help one more time. "Don't worry."

"Dammit Raffi, don't keep me hanging here! Where are you?"

"I'm still in the squad car, and we're pulling into the police station as I speak. I'm fine, but—"

Lorig raises her voice. "I'm coming right now. There won't be any traffic at this late hour."

"That's okay, hon. The police will take me back to my car parked at Rachel's house."

"You heard me! Which police station?" Her shrill voice carries over to the front.

The officer in the passenger seat calls out, "Precinct Twelve, hundred twenty-fifth and Lexington."

Raffi repeats the address into the phone and before hanging up, adds, "I love you." He smiles, telling himself, *she's always there for me.*

At police headquarters, for at least thirty minutes, he pours over several binders holding photos of criminals, nodding with a negative response with each turn of the page. Two thirds into the log, he stops at a photo. Pointing excitedly, he shouts. "That's him! Like I said, his neck was inked with a scorpion and he wore a diamond stud in the right ear."

"You're sure?" the officer questions. "Scorpion tattoos are very common."

"Not this one." Raffi's finger traces the inked work of art. "Look, this one's unique. See the skull in the background?"

The officer studies the photo. "That *is* different."

"Yes," Raffi insists, scanning the long criminal record listed under the picture. There's no question he's the thug that shot Marcellus in the hospital bed, and beat him in Rachel's apartment.

After a brief questioning, he's allowed to return to the fluorescent-lit reception area and finds a dozing Lorig slumped on a hard bench in jeans and no makeup. Her natural beauty shines through, melting his heart. *Stay cool, don't frighten her.* His greeting is casual. "Hey, babe."

She jolts upright, alarm written on her face. "Raffi! Your face is all bruised! What happened?"

"I'm OK, but I'm worried about Rachel and Twila."

"Please, Raffi, what's going on!"

"Long story. I'll tell you once I get hold of them. Right now, drive me to Rachel's to pick up my car."

Tears roll down Lorig's cheek and he sees fear in her eyes. Approaching her car, he comes to a halt, flushed with an overwhelming sense of gratitude. Lucky to be alive, he wraps his arms around her. *Thank God she's in my life.*

She faces him, her eyes questioning. Without saying a word, she returns his embrace, crying on his shoulder. No words are spoken, but she senses all is not right.

On the way to Rachel's house, he dials Harlem Hospital while Lorig sits stoically at the wheel driving. The hospital switchboard connects him with Twila's room.

"This is Raffi, Twila. Are you and Rachel okay?"

Twila's voice shakes as she speaks. "Oh Raffi, I'm so glad to hear your voice—glad you're alive." She takes in a deep breath, taking control. "I'm okay, just a fractured ankle. Luckily the gunshot to my shoulder is only a flesh wound."

"That's good, but what about Rachel?"

"She's okay too. A friend came to the hospital and picked her up. Rachel is staying with her tonight, but said she'll call you in the morning."

"Do you know what happened to the duffel bag?"

"No. The hoods probably have it. Anyway, I'm thankful to be alive." She sighs, her voice lowers. "Sorry to get you involved in this mess. It's almost midnight, and we both should get some sleep."

He ends the call and glances at Lorig, who continues driving and listening intently to the one-way conversation. He leans over and kisses her cheek. "Take me home. I'll pick up my car from Rachel's tomorrow."

Once inside his apartment, Lorig sits on the sofa, watching him pace the floor excitedly, describing how the thugs broke into Rachel's apartment looking for the bag of money. Exhausted, he finally sinks on the sofa next to her, his hands covering his face.

Lorig caresses his arm. "I was petrified when you didn't answer my call. Thank God you're safe."

Raffi goes limp, a sudden calm washes over him, lucky to have escaped the threat on his life. Lucky to be sitting next to the woman he loves. He brushes away the tears in her eyes with his fingers, reading the love in her eyes. Tenderly, he smothers her with kisses, pulling her down atop him on the sofa.

Her body trembles, fear fills her eyes. "You're safe tonight, Raffi, but what about tomorrow or the next day? Those creeps are still out there. How can I be sure you'll be out of harm's way?"

That dread has already crept into his thoughts, but he must convince her otherwise. "Lorig, I can cross the street tomorrow and get hit by a taxi or whatever. There's no guarantee in life."

She pulls away; her lips form a pout. "But you can't always count on beating the odds."

Teasingly, he grabs her again, holding her close. "And what are the odds of you staying with me tonight?" He's wanted her for so long. What would she say?

Her gaze suddenly softens, and her silence encourages him. He strokes her cheek gently, kissing her. "Please stay," he whispers.

She holds him, tears glazing her eyes. "I could have lost you before I had a chance to say I love you."

They cling to each other; she crying, he emotionally moved by her admission. That night they make passionate love as if they'd never see each other again, sleeping deep in each other's arms.

~ * ~

After a simple breakfast of orange juice and cereal the following morning, along with shy laughter and many kisses, Raffi sends Lorig off to work—she doesn't want to call in sick because a change in routine is hard on the kids.

He lingers over the last of his coffee, his heart bursting with love. He tries hanging onto the joy, but reality raises its ugly head. Certainly Sanders' henchmen know of his involvement with Twila and the damning evidence in the duffel bag.

The image of the tattooed assailant who attacked him in Rachel's apartment flashes in his brain. By God, the man is a ruthless killer...shooting Marcellus, the young drug dealer, in the head as he lay in the hospital bed. If the cops hadn't come when they did, he'd be dead too.

He checks his watch, wondering where the morning has gone. Quickly, he clears the dishes and leaves to follow up on the few patients he has in the hospital. Then he'll go to see Rachel.

On his way out the door, his cell rings. It's Adam Wolfe.

"Hey Raffi, I heard what happened last night. Are you OK?"

"I guess so—they were after the duffel bag."

"What duffel bag? I thought it was just a break-in and shooting."

Raffi hesitates to tell Wolfe about the incriminating information in Twila's possession. The reporter might inadvertently leak the information in the press, putting Twila in a precarious position. To protect Rachel, Twila, and himself, he first has to connect Sanders to the crime. Except for the implicating evidence, there was no other link to Sanders.

"Look Adam, it's a long story. What is it you want to talk about?"

"There's breaking news about Patsy Sweet—the congresswoman who took blood money from the Turkish coalition. Are you free around ten? I can meet you at the hospital cafeteria."

"I'll see you there," Raffi replies. Ironically, it's Jasmine Battia who exposed the illegal payout, and now she was the center of the controversy—instead of Sweet.

The conversation ends and Raffi dwells on the political corruption around him. Where is the justice? Jasmine is silenced by presidential order while Turkish nationalists threaten her life. Hiding under the cloth, Reverend Sanders pilfers money from small businesses while shacking up with a woman who isn't his wife, and beating her as well.

He puts on his coat, making a resolution. *Something has to change.*

~ * ~

Raffi quickly spots Adam seated in the hospital cafeteria, a can of cola in his hand. With the breakfast rush over, the room is nearly empty and free for talk. He fills a cup of coffee and slips into a chair, facing the reporter. "So, what's the breaking news?"

The reporter nods a hello, not wasting time. "The Ohio Ethics Commission determined Patsy Sweet violated the law by accepting money from a foreign lobby."

"Well, that's good news—getting a payoff to vote against the Armenian Genocide Resolution is not what she was sent to Congress to do. Now what?"

Wolfe's bushy eyebrows arch in annoyance. "Although she's found guilty on three of the five counts, supposedly her *intent* was not to violate ethics laws. Can you believe they determined she only used bad judgment?"

Surprised, Raffi puts down his cup. "So they let her off the hook."

"Yes, they did. The decision went to the House for final adjudication and they accepted the Ethics Committee's verdict not to sanction or prosecute her."

Raffi shakes his head in disgust. "So she gets off to run for office again without a blemish?"

Wolfe lets out a sarcastic laugh. "She's required to return the Turkish PAC money, over four hundred thousand dollars, but can draw it out of her political contributions."

Raffi taps his fingers on the coffee cup impatiently. "What a convenient resolution."

"Yes, but there's a hook."

Raffi throws Wolfe a questioning gaze.

Wolfe takes a swig from the can before speaking. "Sweet's congressional zone is getting redistricted with her home base being phased out."

"So the Ethics Committee defends her actions to sell her vote and then closes her district to avoid embarrassing questions."

Wolfe rises and pats Raffi's shoulder. "Welcome to Washington politics, Doc."

~ * ~

Later that morning, Raffi climbs the steps to Rachel's apartment just as two glaziers finish replacing her shattered front window. They finally secure the panel in place.

"Nice job," Raffi calls out.

One worker climbing down the ladder smiles, handing him a business card. "We do good work. Call if you need us."

Raffi nods, slips the card into his pocket and enters the building. Rachel greets him at her front door, in jeans and a gray t-shirt with dark hair tied back in a colorful scarf. Her taut expression confirms the previous day's traumatic episode. She nervously grabs his hand, ushering him into the apartment.

"Thanks for coming, Raffi."

"I got your message," he says, his eyes darting around the apartment. Linen and clothing hang out of open drawers; lamps, tables overturned.

Rachel picks up pieces of a broken vase as she speaks. "The hoods did a thorough job searching for the duffel bag. Been trying to clean up this mess all morning."

Raffi places a hand on her shoulder. "Thank God you and Twila are okay."

She nods, placing the bits of pottery into the trash. "I telephoned the hospital this morning and she'll be discharged later today. I convinced her to stay with me—I have bulletproof glass and new locks—nobody will be breaking in again."

Raffi gathers linens from floor and places them on the buffet. "Sorry the police never found the duffel bag. Those crooks must have gotten it."

Rachel stops cleaning, letting out a wry chuckle. "The police don't have it and neither does Sanders."

Raffi stands dumbfounded. "Where is it?"

She teasingly shakes her head. "Can't say."

"Don't you trust me?"

"Raffi, of course I trust you. But I want to protect you and Twila. What you don't know won't hurt you."

The lines on her brow suddenly deepen with concern. "At first I thought the bag only held the black book and shakedown money, but there's more. After Twila was shot, she begged me not to give it to the police. Told me to hide it because Sanders has connections at the police department. She doesn't trust them."

"You think so?" *This all sounds like a fiction novel.*

Rachel is adamant. "Yes, it's true, Raffi! She recognized one of the cops guarding us at the hospital. She thinks he's one of Sanders' cohorts."

Raffi's stunned his pulse races. *The wolf guarding the henhouse.* "What else is in the bag?"

Rachel lowers her voice. "Besides the monthly payoff ledger, it holds two overseas bank accounts registered in Sanders' name."

"How in the world did you hide the bag in all that confusion?"

"After I jumped out of the window, I threw it into the shrubs. Early this morning, I moved it from the pines and put it in a safe place."

Raffi laughs, a glint in his eye. "You are one brave woman, Rachel. You've done yourself proud."

Rachel grins, revealing the dimples on her pretty cheeks. "The greedy bastard. Thinks he can get away without paying good old Uncle Sam his share? That's why he put it in untraceable overseas accounts with secret banking numbers."

Raffi catches the satisfied grin crossing Rachel's face. *It all makes sense.*

She wipes the moisture from her brow. "God, I'm dry from all this excitement. Can I get you a soda, lemonade?"

Raffi stands in a reflective mood before speaking. "So what are you going to do with it?"

Rachel heads to the kitchen, calling out over her shoulder, "I haven't decided."

He follows, watching her fill two glasses from a pitcher. She turns to face him, her eyes sad with grief. "Sanders is why my Jeremy is dead. I swear to God, I want this evidence to nail him to his own cross."

Raffi pauses, his heart heavy, the image of Jeremy dead in his arms. "Rachel, whatever you're planning, you've got to be careful."

Rachel takes a long swallow and then puts the glass on the kitchen table. "I'll think of something."

Raffi holds her by the shoulders. "You and Twila may be wise not to trust the police. I have a suggestion."

Rachel's frown tells him she isn't eager to hear his proposal, but he persists. "Hear me out. Our hospital lawyer will make contact with the district attorney. Once everything in that bag is legally documented with copies and the evidence protected, you'll also be protected. Then we can pursue criminal charges against Sanders."

Rachel's lips curl, suggesting she isn't comfortable with his idea. "I'll think about it, Raffi, but in the meantime, please do me a favor."

"Sure thing. What is it?"

"Get me a security guard. I need to sleep at night."

# Forty-two

The next morning, Raffi finishes operating on an elderly man suffering from bowel obstruction caused by colon cancer. He steps away from the OR table, orders the resident to write the ICU postop orders and then heads to the surgical lounge to dictate the operative summary.

On completion of his report, his attention is drawn to the headline in the *New York Times* lying on the desk. *French Senate to vote on Armenian Genocide.*

His heart skips a beat, remembering Adam Wolfe's warning about Jasmine Battia's safety. With the increasing international recognition of Turkey's long standing ethnic cleansing of Armenians, he worries its government might take desperate measures to silence the congressional payoffs.

He begins reading the article when the circulating nurse enters. "Dr. Sarkissian, your next case is delayed. Anesthesia is responding to an emergency call."

"Let me know when you're ready," he replies, turning to the editorial page. He searches for comments critical of Turkey but none are printed. Annoyed that the political winds don't favor casting Turkey in a negative light, he tosses the paper back onto the desk. The odds are against Battia finding justice. Frustrated he has no solution; he picks up his phone to call Lorig but remembers she's at school.

His next thought is Rachel and he dials, hearing the tremor in her voice. "Are you all right? Where am I reaching you?"

"I'm in my apartment trying to make arrangements for Twila to stay with me."

"What are you going to do about the bag?"

"I don't know."

"Rachel, consider my suggestion to speak with our hospital attorney. Mr. Gold can take the evidence to the DA without involving you."

Her voice shakes. "I told you, I don't trust the police. My heart pounds whenever a stranger enters our building."

"You think Sanders is having you watched?"

"They'll do anything to get the bag. His goons are just waiting to pounce on me."

"Don't panic. Let me speak to our hospital attorney."

Rachel hesitates. "Maybe the hospital doesn't want to get involved with a man of the cloth, especially with all the legal shenanigans. What about speaking to Traci Doss's lawyer?"

"Grant Perry? Maybe I should talk to Traci first."

"How is Traci? She never came to Jeremy's funeral."

"Probably because she was still convalescing after rehab."

A brief silence follows before Rachel speaks. "I never asked, but do you think she's the anonymous person who paid for Jeremy's funeral?"

"I have my suspicions."

"Raffi, maybe you *should* call her. We might need her help down the road."

Rachel's words make sense. He's heard nothing from Traci lately or her doctors about her progress and hasn't checked. Subconsciously he's afraid to hear she's back on drugs. Plus the fact that Lorig shared some of Traci's problems the night of her overdose and Raffi doesn't want to drag that drama into his and Lorig's relationship.

"I'll call her, but Rachel, I want you to be with me when I see her."

Rachel questions, "Why do you need me?"

"Because she probably trusts you more than me." Raffi understands Traci. In her mind, he's one of many men who have let her down.

~ * ~

Raffi's nurse, Mary, tracks down Traci who agrees to meet him at six in the evening at her Central Park West apartment. He dials Lorig to tell her his plan, but senses she's annoyed by the tone in her voice.

"Look Raffi, you're not the law, you're a doctor. You're getting in too deep with these low life politicians and criminals. I'm worried."

Raffi brushes off her warning with a chuckle. "I promise to be careful. Rachel needs me and I feel I owe it to Jeremy." *And if this brings Sanders down for good, then it's worth taking a chance.*

"I can't talk you out of getting involved?" Lorig doesn't wait for him to answer before pressing on. "You can't help it, I know, but be careful. I love you."

He hangs up; her last words ring in his ear. After this episode, he promises himself, Lorig will come first.

~ * ~

Raffi double parks outside Rachel's apartment and blows his horn, waiting for her to appear. Within minutes she hurries down the stairs and slips into his car, her gaze directed to two men in hoodies lurking across the street. "You see those guys? They just ran out of my building."

"Don't worry. You're safe with me and we have business to attend to." He guns the car and to satisfy Rachel's fears, weaves in and around traffic in an effort to lose anyone who might be following. Within thirty minutes they pull up to the front of Traci's apartment building.

The doorman approaches. "Sir, you can't park here."

Rachel lowers the passenger window. "Miss Doss is expecting us. Where can we park?"

The doorman's brow wrinkles. "You won't find Miss Doss at home. She just left." He points to a silver sedan pulling away from the curb several car lengths ahead of them.

Raffi surmises Traci's up to no good and leans toward the open window. "I'm Miss Doss's physician. Did she appear alert, steady?"

The doorman hesitates. "You're her doctor?"

"Yes. I need to make sure she's all right."

He rubs his chin; a puzzled expression plasters his face. "Well, Doc, I must admit, she stumbled a bit climbing into the car."

"Thanks," Raffi replies, quickly stepping on the gas to chase the silver sedan.

Rachel's brow wrinkles. "Where could she be going?"

"We'll soon find out. I have a strong feeling she's hooked on drugs again." Guilt makes him reckless as he speeds, following the sedan.

"Watch out!" Rachel shouts as a taxi races in front, cutting them off.

Raffi tightens his hold on the wheel, swerving to avoid a collision. "Sit tight, we can't lose her."

Rachel grips the armrest, taking in a deep breath as Raffi races through a red light, tailing the silver sedan all the way to the East side on 27th Street until it slows and slips into an empty parking space.

He quickly pulls up and double parks adjacent to the sedan, blocking the driver's door. Jumping out of the car, he dashes to the passenger side, and swings open the door. His suspicions are on target. Traci is lethargic, leaning back on the seat.

Her eyes are glazed. "Raffi! What are you doing here?"

Dilated pupils, slurred speech indicates what he fears. Pills, heroine, alcohol?

In anger, he shouts, "Dammit, Traci!" He wraps his arms around her, trying to lift her out of the car.

The large, bearded man behind the wheel gives a guttural snarl, attempting to open the door blocked by Raffi's car. "Who the hell are you?"

"Her doctor, so you better take your damned hands off her," Raffi shouts, struggling to carry Traci out of the car.

The man amazingly pulls his hulky body over the center console and jumps out onto the sidewalk, knocking aside an overflowing garbage can at the curb. He flings himself on Raffi, pushing him onto the concrete pavement, and knocking Traci head-first to the ground.

His massive boot presses Raffi's chest, and he pulls out a gun. "What the fuck do you think you're doing?"

Raffi can't believe he's staring at the barrel of a pistol, *again*, but this time Trace's limp body lies sprawled on the walkway next to him. Fear is his enemy, and he musters up the toughest voice he can deliver. "Pull that trigger and you're a marked man," he shouts, as the cold metal of the gun presses against his temple.

Rachel's high pitched voice screams into her phone. "A man has us at gunpoint on the corner of East Twenty-seventh Street and Third Avenue. Please come quick."

The bearded driver turns toward Rachel, surprised by her presence and turns the gun on her. "Who the hell are you?"

Rachel bee-lines it out of reach of the gun's target, hiding behind the cars just as the sudden wail of police sirens sound in the distance. The drug dealer sticks the gun into his belt, bends over and picks up Traci.

Raffi gets up, fighting him off. "Let her go, you shit!" he curses.

Out of the dark, two teenagers appear. One points a weapon at the bearded gangster. "What you done to that girl, mister?"

Startled, the man releases his grip on Traci, who falls, again striking her head on the pavement with a thud. He stands over her body, fear plastered on his face. "See what you did," he shouts, and then runs down the street, disappearing in the shadows.

Raffi's breath comes heavy, and he jumps up, gathering a senseless Traci in his arms. "Traci, talk to me, it's Raffi," but she's unresponsive. *She either suffered a concussion or is zoned out on drugs, or both.*

The two teenagers stand, peering over them. "That your girl, white boy?" the one with the gun asks. "Better get her to the hospital."

With the flashing red and white lights approaching, the youth tucks his firearm in his trousers. "Let's get the hell out of here." The two run from the scene as Raffi nests his jacket under Traci's head. He searches for Rachel, who reappears from behind the Lexus.

Breathless, she kneels by Traci, facing Raffi. "I called nine-one-one and gave directions. Do you think she's dead?"

Raffi presses his fingers on Traci's wrist, feeling for a pulse. "Chances are good she'll recover once we get her to the ER."

Tires screech and lights flash, announcing the arrival of the police. An officer scrambles out of the squad car and approaches Raffi, his arms extended holding a gun. "Hands up. Stay where you are!"

Raffi does as ordered, and pleads. "We need an ambulance to take my patient to Manhattan Medical."

The officer questions. "You're a doctor? Identity, please."

Raffi takes out the license from his wallet, shoving it toward the cop. "I'm Dr. Sarkissian and I just stopped a kidnapping."

The second officer approaches, speaking into his two-way radio, witnessing the scene. "Officer Clancy, here. We need an ambulance at Twenty-seventh Street East and Third Avenue."

The officer holding the gun points to the double parked Lexus. "Is that yours?"

"Yes," Raffi answers.

He points to the silver sedan at the curb with the open passenger door. "Who owns this one?"

"Don't know," Raffi answers, "but when you find out, that'll be the kidnapper. And this is heiress Traci Doss."

# Forty-three

Raffi enters his apartment at midnight, after the two hour police interrogation. He checks with Rachel, satisfied she was driven safely home. With an early surgery schedule the next morning, he struggles to sleep, plotting how to get Sanders' incriminating evidence into the DA's hands.

Finally falling into a deep sleep, he hears the annoying alarm ring as the morning light comes through the window. He plots his day. Do morning surgery, and then check on Traci in the hospital. Fortunately, the internist he selected agreed to make her a medical admission rather than a drug addiction case.

He finishes his case, quickly heads to the medical floor and reads her chart in the nurses' station. *Aggressive violent behavior, hallucinatory meltdown noted. To be gradually weaned off drug dependency.*

He finds Grant Perry and a nurse standing at Traci's bedside when he enters her room. Sitting upright with the head of the bed raised, she appears surprisingly alert. The nurse holds onto a clipboard as Traci signs documents.

Perry turns to greet him. "Just one more signature and I'll be out of your way, Doc."

*Has Traci been lucid enough to call her attorney?*

Traci holds the pen, her hand shaky, and scrawls her signature, after which the nurse signs and hands Perry the clipboard. "I've witnessed all the signed papers, Mr. Perry. Will that be all?" the nurse asks.

"That's it for today, thank you," Perry replies.

After the nurse leaves the room, Raffi's questioning eyes narrow. "How did you know Traci was in the hospital?"

The attorney slips the documents into his brief case, giving Raffi a hint of a grin. "I guess you didn't read the morning paper," he says, locking his leather case. "Traci is big news wherever she goes. Last night's police report was picked up by a reporter. By the way, your name was mentioned."

Raffi flinches inwardly. Having his name constantly in the press isn't helpful to his professional career. But right now, his concern is for Traci, and he faces her.

"How are you feeling?" he asks. "Do you remember what happened last night?"

Her voice carries a snooty ring. "Don't care to know. I just want to get some sleep."

Raffi reads the haggard look on her face. *Drugs or pride has a hold on her.* "Rest for now, Traci. You'll feel better in a few days."

He motions Perry to follow him into the hallway and once outside the room, ushers him into a secluded nook. His voice lowers to a secretive pitch. "As Miss Doss's legal advisor, perhaps you can help."

"Please explain."

"A friend possesses a bag holding incriminating evidence against Reverend Sanders. This material needs to be brought to the attention of the district attorney without endangering my friend."

Perry's gaze remains focused, legally cautious. "What is it you want?"

"We would like you to approach the DA with his assurance the person holding the evidence will be protected. That person has been personally threatened by Sanders and doesn't want to be another unsolved statistic."

Perry hesitates a moment, lowers his chin, deep in thought. "This is a very sensitive issue, Doctor. Why ask me? Call the DA yourself."

"I feel we need legal protection and I'm sure Miss Doss would approve—in her normal state. That's what I was to discuss with her yesterday when that pusher attempted to kidnap her."

The attorney looks down at the floor, without making eye contact. "You realize I'm not a criminal attorney. Perhaps you should—"

Raffi cuts him off, pushing for help as one friend for another. "You're well aware of the favors I've done for Miss Doss. It's a simple request. Call the DA and have him provide police security. That's all I ask."

Perry hesitates a moment before agreeing. "I'll need all the details."

"I'll provide that. As our legal representative, you will relay the information to the DA."

Perry's brow knits with concern. "I'll do it, as long as it's legal and straightforward."

Raffi grasps his hand. "Thank you." He pauses for a moment and clarifies. "Of course you agree there won't be a fee."

Grant Perry's frown turns into a genuine smile. "Of course not."

~ * ~

Raffi hadn't heard from Lorig all week, not that he has any free time to share with her. Until she calls one evening.

"Raffi, I need to talk to you." Her voice comes across edgy, demanding.

"Lorig, what's up?"

"Not over the phone. Where can we meet?"

Unlike the accustomed warm hello, her brusque tone bothers him. But he keeps his cool. "What about your favorite Italian restaurant up the road from you? I'll pick you up."

"That won't be necessary. I'll see you there tomorrow at seven."

He picks up the phone to call her several times the following day, but hesitates, quickly hanging up. *What's upsetting her?* Everything was great the night she spent with him at his apartment...so he'll just have to wait until he sees her tonight.

That evening he drives over the George Washington Bridge and follows the familiar 9W road north, his hands white knuckled on the steering wheel. Had he hurt her in any way? He searches his mind. The only way to find out is to confront her face to face.

Beside a few guests, Casa Luna, the restaurant where they had their first date, is quiet with only a few tables occupied. His eyes roam the room, spotting her alone at a secluded table, nursing a glass of wine. He approaches, catching her determined expression.

"Hi, hon. Sorry for not keeping in touch, but things got crazy at the hospital."

She twists her glass on the cocktail napkin; her eyes focus on him. Her voice carries a slight tremor. "Raffi, sit down and listen. What I have to say won't take long."

Throwing her a puzzled glance, he slips into the chair opposite her, his heart beating against his chest. He waits for her to speak.

Her voice softens; she continues to play with the napkin. "Raffi, I've thought long and hard about what I'm going to say." She hesitates, taking a hard swallow. "I've come to the conclusion our lifestyles are too different to sustain a long term relationship."

For a moment, he doesn't understand her message, coming so swift, without warning. *Is she breaking up with me?* He reaches for her hand, but she pulls away. His eyes lock onto hers. "Lorig, I love you. We're so good together!"

Her voice trembles; she stares down at her glass. "Raffi, you know I care for you, but I have doubts." She raises her head; a tear runs down her cheek. "Our time together has become unpredictable, filled with violence, confrontations. I have a continuous knot in my stomach, keeping me up at nights worrying what'll happen next."

Stunned, he pleads, again reaching for her hand. "Lorig, please forgive me. From now on, things will be different."

"Nothing to forgive," she replies firmly. "You're immersed in the reverend's politics, Traci and her world. I don't feel any of this has anything to do with *us*." She wipes the moisture from the wine glass, and continues. "What was last week all about? Your name in the paper, linked to a woman who might as well be in a crack house."

Demoralized, he pleads guilty as accused, but replies defensively. "I didn't plan for that."

Tears fill her eyes, and she finally slips her hand on his. "You mean well, Raffi, but I can't live an unpredictable life filled with dangerous encounters."

The anguish on her face hurts him to the core. "I love you, Lorig. Doesn't that mean anything?"

She wipes tears away with her hand. "That's why this is so hard for me to say. I love you too, but there are things I need in my life. A sense of stability, children, a normal family life, friends who are ordinary people."

He has to convince her that he wants the same things and leans forward, tightening his grasp on her hand. "Okay, honey, let's start over. Plan something you want to do with your friends this Saturday. I will make myself available."

She removes her hand, pulling out a tissue from her purse. "That time is over, Raffi. I don't want to be hurt anymore."

Her words cut through him like a knife. He wants embrace her and extends his arms but she pushes him away, jumps up from the table and rushes out of the restaurant.

~ * ~

Raffi fights back anger and frustration over his sudden breakup with Lorig. He sits at the nursing station staring aimlessly at a patient's chart when the desk secretary breaks into his trance. "Did you hear your page, Doctor? You're wanted in the administrator's office."

"Thanks," he says, rising. "Please call and tell them I'm on my way."

As he rides the elevator to the executive offices, he worries that he might be doing just what Lorig feared. Getting involved in other people's problems. Why did he ask Grant Perry to take the reverend's incriminating documents to the district attorney? Lorig is right. He has no reason to get involved with the reverend's underhanded politics. By the time he arrives at the administrative offices, he's convinced himself he'll have nothing further to do with anything but medicine.

He enters the office, and faces Detective Daley seated with Barry Gold, the hospital attorney.

The lawyer rises to greet him and gestures to the empty chair beside the desk. "Thanks for coming, Doctor. Something just came up that Detective Daley and I feel you should know."

Raffi stops in his tracks, unprepared to deal with another unexpected challenge, and then takes a seat.

Gold clears his throat, giving Raffi a penetrating look. "Grant Perry from the law firm, Conway, Albert and Noble, gave the DA some incriminating documents that reportedly belong to Reverend Sanders. Before pressing charges, the court needs to know how those records were obtained."

Raffi shifts uncomfortably in his seat.

"Mr. Perry states you gave him the material but the DA wants to know how you got them," Gold repeats.

Apprehension settles over Raffi, his tone defensive. "I didn't steal them. I only delivered the material."

"Who gave it to you?" Daley questions.

Raffi shakes his head. "I can't say."

Daley squints. "You do understand any public exposure of illegal activities by Sanders is like clubbing a hornet's nest. We need the facts or else it's a no-go."

Raffi reads suspicion on the detective's face. "Does Sanders know you have this material?"

Daley nods. "His attorney claims they can prove it was stolen and requests it to be returned."

*How did Sanders learn the DA has the incriminating evidence?* Raffi repeats, "The stuff was not stolen!"

"Then tell us how it came into your possession."

Raffi stands his ground, aware that both Twila and Rachel need to be protected. "I don't want to endanger my source. Lives could be in jeopardy."

"Everything will be kept confidential," Daley replies.

"Confidential? Then how did the reverend's attorney know this information was in the hands of the DA? No doubt it was leaked by the reverend's spies in the police department." *Twila had been right to be concerned.*

"I can't answer that, Doc. But you'll have every protection the law can offer," Daley replies.

Raffi's eyes narrow in anger. "I don't want to have anything to do with the reverend. Let the DA handle it."

The attorney peers over his glasses. "Unfortunately, you are already involved. The reverend filed a lawsuit against the hospital naming you as a co-conspirator. He claims you orchestrated the robbery and used the hospital as a cover."

Raffi cringes inwardly, possibly facing another lawsuit.

The ring of Daley's cell phone breaks the tension, and he answers. He listens, his face turning a ghostly white.

"I'm on my way," he says, and then turns to Raffi. "A cleaning lady just found Jasmine Battia dead in her apartment."

Raffi gasps in horror. "Dead? From what?"

Daley shakes his head. "A bullet."

# Forty-four

Raffi follows Daley's unmarked car to the lower East Side and pulls up in front of a five story brick apartment building. He convinces the detective as her doctor he could verify the murdered woman's identity.

The street is blocked by an ambulance and patrol cars as Raffi steps out of his vehicle. An officer approaches, throwing him a stern look. "You can't park here."

Daley flashes his badge. "He's with me." With that, the officer nods and steps away.

With Daley, he rides the elevator to the top floor. The pungent odor of garlic brings back memories of his days as a youngster living on the second floor Brooklyn apartment and Mrs. Dooley's cooking.

A barrier of yellow tape surrounds the entrance to Jasmine's home. Crime investigators are busy dusting for fingerprints, snapping pictures and searching for clues as he follows Daley into the apartment. A sudden wave of nausea hits him. Although he has seen his share of gunshot victims and stabbings, never has he witnessed the murder scene of someone he has grown to know and respect.

Jasmine Battia lies curled on her side as though sleeping peacefully. On closer examination, Raffi sees the bullet hole, clearly visible at her left temple. Dry blood coats her face. He stands silently over her body, recalling the terror in her eyes the day she came into the emergency room. His heart feels heavy, aware Jasmine's greatest fears have become reality. How can he stand by and do nothing?

Daley approaches Raffi after consulting with the CSI investigator. "The shooter entered through the bedroom window. He must have scaled from the rooftop of the adjacent building."

Raffi's skin crawls with goosebumps, imagining the murderer's fanatic determination, and turns to the detective. "But we're on the fifth floor. What's the drop to the rooftop from the other building?"

Daley rocks back on his heels, rubbing his chin. "This had to be carefully planned. Not the typical rash breaking and entering."

Raffi's mind races to the most obvious conclusion. The murder has to be linked to the Turkish lobby, but how can he prove it? He must clue Daley of the connection, but hesitates. Will he be taken seriously? He has no choice but to try.

~ * ~

Raffi sits slumped over his desk, reflecting on the events that transpired over the past week. He can't shake his guilt and frustration over Jasmine's death. Mired by negative thoughts, Lorig's smiling face surfaces, and he becomes even more depressed over their unexpected breakup.

He glances at the stack of medical charts on his desk, giving him some sense of comfort. His increasing surgical volume proves the split from Harold Flint is a distant memory to the medical staff. Opening a chart, he begins dictating when his secretary's voice crackles over the intercom.

"Adam Wolfe is in the waiting room, Doctor."

After losing Lorig, he promised himself to avoid all future political entanglements, and hesitates before answering. But

Wolfe has become a wealth of information and his curiosity gets the better of him. "Send him in," he replies.

The reporter appears at the door, his shirt collar unbuttoned and his tie hanging loosely over an unkempt suit. Raffi surmises Wolfe's indifference to neatness is due to his dedication to investigative reporting, leaving him little time to worry about outward appearances.

The reporter sits across from Raffi, his expression intense. "Thanks for seeing me, Doc. I won't be long. I have some hot news about Jasmine Battia's death."

Raffi catches the knowing look in the reporter's eye. "Did the police dig up something to clinch it?"

"Hell no! The State Department sealed all the records."

Raffi scratches his head. *The State Department?*

"So what did you find out?"

Wolfe pulls a letter out from inside his jacket and hands it to Raffi. "After meeting Jasmine in the hospital, I hounded her for names of people working for the Turkish Embassy who might want to hurt her. She refused at first, but then last month she sent me this note with pictures."

Raffi reads the name of the person Jasmine believes was stalking her, and returns a puzzled gaze. "Who is this Akim Tobuglu guy? Is he a diplomat?"

The reporter leans back, tipping his chair. "He's supposedly an embassy security guard, in this country for only a few months. Strangely, in less than twenty-four hours after Battia's death, he flies back to Turkey."

Raffi runs a hand through his thick hair, letting out a soft whistle. "That certainly makes him a person of interest."

Wolfe leans over the desk, his dark eyes dancing with excitement. "Battia's suspicions have to be on target. She got a cell phone picture of him, and her friend at the State Department tracked down his name."

Raffi gazes at the reporter, drumming his fingers on the desk. "I'm trying to connect the dots, Adam. If Tobuglu was hired by the

Turkish Embassy to silence Battia, why would the State Department want to seal police records about her murder?"

"Your guess is as good as mine, Doc. It could be politics as usual. Turkey's *supposedly* our ally and the State Department doesn't want to rock the boat."

Raffi fists his hand in anger. "We can't let them get away with this, Adam! We gotta do something! Turkey's gotten away with murder for too long."

Wolfe pulls forward in his chair, his voice uncertain. "We're talking high powered international stuff, my friend. It's getting way out of my league."

"Come on, Adam, this is what investigative journalism is about. To get at the truth, no matter what it takes."

Wolfe nervously tugs at his collar. "But we need well-documented evidence to link this Turk to Battia's murder. Not just hearsay."

A bold and daring thought flashes in Raffi's brain. What provides evidence? Photo recognition, as in those mug shots he'd pored through at the police station, and fingerprints. "Adam, I remember they were dusting Battia's apartment for fingerprints when I went there with Daley. Immigration must have taken Akim Tobuglu's fingerprints when he came into the country. Ask for the Turk's file."

Wolfe lets out a sarcastic snicker. "Be real, Raffi. No way will they release information like that!"

Raffi presses on excitedly. "There's a good chance those fingerprints taken at Battia's apartment will match."

Wolfe taps his fingers on the desk, deep in thought. "I have a close buddy in Immigration who owes me a favor. Maybe I could try." He hesitates a few seconds, and then pounds the desk. "We're talking global politics now, as well as murder."

Raffi persists, unable to contain his excitement. "That's what makes this a fantastic scoop—exposing the corruption running through Congress." He pauses, looking squarely at his friend. "You're not afraid to get involved, are you, Adam?"

DR. RICHARD A. BERJIAN

Wolfe shifts uncomfortably in his chair. "You don't have to remind me about congressional payoffs, Doc. I just can't get a handle on this international stuff."

Raffi has no choice. Despite warning his mother to keep her mouth shut, he's instantly driven to do the right thing. Now to convince Wolfe.

His jaw tightens with determination. "Look Adam, I'm in this with you. We can't let Battia's death get lost because of political correctness. Besides, it could win you the highest international merit in journalism."

Wolfe throws Raffi a sarcastic smirk. "Is my life worth a Pulitzer?"

~ * ~

Three days later, Wolfe clutches a heavy folder to his chest as he and Raffi enter the precinct station house. Once inside, they're greeted by a constant stream of uniformed officers and detectives in street dress wearing badges. Conversations in distinctive New York accents fill the room.

Raffi approaches the sergeant seated at a raised desk. "I'm Dr. Sarkissian. Detective Daley is expecting me."

The officer presses a button on the intercom panel. "Hey, Daley, Dr. Sarkissian is here to see you."

Within minutes, Daley appears, waving them to follow him through the waist-high swinging gate. "You didn't tell me you'd have the reporter with you, Doc. Does this mean my name will appear in his paper?"

"That depends," Raffi says. They enter a large room crowded with people at several desks. "Could we find a more private place to talk, Detective?"

Daley's brow knits as he guides them into a small, glass-enclosed cubicle with only a single desk and two spindly chairs. He takes his place facing Raffi and Adam. "OK, why all this secrecy?"

Wolfe speaks first. "It's about Jasmine Battia's murder. We'd like to have access to the fingerprints taken at the crime scene."

Daley doesn't hesitate. "Those records are sealed."

Raffi breaks in. "Why? To cover up a murder?"

Daley raises his chin defiantly. "What proof do you have to call it a cover-up?"

Raffi responds hastily. "None right now, but if you compare the prints taken at Battia's apartment with the ones Adam got from Immigration, you might have your murderer."

Daley's eyes narrow and he remains silent.

Raffi glances at Adam, and then presses on. "Look, Detective, we've had our moments but I always found you to be a straight shooter. This woman was ruthlessly murdered in her own apartment and you have no suspects. Do us one favor. Compare the fingerprints in her apartment to the ones Wolfe got from Immigration."

Daley's brow arches in surprise. "How did you manage that?"

Wolfe strokes the stubble on his chin. "Trust me, I have my sources. I believe the fingerprints belong to a Turkish national who left the country less than twenty-four hours after the murder."

Daley's eyes narrow into a squint. "You know I could get busted for releasing information during an active investigation."

Wolfe speaks with confidence. "Your name won't be mentioned in anything I print."

"But the department will know who unsealed the file. Can't do it. Sorry, guys. "

"Do you want us to get a court order to open the file?" Raffi asks. .

Daley smirks, shaking his head. "You'll never get it."

Having no idea how to get a court order, Raffi confidently extends his hand to Daley. "We'll see about that."

# Forty-five

The call comes at six the following morning and a weary Raffi rolls over to pick up the phone, only to hear Ani's frightened voice.

"Raffi, I'm glad I reached you before you left for the hospital. Can you talk?"

He wipes the sleep from his eyes, sitting up in bed. "Of course, Mom. What's up?"

"I hate to bother you, but Irene Pastorius insisted I call."

Raffi always liked his childhood friend's mother. Memories of playing with Johnny on the Pastorius living room floor in their Brooklyn flat brings a smile to his face. "I'm so glad you've kept your friendship with her all these years."

"Yes, Raffi, she's been like a sister to me, so I took her advice when she insisted I call you. "

Raffi catches the uncertainty in Ani's voice. "Mom, what's this all about?" The delay in her response worries him. With all his personal and legal issues, he hasn't kept in touch and can't remember the last time he's spoken with her.

Ani's voice lowers. "For several weeks, I've had stomach pains. First I thought it was something I was eating, but now it's so bad I can hardly stand it."

Raffi knows his mother is not one to complain. *This sounds serious.* "Look Mom, I want you to come to the hospital this morning. I'll arrange for you to see a good friend of mine, Brad Douglass, chief of gastroenterology."

"Thank you, son. I'll have Irene bring me."

"Great! Keep an empty stomach. I'll arrange things and get back to you."

He ends the call, wiping moisture from his brow. His mom never complains, never gets sick, and the fact that she wants to see a specialist? It might just be a little gastritis, but in his heart, he's worried it could be more serious.

Douglass's answering service connects him, and the GI specialist returns his call quickly, agreeing to examine Ani on short notice. After calling his mother with instructions, Raffi quickly washes, dresses and leaves for the hospital, preoccupied with Ani's illness. She's his only family. Now that he and Lorig have separated, he doesn't have anybody else in his life.

~ * ~

Early the same afternoon, Raffi picks up Douglass's call. "Hi Brad, what did you find?"

The GI doctor speaks in hushed manner. "I can't say the news is good."

Raffi's stomach lurches. "Give it to me, Brad. What is it?"

Douglass continues in the same quiet, measured voice. "I'm afraid your mother has signs of pancreatic cancer. The CT scan shows a mass in the body of the pancreas and the superior mesentery artery is encased, suggesting it's inoperable. Raffi, she needs a more extensive workup and an ERCP to confirm the diagnosis."

Raffi sinks back stunned, his heart pounding. Even with chemotherapy treatments, the diagnosis comes with an expected survival of only six to nine months. He remains silent, digesting the news.

Douglass presses on when he doesn't hear a response. "Raffi, it's not confirmed until she gets the workup."

Raffi's voice cracks. "Did you tell her?"

"Your mom was very insistent, so yes, I told her."

Raffi sighs. "How did she take it?"

"Of course she was shocked, but thankfully her friend was there to comfort her."

Raffi floods with guilt. *I should have been with her.* His throat is parched, and he tries to clear it.

"Brad, thanks for getting on this as quickly as you did. Follow up and I'll arrange an oncologist to see her."

He hangs up, emotionally drained. Both he and Ani have faced their share of challenges over the years, but for the first time, he feels helpless. This devastating news suddenly makes all his other problems appear meaningless.

~ * ~

It's only a few days after Ani's consultation with Dr. Brad Douglass when the bad news is confirmed. Ani has inoperable pancreatic cancer. Even with chemotherapy, he knows his mother's life span is measured in months. Although burdened with this knowledge, he masks his emotional turmoil and continues carrying on his medical responsibilities.

Early one morning, while sipping coffee at the breakfast table and flipping through mail, he spots a flyer announcing an update review on breast cancer. The name of one of the speakers on the panel catches his attention. Dr. Monica Sarian's credits reveal her to be an epidemiologist based at the University of London. Could she possibly be related to his missing father, who carries the same last name? He quickly marks the date on his calendar and registers online.

He keeps mum to not burden Ani with such an improbable connection. Still he hopes this woman might give him information about his father, Haig Sarian.

~ * ~

At eleven in the morning of the day of the medical meeting, Raffi walks into the lobby of the Waldorf Astoria to hear this long awaited lecture by Dr. Monica Sarian. He rides the elevator to the mezzanine floor, following attendees into a large ballroom. Dr. Sarian's name, written on a placard set on an easel, announces her presentation.

After registering, he moves to the front row close to the lecture stand, feeling a wave of anticipation as three people walk onto the platform and take seats behind a table holding a microphone. His attention is immediately drawn to the single woman. Her silky auburn hair falls to her shoulders, framing a fair-skinned complexion. He doubts she could be his half-sister, since she doesn't carry his dark features.

The room quickly fills and a mousy-hair lanky man wearing half spectacles approaches the podium, introduces himself as professor of statistics at NYU and proceeds to introduce the first guest speaker.

His voice echoes throughout the room, and an attendant quickly lowers the volume of the microphone. Clearing his throat, he finally addresses the audience.

"We are fortunate to have Dr. Monica Sarian with us today to discuss the world wide incidence of breast cancer. She is associate professor of epidemiology at the University of London, and she's come all the way from Great Britain to discuss the most recent treatments for breast cancer."

Raffi watches her rise and approach the speaker's platform. Her slender figure is enhanced by a well-tailored powder blue suit. She appears younger than he, which would fit the possibility they could be related.

She speaks in a cultured British accent, looking engagingly into the audience. The scope of her research and her presentation impress him. Related or not, he likes her.

A rousing applause erupts following the talk, after which she answers a number of questions submitted from the audience. At the end of the morning session, Raffi quickly moves toward the stage as she starts to leave and calls to her. "Dr. Sarian, do you have a minute?"

She checks her watch and then replies, "Certainly, let me come to you."

Raffi follows her graceful steps crossing the stage to walk down the side stairway to reach him. He greets her with a warm smile. "Thank you for taking the time, Dr. Sarian. While I'm impressed with your talk, I'm also intrigued by your last name. It's Armenian, isn't it?"

Sarian glances at Raffi's name tag. "Yes, it ends in *ian*, just like yours."

Raffi's eyes light up. "That's the dead giveaway, isn't it? Not to be too forward, but are you related to Haig Sarian?"

Monica Sarian lets out a surprised laugh, her expression warm and inviting. "Why yes, he's my father! Do you know him?"

Raffi's eyes widen, his heart flutters with hope. "My mother talks about a good friend with the same name she knew years ago when she lived in Turkey. She worked as an interpreter in Ankara for the Turkish Defense Department."

Monica brings a hand to her face, returning an astonished look. "This is incredible! My father also worked as an interpreter for the Russian Embassy in Ankara when he was a young man. I believe it was around 1980. Could there be a connection?"

Raffi catches his breath. "Dr. Sarian, we need to talk. May I invite you to lunch?"

Before she can answer, a bald man carrying a briefcase with a raincoat on one arm taps Dr. Sarian's shoulder. "We have to leave for the airport now, Monica."

Dr. Sarian stands fixated, staring at Raffi as if searching for clues to a puzzle. She touches his arm with a familiar gesture. "I will keep in contact with you, Raffi, if I may be that forward." She removes a card from her purse and hands it to him.

Raffi grasps it, then opens his wallet and produces his card. She takes it, slipping it into her purse.

She turns to leave when Raffi calls out, "Wait! Before you go, I have a picture of my mother and myself when I was six years old." He pulls out a tattered photo from his wallet. "Please take this with you and show it to your father. It would mean so much to my mother."

Monica accepts the photo. "Perhaps my father will recognize her. He once confided he befriended a beautiful Armenian woman in Ankara, but had to leave the country due to some unexpected circumstances."

The bald man approaches, tapping on his wrist watch.

She holds out her hand. "I must leave, but I will follow up with you."

Raffi returns her grasp. With that, she leaves.

Unable to contain his excitement, Raffi's gaze lingers on the lovely woman as she walks away with the elderly gentlemen. Could what he's yearned for his entire life come true merely by attending a medical lecture?

# Forty-six

Colonel Haig Sarian sits across from his daughter in her London university office, wearing a puzzled expression. "Now Monica, what's so urgent we had to meet like this?"

Dr. Sarian leans forward in her chair unable to mask her excitement. "Father, I must ask you a very personal question only you can answer."

The colonel's jaw tightens. "Darling, you know I don't keep anything from you. What is it?"

Monica feels butterflies in her stomach and clasps her hands to keep them steady. "Please tell me if I'm correct. You once told me you were a Russian captain stationed in Ankara years ago."

"Why yes, that's true. At the time I was employed as an interpreter for the Russian Embassy."

Monica takes in a deep breath. "I feel I can ask you a sensitive question now that Mom's been gone for five years. Is it true you left behind a love—?"

The colonel cuts her off. "What do you know about that?"

"Very little, Father, but last week while lecturing in New York, I met a young surgeon who approached me, asking about the Sarian name. He said his mother once had a relationship with a captain by the name Haig Sarian in Turkey. Of course I was taken aback and wondered if it was true. Is it possible that she could be the young woman you knew in Ankara?"

Her father sits without commenting, a stunned expression covers his face.

Monica continues, catching the shock on her father's face. "At the time she worked as an interpreter in the Turkish Defense Department and her name is Ani Sarkissian."

Sarian's jaw drops, the creases around his eyes deepen on his still handsome face. "Yes, that was her name. It still pains me to think how I had to leave abruptly without saying goodbye."

Monica bites her lip, recalling the young surgeon's square jaw, his deep set eyes, so much like her father's. Her voice rises with excitement. "This young doctor believes his mother knew you." She withdraws the weathered black and white photo from an envelope and slips it across the desk.

The colonel turns pale, drawing in a sharp breath as he studies the faded picture of a child holding onto his mother's hand.

"Father, that child is the surgeon who gave me the photo. His name is Raffi Sarkissian."

The colonel sits mesmerized, studying the photo as tears fill his eyes. After a long delay, he whispers, "Yes, that's Ani. I never said goodbye because—" His voice drifts. "I had to leave suddenly."

Monica feels a chill course through her. Putting pieces together of her father's early life in Turkey excites her. "This Raffi Sarkissian said you were a very meaningful part of his mother's life and she thinks of you often. She never understood why you left."

The colonel removes a handkerchief from his pocket and dabs his eyes. "We were so young, so in love. It's hard to explain."

There was an edge to Monica's voice. "Father, are in you interested in contacting her?"

He studies the photo again. "Yes, Monica. I owe her that."

~ * ~

Despite Ani's illness, Raffi's mood suddenly lightens when he receives an overseas call from Dr. Monica Sarian telling him her father wants to communicate with him. After a flurry of email exchanges, he and the colonel agree Ani definitely is the Armenian woman he had left behind in Ankara over thirty years ago. Within two weeks, Monica calls, confirming her father will board a British Airways flight and arrive at JFK airport the following Friday.

Raffi decides it's time to tell his mother the news. A month has passed after her first course of chemotherapy, and she's admitted this morning as a twenty-four hour outpatient for her second course of treatment.

He finishes operating by noon, and then makes his way to Ani's room to find her asleep while IV fluids drip into her veins. A nurse carrying a bag of chemo enters, causing Ani's eyes to open.

She smiles at Raffi. "Son, with all you have to do, it's not important to hover over me."

Raffi kisses her brow as the nurse hangs the second IV. "Mom, I always have time for you." Time is limited now and he doesn't want to miss anything.

After the nurse completes her duties and leaves, Ani's brow deepens with wrinkles, and she reaches for his hand. "I know this cancer is pretty serious."

Raffi hesitates a moment before answering. "Mom these drugs are powerful and will help." *To prolong her life, not save it.*

Ani releases her grip. "No matter what, you must promise not to grieve over me. You have a full and wonderful life ahead of you."

His voice shakes, and he clears his throat. "Mom, you can't tell me what to feel." He gently touches her arm, overwhelmed with deep love, and sits on a bedside chair. *Ani, always giving, thinking of others.* He knows what he says will cheer her. "I'm bringing you a surprise visitor tomorrow."

Ani's eyes widen. "A surprise visitor?"

"Yes, someone who desperately wants to see you."

Ani shakes her head, laughing. "I can't imagine who that could be."

Raffi chuckles, glad to see her smile. "Finish today's chemo and get over the side effects so you will be at your best. Did Irene bring you to the hospital today?"

"Yes, she's been a good friend. She'll take me home tomorrow and insists on staying for the night."

He puts a hand on her shoulder and sighs. "Old friends are the best, aren't they Mom?" He gives Ani a cheerful smile, kisses her cheek and turns to leave. "Promise, no more negative talk, Mom."

Her face glows. "I love you, Raffi."

He quickly replies, "I love you too, Mother."

~ * ~

Punctually at nine the following morning, Raffi stands at the British Airways gate watching the arriving London passengers flow out of the exit ramp. The colonel informs Raffi he'll be wearing his uniform since he's still on active duty. His midnight flight will arrive into New York the next morning.

Raffi waits anxiously as passengers flow by but no one resembles the colonel. Finally, a tall uniformed officer with thick dark hair graying at the temples steps out. Raffi waves excitedly, approaching the attractive man. "Colonel Sarian?"

The colonel grins, his jaw firm and strong, and extends his hand. "And you must be Raffi Sarkissian. It's so good to finally meet you in person."

Raffi gives the colonel's hand a vigorous shake. "Welcome to America, Colonel."

The colonel nods. "Please call me Haig."

Raffi can't believe this long awaited moment he always hoped for has finally arrived. A childhood dream now a reality. His voice shakes, feeling overwhelmed, but all he could say is, "Let's get your luggage and then we'll see Ani."

With the turmoil at the baggage carousel, little is said between the two men, but once in the car, Raffi breaks the news. "I didn't want to distress you, Colonel, but Ani is in the hospital. She's being treated for cancer of the pancreas."

Haig Sarian returns a troubled gaze, his voice lowering to almost a whisper. "This is disturbing news. Is it OK for me to visit?"

Raffi grins broadly. "Absolutely! She's not in pain and waits for her surprise visitor."

While Raffi excitedly darts around vehicles to make time in the heavy traffic, the colonel peers out the window, drifting into a quiet meditation. Finally he breaks the silence. "Raffi, I have so much to tell her."

The two men enter the hospital elevator, standing shoulder to shoulder. Both six feet in height, both the same muscular build.

Raffi smiles inwardly watching the colonel roll his shoulders to relieve the tension, whether from nerves or the long overnight flight across the Atlantic. It's a habit he's also acquired, after standing a long time operating.

The colonel straightens his jacket, and breathes deeply as they enter the hospital room. Ani sits in a lounge chair, dressed in street clothes, anticipating her special visitor. Her pink frock brings color to her face. Her hair falls softly to her shoulders.

She looks up in astonishment as they enter, her eyes instantly capturing the familiarity of the stranger before her. She lets out a gasp. "Oh, my God! Haig, it's you!"

Raffi swallows hard to keep his composure, studying the moment of recognition. *The scene right out of a Hollywood love story.* Haig approaches, takes her hand and raises it to his lips. Ani trembles with excitement and begins crying.

"How did you find me?" she asks between sobs.

Haig embraces her, kissing her forehead. "Ani, your son made this happen."

Ani holds him close, choking on her tears. "Haig, I never thought we'd meet again."

Raffi stands by the door, taking in the scene of two people who still love each other. He brushes away a tear with the back of his hand. He hoped to find such a love with Lorig, but it's not to be.

He knows it's time to give them privacy. "Mom, Haig, I'll leave now. You both have a lifetime to catch up on."

~ * ~

Seated at a bedside chair in Ani's hospital room, Haig speaks in a soft calming voice. "I'm so much in your debt. That's why I had to come to explain why I left Ankara so abruptly without warning."

Ani peers into his eyes as he speaks, drinking in his every word.

Haig takes her hands in his, trying to explain. "There's so much I couldn't tell you at the time in Ankara. It would have put you in danger."

His face flushes; he loosens his tie and takes off his jacket. "I was courted by the Russian government into the military as a translator. When I met you in Ankara, I was also a secret British agent. You know well that I had no love for Turkey or for that matter for the Russian Communists, even though they gave me the opportunity to rise up the ranks."

His admission makes Ani flinch but she remains silent, waiting for him to continue.

"When my cover was exposed, I had to leave immediately or face death from a firing squad. My cousin Berj had been apprehended that same day, and I later heard he died in prison."

Ani maintains her silence, studying the deepening lines on his face as he painfully expresses details of his escape. Her silence urges him on.

"By the time I arrived in London, I tried to call you. You had left Turkey and I had no knowledge of where you were. I had to be secretive about exposing my personal connections since I was on Russia's most wanted list."

Before he could continue, Ani's eyes swell with tears and she grasps his hand. "There's something you should know, Haig. I wanted to tell you I was pregnant the day you disappeared." She catches the shock on his face and waits for the full impact of her words to take hold.

His shoulders sag, his eyes wide with surprise. "Ani, I never knew! I never knew you were pregnant!" He holds her hand unable to voice his words. After a silent interval, he asks, "Then Raffi is—" His voice trails off, and he places a hand on her arm. "I've caused you so much pain. Can you forgive me?"

Ani brings his hand to her lips and kisses it. "It wasn't your fault. You're here now, that's what is important." She throws him a wistful look. "Timing is everything. It's astounding how it can change our lives."

She holds back a sob, and continues. "I waited hoping to hear from you, but after a few months, I had to make a decision and decided to leave Turkey to raise our child in America."

Haig lets out a muffled cry, his eyes red with sadness. "You've raised a fine son in Raffi. I should have been there for you and for him."

Her arms reach for him, giving him a gentle embrace. "It's all in the past, darling. You gave me the gift of a wonderful son who's filled my life with joy."

"And you never married?"

Ani lowers her gaze. "I considered it several times. I didn't love them the way I loved you and broke them off. I guess deep down, I hoped we would meet again, but now—"

Her expression turns somber, and he quickly interrupts. "But now we're together, Ani, and we've so much to share."

Her brow wrinkles into a frown. "But you're married, and you must know I have cancer. Just having you here brings me joy."

Haig shakes his head, still holding her hand. "My wife passed away five years ago from liver cirrhosis, possibly due to her drinking. She was a good woman, but lonely. Still, she raised Monica, our lovely daughter."

"Were you a good husband to her, Haig?"

He gazes at her sheepishly. "My work in the British Service kept me away from home for long periods of time. Maybe I could have been a better husband, and that guilt haunts me."

The sound of approaching footsteps causes them to look up to see Irene Pastorius enter the room.

Ani greets her with excitement. "I want you to meet Raffi's father, Haig Sarian."

Irene's face turns white, studying the handsome gentleman in uniform.

Ani's voice is light and cheerful. "He's come from London to see me and to meet his son."

# *Forty-seven*

Autumn arrives, but despite her illness, Ani treasures each and every day with Haig. She feels well enough to show him the sights of New York, take short walks, and go out to dinner and a few Broadway plays.

After two weeks of bliss, Haig receives an urgent call to return to London. She doesn't ask questions, aware of his complicated history. He kisses her good bye at the door of her apartment, promising to return after settling an important business matter. To her surprise, she hears from him several days later, catching the excitement in his voice.

"Darling Ani. I have good news! My request for a diplomatic assignment at the British Embassy in New York has been approved. It may take a couple of weeks before I wrap up some last minute details."

Ani's elated. Her energy returns, allowing her to spend quality time with friends like Irene. After thirty-odd years, her life will be complete having the only man she loved by her side. Each time the phone rings, her heart beats rapidly knowing it's Haig's daily calls.

To pass the time, Ani sits on the bench outside of her apartment, chatting with neighbors whenever the weather allows it. This unusually warm fall afternoon, she relaxes, watching flocks of birds flitter onto telephone lines, preparing for their migration south. Despite weight loss, her love for life is apparent as she counts the days for Haig's return.

Today she waits for Detective Daley, who requested an interview regarding her relationship with Jasmine Battia. She made no secret she had shared a short but rewarding friendship with the woman.

Graciously, she greets the detective as he approaches and leads him into her apartment.

The tall stocky man ducks his head as he enters the door of the basement apartment. She smiles, aware from the look on his face, that he's pleasantly surprised to see the warm and cozy atmosphere.

He stands for a moment, gazing around the modest living room. The finely carved antique bookcase, oriental scatter rugs on old oak floors. His gaze focuses on the wall over the sofa where a framed photograph of a snow-capped mountain hangs.

Ani gestures toward it. "This is an old photo of Mount Ararat where Noah's Ark landed. It overlooks the ancient lands of my people in Armenia. I found it in a flea market and treasure it as a reminder of my roots."

Daley rubs his chin, nodding with surprise. "You have a charming home, Miss Sarkissian. Thank you for allowing me to visit."

She gestures to a chair. "It's my pleasure, Detective. Please sit." She forces a smile, which masks her anxiety to discover the urgency of the visit. "Do you care for tea, a soft drink?"

"No thank you," he replies.

She frowns as he lowers his sizable girth onto her treasured finely-framed antique chair. Why didn't she lead him to the sofa instead? She takes a seat next to him, waiting for the purpose of his visit.

The detective clears his throat, assuming a professional stance. "I'll be brief, Miss Sarkissian. Before you took sick leave from your position, you filed a complaint with your supervisor similar to Miss Battia's. You found evidence of money passing between Turkish diplomats and some of our elected officials."

Ani's voice reflects a sense of confidence. "Yes, Detective, that is a fact. I can prove money was paid to certain congressmen to vote against the Armenian Genocide Bill." Understanding the urgency of the detective's visit, she sits quietly, watching Daley's fingers play with his hat.

He shifts in his chair, as though uncomfortable with what he has to say. "Miss Sarkissian, it appears the Turkish Embassy learned about your accusations. With Jasmine Battia's murder, the department is concerned about your safety."

Ani raises an eyebrow. "You have proof of that?"

"I'm not at liberty to reveal my sources, but the information comes from a responsible informant."

The ring of the doorbell halts their conversation and Ani leaves to answer. She returns with Raffi, who abruptly comes to a halt on seeing Daley seated in his mother's living room.

"What brings you here, Detective?"

Daley rises, still holding his hat. "As you recommended, I requested a court order to compare the fingerprints of the Turkish agent with those found in Miss Battia's apartment. I received them and they match."

"That's good news. Has he been charged?"

Daley shakes his head. "It's not that easy. We'll have trouble extraditing him now that he's back in Turkey."

Raffi shakes his head. "I'm aware of that, Detective, but what does this all have to do with my mother?"

Daley clears his throat. "The complaint she filed exposing the Turkish payments puts her at risk just like Jasmine Battia."

Ani reads the anger on her son's face. Her cheeks flush, making her feel like a school girl caught doing something naughty. "Raffi, let me explain."

Raffi's eyes widen in fury. "Mom, you filed a complaint about the Turkish lobby?"

Ani speaks with self-assured determination. "Yes, son, I did! It's about time history is written correctly. If we don't expose Turkey's atrocities, who will? I can't ignore money going into the pockets of our congressional leaders to gain their silence."

Raffi raises his voice. "I told you not to do that, Mother!"

Daley breaks into the discussion between mother and son. "Doctor, unfortunately, it's too late to argue about the practicality of what she did. Your mother needs security, but I suspect unless she faces an open threat, there's nothing the department can do."

Ani responds defiantly. "What dangers do I face, for God's sake? I'm sick and who knows how long I have to live."

Raffi's tone is harsh. "Don't say that, Mother. You have so many people who love you. " He pauses, his voice wavers. "And I need you, too."

Ani releases a deep sigh, facing Daley. "I'll alert you to anything suspicious. But my biggest enemy at present is not the Turks. It's my cancer."

~ * ~

The call from Mr. Gold comes late in the afternoon the following week. "Dr. Sarkissian, just wanted you to know the hospital made an out of court settlement with the Tommie Jackson family. Now you won't have to face another trial."

The attorney's words leave Raffi with mixed feelings. Relieved there won't be any more court appearances, but at what price? Manhattan Medical performed its mission adequately, so why should the Jackson family as well as the reverend profit with a huge settlement?

He takes a hard swallow. "How much will Manhattan Medical pay?"

Gold clears his throat. "Sorry, Doctor, but according to the agreement, neither party is allowed to make any public statements."

Raffi's face flushes. "What about Reverend Sanders? What does he get out of this arrangement?"

"Sorry again, Doc. Everything's confidential."

Raffi chuckles before speaking. "It looks like the hospital chickened out."

Gold speaks in a matter-of-fact manner. "That's not the case, Doctor. Although the hospital is blameless, the board decided to settle. The cost of litigation, in addition to the bad publicity, far outweighed any courtroom victory."

Raffi leans back in his chair, contemplating this reality. Forget about principle. It all boils down to money.

Gold presses on. "But there is something else you should consider, Doctor. Detective Daley is very concerned about your safety. His sources on the street say you're a marked man."

"What exactly does that mean?"

"It means you might be a target for violent activists. In other words, your life might be at risk."

Raffi's heart drops to his stomach. Jeremy had given his life, protecting him from a bullet.

"Doctor, are you still there?"

"Yes, I'm here, Mr. Gold. Just trying to figure out the cost of seeking justice."

~ * ~

That evening, Raffi picks up the call from Rachel just as he heads home from the hospital.

"Raffi, I can't believe this! I'm holding a letter from the Black College Foundation in my hand. An anonymous one million dollar donation was made in the name of my Jeremy. Who could have done this?"

Raffi immediately knows the donor is the same individual who had paid for Jeremy's lavish funeral. "Rachel, my bet is on Traci Doss. She took a liking to Jeremy in the hospital after the auto accident. You know how personable he was."

Rachel sighs. "Yeah, my man could charm a snake." She laughs, and then lowers her voice. "Oh Raffi, I miss him so much. This is too kind of Miss Doss."

He hears her sniffle and says, "I'm planning to visit Traci. Why don't you come along and ask her yourself if she's the one."

Her tone perks up. "I would like that very much."

~ * ~

Raffi hasn't spoken to Traci in three weeks. She's home in her Manhattan penthouse after another stint in the Columbia University Addiction program. He hopes she's sober, but with her unpredictable track record, he's uncertain. Her calls are less frequent, causing him concern—for better or worse, they're friends of a sort and he has to see her in person.

After several attempts, he finally gets through and sets up a time, after which he calls Rachel. When they arrive in the late afternoon, the uniformed maid welcomes them. "Miss Doss is expecting you."

Traci lies on the living room sofa as they enter, wearing a light blue silk robe over colorful pajamas. Her youthful complexion has given way to a gaunt fatigue. Inquisitively, she looks to Rachel. "Good to see you, Raffi, and who is this beautiful woman?"

Rachel's face lights up. "Thank you for the compliment, Miss Doss. I'm Rachel Johnson. Jeremy Jenkins was my fiancé. I wanted to meet you."

A prolonged delay follows as Traci struggles to sit upright, trying to steady herself. She gazes around, appearing to look for something, her hands shaking. "First, I must have a have a cigarette. Want one?"

"No, thanks," Rachel replies.

Traci coughs, reaches for the cigarette box on the table, removes one and lights it. She inhales deeply and then exhales, watching a stream of smoke float into the air. Then she turns to Rachel. "I remember Jeremy well. His death devastated me. He was a good man—one of the few."

Raffi swallows the barb, and guides the conversation. "Rachel has an important question to ask you, Traci."

Traci's blue eyes come alive and she smiles at Rachel, patting the couch. "Let's not stand on ceremony, darling. My life is an open book."

Rachel sits next to Traci, and casts a modest smile. "Miss Doss, someone was kind enough to pay for Jeremy's funeral and now I receive notice that a generous contribution is made in his name to the Black College Scholarship Fund. I want to know if it was you."

Traci's hearty laugh ends in a cough. "Dear, I contribute to many causes."

Rachel's voice rises; she leans close. "Miss Doss, it's important to me. Jeremy and I were planning to marry when his life was abruptly snuffed out. Who do I need to thank for the kindness?"

Traci continues to hold the cigarette, her stare suddenly turning blank, not speaking.

Rachel looks to Raffi, as if uncertain whether or not to push the issue.

Traci's eyes suddenly roll upward and she slumps forward. Her chin drops to her chest and the cigarette falls from her hand.

Raffi quickly jumps up, lifts the burning cigarette off the carpet and deposits into the ashtray. *What the hell is in the cigarette?* He shakes her shoulder. "Traci, can you hear me?"

Rachel's eyes widen and she backs away from the couch. "Raffi, what happened?"

Raffi slaps her cheeks. "Traci wake up, wake up!" He shouts for the maid, who quickly rushes into the room as he takes her pulse. "Call nine-one-one. She must have taken something and we gotta get her to the hospital."

Rachel raises both hands to her face, watching the maid scurry out to make the call. "Raffi, what makes her do this? My lord, she has everything anyone could ask for."

He throws Rachel a sober gaze, his heart breaking for his one-time lover. "Despite all her wealth, without love, she has no hope. That's why she's hooked and can't escape it."

# *Forty-eight*

It's late October and Haig still hasn't returned, though his daily calls fill Ani's lonely days. Hasn't she made a life for herself all these years without him? Now she's heartened knowing he's alive, thinking of her. Hearing his voice on the phone each day is the whipped cream topping on a lovely dessert.

That afternoon Ani sits with Irene in her apartment after returning from one of her chemotherapy treatments. She sips a cup of tea to settle her stomach and wearily looks to her supportive her friend of many years from across the table.

"Irene, how can I thank you for all you've done for me?"

Irene squeezes Ani's hand in response. "Dearest, you look quite worried today. Is it the cancer?"

Ani's brow furrows, her eyes dark with sadness. "Irene, I don't know how long I have with this illness." She hesitates a moment, finding the words. "There's something I must do while I am still able."

"Darling, what is it?" Now widowed, and with Johnny away working in California, she's become an integral part of the Sarkissian family.

Ani's eyes fill with tears, and she twists the napkin in her hand. "It breaks my heart to see Raffi's quiet sadness. He still loves Lorig and is heartsick over the breakup. When I mention her name, he clams up, refusing to discuss it."

Irene raises a questioning gaze. "Do you think Lorig still loves him?"

Ani sips from the cup and lowers it on the saucer before speaking. "That's what I must find out. If Lorig still loves him, then there's a chance for them. If not, so be it."

Irene is not one to waste words. "Ani, speak with Lorig! Are you going to let foolish pride prevent their happiness?"

After Irene leaves, Ani takes her advice and opens her address book to find Lorig's telephone number. Holding a tight grip on the phone, she dials Lorig's cell and hears her voice on the third ring.

"Hello, Lorig, this is Ani Sarkissian, Raffi's mother."

Lorig has a slight edge to her voice. "Miss Sarkissian, I'm surprised to hear from you." A hesitation and then, "Is Raffi OK?"

Ani lets out a gentle laugh. "Why yes, his health is fine." She wants to say his heart is not but continues. "Please call me Ani. All of Raffi's friends do. Could you do a favor and come to my apartment so we can talk?"

There's a moment of silence until Lorig replies. "You're getting me concerned. Something's wrong!"

Ani hesitates. "You should know I'm not well. I'm receiving chemotherapy to treat my cancer."

Lorig's voice drops. "I didn't know. I'm so sorry to hear that."

"After taking chemo today, I'll get considerably weak in the next two days. I would like to see you soon, possibly tomorrow?"

Lorig's tone softens, carrying a distinct sound of compassion. "Of course I'll come to see you. Maybe there's something I can do for you. I mean, like shopping—whatever you'd like."

Ani's heart races with joy. After giving her the address and agreeing on a time the following day, she hangs up with a new-found hope. Life is too short to allow two wonderful people to throw away a meaningful future together.

Lorig arrives on Saturday afternoon, and after ushering her into the apartment, Ani gives her a warm embrace. "Thank you for coming, but I must apologize. The chemo makes me nauseous so if I suddenly have to leave the room, please understand."

Lorig hugs her in return. "No need to apologize, Ani."

Ani leads her guest into the living room, her eyes glowing with Lorig's warm reception. She holds a steady gaze facing the young woman and begins the conversation as they sit next to each other on the sofa.

"Lorig, having us meet is my idea, not Raffi's. Since you two parted, I've noticed a change in his state of mind. He's quiet, subdued, melancholy." She pauses to lend emphasis to her words. "I know my son. He puts on a courageous face at work, but inwardly, he's crying his heart out."

Lorig drops her gaze, and lets out a sigh. "He never tried to reach me. We could have talked."

Ani gives a motherly touch to Lorig's shoulder. *Could this young woman embrace the chaotic life of a surgeon?* She presses on. "I raised Raffi without a father and sense his every mood. Right now he's overwhelmed with the notoriety surrounding him. But when he's alone, he's despondent and needs someone he can rely on. For a while, he thought it was you."

Guilt tracks Lorig's face and she nervously brushes her long hair behind one ear. "Ani, I am so sorry for what's happened. I just couldn't handle all the unknowns that kept taking hold of our lives. I'd stay up at night, worrying about what would become of us. I felt the need for—" and then with hesitation she continues. "I need security." Her voice cracks over the word. "And that's why I cut the cord between us—but I miss him too."

Ani persists with determination. "Even more reason for you to open the door again. I won't be here much longer to see grandchildren, but at least I'll have the peace of mind knowing Raffi will have someone like you in his life."

Lorig's pretty eyes well with tears—and shame.

Ani has to ask the question that matters most. "Do you love Raffi enough to open the door for him?"

Lorig's insides twist with shame, her voice wavers. "He's in my thoughts each and every day. I miss him like crazy, but I'm afraid to call. He must hate me for doing what I did."

Ani's hopes soar. Despite the anguish on Lorig's face, she doesn't let up. "If you're to love my son, you must understand him. He's grown up in a different world than you. Even as a child, he always wanted to help, to give of himself. He picked medicine over music because of that. His work, his patients, are important to him. But he needs a supportive woman at his side if he's to succeed. Lorig, please be the one."

Ani reads the suppressed emotions crossing the young woman's face: love for her son is evident, but so is her fear of being hurt. Ani knows she risked much loving Haig for all those years but now she's rewarded having him in her life again.

She gently holds Lorig's hand, her dark expressive eyes flashing wisdom that comes with age. "Lorig, love is giving and accepting another for who they are. There is always risk, my dear."

Lorig sits speechless, and then rises abruptly and hugs Ani, choking back tears. "Thank you for sharing with me. It's getting late, I've got to go."

~ * ~

Lorig rushes out of Ani's apartment, her body shaking with grief. She hasn't heard from Raffi since the breakup and assumed he's fine, happy even, without her, while she's been miserable. She runs to her car parked a block away, and stops, fumbling for her keys. Guilt floods her, tears sting her eyes. *I've caused such sorrow, such hurt. Am I just like Traci? Self-absorbed, driven by my own needs?* The thought sickens her, and she breaks down crying as she slips into the car.

She continues driving and crying at the same time, paying no attention to the honking horns of cabs and travelers on the busy streets of the city. By the time she crosses the George Washington Bridge to New Jersey, she takes control of herself, parks her car in the driveway and enters the house.

Alice Balian calls out from the kitchen. "Lorig, did you have a good visit with Miss Sarkissian?"

Her eyes still red, Lorig remains in the foyer, not entering the kitchen to face her mother. She realizes it has taken strength of mind and body for Ani to reach out to her on behalf of Raffi, without his knowledge.

"Yes, Mother, it was a good visit," she calls out. "She's a courageous woman, a great mother."

"Well, aren't all Armenian mothers?" Alice replies with a laugh.

Instead of going into the kitchen, Lorig runs up the stairs to her bedroom, throws herself on the bed and cries into her pillow. What kind of a wife and mother will she be? *Am I a giver, or a taker?* She's yet to find out.

~ * ~

Raffi spends several sleepless nights remembering Detective Daley's warning that he might be targeted by the reverend's henchmen. And then there's Wolfe's warning about the Turks who killed Battia...both danger threats. But he goes about his daily schedule as usual, and after a week, other pressing matters occupy his thoughts. On several occasions he notices a grey BMW pull up behind him as he leaves the parking area across from the hospital. The vehicle lags one or two cars behind as he drives onto the street and then it cuts around and speeds ahead. Is he paranoid or is someone watching his every move? After all, he was instrumental in fingering the reverend's illegal activities.

One evening, after a full day of surgery along with a complication that kept him in the hospital late, he walks across the street to the parking garage to head home when he remembers his refrigerator is bare as Mother Hubbard's cupboard. Tired and out of sorts, he enters his car, drives out of the garage, and turns into a side street toward a small market he patronizes close to his apartment. He likes the owner, Plato, a friendly Greek, who keeps his store open for late working customers.

The grey BMW suddenly appears in his rearview mirror, following closely behind him. Goose bumps run along his arm; he's convinced the reverend's men are out to get him. Maybe Lorig is right and he wonders why he ever put himself in such a position.

Angrily, he pounds the steering wheel, concluding he's had enough of this cat and mouse game. Abruptly, he swerves into the small two car parking area of the Greek's grocery store, prepared to confront the pursuing goons. To his surprise, the BMW races on, disappearing in the darkness. Relieved, he lets out a soft whistle, recalling his childhood. The monsters he'd see in the dark of his bedroom were only shadows of branches outside his window. He chuckles to himself. *Is my imagination still playing tricks on me?*

As he enters the small but well-stocked market, Plato greets him with a broad smile partially covered by his thick handlebar mustache. "Dr. Sarkissian, I waited just for you. How was your day?"

"Thanks for asking. Busy as usual, but I'm starved. What do you have left for a hungry soul?"

"You're in luck. Still have a few kebobs and rice pilaf. Look, I'll be shutting down so take all I have left. My dear wife makes the best—nothing but the finest ground lamb."

Raffi smiles; the Greek treats his customers like family. "There's a place for you in heaven, my friend," he says. After the food is packed in a large brown bag along with other staples, Raffi waves good bye and walks to his car, anticipating the only decent meal of the day. Suddenly an athletic jogger approaches, a knit cap pulled low over his head, something in his right hand. The instant the runner closes in on him, Raffi spots trouble and shoves his brown paper sack at him, causing the groceries to spill onto the sidewalk. The runner bends and lifts a syringe off the concrete and continues his jog, disappearing into the distance.

Raffi stands alone in the parking area, shaking. Sweat pours out from every pore of his body as he stoops to salvage whatever dinner he can. *What the hell was that about?* The reverend's men use knives, clubs, guns, but nothing as sophisticated as a syringe filled with who-knows-what? Death by poison could only be attributed to some foreigner intent on killing an enemy.

It finally hits him. The jogger, the BMW, have to be part of the treacherous Turkish plot to do away with anyone exposing their covert scheme of buying influence. Jasmine Battia's death had been a carefully planned execution, and possibly his friendship with her places him in the same danger as Ani. Now that his mother's terminal state relegates her to a sick bed, he possibly might be the Turkish lobby's next target. By silencing him, their underhanded schemes interfering with America's elected officials will remain behind closed doors.

He places the brown bag with some of its contents on the back seat of his car and moves behind the steering wheel, his heart hammering against his chest. His mind transfers to the ex-Russian diplomat in London who stood in a crowd prepared to cross the street when someone suddenly injected him with a paralyzing agent. The victim developed rapid paralysis and respiratory distress. His life was saved by immediate hospitalization, although he never recovered to full health, enduring generalized weakness and episodes of mental confusion.

Raffi shudders at the thought. He doesn't have the syringe as proof, but he's convinced he came close to being another victim. Definitely, he has to talk to Detective Daley.

He starts the engine and slowly backs out of the parking space, his heart still pounding. As he turns the corner, two police cars with lights flashing block the narrow side street. He comes to a halt behind a car and gets out to discover the cause.

Just then an officer approaches. "Sir, please remain in your car."

"What's up ahead?" Raffi questions.

393

"A pedestrian accident. We'll detour you once the ambulance arrives."

"I'm a doctor. Is he hurt bad?"

"Afraid so. According to the driver who hit him, the kid darted out of nowhere as he turned the corner."

"Is there anything I can do?"

"It's too late. Looks like the kid's dead. The ambulance should be here any minute."

Suddenly sirens blare at full force announcing arrival of the fire department rescue squad.

Raffi watches the emergency team place the lifeless body on a stretcher. As they carry the victim to the vehicle, he spots the knit cap still on the kid's head.

The ambulance leaves and the police officer waves his arm, signaling the queue of cars to move."

Raffi puts his car into gear and pulls away from the scene. His thoughts harden, his stomach turns. Is he now the Turkish target? The Turkish Embassy must be put on notice. But he has no proof. How far would that get?

He finally enters his apartment, carrying what's left of his dinner. Exhausted, he wipes his brow. *How did I get mixed up in this international quagmire?*

~ * ~

The following morning, Raffi calls the detective, describing the attempted threat on his life. Daley's voice has a finality to it as it comes over the phone.

"Look, Doc, the kid's dead. What do you have for proof?"

"That's not the point, Detective. I need protection."

"Of course, Doc. I'll contact the State Department and the Turkish Embassy to get it on record. The department is still embarrassed by Battia's death. We should have given her better protection."

Raffi hangs up; a frown lines his brow. Despite the morning conversation with Daley, he's still in limbo. Without evidence, will anyone take him seriously?

Annoyed, he fingers the phone in his hand, and then checks his watch. He still has time before rounds and dials Adam Wolfe. If anyone can uncover who's behind the attempt on his life, it's the sleuthing reporter.

Wolfe picks up. "Doc, what's with the early call?"

Raffi explains the incident the night before and the weak response from Daley.

"Adam, to put it bluntly, how can I prevent this from happening again? Remember Battia?"

Adam hesitates, clearing his throat. "I think we're pursuing an endless quest trying to influence US politics. But I do have some good news."

"I could use some right now, Adam. Shoot!"

"A reliable contact of mine in the State Department confides that since Battia's murder, our government officially states that any untoward act by a foreign agent against an American citizen will have severe implications."

"That's good news. But why do we pander to Turkey, labeling them an ally?"

"Simple answer, Doc. Geopolitical interests have nothing to do with morality. But nothing stays the same, whether in predicting weather or politics. Since Turkey's shift toward an Islamic State, our government is re-evaluating its relationship with them."

Raffi huffs a frustrated sigh. "So possibly I'm off their radar?"

"Raffi, go live your life. Make sure Daley reports the incident to the State Department and they'll speak to the Turkish Ambassador. That should set up warning lights to the Turks."

Raffi shakes his head, not convinced. *The game of genocide denial is in Turkey's DNA, but at least this is a step in the right direction.*

"Thanks for listening, but let me end with this: until they stop imprisoning journalists for speaking out, until there's open and free debate, Turkey cannot be trusted."

He ends the call, telling himself, *keep your nose clean and stay away from politics if you want to stay safe.*

~ * ~

The colonel finally arrives in New York shortly before Thanksgiving. Raffi is heartened to see Ani and his father share their days together. Desperately missing Lorig, he finds release spending the little free time he has with his mother and most recently discovered father.

Tempted to call Lorig several times in a moment of weakness, he stops in his tracks, deciding it's of no use. She probably needs someone who will pamper her, have more time for her. How many times has he taken her out on the spur of the moment? Not many. Instead, he keeps her waiting while he attends to some emergency or crisis. In time, he blames himself for the breakup, and wonders if he will ever see her again.

Another heartache is Ani's rapid weight loss. Fatigued, she dozes off unexpectedly in the middle of a conversation. Months into her treatment, the intensity of her pain increases and she takes to her bed a good part of the day. Completely dependent on narcotics, she endures side effects of nausea and appetite loss.

He watches his mother's decline with sadness, though gratified the two lovers have found each other after a lifetime apart. However, the inevitable becomes reality one afternoon while visiting Ani and the colonel in her apartment. He enters to find his mother violently throwing up, signaling her days are numbered. These are moments when Raffi yearns to share his sorrow with Lorig, but still hesitates to contact her.

With Ani back in the hospital and Christmas nearing, Raffi looks forward to sharing dinner with his father in the doctors' dining room. Together they talk of their life experiences as only a father and son could share. During those encounters, Raffi tells Haig about his love for Lorig and their breakup.

The colonel brushes his chin, slow to respond. "Son, give it time. If you both care for each other, genuine love doesn't suddenly vanish. You must not give up; be persistent. Fight for her!"

Raffi is pondering his father's words when the overhead speaker breaks into his thoughts, and he moves to a wall phone.

Grant Perry, Traci's attorney, is on the line. "Doctor Sarkissian, I have some shocking news that's not yet public. Traci Doss was just found dead in her apartment."

The news catches Raffi off guard. No matter how he insisted, she refused to return to rehab.

"Don't know the details yet," Perry continues. "The housekeeper returned from shopping and found Traci sprawled across the bed, not breathing. We'll have to wait for the coroner's report."

Raffi's voice cracks with pity. "It's no mystery what they'll find."

"I agree, Doctor. You should know the police are holding a handwritten note addressed to you. It was on her desk in the bedroom."

"Have you read it?"

"No, they'll release it only to you."

Raffi's emotions churn from anger to guilt. *Is there something I could have done to prevent what happened?* He has no answer.

The attorney presses on. "We both know her unpredictable temperament, her stubborn streak." He lets out a long sigh, choking up. "But deep down, Traci tried to be a decent person. She had me set up a scholarship fund to the National Association of Black Colleges in Jeremy's name. You know she liked him a lot. He visited and joked with her during her hospital stay after the accident, making her laugh."

Tears stream down Raffi's face as he reflects on his love-hate relationship with the heiress. Despite her erratic and extravagant lifestyle, she was a vulnerable innocent searching for love in a mercenary world.

He hangs up, returns to the table and faces the colonel. "Traci Doss, the cigarette heiress, is dead."

The colonel blinks. "The young lady who's always in the tabloids?"

Raffi nods.

"Blimey, she was so young."

At that moment, Raffi senses the sheer joy of love. Love for Ani, Lorig and even Traci. Soberly, he gazes into the colonel's eyes. "Thank you for your advice. Life is too precious to squander. I've decided to fight for the woman I love."

~ * ~

Although Ani's death is expected, Raffi suffers days of despondency over her coming demise. He remains in Ani's hospital room with Haig at his side, watching her slip away painlessly into a deep sleep from morphine administered by the hospice nurse.

After she takes her last breath, the nurse turns to the two men sympathetically. "You may spend time with her while I make preparations at the nursing desk," she says, then leaves the room.

Raffi rubs his red-rimmed eyes and leans over his mother, kissing her forehead. His voice trembles. "Mom, you're at peace now." Uncontrollably, he lets out a gut-wrenching sob. "You will always be in my heart."

A tear rolls down Haig's cheek and he embraces the grieving son. "She was so proud of you. Your mother was a strong, courageous woman and raised you well, even without a father."

The two men stand soberly gazing at the woman they both loved. Although it took a lifetime, they each sense her love is the bond that ties them.

Raffi wipes his eyes, leveling a sober gaze at his father. "You brought her tremendous happiness in her last days, and I thank you for that."

In the fading daylight, father and son stand by Ani's bedside sharing their grief, comforted by the joy she brought them.

~ * ~

With Christmas days away, Raffi lingers before his hospital locker deep in thought before changing into street clothes. Tonight is Ani's viewing at the funeral home and he reflects on what he should say. It's Haig's presence and consoling support that has sustained his emotional sanity during the last few days. But despite that, he feels alone, refusing to call Lorig with more bad news.

With a heavy heart, he makes his way out of the hospital and heads to the subway to attend the seven o'clock viewing at the funeral home. The priest from the 27th Street Armenian Apostolic Church has agreed to say a prayer, as well as officiate at the funeral service the next day.

He enters the subway, blending into the crowd of passengers carrying packages of holiday gifts. He'll always remember this saddest Christmas but can still share it with his father. When the train stops at his station, he walks out, rehearsing his message. By the time he enters the funeral home, he knows what he has to say.

Haig greets him at the door. "I waited for us to be together when we pay our respects to Ani. Monica sends her love."

A choked-up Raffi embraces his father. His voice lowers to a whisper. "Now more than ever, we need to stay strong for each other."

The two men enter to find many guests already present. Mournful recorded organ music plays in the background as Raffi approaches those present and introduces the colonel. Irene Pastorius, Adam Wolfe, Rachel and Twila. They all embrace him, paying their respects. Friends from church, acquaintances and others he never met. A diverse smattering of co-workers from both the UN and FBI come to say good bye. Their presence confirms how much Ani is respected and even loved.

As Raffi and Haig take in the last image of Ani, David Frohman approaches placing a hand on Raffi's shoulder. "I feel blessed to have known your mother. She was an independent woman and I respected her very much."

Raffi nods. "Thank you, David. Please meet my father, Colonel Sarian."

The three men stand before the open tufted casket as Raffi makes the sign of the cross. The line thins and the mourners take their seats. The neat bearded Armenian priest, dressed in a tailored black suit and white collar, moves in front of the casket. An assisting deacon stands at his side, chanting the traditional Armenian liturgy along with the priest. After the priest renders his final words of prayer, he invites people to speak.

Raffi is the first to stand and face the gathering. His voice is steady and clear. "Ani has been more than a mother to me. She was my friend, my mentor. She left her humble home in Turkey as a young woman with one mission in mind. Her long journey took her to Switzerland and then America to make a home for me. With her gentle persuasion, she enabled me to follow a meaningful path in life. No matter all my personal and political challenges, I will constantly be enriched by her wisdom. Her values sustain me and for that I am grateful. Thank you all for coming to share my loss."

People approach Raffi, give their condolences, and then leave. He picks up his coat, prepared to leave when he spots Lorig standing in the doorway. His heart beats wildly as she approaches, tears running down her cheeks.

She throws her arms out to him and he grabs her, drawing her close. She speaks between sobs, her body shaking. "Raffi, I've been such a fool. Can you forgive me?"

In that moment, all becomes right in the world. Despair instantly turns to pure joy, and he whispers in her ear. "Lorig, please stay with me always."

She nestles her face on his shoulder, still crying softly. "I promise, Raffi. I want to be a giver. Through thick or thin, I will never leave you."

The colonel watches from the rear of the room, beaming as the two embrace.

Raffi signals him to approach. "Father, meet Lorig, the woman I'm going to marry."

The colonel smiles, taking Lorig's hand. "Life is about finding love. But giving love is a lifetime endeavor and nothing should ever take it away."

~ * ~

Daley enters Raffi's office and sits facing him across the desk. "Thanks, Doc, for taking the time. Sorry about your mother but I want to update you on Sanders' complaint against you for the theft of his personal property." The detective pulls out a sheet from his folder and shoves it toward Raffi.

"Here's a request from the DA's office. After investigating the facts, they proved Sanders had been collecting protection money from small shopkeepers in Harlem for years. The prosecutor wants to know if you'll testify for the department if they file an action against the reverend."

Raffi ponders the question as he scans the document. "I have no interest in doing that, Detective. I'm not a litigator. I'm a surgeon and don't want to take any more time from my patients."

Daley lingers before rising. "Just thought I'd ask. The DA has enough evidence to throw at Sanders." He removes an unsealed envelope from his pocket and hands it to Raffi. "This is addressed to you."

Raffi grasps the letter, immediately recognizing Traci's handwriting. "I see you've already opened this."

Daley nods in the affirmative. "We had to confirm the coroner's findings that Traci died of a self-induced drug overdose." He throws Raffi a compassionate nod. "Sorry, Doc, we had to read it."

After the detective leaves, Raffi leans back in his chair, removes the handwritten letter from the envelope and reads.

*Dear Raffi,*

*I ask myself. Is life just a façade? By the time you read this, I will no longer be a part of yours. Loving you was both a blessing and a misfortune. For a woman who could buy anything, I couldn't win you. Funny, my immeasurable wealth that helped so many has been a curse in my empty loveless life. But no matter. From the first time we met, you were different from the gigolos and phony wannabees who pursued me since I can remember.*

*As for my drug habit, I won't apologize for that. In a way, it helped me survive the pain I've felt since childhood. Funny that I say this because it also blinded me from living a healthy secure life. I've come to realize I could have given more of myself rather than my money.*

*Do not be sad, my friend. If Lorig is the right fit for you, don't ever let her go. Thank you for the fun times we had together but I can't go on living like this.*

*Traci*

Raffi chokes up; his eyes fill as the receptionist buzzes him.

"Dr. Sarkissian, Lorig's on the phone."

He clears his throat, composes himself and picks up the phone. Her arrival at the lowest point of his life still seems like a gift and they haven't stopped talking since.

"Hey, Lorig."

"Raffi!" Her voice is light and upbeat. "I'm inviting you and your father to join me and my family for Christmas Eve service at St. Gregory's."

"I'd like that." He tries to sound upbeat but his mind jumps ahead to the future. "I've been doing a lot of thinking. What would you say if we moved out of New York City?"

Lorig hesitates and then erupts with laughter. "What do you mean? You've done well for yourself in Manhattan, so why would you want to leave?"

"I've been mulling over my original plan to open a practice at the Jersey shore."

"What made you decide that?"

"I've come to realize city living is not for me."

"Raffi, are you doing this for me?"

"For you and myself. Quality of life there will be better for us and our children." He waits for a response, but hears none. In the months they'd been apart, he missed the family they talked about creating, the life they planned together. Traci's note drives the message home.

"Lorig, did you hear me?"

She answers softly. "Raffi, thank you, but it's a major sacrifice you're making. Not as much money or prestige."

Raffi smiles, glowing inwardly. "My dearest Lorig, when you love someone, there's no such thing as sacrifice."

# *Forty-nine*

It's late spring by the time Raffi sits in his newly opened office at the Jersey shore. His friend Ray still had enough office space to offer him, keeping down his overhead. He pays off most of the loans on his medical equipment and ships them down by van to his new location.

He lets out a satisfied sigh, taking in a deep breath. All is falling into place. Lorig's teaching contract ends in six weeks, after which they'll marry. She travels from north Jersey every weekend to set up their apartment in a condominium close to the hospital. Their marriage announcement is made at an informal gathering given by Ray and Carol, introducing them to their new community. They plan a beach wedding on the Fourth of July, and a honeymoon week on Nantucket before returning home.

His only regret is not having Jeremy at his side. That dream died the day a misguided youth, ravaged with hate, foolishly took the life of his closest friend. A lump catches his throat. What a great team they would have made.

It's close to five and the sun is slowly sinking on the horizon as his thoughts drift to Ani. His life's foundation is built on her crucial guidance, and his heart aches, knowing he can never repay her for all the love she gave.

He rises from the desk and looks out of his office window, gazing into the distance. A sense of gratitude mixed with melancholy overcomes him as he listens to the roar of crashing waves, a short distance beyond. He recalls the first time he laid eyes on Lorig. The image of her honey silk hair flying in the ocean breeze as she strolled the beach with her friends is still fresh in his mind. Life is stranger than fiction and he couldn't have written a better love story.

Occupied with his memories, he leans both hands on the windowsill, still gazing into the horizon, when Traci abruptly enters his thoughts. He carries a soft spot in his heart for the woman who had struggled all her life to find a genuine relationship. In her search, she became mired in the financial power she wielded. In the depths of her soul, he concludes, she yearned to be a giver. What she did for Jeremy and Rachel truly came from her heart.

Ready to call it a day, he returns to his desk to gather the mail before going home. Flipping through the advertisements and medical literature, he comes upon a copy of *The Manhattan Medical Journal*. Dr. Harold Flint's picture on the front cover smiles at him. The mayor of New York City stands next to Flint, awarding him an honorary key on his retirement. Headline reads, *Noted surgeon honored for major contributions to Manhattan Medical Center*.

Raffi nods, reflecting on his relationship with the man. Despite Flint's influence, his ex-associate is driven by political power rather than dedication. Thankfully this kind of physician is fading out. With the rapid growth of managed care and government medicine, businessmen now run the profession rather than physicians. In the end, Raffi has to conclude, despite everything Flint contributed, he's no giver.

The ring of his phone abruptly interrupts his thoughts. It's Lorig and his heart leaps as always on hearing her voice.

"Raffi, I'm so glad it's Friday. I've had an exhausting day at school. Traffic on the Garden State Parkway will be heavy, so I'll be a little late."

He sits down, leaning back in his chair. "Travel safely, darlin'. Just sitting in the office reminiscing about my interesting year at Manhattan Medical."

"Interesting?" She bursts out laughing. "You could write a book, mentioning some of the lowlifes you met along the way."

Raffi lets out an amused chuckle. "Oh, you mean the notorious Reverend Sanders?"

"He, among others. Thankfully the DA rejected his charge against you about his so-called stolen property."

"I guess there is some justice left at the end of the day. No question, Sanders' actions amounted to illegal bribery."

"Hard-earned justice, mixed with a miracle," Lorig declares. "I'll see you at the apartment by seven, ready to start the weekend. Love you."

"Love you too." He ends the call, telling himself he's a lucky man.

But not everyone is as lucky. How lucky was Jasmine Battia to bravely expose Turkey's payoffs to deny the Armenian Genocide? In return she was silenced by an assassin's bullet. She definitely was a giver.

His medical assistant, Nancy, knocks. "Doctor, the ER is on the phone."

Raffi picks up the call. "Dr. Sarkissian, here."

"Doctor, I have a twenty-eight-year-old male admitted with bowel obstruction. He's a migrant worker, fearful of being caught because of his illegal status."

"What's his history?"

"He's had multiple surgeries resulting from gunshot wounds, but refuses to give any additional information. How soon can you be here?"

Raffi checks his watch, a waterproof Nixon he bought for less than a hundred bucks and good for surfing. His Rolex has long been gone, most likely on some thief's wrist.

It's close to six. "Give me ten minutes," he replies. This story will repeat itself over and over again. An uninsured patient in distress, needing medical care. Throughout his professional life, he cared for hundreds of patients, rich and poor, responsible and irresponsible. Why should he question if he's a giver or a taker? No one has to tell him.

He rises, clicks off the lamp on his desk and looks to his medical assistant in the reception area. "Nancy, it's time you go home to your family. I'm heading to the hospital to see a patient who probably needs surgery."

Nancy's eyes glow. "Wonderful, Doctor. See, you're starting to get busy." Then she pauses, a frown crosses her brow. "Does he have health insurance?"

Raffi doesn't want to dampen her enthusiasm. "I think so."

"Do you know what kind?" she asks.

He smiles to himself, and stops at the door, facing her. "I think it's called United Nations Insurance."

Nancy replies. "Good." She stops abruptly and frowns. "What kind of insurance is that?"

Raffi turns before going out the door. "I guess we'll just have to wait and see."

# *Meet Dr. Richard A. Berjian*

 Richard Berjian has practiced medicine in both community and academic medical centers. He served as senior research cancer surgeon at Roswell Park Cancer Center, Buffalo, NY, and also held the post of Chairman, Department of Surgery at University of Medicine and Dentistry of New Jersey, School of Osteopathic Medicine. *Givers and Takers* is his third published novel. He resides in Stuart, Florida with his wife, and besides writing and golf, he is actively engaged in a research project.

# *Other Works From The Pen Of Dr. Richard A. Berjian*

*__Behind Hospital Doors__* - A suspenseful novel highlighting a young surgeon's worst nightmare when his integrity is challenged by hospital politics and medical incompetence. It's also a story of the consequences that result when the doctors and nurses we trust confuse their personal lives with their professional duties.